I0819867

SEASON OF THE WITCH

Novels published by Midnight Fire Media

Your Own Fate
Night on Earth
Dreams Belong to the Night
ShadowWalk
Alarums of Reality
Afterglow Dust
Black Dragon
Falling
Thunder road - Ice and Fire

The Janus Clan series:

The Defenseless
The Slaves
Birds Flying in the Dark
At the End of the Rainbow

Poetry:

Amos Keppler: Complete Poems 1989 – 2003
Secrets - Descriptions of what cannot be described

(A few of the) novels to be published:

Afterglow Rain
Red Shadow
Lewis of Modern York
Fangs and Claws of the Earth
Forsaken
Resurrection Dreams

For an incomplete list of current and current future Amos Keppler and Midnight Fire Media projects see the back of the book and the Midnight Fire/Midnight Fire Media web pages.

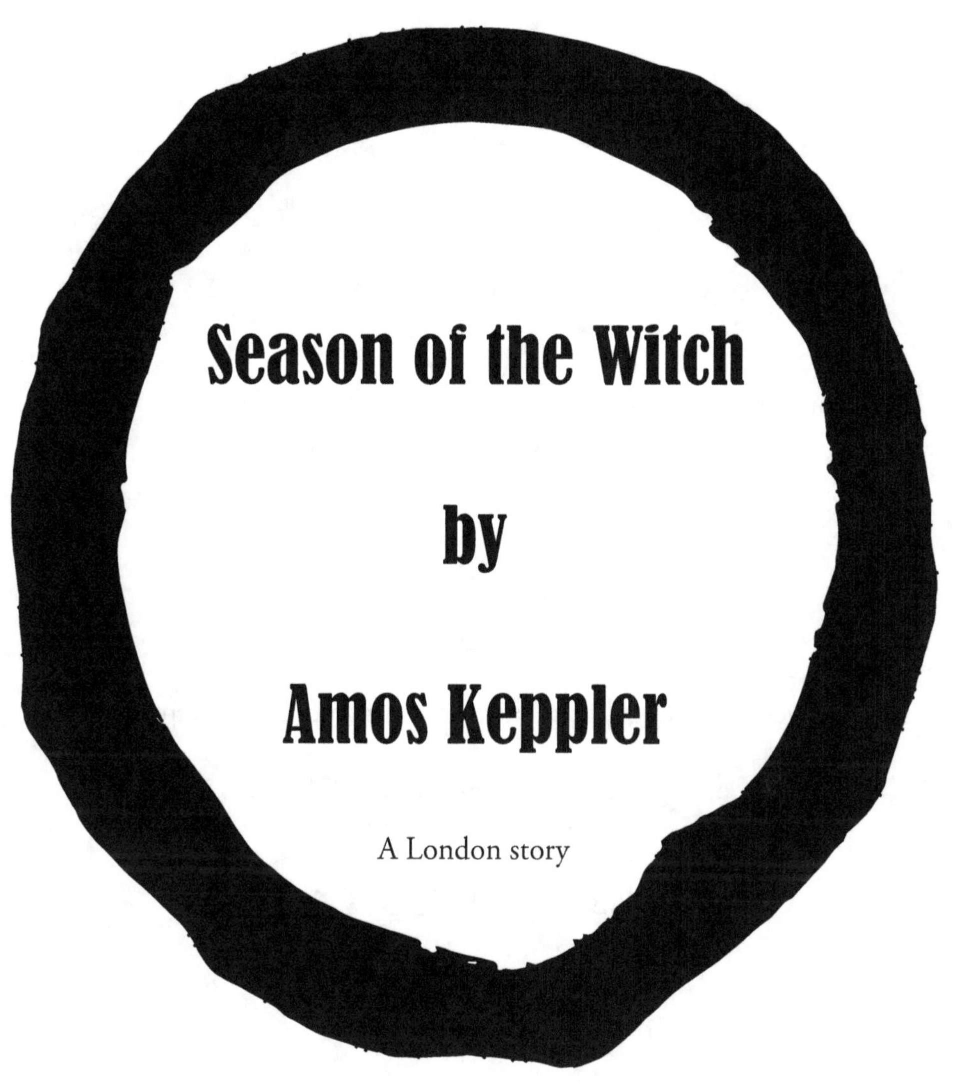

Season of the Witch

by

Amos Keppler

A London story

∞

MIDNIGHT FIRE MEDIA
2017

Midnight Fire Media

http://midnight-fire.net/mfm
For more about Season of the Witch and Earth and sky, day and Night:
http://midnight-fire.net/esdn

E-Mail:
Amos13@midnight-fire.net
manofhood@yahoo.com

Cover, text, design, premedia, art and photos Amos Keppler

ISBN 978-82-91693-22-4

Part one:
Awakening

«Go, tread the path of no return» Richard III - William Shakespeare

Chapter One

The image of the tree will haunt me forever.

The gray hairs weren't really visible, except on occasions where light hit the head in certain ways.

Lori stood in front of the mirror, dressed in a thin wardrobe, a morning gown, turning her head, observing herself from all possible angles. The early morning, the early spring reached her through the open window. She was brushing her hair. The distant look in her eyes reflected the faraway thoughts in her mind. There was a scent of sorrow in the air.

I'm turning forty today.

The thought brought strangely little worry or anger, just small bits of waves on the calm surface. Not even anxiety. Was that healthy, was that right? The arm, not tired, lowered itself, until it rested on her hips. She heard steps behind her, steps she knew intimately. She could tell the slightest change of mood by listening to those steps. Tom embraced her and kissed her on the neck.

– Good morning, honey, he said, yawning slightly.

Tom's American accent played in her ears. It was still quite distinct, even after decades of living in the UK.

– Good morning. She turned to him and gave him a kiss on the lips.

The world started turning again. She heard the whine as the steam pushed itself from the coffee machine. The boys were running in the hall again. The girl shouted at them. The first two slices of toast had almost completed their run in the toaster. They would be toast soon, if no one took action. She giggled.

The running, the shouting stopped. The boys, the girl entered the kitchen a bit sooner than they usually did. Tom, sitting down with his newspaper, looked up from it with a sympathetic smile on his face.

– Would you like to share that with us, honey?

– No, she said, shaking her head. – I won't… It was nothing, wasn't anything important.

He looked at her with a slightly pointed look.

– You… won't? He said perplexed.

– No, she said, shaking her head decisively, smiling sweetly, soothingly, to them.

I won't, she thought. It's mine. It belongs to me, me and no one else.

She went to the bathroom, lifting up the cloth covering her thighs and sat down on the toilet. The sweet pain of relief in her bladder made her stretch her body in pleasure. The bathroom wasn't dark, wasn't bright. It conveyed a certain twilight… quality that she had always found pleasing. Another mirror. She didn't stop by it, but passed it by, somewhat satisfied with just looking at herself at a glance.

Her face. Her face seemed almost completely covered by her dark hair. Her short hair covering her face. It was its shadow. A shadow covered her face.

The children helped put food on the table. Responsible, very modern teenagers. Tom left his newspaper for a moment to help. A few minutes later they were all approaching the desk, picking up their scrambled eggs. The unborn chickens screamed in the pan, as they died unborn. She grabbed her forehead, starting the exercises, repeating her Mantra, started breathing, out and in, in and out, slowly calming down. The toast had burned, but only slightly so. It tasted good. Everything in her mouth tasted… good, as she chewed and chewed and chewed.

Tom stood up, in a solemn manner. They had all risen, risen earlier from bed, too, today, especially for this.

– Happy birthday, honey, he said, as he gave her the little square package he had found in the closet.

– HAPPY BIRTHDAY, MOTHER, the kids echoed in a slightly noisier manner.

Rusty the dog barked once, very polite and controlled.

Jeff ran off and returned virtually immediately with the cake. There were forty small candles stuck in it. The boy lit them all with a lighter, just a little bit shy.

He hasn't started smoking, has he? Just for a second panic threatened to overcome her. She held back another giggle.

You're hysterical, she told herself.

They sang «Happy Birthday to you» and it all felt sort of distant to her. Did they really mean it, or were their smiles and song only a phase, a pre-programmed duty? She saw her mirror image reflected in the window, in the twilight outside. The hair seemed completely gray, the face full of wrinkles. Did she see herself, her true self?

She wanted to shout loudly to the fucking kids and the joke of a husband to stop, stop, stop…

Was she having a nervous breakdown?

She kissed everybody goodbye and ushered them out the door.

– You're late, she warned them.

– We're entitled, husband said. – You're entitled.

– My, what a nice thing to say. She threw herself at him, embracing him, giving him a smothering, lustful kiss on the lips. – Mmmmm

He freed himself, clearly flustered. What a cutie, what a cute boy… He walked down the isle waving, holding on hard to the dog's leash. The kids had already disappeared around the nearest corner. He waved to her as he disappeared into the garage, and repeated it when driving the car out and away.

The room had fallen silent around her. She occupied the kitchen alone.

She migrated to the mirror once again, started combing her hair again.

Her father had once told her, by the end of his life, while prompted by her, how he experienced the years, how time tended to speed up the older you got. His experience had been that the latter half of his life had been much shorter than the first. Figuratively speaking, of course. She believed that… now.

She didn't really have anything to complain about… did she? Their personal economy was good, even outstanding. Unless something drastic happened they were secure for life. Her body didn't merely look fit. She ran ten miles three times a week, without really exhausting herself. Her looks and the shape of her body suggested a woman in her early thirties. The speed of the brush through the hair accelerated just a bit. She had three kids, a good job, a husband, two cars, a dog, a parrot, a recent personal computer, the fastest possible Internet connection…

– HAPPY BIRTHDAY TO YOU, HAPPY BIRTHDAY TO YOU, Trish, the parrot squeaked.

The hand stopped the brush's journey through the thick, black hair. The arm fell slowly from the side of her head and came to a rest along her side.

She took the morning shower, carefully shampooing her hair, massaging the scalp, getting rid of whatever cobwebs still present from the night's sleep. Soap was distributed everywhere on her skin, at least every spot she could reach. Her attention, preoccupied wandered her body with her hands, her sensitive hands touching her sensitive skin. She imagined she felt every single touch or rub. Rinsing removed the layer of soap. She applied another round of it and rinsed both her skin and her hair. It felt pleasant, so pleasant. Delaying the end of it added to the pleasure and made her postpone the end of the shower further. Hands reluctantly turned off the water flow. She stepped out on the bathroom floor. Steam covered the mirror, covering her mirror image. She stood there and looked for a few seconds, while steam covered her features. The features beneath the steam and the mist seemed to shift and change.

Ten minutes later she returned to the kitchen, well dressed and well groomed. She had learned to be thorough, meticulous when dressing. Jacket, matching pants, white blouse, black tie. She did today's make-up, fastening the hair, becoming a different person, feeling more like herself.

The most recent high-end Tesla awaited her in the garage. She closed the door using an electronic lock. The garage door closed itself automatically before she had reached the end of the driveway. She suffered a few minutes slow drive through rows of light-colored painted houses, the nice little neighborhood, before reaching the highway. A relieved sigh escaped her lips. She enjoyed the ten minutes' drive at top speed before swinging off to one of the many industrial parks in the area. Ten years ago, this had been pristine land. Now it was covered with the most modern architecture, buildings containing the most recent technology.

On the passenger seat, there were lots of magazines. She, like any up and coming hungry, ambitious executive, read a number of computer and web publications, both off and on The Web in order to keep up with the faster than light evolution of equipment and trends. The recession a few years ago had hit the industry hard, but she had managed where others had not and in time, like the industry itself bounced back, stronger than ever.

The building of glass and steel and plastic and concrete rose in her vision. A pre-programmed system triggered by a laser beam recognizing the computer chip on her car made the heavy gate to the garage complex open. She drove inside without slowing down. The space where she stopped, the space wearing her name, not that of a car number was one of the closest placed to the elevator. She didn't lock the car door, hardly even bothered closing it. Heavyset guards were posted all over the building, all over the garage. She could easily see them without looking as she walked the few steps to the elevator.

The elevator doors slid open, effortlessly, virtually soundlessly. She stepped inside. The doors closed behind her. She sensed a slight shake as the small cube rose, as it slowed down, nothing more. The modern, stylish office space welcomed her. No one welcomed her. She nodded to the young man and woman behind the desk in the reception area and proceeded further into the luxurious space. She passed a considerable number of doors before entering one, almost at the end of the hallway. A well-dressed, well-groomed man rose eagerly from his chair.

– Good morning, Mrs. Russell, he greeted her.

– Good morning, Paul.

She walked into her office, a big, bright room with a view of the scarce remaining forest. He walked in her tracks waiting the appropriate seconds, a very skilled young man. She found, as she turned to face him that she wanted to ruffle his perfect, hundred pounds haircut.

– So, what have you got for me today, Paul? She said in a clearly mocking tone.

My God, am I flirting with him?

He reddened. She upheld her cool, professional mask. It didn't cause her any difficulties. It never did.

– Your scheduled appointments for today are all on, he said. – I've received confirmation from everybody, except Mr. Reddham at two o'clock. His secretary said she would contact me promptly when a possible solution was at hand.

– So, what is wrong with Mr. Reddham today, Paul?

– She didn't say, but told me that the meeting would probably have to be postponed until next Tuesday. And that concludes all the bad news. There are no surprises, or unscheduled meetings for today, Mrs. Russell. There is your one o'clock, which you ordered me to remind you off several times during the day, which you may feel confident that I shall.

She looked at him with her cool professionalism, wondering if he attempted to flirt with her.

– And then there's your birthday party, of course. He brightened even more. – There have been a few late additions, more people eager to give praise to the vibrant jubilant…

The flirting notion lingered. She dismissed it, turning and sitting down behind her desk, as he correctly and promptly left the room, leaving her alone.

As long as she could remember she had always thought of herself as alone here. She had always thought of herself as alone, but especially here. Since starting her climb up the corporate ladder, she had preferred the meetings, the hectic schedule keeping her from dying of boredom. She looked at her watch. Still twenty-eight minutes to the first, scheduled meeting. She started counting dust particles in the air, but her eyes were drawn to the window. The view fascinated her, somehow. The wilderness across the river, so close to one of the world's most modern industrial parks stood out in her eyes. Time eluded her. As she looked at her watch (again), it still showed 9.32. But that was impossible. She shook her arm, quite unnecessarily, since she had established that her watch wasn't broken. The numbers did change. Time did crawl.

She studied the shadows of the clouds drifting across the carpet. There were no clouds crossing the sun. In fact there were no fucking clouds in the entire sky. No matter how much she rubbed her eyes, she saw clouds drift across the carpet. In her ears, she heard an atonal sound. Nothing rhythmic at all, but something tuning in and out, in and out, in and out…

The buzz from the intercom put a stop to it. Good, focus on what's important. Focus.

– Yes?

– It's a message from Mr. Coleman. She heard Paul's distant voice. – He wants to see you in his office.

– Tell him I'm on my way.

She walked straight to the bathroom, to the mirror.

The renewed styling process wasn't really necessary. Everything, the hair, the lipstick, the makeup, the tie, the composure had stayed in place. She did it anyway, as a sort of exercise in an ongoing effort to calm down.

Marco Coleman's office didn't have more space, really, but to those who realized that the important part of life was in the details it clearly rated a level or so above hers.

– Good morning, Lori, he said casually.

– It is a wonderful morning, Marco, she replied.

Another person, another chief executive might have gone on about the weather for a while, before coming to the point of the unscheduled meeting, but not Marco Coleman.

– It's Mr. Reddham again, isn't it? He said, flaring up just a bit, for the desired effect.

– He's a bit of a bother, sir, she said in the same straight tone. – Nothing I can't handle. I did give him a bit of a leeway, a bit too much, perhaps, before reeling him in, but he won't cause trouble. I'll see to it that he never needs to be… encouraged again, sir.

– Good, good. He waved his hand dismissingly. – I know I can count on you, Lori. You're so good that you'll probably make the poor guy wet his pants and not even be aware that he has done so…

He wouldn't have called her in just for this. He wouldn't have called her in for this at all. She waited patiently. The numbers on the clock moved swiftly and correctly, at the correct speed.

– The reason I called you in here today, quite frankly, he stated casually, – is that I'm looking closer at all our executives to find the best person qualified for one of our upcoming tasks.

– The Rodham-project, she enlightened him.

He actually smiled. It wasn't a pleasant smile. But the fact that he smiled at all spoke volumes.

– I guess I shouldn't be surprised that the company windmill is turning, he grinned. – Truth to tell I would've been surprised and disappointed if it didn't.

– I'm the perfect corporate shark for the job, sir, she grinned.

– Perhaps, he said, purposely distant. – We shall see.

He sat down by his desk, thereby becoming more imposing. A bit unnecessary with her, she thought. She had admired him since her teens.

– In the meantime, I will stress what I've stressed to all you boys and girls, what you already know perfectly well: Not even a hint about the Rodham-project must venture outside these walls. Clear?

– As clouds, Sir.

He laughed out loud. She smiled politely.

– Yes, the clouds. He shook his head. – You can see them at a certain angle. Very creepy, isn't it.

– Indeed, Marco, she replied.

– I would have driven the fucker who made the windows out of business a long time ago… if I didn't thrive on the strange and unexpected. Most of my competitors would have scoffed publicly at such a notion, but they know that it is a necessary factor in any business.

She felt a tingle somewhere, a sort of (unnecessary) reminder of why she admired him so.

– You're really lucky today, he said, suddenly, unexpected. – First there's your one o'clock, then the unfortunate Mr. Reddham giving you one more hour.

– Yeah, lucky me, she said mockingly

– You know I don't mind, he said hastily (too hastily). – I don't want my associates chained to the desk. That's bad for business. Your time is your own.

– I'm seeing a therapist, Marco, she pointed out mildly, quite unnecessary, shrugging.

He knew perfectly well about her «one o'clock». His investigators saw to that.

It wasn't a big thing anyway. Most executives went to see a shrink for at least one period of their career in an effort to set themselves straight.

– A soft couch, dark blinders and pleasant relaxation. He gave her his Big Smile. – How I envy you.

– Thank you, good sir. She curtseyed. – You're making me quiver all over…

– Hopefully, that feeling will only add to itself when you see what we've done to make your birthday party something truly special tonight, to truly make you feel appreciated.

– I can hardly wait, Marco. She flashed her smile.

Was that another hint of mockery in her voice? She had to watch herself.

She left the office, alone again, his shadow no longer warming her.

The sun felt warm on her face. After her one o'clock session had ended she had plenty of time before she had to go back to the office. The present workload was light anyway. The pressure didn't let up for a minute, of course, but it was like Marco told them. They were in charge of their own destiny.

A young woman is walking through the streets, streets of wonder, streets of fear. The young woman is looking around in excitement. Everything seems *new* to her. There is so much to see, to feel, to experience…

Lori looked at her watch, almost shocked. It showed much more than she had anticipated. She had no idea she had walked around that long.

Time flies when you're having fun… she thought.

It was like some of the time had simply… disappeared. That thought sent a shiver through her and a sort of panic buzzed in the deeper recesses of her mind.

She shook her head, mentally calming herself. There was really nothing to panic about. There was still a long hour before she was supposed to return to the office. She even had time to grab a quick bite before returning.

On impulse, she visited an Indian restaurant. She had never eaten at any sort of exotic dining place before, but suddenly she wanted to. The door was heavy, hard to open. She needed an extra pull in order to get inside.

The door closed silently. She resisted an irresistible pull to turn and see if it actually closed. Just inside she was met by a huge sign:

PLEASE WAIT TO BE SEATED

Such statements were far from unusual in restaurants, she recalled. So why notice it at all?

Something seemed different, very different.

This early in the afternoon not many guests had shown their hungry mugs. She shook her head slightly, wondering about herself. But the room had only one waiter present and he took his time approaching her.

– Dinner for one, please, she told him.

– This way, please, the waiter said courteously.

She followed him to the back of the room. There were no windows there, very little light. Her stomach rumbled.

– I'm really hungry, she said nervously, apologetically.

The waiter, probably used to strange dinner guests didn't comment on it.

Music, some horrible pop tune in the background distracted her. It took a while before the food was put on the table, and she started… started devouring the content on the plate. She knew she had been hungry, but hadn't had any idea of how much. The foreign flavor enticed her, making her mind go in new and interesting directions.

– Do you *know* how long it has been since I've done anything even remotely resembling variety? She bespoke the waiter. He smiled politely at

her. – I truly enjoyed the meal, thank you.
– Thank you, he replied.
Perhaps he wasn't really used to guests praising the food or at least not anybody doing it with any sort of sincerity?
She sat there, resting, savoring the sensation of the food being dissolved in her stomach. She shook her head over the strange choice of words, but that was how it felt. And her ears picked up the noise from the street, the sound of forks and knives against the plates just as easily as her sense of taste and smell seemed to have grown.
And then it happened.
Someone made love somewhere close, perhaps in the backroom, perhaps another room, but close. She got a… funny feeling in her stomach. Bells were ringing in her ears, in her head. Suddenly she sat there, drenched in sweat.
She raised her hand. The waiter reacted on the signal pretty quickly. That pleased her somehow. She had been to restaurants where one needed to sit there with one's hand raised for minutes before anyone reacted.
– The bill, please, she told the waiter.
– You don't want coffee or desert or anything first? He inquired.
– No, thanks, she said pleasantly, – I'm stuffed.
She sensed a familiar pain in the intestines, of her stomach acting up. She had had trouble with her digesting system from time to time during the years. It had never represented a real problem, as she had learned to recognize obvious signs, and acted in time to avoid unpleasantness. At one occasion it had happened suddenly, during a board meeting, but she had managed to keep it in check until she could reach a toilet bowl.
– Where, may I ask is the toilet? She inquired as he brought the bill and she paid him.
– Down the stairs by the kitchen, Madame, he said eloquently.
She descended quickly, but not furiously the stairs. The ladies' room was first, just around the corner. Gratefully she rushed into the room, into the stall, closing the door behind her, pulling down her skirt and panties and sat down. Her not so agreeable cargo spit itself out almost instantly, mostly a thin soup of shit. She felt the characteristic relief and the draining of strength. Experiencing this diarrhea-like thing always made her feel drained afterwards. More was coming shortly thereafter. She shook her head in distress.
Silence greeted her, when no more shit fell from her sore ass.
As she rose, drying herself, pulling her skirt and panties back up cold sweat still pricked her skin.

She met an oriental, non-Indian kitchen maid on her way up.

– He's not worth it, you know, she told her.

She couldn't tell who was most surprised, the maid or she herself.

The waiter cast a worried glance in her direction as she ascended the stairs and was about to leave the place.

– Don't worry, she told him. – I don't think the food caused it. I have a history of stomach problems. Nothing serious, but a history nonetheless.

She cast one more look at the maid. The young girl wouldn't look at her. Lori, amazed at herself imagined she saw fear in the other's face.

Lori, outside in the streets took a deep breath, instantly being rewarded by that folly by a long hard cough. Cars went back and forth, up and down the busy street. The sight made her eyes water, and her head spin. The headache attacked suddenly, overwhelmingly. It always did. She leant against the brick wall, fumbling in her purse with shaky fingers. The small box with painkillers was easily opened. She swallowed using the spittle flowing in her mouth as aid. She stood there, breathing, for what she imagined was minutes, but just as well could be hours. Sweat poured from her brow. Looking at her own reflection cast in the windows, walking back to the office, she glimpsed a pale, stricken face. Her expression, slowly relaxing took on a dull, lucid quality, as the poison spread through her system, dulling her senses.

Paul met her with his sweet, worried smile virtually the moment she returned to the pre-office office.

– The headache? He asked.

– The killer headache, she corrected him gently.

– And there's still no reason to be found?

– I've been to a dozen specialists, she sighed. – They're calling it by a dozen names. Migraine, electronic disturbances, stress-induced disruptions. They've been unable to find anything physically wrong. One brave boy finally dared suggesting it might be somatic.

Of psychological origin. That was what had pushed her into seeing a shrink. The pills helped, but they made her giddy, unfocused. She hated them.

She stood before the mirror inside her office's private toilet, washing her face, rinsing it with cool, flowing water. She could smell the chlorine, the «purifier», but right now it didn't seem to matter. The hair had gotten wet, too. It hardly did anymore. She had, during the years developed an almost full-proof method of rinsing her face without getting her hair wet, a feat unparalleled in the annals of young female executives for sure.

The stairs to the roof shook under her feet. It always did. Broad stairs, elegant surroundings. Marco held some of his parties here, during dry, quiet summer evenings. She stopped by the rails, the solid fence, forcing herself to look at the streets so far below. The sense of vertigo hit her almost instantly. She had had problems with heights since early adulthood. It wasn't exactly overwhelming. She could control it with just a slight force of will, but it made her dizzy and her knees weak, as if her entire body, all her limbs turned to rubber. Just one step up a ladder and there it was. It always made her smile and shake her head. She had confronted it countless times, in vain. If anything, it turned worse the older she got.

It was like an abyss, a vortex down there, pulling her in. A part of her wanted to jump, to fly. The desire was there, in her mind, undeniable.

She sat behind the desk at her office, attempting to focus on the work, a completely wasted effort. Her three o'clock, her four o'clock sat there speaking, but she didn't hear a word of what they were saying. She sat there alone, burying her face in her palms, smearing the make up all over. Another visit to the toilet, another face job. She used her brushes and tools in an expert manner, refined through many years of do or die. As she passed Paul on her way out she knew she was, once more the epitome of a presentable executive.

Day turned to evening, turned to night. Lights invisible during the day grew to prominence. She was back on the top floor. So was a host of elegantly dressed people, men and women dressed for success. She sipped the wine. It was bland and she put it back on the tray, silently scolding the waiter. The servant hurried off with a rushed apology.

– I'm sorry, Mrs. Russell. Please accept my most sincere apology.

She hardly heard him, brushing him off by ignoring him.

The top floor was filled with people, a few friends, business associates and family.

These parties were really used as a social call, a way for local, national and international sharks to meet informally.

She danced with Tom, her husband for close to twenty years. The music was a slow, jazzy tune (they always played jazz at such gatherings and she had no idea why).

Jeff passed by, her son, the young man. He was dancing with a girl, flushing when noticing his mother's stare.

Tom looked at her. She met his eyes and he looked away.

Marco broke in and led her away, led her astray.

After a while, after two dances he led her to the punch bowl, filling a glass for her.

– Enjoying your party? He inquired lightly.

– Are you kidding? It stopped being my party weeks ago…

He turned her body one, two, three times. Dizzy, she fell into his arms.

Their eyes met.
– I'm enjoying myself, though, thank you very much, she added with a flashing smile.
The dance ended.
– You seem… different tonight, Tom said a bit hesitatingly, a bit jokingly.
– I'm turning forty, Tom, she said lightly. – It's not every day a woman is turning forty. Don't you think I'm entitled?
They laughed, heartedly, a bit sore, a touch of vulnerability.
Everything seemed jagged tonight. That was how she experienced it anyway. Time seemed to have lost itself. Events went back and forth, crossing each other. And no one's watches showed the same. Images, sounds, impressions were fragments, no more real than something on a black hole's event horizon.
She couldn't tell if she walked out on the balcony before or after dinner, before or after the first dance. There it was again, before her, the rail. The dizziness assaulted her instantly, as she looked down at the city.
People enjoyed the dinner. They always did at Marco's. He was almost like a restaurant owner. He didn't own any restaurants, but if he had he would have been one of those restaurants owners actively participating in the festivities.
Lori found herself out on the balcony. Again?
The texture of the world below, the city, the river and the wilderness across the river turned so very distinct in her eyes. She felt like she was able to see every detail in the painting before her.
Marco called everybody's attention, hitting a glass with a spoon. Lori sat with her husband and children at the place of honor at the long table.
The room turned silent. He had that effect on any room, on anyone ever present in any room.
– This is Lori's night, he cried.
The sound of applause filled the room, the jagged room, as everybody looked at her and smiled at her (the sharky smiles). Lori kept smiling as she touched her forehead, something that could be taken as a sign of modesty.
– I first met Lori Russell twenty years ago, Marco continued, after the applause had faded. – She was just Lori Michaels then, young, energetic and eager to learn the ropes of modern business. I'm happy to say that she met or rather exceeded all my expectations…
Lori found herself on the balcony. The streets and buildings seemed to become a monster, opening its jaws, eager to devour her. She felt its teeth, its sharp and pointed tear and pull. Very, very dizzy she was convinced she would tip over the rail and fall far, far down.
– She will be the head of a new division we jokingly, affectionately call

Genesis. Congratulations Lori. May your next 20 years with the firm be as profitable as the first.

Lori rose and bowed, to the wave of applause.

– *The Rodham-project,* a female voice some seats away exclaimed hardly audible in the middle of the ruckus and rows of people eager to congratulate the new head executive.

It looked like the word was already out. Lori wasn't surprised and she doubted Marco was either. He loved to play his little games, games where he had absolute control.

– Congratulations, girl, you've deserved this. Rhonda Lasko, the head of Research, congratulated her with absolute insincerity, not even bothering to hide it. – I look forward to work closely with you in the future.

– Thank you, Rhonda, Lori replied sweetly. – I do, too.

There was more dancing. Finally, the band had been excused and some moody pop song flowed through the speakers. At least she found it moody, as she, caught in its rhythm threw herself around and moved exuberant on the floor.

She danced with Jeff during a slower tune, feeling his young, tense shoulders at her fingertips.

– Mom? He began in an inquiring tone.

– Yes? She encouraged him lightly, but not eagerly.

– Why does always Rhonda speak to you like that? She's so insincere that if she was more so, she would be a sharp bloody knife, that's what she would be.

Lori laughed straight out, quickly giving him a warm smile, to assure him that she did laugh with him, not of him. He had always been a clever, but moody one.

– They give you the best of smiles, honey, she said with regret, – but behind their masks they hiss. It's the way of the world, I'm afraid.

He nodded, in a very somber, very adult way. He was a very somber young man. Occasionally so much that it worried her.

But she could speak to him, in confidence, about her worries, her fears.

– Jeff? She said some time later. – Do I seem different tonight, compared to other nights?

He considered it carefully before shrugging.

– You probably do, even though I can't put the finger on anything and say that this, this is different. But you're turning forty, mom, you're entitled.

She kissed him, a motherly kiss. She hugged him, a very motherly hug.

… fragmented. Everything seemed fragmented, a jigsaw puzzle where a piece would always be missing. She shook her head. Nothing was real, except the walrus dancing among the other polite, sickeningly polite guests. She threw herself back and laughed throatily as she danced in Tom's arms. Lori Russell wondered then, if there wasn't a look of worry there, in the depth of her husband's eyes.

She stood alone on the balcony, looking back at the people inside. They could see her, she was certain of that, but no one joined her, kept her company. There were a lot of subordinates sucking up to the new boss, but no one out here, on the ledge. Marco was here, his shadow always looming over her. She was young. It was bright day and it was the height of summer. He had only recently completed his new, proud headquarters, his aerie. The workmen still kept it going, going over the last details, making sure everything was done, was perfect. She had come here with her class of other students for a tour of the building, or the business world. After a while he had singled her out, brought her with him on a personal tour. She had no idea why and she was full of questions, full of curiosity and fear. Looking sidewise, shyly at him.

He had taken her to the roof, had shown her his domain, the world below. Almost overtaken with dizziness, with vertigo she had sought support and he had taken her in his protective embrace.

After a while he had said the words, and it was as if she had been waiting for them, for him to speak them for an eternity.

– If someone stood on that ledge, would you push him or her off?

– Yes… I would, she said dreamily, slowly closing her fist, her voice and eyes clearing, as she turned to him, turned to him, turned to him. – I would, damn you.

Until then it had all been a very pleasant, very relaxed, very normal conversation with the shy young girl and the confident magnate, giving advice, giving road maps for his success. Nothing obvious had been leading up to this. Nothing but everything, she realized, as she stared into his enormously deep eyes, as his stare penetrated her, releasing all her neurosis and fears. She was never sure these sentences, these words had actually been said, been uttered. She still wasn't.

She looked down at her hand, her raised hand, her fist, slowly relaxing it, staring at the blood; the blood on her nails, the bloody palm. For it to be such amounts of blood she would have had to dig real hard and deep. The remote look in her eyes remained as she licked her hand clean. The blood continued flowing. She took the gloves from her belt and put them on. Expensive quality gloves made of alligator skin. Marco had bought them for her. She stared intensively at the gloved hand. Inside, this glove was soiled, soiled by blood. But nothing showed on the outside. She shook her head, dismissing the thought, putting on her best smile, before returning to the party.

The party in her honor. The buzz in her ears was all for her. She smiled.

Tom drove them all home. Giddy, as she was by all the champagne they had decided to let the other car remain. It was a big car. It housed all five of them easily. Lori sensed the space, the infinite space around them and giggled. Toni's giggle was like an echo of her own. Lori looked at her daughter. Were all girls like this, so shy and insecure and needy?

– … and then he showed me the steps, the dance, and it was like I danced for the first time, like I felt my feet for the first time.

She suddenly looked anxious at all of them, as if she had committed some unforgivable sin stating her love for the dance.

The house greeted them, dark and moody. All the lit lights couldn't truly redeem that. Lori went to the bathroom, removing her gloves. The wounds had stopped bleeding and had started inflating the skin around them. She washed the hand and found bandages.

– What happened? Tom stood behind her. She could easily spot his worried eyes in the mirror, in the dark room. The dark room seemed bright, seemed Shadow and she had no idea what brought these thoughts on.

– I broke a glass and cut myself when picking it up.

She wasn't sure if she sounded as if she was apologizing for her own clumsiness, but that was how it sounded to her.

– Very clumsy of you, he joked.

– Very clumsy of me, she agreed.

She turned to him, pushing herself close. The kiss on the lips was hot, sultry. He withdrew a bit, clearly breathless. She laughed throatily, pleased.

Lori later remembered the small, short birthday party in the living room as strangely satisfying.

Fragments. The day had been all fragments. And now came the night, more fragmented then ever.

They presented her with her gift, a square, light package with a certain repressed solemnity, with all the honors of a military unit without uniforms. She giggled again.

Mine. The joke is mine.

Their closest neighbor played his black metal records, his own music, as loud as ever. Lori couldn't make out the lyrics, she never could, of the loud and invasive music.

– That son of a bitch, Tom mumbled.

– *Dad…* Toni giggled. – He's just playing music.

– That ain't music, dad mumbled.

– Dad, you're speaking in *contractions,* Jeff gasped.

Tom closed the windows, all the windows with a very definite attitude.

Lori found the awkward silence afterwards quite strange and puzzling. She started unpacking the gift as the others' attention slowly returned to her, as their faces once more lit up in expectation.

The hidden content in the box was slowly revealed as she like a girl tore off the paper, revealing a jigsaw puzzle. She blinked, as she looked at each and every one of them, of her family.

– I've always *loved* puzzles, she exclaimed.

With an exuberant cry, she embraced each and every one of them.

She said something, as she was standing by the window in the bedroom, nude. Tom sat on the bed, wearing his pajamas.

– What did you say? He asked.

– The waves are sometimes very ordered, she replied. – There's hardly any change, except the occasional ripple on the surface. But drop a single stone in the water and observe how the ripples spread, changing everything.

I can see it, she thought. Can I see it?

She heard the muffled sound of the voice through the window, that of Richards Marx, the neighbor Black Metal singer.

Satan comes riding
On the big pale horse
Life and Chaos
Follow in her wake

– I don't think that was what you said, he said, Tom said. – It was a shorter, definitely shorter sentence. And it wasn't exactly the most rational wording you've used either.

– Perhaps you're right, she shrugged. – I wouldn't put it past you…

To hell with it. She turned towards the bed, but which way she turned she couldn't say.

She found herself somewhere remote, unknown and realized that she was able to breathe, breathe better and fuller than ever before.

Birds flapped their wings. The sky above her was filled with birds. She stood outside somewhere, in a place she didn't recognize. There was a loud roar in the distance. She stood at the top of the office building and a lion crossed the parking lot. Then she was down there, on the parking lot, and thousands of birds blocked the sight of the sky.

The entire family had visited central parts of London this Sunday. They had ended up in St. James's Park, with all the birds. Lori knew what was coming. She felt a strange dread. Dozens of birds blocked the path, picking crumbs humans had left them. Lori and the children kept walking the road, walking close to the birds, even right in their midst, but Tom freaked out and took a detour.

– Are you for real? Lori frowned, suddenly, unable to help herself, looking at him with unkind eyes.

He ignored her and stepped off the road and onto the lawn, walking all the way around the big tree, in a long bow around the birds. It dawned on her that they frightened him.

She looked startled at the man she thought she had known.

The birds surrounded her and the children, and she stopped. Most of the birds didn't seem to have a purpose doing it. They just prattled and squeaked, moving around in a random pattern. But five of them, five of the really big avian, black-feathered creatures stood there facing her.

Long afterwards she visualized the long moments she had spent with the birds, unable to get it out of her mind. It seemed unreal. They were looking at her with their black, black eyes, as if they were trying to communicate with her, to tell her something, something important.

The children hadn't been afraid either, but looked at the spectacle with curiosity and interest.

She dreamed about herself in the elevator. That dream was always the same. She wasn't certain that was truly a dream either. In that dream she left the office, about to leave the building. A long day at the office had ended. She was exhausted, but felt strangely light on her feet. The shadows (created by the clouds not there) danced around her. She pushed the button to the garage complex. The elevator descended below her feet, below her intended destination, to the floor below. The door opened. There was nothing there really, nothing more than a few cardboard boxes and a lot of dust. It obviously hadn't been in use for years. The dust… She saw, observed how it whirled in the air. As she breathed she felt the dust in her nostrils. She pushed the button to the garage complex once more, not more than slightly irritated. The inefficiency of pushing the wrong button had always irritated her. The door closed and there was movement once more, but as always she couldn't really tell if it went up or down. The door slid open and she could step out in the garage complex. She had almost walked all the way to the car… when she stopped, freezing in her tracks. And then, just then, she realized the obvious.

There was no floor below the garage complex.

And then she woke up sweating, without really knowing why the dream, vivid as it was had such an impact on her.

It was early morning, May first.

Chapter Two

– It was… unsettling, she said flat out, lips shivering, eyes wandering.

Helen Weaver, the therapist, her one o'clock appointment waited calmly in the chair on the other side of the desk.

– Okay, it was *scary,* okay. Is that what you wanted me to say?

Weaver gave away nothing, as usual.

– Why?

– I don't… know.

She sat in the comfortable chair, irritated, also with herself.

– But you've had the dream before, haven't you?

– Yes, but this time it made me… uneasy. I know I've used that word before, but this time I really mean it.

She waved her hands vigorously.

– And the visit to the Indian restaurant, too. It's so unlike me. I've always tended to agree with those stupidly enough claiming that as long as the English have Yorkshire pudding and such a well of culinary delights, there's no need for us of European-English descent to go exotic anywhere.

– But still people do… occasionally. Why do you think that is?

– I guess they do want a slight variety in their daily life. At least that's how it started. Now, going to an exotic restaurant isn't really that exotic anymore, anyway. It has merely joined the relatively short list of people's acceptable chores.

– Perhaps people need regimentation? Helen commented.

– Yeah, like a shopping list, perhaps, Lori snorted. – To not forget anything important, to not remember anything not on the list.

– Why do you say that?

– Why do you ask? Lori retaliated.

– It's my job to ask questions, you know… Helen laughed a bit. – You're paying me quite a lot to do so.

The woman in the patient chair leaned back in it, noticing its soft embrace.

– I don't know. It just felt right at the time.

– But does it feel right now, when you think about it, when you're pondering it?

– No, it doesn't. She shook her head, in bewilderment, in fear.

– You must help me out here, Lori, Helen said pointedly. – If you don't help me, I can't help you. This is a two-way street, you know.

– Of course, I'll help you out, Helen, Lori said meekly.

– You turned forty recently…

– Yes.

Lori closed her eyes. The chair was so soft.

– Well, it's a matter of record that many a personal crisis begins at that age.

Lori jumped out of the chair and started pacing around the room.

– So now you are trying to suggest that I have some sort of midlife crisis? She waved her hands exasperatedly. – Men get those around forty, supposed psychological changes brought on by chemical changes. And it concerns far from everybody. I've seen quite a few, being conscious about possible pitfalls not being affected at all.

– Mortality, Helen said. – We start feeling our mortality.

Lori stopped, smiling a bit.

– I'm afraid you have to do better than that… or I will have to kill you…

The therapist visibly reacted to the other's intense staring eyes.

Lori still felt a bit ashamed while driving home from work a few hours later. Helen, like many people without imagination couldn't handle irony well. She felt ashamed, but she was also bursting with laughter, and the close to hysterical good mood wouldn't let up.

After leaving the M3 motorway she let go of the wheel and raised her arms above her head, a short moment before once more grabbing the wheel tight. She laughed aloud, even though she imagined everybody was able to hear it above the roar of the engine, the many machines on their way home to supper.

Not long after that she heard the penetrating sounds of sirens. She looked in the mirror. Blue lights flashed right behind her. She sighed and pulled over close to an old, abandoned factory more than ready for renovation. The police car stopped behind her. The constable stepped out of the angry car fairly quickly. She pushed the automatic button, and the window rolled down.

– Is there a problem, officer? She joked, as he approached her side of the car.

He didn't appreciate her wit or her bad attempts at it. She blinked. Suddenly the man's face changed dramatically, transforming into what she would swear was a demonic expression. And the world itself seemed to change around her as well. Changing, but not changing, like his face, just an ordinary face. She blinked. His face had reddened quite a bit, but that was all.

I'm awake now, am I not? She wasn't sure she had asked it aloud, and waited in anguish for him to speak.

She felt like she had been transported into an American movie, with its often-absurd scenes. That belief didn't leave her.

– You swerved from side to side in the road, Madam. You were driving recklessly to the point of no control. May I ask if you've been drinking alcohol the last few hours?

No, you may not, she thought.

– I haven't been drinking, she said. – Not a single drop. You may test me if you like.

– That won't be necessary, Madam. I can see with nothing more than the power of my observational skills that you're not under the influence of any substances, illegal or not.

What a dork, she thought.

– However, I do feel I must caution you. Inattentiveness while driving has led to many accidents, you know.

– I know. She nodded solemnly. – Thank you, constable.

– You have a nice afternoon, now, Madam, he bid her farewell and left.

She started the engine before he started his, and drove off before he did. Most people were too intimidated by the police to do that, but she wasn't. She most certainly wasn't. With a mighty roar, she speeded up down the street, her laughter shrill and loud. Passing the Hampton Court railway station, she slowed down a bit, staring in the general direction of Central London. Something stirred within her. They didn't really go there a lot. She had always felt strange about that. Living that close to a large city and hardly go there. Twenty minutes away with train, and it could just as well be on another planet.

Deviating even more from the norm she drove around in the neighborhood a bit. She remembered riding her neighborhood on an old bike as a child, always riding a little longer each new day.

It didn't really bring any revelation. The familiar mixed with the suddenly strange in her eyes. She made another pass.

And now it did give her more, enough for her to frown. The man mowing his lawn stared at her with his sticky eyes. He had always looked ridiculous to her with his big belly and Hawaii shirt. Now, he looked… sinister as well.

Those eyes haunted her as she drove the car into the garage and walked into the house, the silent house slowly waking up with children and husband.

– A copper pulled me aside just after the M3 today.

The very familiar interior of their somewhat stylish brick house surrounded her.

– Oh? Tom lifted his eyes from the paper. – Nothing serious, I hope?

It wasn't really a question. He wasn't really worried. He knew that his cute little bitch of a wife wouldn't do anything truly illegal or wrong.

Wife and husband sat by the dinner table. The kids had finished their plates in the usual fervor, and disappeared to their usual obscure activities.

– It was for reckless driving. He tried to intimidate me, but it didn't work, I'm happy to say. It's been many years since I've been intimidated by coppers.

He hesitated. She waited.

– It's good that the children don't hear you speak like that…

– Talk like what, Tom? She said it sweetly, with the tongue dripping of honey.

– With such disrespect of authority.

She wanted to reply to that, she really did. She very nearly did, but forced herself to calm down, to hold back the sudden, shocking rage within her. Several minutes went by, endless seconds while she waited, and finally rose from her chair, smiled to Tom, and walked to the bathroom. She was still breathing faster than normal when she stood before the mirror, looking at herself, studying herself, without seeing anything more than her common, mundane face.

She heard piano music somewhere, brittle tones and chords cutting her up, putting her back together again. Richard Marx played one of his savage tunes on the piano, always a great, harrowing experience. She couldn't keep herself from grinning. Thought followed action instantly. Thought was action. She sat on the train leaving Hampton Court, heading for Waterloo Station at the center of London.

– I'm going out for a while, she had told Tom, kissing him on the cheek.

He had just nodded, and kept reading his newspaper, like an old man on a retirement home. She had left quietly, with hardly any noise, and walked the stretch to the railway station.

People didn't talk on the train. She had noticed that before, of course, but now the current passengers confirmed it to her. Oh, they exchanged pleasantries and such, but they didn't really talk. Some were reading the newspaper, others a book, while others again just sat still, staring at nothing.

It had all happened so fast, she thought, she once more pondered. From the moment she had made the spontaneous decision and until its execution.

Such a short time.

She started listening in on the conversation with half an ear, at least that.

– Hampton Court is such a great, picturesque train station, a woman said to her yawning companion.

The yawning companion turned into Tom, she into the woman.

The piano music rose again from somewhere, haunting and close, hauntingly close. She saw no player, nobody listening to a recorder anywhere, as if the music didn't come from anywhere in the coach, but from somewhere outside… or elsewhere.

The rural areas of southwestern London flashed before her eyes. There was rain in the air this afternoon in early May. Rain and air were hot. Just sitting still inside the stuffed coach, with the many people migrating to London for the evening was an effort. All the open windows were to no avail. The pervasive heat and humidity penetrated everything and everyone.

Buildings were gray. Air was gray. The first signs of the approaching darkness came earlier because of the rain-heavy clouds covering the sky. Lori sat by the window, staring out.

– Night is coming, she said aloud.

They heard her. She knew they did. Lori and Tom looked at her across the divide of the isle. The flickering in their eyes changed ever so little. But they gave no overt sign of having heard her. Irritation, relief swelled simultaneously inside her.

She produced her cell phone and used its camera to brush her face, a lifesaver before and during more than one board meeting all these years. As she had stared out of the window, she now studied herself. She had tied her hair in a ponytail, a refreshing change from the strict executive look she had adopted. Part of the black tresses fell forward, connecting with the brows. She had dressed casual, in pants, jacket and shirt she had found deep in a drawer. And Tom hadn't noticed… Or he had pretended not to notice, the bastard. She shrugged and grinned. Most of her satisfaction stemmed from the fact that most people at work would have had difficulty recognizing her, though.

And she wasn't really that different. It was the same face, the same hair, still the strands of gray in the black.

– Yes, Night is coming to London, the man in the seat adjacent to hers said. – You're heading for London, I presume.

Something about the way he pronounced «night» appealed to her.

She nodded, amazed by his bravery. She would never have had the nerve to speak directly to a total stranger like that.

– Where else would I be going? She replied. – You could just as well have asked me if I intended to leave the train.

– You have a point there, he nodded.

She caught a glimpse of her wedding ring, at the edge of her vision. Its golden surface flashed in the blinking light of the failing ceiling lamp.

The train stopped at Waterloo and they both left quickly. After a short walk they turned left and towards the Tube, the underground leading to other central parts of London.

She stopped a bit, suddenly wide-eyed. It was as if the hall, the main hall of Waterloo Station… welcomed her, as if she was embraced by its air, its floor, walls and ceiling, by its metals and compounds. She drew her breath, and she sensed the dry air move between her lips, sensed it reach her lungs, and, finally, her bloodstream. She started walking again, paced a bit to catch up with the man in front.

– So, will you stay in London? She walked by his side and spoke to him with her hands tangled behind her back.

– I will tonight, he replied.

Air was sharp knives, cutting her, causing the most pleasant of sensations.

She took his arm. They stopped.

– There's something I probably should tell you, she told him.

– You're such a nice and obedient wife, he grinned.

– I don't want to fuck you, she said.

She didn't exactly blush. She was a bit too experienced for that. But she found she really cared and wondered what he would say next.

– I just want to have some relaxing fun, okay, Marc?

– What a coincidence, he replied. – Relaxing fun was exactly what I, too, had in mind.

He stuck his hand in a pocket for a while. When pulling it back up he held in it a golden, but worn wedding ring.

– You don't know this about me, yet, but I love honesty.

He put the ring back on his finger, and she saw shame in his eyes.

They took Northern Line to Leicester Square station, emerging deep into the very heart of London. Her eyes widened once more, as they ascended the last, few stairs up from the Underground.

– Can you smell it, she asked him, – the heavy scent of spices in the air?

He nodded and smiled, and it was like his entire face lit up, and changed.

– It's amazing, isn't it? She shook her head. – I've been here more than a few times before, but yet I feel it: An undeniable sense of it being the first time, like I'm some adolescent tourist never having visited a big city before.

– I've been told that London may have that effect on people, he said.

They crossed the street, heading towards Leicester Square. As they were moving people were moving in all directions around them, like a huge, dynamic entity of individuals. Lori shook her head in wonder.

– And I don't mind. He took her hand. – I don't mind at all.

Many people crossed back and forth in front of the Vue Cinemas. The queue mingled with those passing by, until they all turned interchangeable. At Leicester Square, the velvet glove of music started surrounding them. There were several musicians and groups of musicians standing by the fence to the «recreational area», the small, but dominant park at the square's center. The music from one group faded out, while that from another faded in as they walked by, towards Piccadilly Circus. Lori saw flashes of red, of brown, muted but so very, very strong.

– You should wear your ring always, she said casually, chidingly. – The odds of bedding females improve that way.

– Are you serious? He asked perplexed, nonplussed.

– I am indeed, she grinned. – Haven't you seen them, how they flock to the tied men, leaving far more of the others pretty much alone? Some men wear rings, even though they aren't married because of that very fact.

– I've never really thought about it that way. He shook his head in wonder. – But I do believe you're correct.

There was a guitar solo somewhere, played from one of the stores. She started dancing, hesitatingly at first, then with growing confidence. She danced as she walked, by the stranger's side.

This May night was as most May nights in London, hot and dry. Rain might have touched the southern suburbs, but here there was no sense of moisture, either in the air or on the ground. The city was that big. What was true in one place might not be in another.

A single car passed behind them, in the street they had crossed, Charing Cross Road. She imagined she was able to single it out, to recognize its signature. It had stopped. She knew. She couldn't see it. She wouldn't be able to do that, even if she had turned her head. But she knew. Leicester Square was off-limits for cars, but she experienced it as if the car had stopped right behind them.

She slipped slightly closer to Marc, laughing about something he said, while the sense of hyper-reality prevailed. They sat by a table in one of the area's countless restaurants and entertainment facilities, enjoying each other's company. From the speakers there was music, from the room the sound of voices. The restaurant was upstairs, the pub and dance hall downstairs.

– This is an okay place, she nodded pleased. – One can hear oneself think, and one is able to conduct a conversation without it being necessary to resort to shouting.

– Shouting can have its uses, he grinned, – but not when one wants to have a… conversation.

– I can hear the buzz wherever and whenever I go, you know. She smiled at his pointed, overt flirting. – Sometimes I even imagine I can hear what's beyond it, but then it's drowned in a cacophony of noise.

She frowned a bit, before shaking her head, dismissing it all.

The waiter put the plates before them and they started on the meal. The room had been hot from the moment they entered it, and during that half an hour they had been sitting by the table, enjoying each other's company the sweat and moisture from those dancing below had risen to their floor, and made everything even hotter. Lori started sweating shortly after her first bite, the first spicy, hot piece of food. She shook her head, shaking loose her hair. He lifted his glass in a salute. She did the same.

– What should we toast to? She inquired.

– To Life, he said. – To no more wasted opportunities.

– To Life, she whispered, suddenly very, very dizzy. – To embracing every little opportunity, enjoying it without limitations.

Glasses met and parted with a sharp, singing sound. She tasted the red wine, the blood red wine a few times, before finally devouring it all.

He reached for the bottle, but she stopped him, grinning.

– Allow me…

She poured the glasses to the brim, to the point that when they had another toast it spilled across her hand.

The wine and hot food exploded in her stomach, in her gut. She imagined it started spreading beyond the stomach, to all parts of her body. And it felt so right and so wrong.

They ended up downstairs, eventually. And on the dance floor. The surroundings of the restaurant dissolved and rearranged itself into that of the shadowy dance floor, surrounded by a mass of swirling bodies. And when they embraced each other and started dancing dirty and tight it felt like the most natural thing in the world.

They sat by another table having more wine.

– It's funny, she said. – I've had red wine, even this particular brand of red wine several times before, but it has never tasted quite like this.

He looked at her, attentive and clearly interested. She felt a warm breeze inside.

– I mean… it's like the very quality, my very perception of it changes the moment I taste it in my mouth… as if I can perceive its rich content for the first time in my life.

And then, completely out of the blue:

– I know there is something going on, she told him.

– And what, my pretty bird is that? He inquired.

Had he just called her his pretty bird?

– I've sensed something for some time, now. She struggled with the words. – I just don't know what. I go to sleep at night, and I can hear music. Then I wake up. And there it is, the music.

She shook her head.

– I go to a shrink, she admitted shyly.

– Who doesn't? He smiled, touching her cheek.

– Your hand on my cheek feels so good, she said, grabbing and kissing it.

Two women approached their table. Lori looked confused at them, as if she hadn't been present in her own skin or something just now.

– Hi, one of them said hesitatingly. – All the tables are full. Is it okay if we sit here?

Marc looked at her, referring to her. The feeling of his hand on her cheek still lingered on her skin, her suddenly so very sensitive skin.

– Sure, she shrugged. Then reconsidering, rethinking her statement, clearly not pleased with the first: – Please do sit down. Be our guests, on this river of life. Let us all enjoy ourselves thoroughly tonight.

They looked at her, uncertain, more than a bit taken aback by her candor, by her heat. They sat down, smiling, as Lori turned the two remaining glasses on the table downside up and filled them with wine, filled them to the brim.

The two women looked at each other, before nodding and accepting the offer. Lori lifted her glass, Marc, too, and they all participated in the toast.

– To the Night, Lori stated, and smiled to them as if they were all old friends.

She felt dizzy, a dizziness not related to her alcohol intake.

– TO THE NIGHT, they all choired, the sound of the glasses meeting and parting no longer muted by the surrounding noise.

They all laughed, abruptly, almost shockingly. Laughter faded, but didn't die.

– This is Kelly, the youngest of the women said. – I am Lynn Jenny. Call me Lynn.

– The gentleman is Marc, Lori presented. – I'm Lori. Nice to meet you all.

– Lori, the mermaid, Lynn said. – Pleased to meet you.

Lori took the outstretched hand. It was like both their hands were shaking. Lynn pulled hers back with an apologetic smile. Lori stared into the foggy, gray eyes for a moment, but saw nothing, nothing at all, and she shivered in the hot night.

– Here's to this evening. Marc lifted his glass. – May it become something extraordinary.

The three others lifted their glass, and once again all four met and parted.

The wine exploded once more in Lori's stomach. She gasped hardly audible. The others didn't notice. At least they gave no notice of having noticed.

The evening progressed, and they all clearly enjoyed themselves, as they sat there, conversing as if being old friends. Kelly danced with a guy for a while, a wild dance, catching the attention of the entire assembly. The guy pulled back, clearly embarrassed by being in the center of the action. Kelly returned to the table, with only the slightest disappointment visible in her grin.

The four of them sat there, staying put. Fog and smoke drifted in the air, hiding them from possible onlookers.

– It is strange, Lynn whispered. – It is as if we are alone in here, as if the others are elsewhere, or we are.

– It is as if we're… missing something, Lori said, attempting to concentrate through the alcohol haze.

Elsewhere, she thought.

– Or if they are missing something, Marc grinned.

– I have a sense of having… missed something. Lori kept talking, as if he hadn't.

– What? He took her hand.

– I don't know, okay, but it started… I realize now it started just after April 30th.

– April 30th, you say? Lynn inquired.

– Yes, I've had a dream for a long time, and it… changed that night, changed into something alive, something real and potent.

She looked at them, deliberately staring at them, challenging them to openly ridicule her.

– April 30th, the night to May 1st is the Beltane, Lynn told her lightly.

– The *what?*

– According to ancient pagan beliefs it is a night of the witch, one where she or he, and the coven, the circle is communing with spirits, alive and dead, a night where the borders between worlds are weakened and everything is up for grabs.

– You seem to be so knowledgeable, so sure about this. Lori shook her head in wonder.

– I'm not the one with the lucid super dreams, Lynn grinned.

They all laughed, and it was a relief. Lori sensed just a taint of vulnerability in the laughter, and forgot it the very moment it happened.

There was more dancing. A lot of dancing. Everything seemed to blur, turn indistinct, as she whirled around and around. She sat in her chair, watching Lynn and Marc go at it, sat in her chair breathing, breathing hard. Legs felt like lead. The floor seemed to not be there, as she watched the dance, as she danced. Marc reached out for her, and she joined him on the fluffy, polished floor, where mist seemed more real than wood.

The two of them moved together, there on the floor. She couldn't hear the melody, couldn't hear the song, only that there was one. There was a slow, slow beat, the rhythm spreading with such a pleasant speed through her body, through her mind, and her mind's eye. There was Marc's face, and one, tiny moment it was the only thing she could see. Sweaty, wide-eyed and hard-breathing she put a finger on his lips, stopping him from kissing her.

She returned to the table. Lynn sat there. She didn't see Kelly.

– What you said about weakened borders… She spoke to Lynn, more than a bit distant. – Generally speaking, I do believe you're right. People say the world is a brick wall, but I don't think that's true. It's more of something resembling… resembling ghosts and shadows… if you ask me.

Lori heard herself speak. She listened hard, but understanding eluded her.

– I think you're on to something there, the other woman nodded solemnly.

– Even if there aren't really any real witches in the world, I do believe there is room for a deeper understanding of reality at large, Lori Russel said matter of fact. – It is quite counterproductive to stick rigidly to old convictions.

– Spoken like a true executive, Lynn grinned, grinned widely.

Lori frowned.

– I didn't tell you that I was an executive. I didn't tell you that, did I? Apprehension was suddenly audible in her voice.

– Are you kidding me? It's very obvious. You don't need to tell anyone. The thickest of idiots would see it at first glance.

They giggled, in united enjoyment of the moment. The two of them had such… such a great rapport.

More time passed. It passed, now, without her needing to look at her watch. She watched Marc, attempting to relax, in an attempt to get the labored breathing under control.

– He's a good dancer, isn't he? Lynn (that sharp-eyed bitch) said good-humored.

– You dance with him, Lori said coolly, controlled.

– Are you sure? Suddenly Lynn could no longer conceal her excitement.

– Why shouldn't I be? Lori Russell breathed evenly, now. – I must leave anyway. It's an early day tomorrow.

– Poor rich thing, Lynn mewed mockingly, shaking her head.

– Will you say goodbye for me? Lori grabbed her jacket and purse, already on her way.

– Yes, Lori, the other said lightly. – I will do you that huuuuge favor, and you will owe me one…

Lori looked for Marc on her way out, but didn't see him. Then she was outside, the sharp, hot night embracing her on all sides. There was no one else outside. She was there all by herself.

She encountered others, other late birds, as she stumbled the few, long steps towards Leicester Square Station. Steps were treacherous. She had to focus for every step to not fall, more totaled then in a long time. It felt like a long way down, down below the ground, where trolls and demons awaited her with hungry mouths and sharp fangs. She shuddered, unable to help herself. The enormous amounts of alcohol she had ingested had dulled her motor functions, but her mind and senses, her perception, incredibly enough seemed as sharp as, no, sharper than ever, and she experienced everything in a kind of hypersensitivity mode. She shuddered, even as the hysterical good mood persisted. Even though she saw people and their faces in the diluted form of alcohol-poisoning she could make out their features amazingly well. She saw Lynn and Marc dance, and they were both looking at her with vicious smiles, and she didn't understand.

The train met her the moment she stepped out on the platform. She made sure it was southbound. Lori Russell made her way home after a late night out, like thousands of Londoners. Waterloo Station looked even more abandoned than Leicester Square and Leicester Square Station. There were lots of people here, but it looked empty to her.

– Explain that one, Lori, she mumbled, – you crafty bitch.

Leicester Square and Leicester Square Station had actually been teeming with people eager to catch the late train home. She just hadn't experienced it that way, as if she saw something few others saw.

She knew they looked and glanced at her, but didn't care. It was an effort boarding the train to Hampton Court and not one going to Timbuktu or somewhere, but she managed (she believed).

All the windows remained open, but it was still just as hot. There was no wind, not to her, even though she could observe how people's hair blew and obscured their features further.

She had a conversation or two during the ride, even though she couldn't say if it was with others or with herself. Everything turned into a blur. Only the big, happy smile on her lips felt real.

The quiet of the house assaulted her. She stumbled in her own shoes, as she attempted to kick them off her feet. She had to sit down in order to remove them. But even that felt like an effort. She giggled, couldn't stop herself, couldn't help herself. She rubbed her right thigh, fast at first, as if she was scratching herself. Then the movement slowed down, becoming more like touching. She touched herself. An involuntary gasp pushed itself out from between her lips. She touched herself, and now her hand lingered, lingered between her thighs. Another squeezed a nipple. It became hard and sore to her touch. She noticed how the other hardened by itself. Her skin had suddenly become extremely sensitive, enough to feel how the warm, pleasant draft played with it all over the body. She rose and undressed as she walked, as she entered the bedroom. Tom lay still in bed. She could just about make out his breathing in the dark, silvery light from the crescent moon. It was as if she was able to spot multiple images of a crescent moon on her body. Her nude body. The thought sent a shiver of excitement through her. She crawled into bed, grabbing Tom in the shoulder, shaking him awake. He looked confused and befuddled at her. She started kissing and touching him, casting him hot and musky smiles.

– *I want to,* she whispered in her husband's ear.

She couldn't remember falling asleep, but she remembered waking up. The moon hadn't really moved that much in the sky. Tom had fallen asleep again. She crouched on the other side of the bed, clearly disengaged from him. She rose silently, walking to the window. The sound was unmistakable. The sound of music, the music. She covered her ears with her hands. It did no good. The music didn't come to her through her ears. It came through the floor, the ground, spreading through her body, invading it like the air she breathed, the food she ate, the water she drank. She released a moan, before sitting down there on the spot, by the window, shaking her head, shaking her head constantly until morning finally came, and she fell asleep there on the floor, boiling in the early sun's fire light.

Chapter Three

– I'm walking through Queensborough Passage in London. I always walk through there. There's a door ajar, and mist is steaming from walls and ground. Everything is unfamiliar and spooky. A car is driving by. The lights are on. I can see the driver's seat clearly. There's no one in it. I realize I'm having another dream. I'm walking down a street a hot, pleasant afternoon. The light, the colors are muted into a deep yellow like in an old photo. The city noise surrounds me. There's an eerie quality in the air I can't make out. I stop by a tree, an old dead tree, and the moment I stop everything is falling silent. A car approaching me from down the street gives away no sound. The tree comes alive before my eyes. I can hear birds' singing and everything is changed. The tree, growing in all directions, becomes a forest and the sound of the birds' voices is deafening in my ears.

– The burning skull is floating in the air before me. I don't know if I'm walking, if I'm moving or standing still, but there it is, just slightly above me, a few steps ahead, as I'm tilting my head.

– I walk in and around Hyde Park. The concrete in the subway is covered by green grass. It still seems like an ordinary park at first, but something is happening. I enter the park at dusk, a strange and foreboding place, where everything is changed. I hear the sparrows and see the ravens. The surroundings are changing around me. I can see, can sense the branches grow on the trees. The sparse trees are multiplying, turning into a forest.

The voice was calm, measured, dreamingly, as if coming from far away, and not from her at all. She smiled, in a kind of distant way. Even the smile didn't feel like her own.

Helen Weaver smiled, too. The office was, as always, a cool and pleasant shade.

– So, what's *wrong* with me?

– Yours is a classic case of what we call disassociation, Weaver replied softly. – Even though yours is slightly more… pronounced than any I've ever encountered.

She could hardly keep the excitement from her voice.

– You start imagining your own, separate world, and after a while it becomes more real than the real one. That's when the line of danger is crossed. It doesn't have to be dangerous, though. Most of us go through our lives daydreaming, without it ever turning into something more, but it's clearly bothering you. That's not good. On the other hand, it's also a positive sign. You don't want this in your life. You can't deal with it on your own, so you seek help mastering it.

– I *felt* it, Lori said, raising her voice slightly, with a pointed, accusing stare, – when dancing with the charmer, unmistakable, the illogical quickening of the pulse, the heat to the head, the softening of limbs, like a schoolgirl having her first, helpless fucking crush.

The venom in her voice shocked her. She closed her eyes, biting her lower lip.

– And I wonder where all the anger stems from.

– Where is it coming from, Lori?

– You tell me. The pointed stare got even more pointed.

Helen sat there a bit. Lori thought she spotted fear in her eyes.

– Well, it's more of the same, really. You don't feel your world is your own anymore, so you grow sullen, angry. You fear things have changed. You want it to be like it was, like you were, feel like you used to feel.

Lori sat on a bench, in the park, in the industrial park in which Coleman Enterprises was a distinct part. There was wind. The wind blew her methodically done hair to pieces and disorder.

She didn't mind just then. She just sat there, letting the wind blow.

It took some time, and some doing, but she finally returned to her office, her hair, though hastily fastened still disheveled.

– Hi, Paul, she called out mischievously.

– Hello, Mrs. Russell, Paul greeted her with his professional smile in place. – Your… guest has arrived, a little early, as she, herself pointed out.

My guest? Lori thought. The slight hesitation in the secretary's voice, the slip in his professional mask didn't escape her.

– Thank you, Paul, giving him a dazzling smile.

With one hand in her pocket on the stun gun, she hesitatingly opened the door in front of her. Closing it behind her. Her once so comfy office suddenly looked vast and alien. She looked around her, but saw no one. Touching and shaking her hair she went to the restroom, her own private, comfy restroom. Lynn Stafford stood there, in front of the mirror, dressed in strange clothes, looking strange, doing her lips, turning with a dazzling, immediate smile.

– Ah, *there* you are, I thought I would have to wait *forever*.

– Hello, Lynn, Lori said slightly caustic.

– Hello, Lori, it's so good seeing you again. I just wanted to pay you a visit after the great time we had the other night.

Lynn didn't look quite… normal where she stood, with her ever more dazzling smile and outlandish clothes and appearance.

– Yes, this is how I usually look like, she grinned. – The other night I made myself normal as a favor to Kelly. She isn't exactly comfortable with the more… unsavory aspects of my life.

Lori made coffee at the office, showing her new friend to the table by the window. She could have called Paul and made him do it, but she… she preferred not to.

He, he, she thought, and could almost hear her own laughter.

Lynn made a quick glance out the window, before sitting down, crouching in the chair.

There was mostly silence while the coffee was brewing, the whistling sound the only one. Lynn walked a few times to the window and looked out of it, but not saying much.

– I like your office, Lori, she said jokingly. – It's big and spacious, truly worthy of an executive with the future at her fingertips.

Lori brought two cups to the table. She sat down, and Lynn joined her.

– Thank you, Lori, I love coffee.

– How did you find me, Lynn? How did you get past security and my secretary?

– Oh, I could have said I saw your name and picture in the newspaper, but that wouldn't really be true. You see, I am a witch…

– A *witch?* Lori said astounded.

Lynn's outlandish clothes and appearance suddenly didn't seem so outlandish anymore.

– A pagan witch, yes. It was I who told you about Beltane, remember? Witches easily see through appearances, to the truth below. I must say I'm astounded by myself occasionally. It isn't anything conscious, you know, not usually there isn't. I knew what train to take, what station to leave the train, and everything. Bluffing my way past cute guards and secretaries is peanuts compared to that, don't you agree…

She leaned over, leaned really close. She sat relaxed in the chair, not coming closer at all.

– Do you think it was coincidence that brought us together? It was not, you know, because you're a witch, too. A witch is born, not created.

– No, I'm not. Lori shook her head in dismay, sipping her hot coffee. – Certainly not.

– But you are. I can tell. I've always been able to tell. The shit the shrink tells you, all her… outlandish explanations… it's just bullshit, all of it. Your dreams… everything you deem weird happening to you lately. All of that are just the first, premature signs of your awakening.

Her calm, the casual, relaxed way she was outlining her claim, it was all so unnerving. Lori stopped sipping her coffee, devouring it all in one, huge slurp. The hot fluid flowed down her throat, almost making her cry out in pain.

The apprehension in her gut wouldn't let go.

– It's a shock, Lynn Jenny knows that, Lynn Jenny said. – Don't think I don't know that. Telling isn't realization, and realization isn't acceptance. Acceptance isn't happiness, isn't embracing. I've gone through it all, all the stages, and believe me, I know how you feel.

– I don't feel, Lori heard herself say.

– The numbness will pass. As I said, I know what you're going through. I, too, discovered, realized my gifts fairly late.

– There's no such thing as witches. Lori shook her head. – I'm sorry, but there just isn't. It's just an old fantasy that has gained an unfortunate foothold in the modern world.

– Sometimes I wish that was true. The younger woman patted her hand. – There are moments I desperately wish that was true.

– I like you, Lori grinned, shaking her head some more, attempting levity. – Compared to my other friends you're a fresh breath of wind. We're all insane in some ways. I've got no problem with that.

– So, you're hiding behind that, are you?

Lynn rose abruptly, the insane glee in her eyes momentarily multiplied. Lori froze, suddenly unable to move. Something happened somewhere, and she couldn't tell whether or not it was close or far away. Lynn's shoulders sagged, the body forming a resigned posture.

– As I said, she said softly, – how can I expect you to accept all this at face value, and without initial reservations? Even I wouldn't. I didn't.

Lori rose, too, putting a hand on the younger woman's arm, attempting to comfort her. She obviously needed comforting.

– It's just that I've seen things, you know, experienced stuff that truly makes your dreams, your beginning anxiety the drop in the ocean it truly is.

She walked to the window, looking down at the outside guest parking lot.

– I know there is something going on, she mumbled.

She walked to Lori, embracing her.

– This was fun, she said. – We must do it again, some time.

– Some time, Lori agreed.

There was… warmth here. Lori felt so warm, almost unpleasantly hot. She stiffened in the other's arms.

Lynn looked at her with her huge, opaque eyes.

– You *know* me, she said triumphantly. – We know each other. We've always known each other.

She stepped back. Lori remained there, on the spot.

– You're dressed like a Gypsy, Lori stated. – You don't look like it, but you are dressed like one.

– I'll see you around, the woman dressed as a Gypsy said lightly.

She walked to the door, stopping by it for a second.

– There is music somewhere, I know there is, but I can't hear it.

And she was gone. Lori was alone. Alone again.

She walked to the restroom. Her own, private restroom, and she started brushing her hair. She did so thoroughly, methodically, mechanically. It was a process she had gone through a million times before, and she knew it, if not by heart, then by hand. She combed it back by the ears, and started fastening the clips holding it in place. After that she started on her lips and on her face. A few minutes later she nodded relieved. Once more she looked like a modern, female executive.

She returned to her desk, pushing the intercom. Paul replied in his usually, efficient manner.

– I want five more copies of Genesis brought to me, she ordered. –Then call the heads, and tell them I want them here in half an hour. Yeah, and tell Synos, I want him here immediately.

The heads were the chiefs of the five branches. Lasko was Research. Brandon was Acquisitions. Florie was Overview, her old position. Turner Finance. Blackwell Construction. Marco Coleman had quite an unorthodox, funny way of organizing his business.

And Lori had become head of the newly organized Special Operations, according to Marco «the most important branch of Coleman Enterprise in the Twenty-first century».

– Synos is here, Paul reported. She wondered if there was a slight shiver in his voice.

– Send him in, she said coolly.

There was a knock on the door. Synos always knocked.

– ENTER! She cried.

William Synos entered the office. She studied him, scrutinized him, as she always seemed to do. He was English through and through. The name might be foreign, but he wasn't. A tall and skinny looking man in his early forties, impeccably dressed, a closed, expressionless face.

– Good morning, Billy, she greeted him

– Call me Synos, he said dryly.

– Good morning, Billy, she greeted him.

– Good morning, Mrs. Russell, he replied.

William Synos was chief of security, taking direct orders from Coleman. Coleman saw security as paramount.

Lori had seen its accounts, its expenses once. The kind of funds channeled through it was quite substantial.

– We will be holding the preliminary meeting concerning Genesis shortly, she told him. – I thought you should know, as chief of security.

– As you wish, Mrs. Russel, he said. He sat down in a chair, with his back to the wall, and as far as she saw he didn't move a single limb the next thirty minutes.

– *Transport is here, Mrs. Russell,* Paul reported.

– Bring them, she ordered.

A few seconds later Paul opened the door. He entered the room, and stood back a little, allowing the two men to enter. The two men pushed and pulled a table, hard to move even with the wheels it moved on. At its top was a square metal box, a safe. They were a strange mix these two, of accountant and security guard. The table was brought here from Marco Coleman's own office, the most safeguarded place in the entire building. Lori nodded to Paul, and he left the room, and closed the door behind him.

She held up a key. One of the men found another in his pocket. He stuck it in the left hole at the front of the box and turned it. She waited ten seconds. Then she stuck her key in the right hole and turned it. There was a click. The other man started tapping the numerical keyboard under the right hole, a long sequence of numbers. Lori waited thirty seconds, before entering her own, private sequence under the keyboard under the left hole. There was another click, and the door opened. There were five books, thick maps inside. She removed them, skimmed through them and put them on her desk. The man with the key handed her a pen, and a form for her to sign. She did so. Both men bowed. She did, too, and they finally removed themselves from her view. They closed the door on their way out. She was once more alone with Synos. He hadn't said a word during the entire encounter. She preferred it that way, even though she felt his eyes stick to her like glue.

The heads came to her, like flies to the food, the good food.

– Thank you for coming, she greeted them. – Sit down. Make yourself comfortable.

– Thank you, Lori, Lasko said kindly. – I can't speak for the others, but I'm thrilled to be here.

– I think I can speak for everybody, Florie said dryly, – when I say we're all pleased to be here.

I'm sure you are, Lori thought. You would just prefer that I wasn't.

She didn't sign to Synos, she was positive she didn't, but he started distributing the five copies of Genesis to her guests. He looked at them as if they were wet paper, and they looked clearly uncomfortable.

He handed them five more documents and a pen. They looked at it briefly before signing it. It was basically the same legal paper of responsibility and nondisclosure Lori herself had signed.

They looked at her, up to her, five human sharks on the hunt. And as the shark they never changed, but just continued the hunt on their eternal swim.

– Welcome, gentle beings, she said to them in a sort of repeated quite official greeting, grinning widely, – to this initial, introductory meeting concerning the Genesis project. Yes, you are correct, this is the so-called Rodham report whispered about on the grapevine the last few years. As you know this is about genetic engineering, about development and application of this new and exciting technology...

She stopped a bit, for effect.

– But it is also more: It's about economic, social implications of it all, in short how we're going to live our lives just a few years from now...

She felt spent, exhausted afterwards, she always did, sitting there, alone in the room. There was the shadowy, ever-shifting pattern on the floor to study, and she did. She looked at her watch. Her day was done, really. Just a few minutes left, and such trifle matters was, as always, as Marco was very fond of pointing out left to her discretion. She was on her way up, when she cast a look at the desk, at her desk, cast a look at the table again. There was a note there she hadn't noticed before. No one had been close to the desk, not even Synos, and certainly not the five others. She picked up the note, doing so without really needing to do so, she could easily read what it said:

YOU CAN HEAR THE MUSIC

And there was a smell of ashes lingering in the air.

Lori is walking through streets of Central London. The scent of ashes remains in her nostrils. Spring remains hot, almost to the point of being a summer. She's dressed in her office suit, with a tie, warts and all. She's strolling on Piccadilly. This is one of the more exclusive parts of town, where people in such clothes are more common. Here are several of the more than exclusive casinos in town, where people below a certain earning and class have no change of being admitted.

She walked inside the Mayfair Casino. It greeted her with a cool, pleasant temperature and atmosphere, far from the smoldering heat outside. The interior laidback, but expensive. Pleasant, pale colors, as an interior architect would have said. Lori had conversed with several interior architects lately.

– Good afternoon, Madam, the young man behind the counter greeted her, – how may I be of service to you?

She smiled to him, on the verge of the smile being a grin.

– I can think of several possible ways, she said lightly.
– Madam…?
– I would like to apply for membership, she said pleasantly.
– Certainly, Madam. Would you care to sit down for a moment while I notify our member manager?
– Certainly, my good sir. I know protocol must be observed. You stroll along.
He was blushing. All the aged bitches passing through here, making him used to such implied language, and he was still blushing. She sat down in the deep chair, parting her legs slightly. He didn't dare look at her, and she felt pride.
He returned after a couple of minutes, empty-handed.
– The manager will be here shortly, Madam, he bowed.
– That will be fine, she nodded to him.
It took quite a while for the Manager to show. It was surely customary to let prospective members sweat a while. Lori understood such tactics well. She used them herself.
– Hello, a taut, serious minded woman in her early thirties greeted her.
– My name is Corinne O'Donnel. I am Member Manager on this casino facility. What can I help you with?
– My name is Lori Russell. I would like to become a member of Mayfair Casino.
Lori took the offered hand, accepted another hand of fake friendship.
– Certainly, come over here, please. Lori nodded, and followed the woman across the room, without really stopping or influencing the other's one-way speech. – You just need to fill out the application form and you will be admitted right away.
The procedure took about ten minutes. Then Lori was let inside the cool, pleasant room of spinning wheels and blinking lights, and well-dressed people. She didn't stay long, only long enough to get a feel of the place, bet just a little, study the people and wonder why she was here.
The sun kind of blinded her when she stepped back outside.
She crossed into Hyde Park, walking north. She didn't really know how she got there, but she found herself at Speaker's Corner, and at Speaker's Corner she saw Lynn, Lynn at the stool, saying her piece. Lori didn't know if she had been speaking for a while or had just started, but her words faded into Lori's hearing range like waves on a shore.
– … There once was a girl touching a tree, touching it in ways she never had believed possible. And in so doing she learned who she was. She learned to listen, not only to trees, but to the whispering grass and the soft soil as

well. And most important of all: To the wonderful and terrible Magick song of the Universe. She learned that this world is merely an illusion, no more real than a mirage or a lie.

There were not many present today. There rarely was, these days. This was supposed to be a place of free speech, where people could say whatever they wanted. As long as they didn't insult the British queen they could say absolutely everything, without being arrested or persecuted. That was the theory, anyway.

During the sixties, huge rallies had been held here. Now there were merely echoes left.

– And she is just one, one of many, bringing on the true New Age. Not the lazy and superficial many are talking about in relaxed ways and with stars in their eyes, but one screamed from the rooftops, from the shadow cast by the forest. The forest is waning, people claim, cut down by the greed in people's hearts. Well, that may be true in a purely physical sense, but what it represents can't be destroyed that easily. Civilization has for a long time been destroying everything making life worth living… and now payback is coming. Nature is commencing payback on its malefactors. Dirty Jenny says so. Dirty Jenny is right, right as rain.

There was laughter among the «audience», the spectators, even though it had a brittle, insecure quality. There was something about the woman on the stand, making her different from all the other quacks speaking here. Lori felt it, too, felt the painful thud in her head.

– Civilization? She asked Lynn later, with a distinct question mark behind her sentence.

– Precisely, Lynn replied. – Most critics of society don't go far enough, deep enough, to the root of it all.

They sat by a table on a sidewalk in Covent Garden. Lori heard her, easily heard her voice through all the noise, all the ruckus around them. There was a band of street musicians playing not far away, playing the Gypsy Scale. Not eastern, not western, but something completely different.

Elsewhere, not far away a theater group was acting out their drama of life and death. There were often performers doing their stuff in Covent Garden. Lori could recall everything starting up at three o'clock at night occasionally. It felt like night, right now, in the middle of the sunny afternoon. She saw Lynn sit there, as if cloaked in shadow.

– Critics? Lori said.

This time there was no vocal reply. Lynn just looked at her.

They had their dinner. Vegetarian, strong, tasty, spicy. Lori shuddered somewhere deep inside. She hadn't had vegetarian for a long time. It was as if the food itself was changing something within her, changing her on a cellular level. New food, new woman.

And now Lynn spoke. And her words cut through the other like a razorblade.

– Something incredible is happening. Can't you feel it? Everything is changing.

– Changing? Lori laughed out aloud. – Perhaps superficially. On a fundamental level, nothing will ever change. You are kidding, right?

– The world is changing all the time, Lynn said quietly. – The question is in what direction and who is doing the changes.

There was a short impasse. Lynn grabbed her hand.

– Now, there is thunder without lightning, lightning without thunder, she whispered, – but that won't last, that won't last.

Lynn had very distinct features, the straight nose, the jaw, the suggestion of remaining puppy fat on her cheeks, revealing that she wasn't as old, as sophisticated, as she might seem. Her eyes could look gray in a certain light, but Lori now realized they were black, coal black. It was night in there, always night.

– How long have we known each other, would you say? Suddenly a hoarse voice, filled to the brim with impatience. – How many nights?

Lori thought about it, she really did, but couldn't muster a reply before the other continued.

– Just a few days, right? And still, it feels like we've always known each other… right?

Lori just nodded, numb, and with thoughts racing like a turtle.

– We've known each other through eons of time and space, of vastly different realities and universes. We will still be together when the stars are cold, and it's time to move on to the next cycle.

And Lori finally realized that Lynn Stafford was a very troubled young woman.

Lynn looked at her, looked straight through her. Lori felt a series of shivers down her spine. She had never felt anything quite like it.

– Look around you, Lynn indicated their surroundings with her hands, – what do you see?

– I see people, a lot of people.

– Oh, yes, but there are more to it than that, isn't there?

– I see people, Lori insisted. – Nothing more.

– You stupid *cow*. Look!

And Lori Russell looked. There were guests sitting. All the seats outside were taken. But weren't there also others, standing, looking at her, with their cold stares?

– Aside from that I see only shadows, she said irritated.

– What you see are spirits, living and dead, studying us, Lynn Jenny insisted eagerly.

– Spirits?

– Spirits. The other one nodded.

– No, I don't see «them». I don't see anything special.

– They're curious, you know, very curious, and more than anything *we* make them so.

– Who, Lynnie, *who?* Lori could hardly keep the irritation out of her voice.

– You'll see them, see them soon, through pain, through release. Their interest in us is quite understandable. We are, after all the coming Power, the Earth and Sky, Day and Night. And in their shadow state they see and know far more than they're usually doing.

Lori leaned back in her chair, touching her head, closing her eyes. And she saw the horrible disappointment, the terrible rage in Lynnie's eyes.

Lynn rose abruptly, anger and desperation visible in her eyes and stance.

– You don't believe me, she said aloud.

– Yes, I do, Lori protested. – I…

– You don't believe me. You think I'm crazy, that I am fantasizing it all, all this, but it's real, you hear me, far more real than the world you approach with disgust every day.

– I think you need help, girl, Lori said curtly.

– I'm leaving you now, Genesis, the young woman shouted, – leaving you in p-pieces.

Lori felt as if she had been struck.

The girl turned and headed for the exit, before turning once more, before the doorway.

– You'll be *sorry*. You will want to find me, but I'm nowhere to be found.

And she faded away there and then, in her tracks. Lori couldn't recall actually seeing her walk through the door. She ran outside, but there was no one even resembling her friend there. And then Lori stopped, frozen and still. She could recall them sitting on the sidewalk outside. But then, without transference, without thought they had been sitting inside eating, speaking, talking about shadows.

Lori screamed. She opened her mouth and she screamed. But there was no sound, no sound at all. She fell to her knees, hiding her face in her shaking, shaking hands.

Lynn is crossing the parking lot. It is an empty parking lot. As if it is night, not a sunny afternoon. There's a black car at the end of the open space, waiting for her. The door is open. It's opening wide as she's approaching it. The car is black, and it's swallowing her whole, digesting her, and spitting her out in pieces.

She sat down in the empty seat beside the driver. Marc turned to her, and they exchanged kisses. Lynn sensed a hot breath, from him to her, or from her to him, she wasn't certain.

– So, it was a productive ten minutes, I gather, he chided her.

– I don't really know. She smiled shyly to him, averting her gaze.

She considered it, considered her words carefully, finally speaking out.

– I sat on the toilet bowl, doing my thing. She frowned. – I was dreaming, dreaming that I was somewhere else.

He started the engine, giving her his confident and calm smile.

– Well, I would guess that wasn't really that strange, he kept chiding her.

She wanted to tell him, tell him everything, but something held her back. She leaned closer to him, kissing him on the cheek, masking her true feelings.

The car moved, without her able to recall it starting. It left the parking lot. Everything happened so slowly. She saw his face, she saw his eyes, the flash behind them, and she recoiled. He didn't notice. She sat up in a relaxed manner, stretching her body in a relaxed manner. He drove south, through London's old, antiqued streets. Images flashed slowly before her closed eyes about their dance, their interaction the evening they had first met. Lori was there, too. She was always there. She faded, and it was only her and Marc, Lynn and Marc.

– Where are we going? She asked him. – This isn't the way to your apartment and certainly not to mine.

– It's a surprise, he grinned.

They had gone to bed together that very first evening, in a heated, rushed coupling. She had crawled to him afterwards, a needy, hungry creature, just like he had anticipated. Damn him.

Dark already? Yes. She looked out of the window, and there was twilight. The sun was visible only as darkened rays between the buildings, as they crossed the river Thames, as they drove further south. They passed Waterloo Station, and for a long while after that they still moved. Buildings gave way to fields, and they still drove.

– This is the way to Gatwick Airport, isn't it? She lit up, in a strange way. – We took a cab here some years ago. A friend of mine insisted we shouldn't take the train, that it would be faster with wheels…

– Yes. He nodded in acknowledgement. – This is on the way to Gatwick Airport.

They were on the motorway for a while. Then they were not.

There was this road. They were on it. And then they were not.

Many roads in Britain were buried in the ground. This was one. One could see nothing but the road and the grass-covered skewed walls. Yellow grass, withered trees, the gray, fake rock where the four-legged beasts were faring. She heard it breathe, felt its metal lungs heave and hove.

Lynn started humming, unsure at first. Then it grew, in fullness and strength. She gasped, as if in pain.

– I can hear the music, she gasped. – I can hear its terrible voice. I can see the dancers around the fire.

She discovered that he was looking at her. She discovered the interest in his eyes. It wasn't curiosity exactly, but an interest based on a terrible, insatiable thirst for knowledge.

– You've heard this humming before, haven't you? You don't hear the music, you're unable to, but you've heard its imperfect copycat humming.

– No. He shook his head. – What are you talking about anyway?

They were on the road, the piece of road she had seen just a minute or so earlier. There was a bridge, a road crossing another road. There were trees, and a river running by.

– I know you, she said smirking.

– What are you talking about? He asked it innocently, but she easily saw the smirk behind his eyes.

– I KNOW WHAT YOU ARE!

In one fast, furry move she grabbed the wheel, and pulled hard. They were at the center of the crossing, of the bridge.

– HEY, stop it, you crazy bitch, he yelled, in a voice suddenly filled with fright.

She pulled harder, turning it in one, even motion.

The car turned abruptly and crashed at the protective fence, going straight through it as if it was paper. The car flew, as if it had wings, stopping with a loud CRACK on the road below. Another car crashed into it the moment it hit the tarmac. Dark, fumed flames erupted from two ruptured gasoline tanks. A truck with howling breaks slid across the road, but had no chance of stopping. The three cars exploded simultaneously, in one, enormous outburst of energy. Burning metal parts rained across a vast area, igniting the dry grass instantly.

It burned. Everything burned. Heavy, dark smoke rose in the air, and remained around the bridge and road, lingering in the windless place.

The crouching figure stumbled through darkened streets. Fire rose and fell on the edge of her vision. She could just about make out herself in the store window's imperfect mirrors. Her clothes were in tatters, her face blackened in ashes and blisters, her hair burned in several places.

She stumbled across the street. There was the sound of howling breaks as the cars abruptly halted in their run. There was the howling of rage as the drivers swerved down their windows and screamed at her, spitting their curses and venting their own frustration at her. She walked, that was all she knew, and she needed to continue walking. She knew that.

– There is something going on. She grabbed a man passing by and shook him, shook him hard, staring into his watery eyes. – I must go. I must run. Jenny says so.

He pushed her away.

– Let go of me, you crazy bitch, he screamed, close to panic.

She stared at him, stared into his wavering eyes. And fear riddled him, as he couldn't look away, shook him like a monkey. Then the dull expression returned to her eyes, and she turned away, continuing her uncertain walk.

– Must run, she mumbled. – Must run far.

And as she kept stumbling down the street, she kept mumbling, hardly audible, hardly understandable words.

– I'm Jenny, she cried out, in despair, in her stupor. – Ugly Jenny.

And as she faded into the darkness of the gray night it was as if her eyes grew and encompassed the entire view.

A man was stretched out under a bridge. His body resembled paint on the concrete. One arm floated in the river. Smoke drifted above the water.

Lori tried to open her eyes to Helen Weaver's voice, but discovered they were already open.

– So, what happened, Lori?

– I… don't know…

She sat in the chilly, gloomy office, but it was like the very air around her was alive with fire. It faded only slowly, so very slowly. She wiped her face with her hands. There were presently no outer manifestations of her inner panic, the turmoil raging within her.

– The door leading inside at the sidewalk cafeteria. It was as if… as if it didn't want me there. I wanted to go back inside, but it was like a slap in the face, and as if everything turned dark around me every time I attempted to take that one step forward. I turned and left, and the people at the cafeteria ran after me to get their money, and I… I snapped. What is *wrong* with me?

Helen Weaver tapped her pencil at the paper, an infinitely loud, screaming sound.

– Some nuts and bolts have gone fishing, and it's my job to put you back together.

Lori didn't close her eyes, but she could still see it, still see herself, the ugly, distorted Self in her face as she attacked the female and male waiter. It played itself out time and time again before her eyes, vivid and terrible.

– I would like you to tell you about your childhood, now, Lori.

– Childhood, huh? Lori exclaimed rudely. – That's the key to all you therapists, isn't it, the holy grail for any ill?

– Tell me, Lori…

There was a short recess, while Helen kept prompting her, with her eyes, her soft expression.

– I grew up in Brixton, she said dreamily, – its worst parts. Establishment shills will tell you that Brixton was over the worst by then. It wasn't then and isn't now. We were white trash or white niggers, if you will. Not belonging among the whites, not among the «challenged black». Jesus, these so-called appropriate phrases are truly stupid, are they not?

There was no vocal reply or comment. She shifted in the chair.

– I clawed my way out of there. School, shitty as it was, as it is, became my salvation, my path to liberation. I stayed there, all day. During the evenings, I was at the library, studying. I stole the food I needed from the local grocery stores. I ran long distances in order to alternate between various stores, reducing the risk of getting caught. Years later I joined with the best and brightest children from troubled areas on a guided tour to Coleman enterprises and not long after that Marco… recruited me… And I discovered that I hadn't really been liberated from anything, but merely moved on to a bigger pond of injustice and human degradation. The sharks didn't look the same, being dressed in more elegant suits and dresses and all, but they're sharks nonetheless, predators in a hawkworld where the supposedly strong prey on the supposedly weak.

There was a dog barking outside somewhere. That really shocked her. The office used be to so quiet, completely isolated from the outside world.

The other woman looked at her, looked really hard.

– There has been a lot of pressure at work lately, hasn't it? Helen said quietly.

– There's always pressure at work. Lori grabbed her hair and pulled in it. It hurt. It felt good.

– What's happening is clearly stress-related.

Lori looked at the other woman, in very much the same way one drowning looked at the shore, the shore far away.

– I've felt a bit tired lately and I guess this… the scene at the restaurant really emphasized it.

– You can do something else. You're still young, you know

– And if I'm lucky work only 12 hours a day compared to the 15 I do now, you mean?

She sighed, slipping further back into the chair.

– Look, I know it's stress-related. You don't need a crystal ball to realize the obvious.

– It's just your subconscious mind telling you in a roundabout way that something has gone awry in your life, Helen Weaver said patiently.

Lori looked astonished at her hand. She had just touched her cheek. It was wet.

Helen handed her a tissue. Lori accepted it, looked at it with wide-open eyes, looked at Helen, and back at the tissue. Then, suddenly she turned and crouched violently in the chair, bursting into tears. Her entire body seemed to collapse in the chair and it started shaking, a shaking she could do nothing to stop. She felt it, felt Helen Weaver rise from her chair and approach her, silently. There was no sound, except for the desperate heartbreaking sobs. Helen put a hand on her head and patted her, did it in a comforting, repetitive pattern. Lori felt how she slowly, painfully relaxed. The sobbing stopped. Lori looked up at the other woman, tears and despair still paramount in her eyes.

– I have… wet your chair, Lori whimpered, the sobbing momentarily giving way to hysterical laughter.

– Don't worry about that, Lori, the therapist said softly. – There are worse things.

– But the stain won't go away for weeks, if ever.

– You're the one who is important here, not an old chair. Don't worry, okay?

Lori sniffed, desperately drying tears, in vain.

– Ok-kay.

She sought the closeness to the confident figure above her, and she sensed how she was taken in strong arms and embraced, crying softly until it had run its course. She straightened, sniffing some more, before stopping, finally able to look at the other woman. Unable to conceal her shame, but looking at her. Helen pulled a stool to the chair and sat down close to her, looking at her.

– Listen, Lori, there's no need being ashamed… okay?

– Ok-kay. And Lori hated the inevitable stuttering. She wanted to repeat the word, but couldn't be sure the stuttering wouldn't grow even worse, so she didn't.

– Believe me, Lori, I've experienced plenty of patients break down in that chair. It's not a bad thing, but rather the first, crucial steps towards healing.

– You h-have? It is?

– You better believe it, honey. The steady, strong hand petted the wet cheek some more. – Now relax. I want you to relax.

– Relax… The shaking figure closed her eyes, slipping back into the comforts of the deep chair.

Helen sat behind her desk once more, but she felt so close. Lori felt she could almost touch her, or that Helen could touch her.

– Tell me.

It was not difficult. She just obeyed the leading, commanding voice. Everything slipped way. Her own voice seemed to come from far away. Her own body was somewhere else.

– Not much happened, really. My childhood wasn't great, wasn't bad. At least not compared to the other kids in the street. They let it all get to them, you know, allowed themselves to sink into the mire surrounding them.

– *Tell* me…

The words came easy, slipping away like mercury.

– I remember being in the kitchen with mother, asking her about ghosts, about how they were like. She said there was no such thing as ghosts, that I was just imagining it all, that it was something children did with their overactive imagination.

– Why do you begin with that?

– I didn't begin with that, she pointed out pointedly.

– I would say you did, after a little detour.

Lori closed her eyes. They remained open.

– It just felt… right.

– So, you stopped seeing ghosts?

– No, but eventually my parents turned angry every time I mentioned it, and I stopped mentioning it, and except for the occasional flashback, I stopped seeing them.

Weaver leaned forward. Her elbows rested on the desk and her palms met somewhat above it. She looked at Lori holding her eyes.

– I think we're on to something here, Lori. Your parents obviously did a bad job of dissuading you from your childhood fantasies. We all have them, but most of us let go as we grow up.

– I think you're right. Lori nodded with weary eyes.

The afternoon light moved some more through the blinders. They spoke some more. Helen asked questions and Lori answered. She hardly remembered what she replied or what she replied to. It just felt so good to empty herself.

When she rose, when the hour had passed…

She felt rested, peaceful.

– Can I use the bathroom? She looked at her hands, at the remains of the makeup.

– Of course, Lori. You're my last patient today anyway, so take your time.

Lori grabbed her purse, and hurried to the bathroom, horribly unsteady on her feet. Everything was silent here, even more silent than in the silent office. The running water hardly made any noise at all. She looked into the mirror, at the smear of paint there, kind of relieved. This wasn't so bad. She had looked far worse after some of her rare, but *extensive* excesses.

She sort-of sneaked out of there, like a little child afraid of being punished for some imagined transgression.

– Same time tomorrow, Lori? Weaver called from the office.

– SURE! She called back. – See you then.

Street was noisy, overwhelming. Stores were filled with people. Most people had stopped working at this hour and they were shopping, on their way home from a hard day's work. She was supposed to go right back to the office, she knew that. But she took… a detour. There was an irresistible need to just walk. And she did. There was a market somewhere. She didn't know where. Busy people filled it up, even though there were those taking their time savoring the experience. Lori glanced at the books, as if they weren't there.

HOW TO MAKE PEOPLE CRY IN THREE MINUTES.

The long sentence didn't really register in her conscious mind. She kept on walking.

– It's getting dark, she mumbled, stumbling on.

One of the people close to her actually heard what she said and reacted to it.

– What are you *talking* about? He exclaimed. – It's still a bright, sunny day.

She stopped and looked at him, at the fairly young man, with long black hair.

– Exactly, she nodded. – It's getting dark in the middle of the day. The day is fading and I… and *you* with it.

He pulled away from her with huge circle-round eyes. She stood still, there on the spot, shocked to the bone, without really knowing why.

Her feet moved, but she felt that she didn't. She left the busy shopping street, approaching anew Coleman Industrial Park.

(How they could use the word *park* about this place, she couldn't quite grasp. Not anymore. Suddenly not anymore).

She heard a sound then, a screeching, ugly sound tearing through her like wet paper. The tree, the planted tree, surrounded by concrete. There were green leaves on it, but its branches didn't move in the wind.

And on a branch, she saw a raven.

A big, big bird, so different from all others.

She looked at it, looked closer, and it was as if it wasn't there. And as she watched it rose gracefully from the branch and flew away.

She looked at her watch. Her hour was almost up. Usually she had a lot of time to spare while returning here, but now she was late. She felt a need to pick up speed, to hurry to her office, but didn't. Her movements, her steps were slow, her eyes dull and filled with mist. It was as if all power, every iota of energy had left her, as if she was no longer anything but a shell of a human being. The image of her in the elevator mirror was fuzzy, hardly visible. She couldn't recall stepping into the elevator shaft. She remembered stepping into the reception hall, but after that - nothing.

The elevator went up. For just a moment there she had imagined it had been on its way down. All her senses had told her that. The door slid open. She stepped out into the urban wasteland of an office landscape, heading for her castle and giving everybody a stiff, guarded smile.

Paul wasn't present behind his desk. She heard sounds from the hall toilet, shaking her head, moving on.

Her office felt strange, unfamiliar. The patterns, the clouds on the floor flowed like quicksilver over the carpet. She headed for the desk. That was what she always did when returning to the office. There was a note at the top of the pile of paper, of ashes Paul had collected and brought her in her absence. She looked at it with a mix of curiosity and utter boredom.

Recruitment flyer from Coleman Enterprises to young, aspiring executives: «Do you want to work in a challenging environment, one encouraging growth and growth and personal development»?

She looked casually at the paper sheet. There was a photo there, of a young woman in a suit. In one corner Marco had written: «Your input»?

She grinned, an ironic, bitter taint.

Lori Russel took one step back, two, three…

Then, with a howl of rage and despair she grabbed the desk and turned it over. It hit the floor with a loud crack.

The well-dressed, well-groomed, well-grown woman stood there, breathing hard.

She had thought that that was it, that it would be… sufficient, but it was not. She ran to the table, lifted it above her head, and threw it at the window. It went straight through it. Glass and splinters flew through the air both within and without the office. She saw them fall, fall and join the moving clouds on the carpet, fall to the ground, the industrial park far below, like slow rain on a sunny afternoon. She looked around her with burning eyes. There were chairs, chairs she grabbed one by one and threw at the wall, smashed against the floor. Everything turned a red haze after that.

A thunderstruck Paul stood frozen in the doorway with security guards in tow.

– It's all right, she told them with a forced smile, a forced calm. – I'm redecorating, that's all. Everything is all right. You may leave.

She stood there sweating, a crazy taint in her eyes. Hair was in complete disorder. Clothes, too. Her blouse was torn by the elbow. She had cut herself somewhere, sometime. She felt no pain from the cut, but drops of blood hit the floor, the moving clouds in a steady flow. Arm, it was the arm, of course. She sucked the torn skin by the elbow, sucked blood. It tasted salt and sweet.

The woman with the crazy taint in her eyes stared at them, stared them down.

– You may go, she said sternly.

And they left. She heard them leave, heard the very sound of their existence leave and fade.

She stood in the middle of the room, the center of the disaster area that had been her life. She didn't move. She stood like that, stood there for a long time, sucking the fresh breath of wind through the open window and into her straining lungs.

Chapter Four

She ran. She ran until her legs had become jelly and she was almost unable to breathe… or do nothing but breathe. The park was huge, Bushy Park, Hampton Court Park was.

It felt… good having the wind in her face. She could almost touch the air in front of her, the resistance she pushed herself through. She swayed. After hours and hours of running, after days and years she hardly managed to stand on her feet, but swayed like a leaf in the wind. The surrounding sounds overwhelmed her senses, all the sounds, from the distant traffic, to the birds chirping in the trees. She fell against a tree, breathing, doing nothing but breathing. She looked down on herself. Her clothes were soaking wet. There wasn't single dry spot on the cloth anywhere. She had been running regularly for years, but had never even approached such a level of exhaustion. And it felt good, good, good. She stumbled the first few steps on her way home, but shortly afterwards she started running again, and before she knew it she was once more running flat out.

The shower was a waterfall pulling her down its currents. She soaped in her long, unbound black hair. It reached down to her butt, tickling it and she laughed. To her astonishment, in spite of her close to total exhaustion she had turned horny when reaching the living room. Rusty barked once. She placed herself with her back to the wall with the big towel swept around her. Tom sat in the chair, reading the paper. Even though she made an effort to get him interested, he clearly wasn't. She sighed in disappointment as she walked into the bedroom and started drying herself in a more thorough and methodical manner. Her hair was still wet when she left the house half an hour later. She let it be, let it flow down her back, unbound in the wind.

The wind brought her to the train, brought the train to the city and beyond.

It was Friday night, and the streets of West End in Central London were filled with people.

She saw, saw them all in a kind of sharp edge vision. They moved slowly around her. She moved, moved for the first time in her life. The sense of hyperreality almost overwhelmed her, but she pressed on. The rage in her office… it had empowered her somehow. She no longer had to press on in order to move forward.

Lori took a stroll through West End, visiting the sights, what was deemed the night sights. She visited Rosario first, the TexMex restaurant, bar and dance hall where she had spent most of her time during her previous central

London visit. She looked for Marc, Kelly and Lynn, but saw none of them. She had dinner, prolonging the meal deliberately, enjoying every bite, until she could prolong it no longer. Her eyes sought familiar faces. She walked through the place once more, spotting no one she knew and then she left. There were countless places in and around Leicester Square. She visited them, visited them all. Most had entrance fees. She paid with an indifferent face. Jastic, Shoestring, Culver City, they were all the same. The London disco scene was the same as everywhere else, trite and boring as hell. At first, she spent some time on each place, but after visiting four or five places she just circled once or twice before leaving, hurrying to the next knot on the row.

You'll be sorry. You will want to find me, but I'm nowhere to be found.

She heard Lynn's voice, clear as day.

Jastic surrounded her. And what she heard wasn't music, but a kind of devastating rhythm, and hardly even that. Levels on the wall led to the ceiling, and down there she saw the dance floor. People moved down there, but their faces… their faces resembled wood. There was nothing there. It felt so close, like an abyss reaching out to grab her. Except that that was too kind. The Abyss has many redeeming qualities in folklore and human philosophy, but here there was none. She started descending the stairs, walking down again, and suddenly - before she knew what she was doing she was practically running.

The air outside felt cool against her skin. Before she knew it she had fled outside. She stood there breathing, not able to recall actually having left the building. She could breathe again, having escaped from a place where she could not.

She stood there gasping, bent over, with her hands on her knees. A man approached her and she felt… She straightened, pulling herself together.

– Are you okay, miss?

– Yes, I'm quite okay, thank you. She smiled. He hadn't seen her wedding ring.

– Are you sure? You don't need to see a doctor or anything. There's a hospital close by. I know where it is, and I can take you there.

– That's very kind of you, sir, she said, smiling openly to him, – but it isn't necessary.

Afraid, she realized she was afraid, that she was, in fact terrified. Her heart hammered in her chest. The big and strong man had appeared helpful, but suddenly she had seen the sleazy grin beyond his features. She looked around, looked many times. He had disappeared, and slowly she managed, by an act of will to calm herself.

Her eyes sought and found the underground sign, PICCADILLY CIRCUS. She wanted to go there, to crawl home with her tail between her legs, but she resisted the urge, standing her ground.

– What happened? A woman passing by asked.

– I get occasional bursts of claustrophobia, she lied. – I can usually control it, but tonight, for some reason I couldn't.

It was true she had had some experiences in her youth with claustrophobia, in addition to her vertigo, but never any real problems.

– You rushed out of that place like you had the devil himself on your heels. Can't say I blame you, though. The place is the pits…

The woman shrugged, grinning a bit, not unkind, and kept going.

– I couldn't hear the music, Lori whispered.

Her feet started moving by themselves or so it seemed. She moved on. On a hunch (another hunch) she decided to return to Rosario. Early seventies Hawkwind music surrounded her, and it was like she had come home. And… by the bar she spotted Kelly Andros.

All the endless walking hours this night, her sore muscles, stiff limbs seemed to evaporate in that moment. She slowed down. She finally slowed down, and she approached the other woman in a cautious and nervous manner.

– Hi, she said, in greeting.

Kelly turned.

– Lori? She exclaimed incredulous.

– That's me, Lori grinned.

Kelly's reaction and behavior confused Lori, but then her own probably confused Kelly as well. They looked at each other.

– I was looking for Lynn, Kelly said cautiously, – or anybody who might have seen her or knew where she was.

– So was I, Lori said.

And the rush, the frustration, the impatience she had felt the entire evening finally evened.

– I need to speak to her, Lori said. – I need… very much to speak to her.

– I hardly slept last night, Kelly said. – I awoke on the floor. Martin, my husband found me on the floor in the morning, mumbling curses. The poor bugger got spooked.

The grin more than suggested that she wasn't that sorry.

– Everything has happened so fast, Lori whispered aloud, breaching the dark, loud music. – Since I left home early this afternoon I've hardly been able to catch my breath. I… I have a sense… of myself I've never before had.

– Lynn said we were fated to be together, Kelly shook her head, quickly turning somber again. – Although the way we met may have been accidental, that very meeting set off something that cannot be stopped. And also that we wouldn't have met if we hadn't sought, not only each other, but ourselves. She said we were the New Age, the…

– … the Earth and Sky, Day and Night, Lori part choired, part completed the other's sentence.

Kelly's eyes widened.

And there were seconds there, minutes there, where they didn't do anything but stand still, staring into nothing.

They bought drinks and found a table not too far away from the bar. Catching each other's glances, they giggled and found themselves nodding to each other in mutual understanding, very much like old friends.

– To Lynn. Lori raised her glass of Margarita. – To the most noble, plain-speaking witch in modern London.

– To Lynn.

Kelly raised her own glass. Glasses met and parted, and they drank.

They danced. Strange chords mixed and expanded in them. And this is rhythm, Lori thought. This is life. Her hair was in total disorder. It had been so since she had stormed out of Jastic Discothèque and was even more so now. She saw herself, reflected in mirrors and smooth surfaces and she laughed out loud, and what she glimpsed was a wild, crazy creature. The laughter turned louder.

– I haven't had my hair unbound for years, she mused, in both a somber and excited mood. – It feels so strange, so fucking great.

– I understand what you mean, Kelly whispered.

Lori still heard her, heard her easily. They had another toast.

At some point, they stopped drinking Margaritas and started on pure liquor. They drank Glenmorangie, one of the strongest brands of scotch ever brewed. They drank bottoms up in small glasses. They repeated it many times.

– Now, that is what I call a guitar riff, Lori said, desperately attempting to focus on something, anything in the ever-shifting realities of the room.

I sit here, committing suicide, she thought.

The thought didn't upset her the least.

– I agree, Kelly sniveled. – It beats the living shit out of «today's sophisticated music».

They looked at each other.

– SOPHISTICATED MY ASS! They cried out in unison.

They sat by a table. There were three chairs there. The fourth was missing.

Suddenly… Suddenly Lori felt a trickle down her spine, and it was a whopper of a trickle, more like someone was dancing down her back, leaving chunks of ice. She looked around, experiencing how the entire room darkened, how her vision… cleared. She saw a woman, crystal clear and familiar stumbling across the room, precariously balancing between the tables. It was a Chinese girl, fairly tall for a Chinese. Fairly tall for the westerners' usual perception of the Chinese, Lori corrected herself. She had heard that some local Chinese people could grow just as tall as any westerner.

The girl managed to pass one table, two, three without the impending doom expressing itself, but at the fourth she stumbled into a chair's leg and it was as if a giant invisible hand swept her forward. She landed on the table between Lori and Kelly. The liquor in her glass, in their glasses, that in the bottle, flowed through the air, splashing on them and everywhere. The table collapsed with a loud crack, a drumbeat reverberating through eternity. Lori felt it, in her stupor. And in that stupor, it was as if the gates of eternity had blown wide open. Lynn had spoken about eternity, about the two of them meeting on many worlds, in many realities.

The girl attempted to get up, to focus her swimming eyes, in vain.

– I'm sorry, she said. – I… stumbled.

She started giggling hysterically then.

– You sure did, Lori said.

Lori and Kelly joined in the hysterical laughter.

They grabbed one arm each and dragged the fallen pride to her feet. Skin touched skin. Eyes met eyes.

Skin touches skin, Lori thought. *Eyes meet eyes…*

She gasped. They all did. Suddenly they were no longer in the same room, the room of fun and games and strong drinks.

They sat with a lot of people in a dark room, a room with a cold draft, a place filled with people. They sat with their back pressed to the wall looking at the world with wide-open eyes, looking at nothing, the stench of death ripping their nostrils *to shreds*. People, standing and not, looked at Lori with dead eyes, their faces shrunken and pale, pale as ghosts, pale as Death.

Lori gasped and gasped, open mouthed, cold ice burning her skin, her eyes widening so much that it hurt. The image… the *vision?* It faded, not there more than a second, and probably less, but it felt like… like

An eternity.

Music returned. The sound of glasses meeting and parting returned. The stink of liquor. The barroom itself, with its noise and mayhem. The… the other room had been silent, silent as the grave.

– I remember you, the Chinese girl said.

– I remember you, too, Lori said slowly. – I gave you an… an advice, didn't

I?

– You did, the other one said bitterly, – and a very good one to boot.

She reached out her hand, both her hands.

– My name is Julia Montgomery. Pleased to meet you.

– Pleased… Lori and Kelly mumbled, taking her hand(s).

The three stood there, trembling. Dry leaves an autumn day. Sober as a catholic priest after a Sunday service. In total mutual agreement, they grabbed their purses and hurried outside. Lori threw a twenty-pound bill on the rubble, the remains of the table.

– For the damages, she cried out aloud.

– I've always wanted to do that, she told one of the bartenders as she passed him.

That was only a half-truth, true as far as it went, very common in today's language.

She had wanted to do many things. And now, suddenly she wanted to do everything.

– Jeez, Julia shook her head in curious and cheerful bewilderment. – Talk about a splash. We stink. If a copper comes around now, we will at least end up in the public hotel room for the night. I'm sorry, I knew I shouldn't have pushed my luck after avoiding the first or second table, but stopped and taken stock of me feet.

She spoke «London English» as if born to it, and she probably was.

The «public hotel room» was the nickname for the big cell all drunken females and loose birds ended up sharing at the central Westminster police headquarters.

– Don't worry about it, Lori grinned. – No matter what happens we will survive and we will thrive.

Thrive, she thought. Grow.

The street outside didn't look the same as it had before they had entered the building. She realized she got that a lot these nights, and even days. She shivered in the warm air.

The three women, strangers stopped outside, suddenly embarrassed by the recent displayed exuberance. Lori wanted to say something, anything. She wanted to say so much.

She said nothing. She kept her silence, her shame.

– So, where to, now? Julia queried.

– I know a bookstore that is open late, Kelly said, looking at them both.

– A… bookstore? Julia inquired.

– Precisely. Kelly grinned widely.

It was well into the night when they approached the Witches' Brew north of Oxford Street. Oxford Street itself and the stretch after that had been utterly deserted. Even London slept late at night. But they heard the commotion from far away and when they arrived at their destination, the sidewalk outside was filled with people. Inside it seemed more sparsely populated, but it was so spacious, so big that it merely looked that way.

The place was a bookstore, but also a tavern. There was music, haunting music, but it was possible to hear oneself think, and to speak, easily, without having to shout and strain one's ears. Lori heard the music, the spoken words, and all of it started… resonating within her, in a way unknown and *exciting*. There was a draft from the staircase leading to the basement, a not unpleasant, warm breeze. It ruffled her hair. She was drunk, still drunk, she knew that, but it didn't seem to matter.

They mingled, but stayed together, seeing the sights, feeling hopeful, sensing the general mood, feeling dismay, wandering between celebrities.

– Look, there is Alex Fortane, a girl cried out. – I love him. He's such a hunk.

Julia shook her head, turned to Lori.

– It's disconcerting, isn't it? To find out that even in this place, society's worst qualities are abundant.

She sniffed a bit, before continuing.

– Alex Fortane is a public figure, a self-proclaimed prophet, very much at home with politicians and the filthy rich. He was quite the radical once, but that is long ago. He's supposed to be a sorcerer, too, one «with direct access to the higher spheres». The usual propaganda surrounding self-proclaimed «prophets», I guess.

Lori had actually heard about him. He and his congregation were quite successful, in terms of economic gain. His company, Fortane Limited was even registered at the London/Frankfurt stock exchange.

Julia was quite a different person from Lori's first impression of her that day in the restaurant. She had just seemed like a mundane, flimsy young woman, then. Now, she showed herself to be independent, capable and resourceful.

Lori looked around, truly *looked*. She giggled, taking a couple of unsteady steps, before stopping.

This worked mostly as a place of partying tonight. She supposed it was quite different during the day, but at this time of the night, there were very few books being sold. During these late hours food and liquor were consumed in insane amounts.

More giggles pushed themselves up their throat. Lori felt young and irresponsible again.

The three of them lifted their glasses, and their glasses met and parted.

They kept drinking, but did slow down compared to earlier in the evening. They no longer attempted to commit suicide. Lori felt, suddenly and unexpectedly, a violent, powerful joy swell inside.

– Let's toast to madness, the tall dark woman cried. – May it long live.

– TO MADNESS, Julia and Kelly, and several others nearby joined in.

A few of the more «cultivated» guests frowned in dismay, but mostly their display of bravado was positively received.

The trio, triad mingled further, but stayed close, holding on to each other for dear life. Kelly brightened as they pulled to a stop by the tailspin stairs.

– That's Richard Marx, the Black Metal singer, she exclaimed. – There are indeed quite a few interesting people frequenting this place.

Lori looked at the tall man with the long dark hair, and staring eyes.

– I know, she grinned. – He's my neighbor, and he's almost exclusively playing his own albums through open windows at night. He's making Tom, my sweet hubby, insane…

– You're kidding! Kelly said. – You're kidding, right?

She resembled the typical young girl with a crush on a rock star or celebrity. Lori sighed but played along.

– Not at all. He lives next door. The entire neighborhood has madee several attempts at evicting him, in vain. He has a bunch of lawyers working around the clock to, as he says, «protect him from interfering busybodies».

– Present me. Seeing the other's look Kelly added in a girlish voice: – *Please.*

– Okay. Lori shrugged. – Why not?

She sensed a smile dawn on her lips, sensed yet another first stirring of life within her. Marx stood just a few steps away. It wasn't far, not far at all.

The three of them approached him. The two girls with sideways, nervous glances. Lori with a devil-may-care attitude. She elegantly cleared her way through the queue of admirers and sycophants.

– Hello, Richard, she said sweetly.

She held her hands on her back, pushing her breasts forward, posing boldly for him.

He looked at her with his black eyes, his burning stare, recognizing her, frowning, sensing, clearly sensing there was something different about her, at the very least in her approach to him. An intended sour reply turned to something else.

– Hello, Lori, what an unexpected honor, what are you doing in a place like this at a time like this?

The irony was clearly distinct in his voice, and he wanted it that way. She just kept grinning at him.

– Oh, we were just passing by…

Kelly was panting by her side, her tongue practically hanging out.

– This is Kelly. She wanted to meet you…

He turned his entire attention to the blushing girl, and she turned tomato red.

– Hello, Kelly, he said softly, brutally.

And he grabbed her, pulled her close to him, and kissed her hard on the lips. She gasped, stiffening, before turning limp in his arms.

He led her, didn't drag her away. She looked apologizing back at Lori, before disappearing with him out the door, and undoubtedly to an apartment nearby.

Lori shook her head in wonder, smiling.

– Gosh, Julia exclaimed. – It is actually true. Girls fall for rock stars on the spot.

– It's a fairly known fact that undressing is the price of admission backstage, Lori said dryly.

She felt good, warm inside, a feeling she couldn't name, one she could no longer avoid.

The night ended somehow, sometime. She wasn't sure when. It just melted away, as the store's visitors melted, dissolved into the very air itself, becoming indistinct, like… ghosts.

– This was nice. Julia kissed her on the cheek. – We must do it again sometime.

– We must. Lori nodded.

And then she was alone outside, in the street, the bright dark summer streets of London. Lights and warm skin swirled around her, and she stood there paralyzed, completely unable to move. Everything. She saw everything.

And then she forgot.

She stood there, attempting to catch her breath. But she couldn't, and she wondered if she had died there, on the spot, if she crouched on the sidewalk, unable to move, expiring and fading into nothing.

The car stopped right beside her, with whining breaks.

She turned and met the burning eyes of Richard Marx.

– I think we're heading the same way, he said. – Can I give you a lift?

For just a horrible moment there, she looked at him, absolutely blank.

– A lift? She sniffed. – Sure, why not. Mutual goals and that shit, right.

– That shit, he nodded.

The door opened and she sat down inside. The door slammed shut, and spinning wheels made an absolutely stunning view of the street as Marx pushed the gas(p) pedal through the floor, as smoke filled the streets, as they left it with a mighty roar, and they raced between shifting lights and dark gray walls.

Spinning into the night.

She woke up with a start the next morning, the few, short hours since she had hit the pillow. It was a strange feeling. She didn't feel tired, only... disconnected. As she went through the motions, as she spent the day in a haze, she noticed, once again the first stirrings of impatience within. She went straight from work to the city. Without hardly thinking about it, she left her car at the parking lot and entered the train at Hampton Court station, and headed for London, headed back to London, back to

She had imagined it would be hard to find the bookstore turned tavern, or the tavern turned bookstore, but it wasn't. She walked straight at it, without having to search for it at all. The door was open. The draft from the basement caught her instantly, destroying what little hairdo she had done before leaving the office. She sought deeper within the place, leaving the bright sun from the windows behind.

There weren't many people there today, at least not compared to the crowded house the previous night. There were more than in most ordinary bookstores she had visited, during any given day, though. She walked along the isles, browsing with her eyes, touching with her hands. There were lots of books here, lots of special books. You didn't find this stuff in such quantity in ordinary outlets, that was for sure. She picked one at random, pulling it from the shelf.

PRACTICING MAGIC - an introduction.

It said.

She browsed it, read a bit, turned more pages, read some more.

«The first thing one newly initiated witch should do is to make an altar in her home»...

She put it away and picked another.

MY MEETING WITH THE GODDESS

«I met the Goddess at a low ebb, and that encounter transformed my life».

She read the first sentence and put it away.

A bit frustrated she picked a heap of books, sampling them all in brief succession, before returning them, too, to the shelf. She walked right to one of the counters, with a sign saying

INFORMATION

There was a queue. She didn't really hear anything about what they were saying, the man ahead of her, and the man behind the counter. It was just an unpleasant buzz somewhere in her head.

– You don't understand, the man in front of the counter said to the man behind it. – I want to ascend from this plane of reality, to the higher planes. I want to make sure it won't be a dud.

The guy sounded more than a bit insane. She looked closer at him. He looked quite normal, quite mundane, dressed in blue dungaree pants and jacket, shaven and smelling of deodorant. She shook her head, buzzing out again.

Then she was at the front of the queue.

– Good afternoon, the man behind the counter said pleasantly. – Is there anything I can help you with?

– I've started to believe in the ways of… of m-magic, she stuttered, – and I'm wondering why.

There was laughter somewhere, and she reddened. A schoolgirl. She behaved like a schoolgirl on her first day.

– You're curious of the hidden world, he nodded. – Feeling the need to learn its secrets.

– Yes, that's precisely it, she said eagerly. – You see, I've experienced things I can't explain, and… well, not really experiencing much as much as *feeling* things, you know, and not being sure it's real.

– I understand perfectly, he stated. –You want to get going and you don't know where to start. You want recommendations, right, a point from where you may begin your tutelage? Well, you've come to the right place.

A sigh of relief escaped her.

– Yeah, that's it, she said self-consciously, – There's so much here, so much to choose from, and being the total novice that I am, I find it hard to find anything useful.

– It's all quite natural, he assured her.

He was very good at assuring her.

She sensed something, sensed something being born. It screamed within her.

Her hands touched the books, the paper, her eyes reading nothing. She put them away, pushing them back towards the man behind the counter.

– I'm afraid this isn't very useful.

And by her second use of that word he seemed to get it, at least to a point.

– Useful? He wondered.

– Yes, she said. – I looked for something about witches. But I couldn't find anything. Not about any doing… doing true magic, about someone I could possibly… learn from.

It just… erupted from her, the revealing words, the palatable desire.

And she realized she sounded just as crazy as the guy before her.

She looked at the man, meeting his eyes, desperately attempting understanding, attempting communion.

– Look, this sounds more like Christianity than Witchcraft, she said.
– It's Wicca, he said. – The religion of Witchcraft, the worship of the Goddess.
And now he met her eyes, making contact, staring at her.
– It's about the Goddess, he said. – The central part of our lives, our very reason for living.
It sounded. It sounded…
Fake.
Or perhaps not fake, but contrived, as if even though he believed his own words, it didn't ring true to her.
And she finally realized he was pitching a sale, that he was as sincere as a grassing wolf before a sheep. She recognized a pitch easily, of course, once she managed to pry her eyes open, having done such pitches numerous times herself.
And he was no wolf, only another sheep pitching the grass to other sheep.
She stepped forward, as close to the desk as she could possibly come, doing one, final attempt.
– I want the real thing, understand, not the watered-down version of it.
– I've never encountered anything resembling the «real thing», the man behind the counter said, dismissing her.
She panted, bile stuck in her throat flooding her mouth. Her eyes fell on one of the books.
OLD SPELLS AND CEREMONIES
– I'll take this. It's a start, anyway. Thank you.
She threw some money at the desk, way too much, and hurried out, hurried out of there.
– By the way. She stopped briefly in the door. – My sincere advice is that you should change your name to MUNDANE PRACTICES AND BELIEFS…
The street was breath, was breathing. She rushed off, walking away with long and fast strides. She was sweating profusely. It had begun in front of the counter and had just worked its way up from there. This was different then the rage she had felt when she had vandalized her office. Worse. A terrible sense of loss and disappointment ravaged her.
– Fuck, she mumbled.
– FUCK!
She shouted.
People stared at her, but she didn't care. Slowly, slowly, when seeing their shocked expressions, she started smiling, a wolfish grin scaring them to death.

– I'm not you, she cried. – I'm *more*.

I'm losing control, and I think I like it.

The wolfish grin widened, widened beyond belief.

– You're free as well, she cried. – You're free. You can do what you will.

– Why don't you go to Speaker's Corner? A man glared at her. – That's the proper place for such insanity.

– So, you mean one can only speak about freedom in pre-arranged, authorized places then? She chided him. – That people speak about freedom is insanity to you? That makes sense.

He glared some more, and pulled back, once more fading away into the general background he enjoyed so much.

She looked around at the others standing around her, challenging them to say something, anything. There were no takers. It made her feel good. It made her feel bad.

After a short walk she reached the new, shiny Tottenham Court Road station. She walked inside it and all the way down to the trains, down the stairs and escalators, and sat down in a seat. Not on a train, but by the platform wall. A train, several trains passed by. She sat there, reading the book.

Trains passed and passed again. She hardly noticed all the people leaving and entering the coaches. There was the occasional gush of wind, as the trains arrived and left, the sounds of steps, of voices. Then there was silence. She didn't look at her watch, but when she finally rose again many trains had passed. Determination showed in her face, in her flashing eyes, and she went back upstairs, moving in the midst of people, almost suffocating among them all. Well outside, able to breathe again, somehow, she threw the book in the first wastebasket she encountered. It wasn't hard finding one. The Westminster Borough put great emphasis on keeping garbage off the streets.

Finding an Internet Café wasn't hard either. She sat down and started searching for interesting topics… and left about an hour later, filled with frustration. She had found a few sites that could be interesting, sent a few emails, but mostly it stank, reeking of mediocrity and normalcy.

«We should meet», she sent to mark247@yahoo.com. «People with such special interests should exchange both ideas and company».

She signed it with «Lori».

Feeling very daring.

His site was about everything from occultism to paganism and witchcraft, and he claimed he resided in London.

«Today's world is merely a trifle», he wrote. «It's nothing compared to the infinity of the Universe, of all worlds, including Earth, past, present and future».

Again, she felt a little better, a little worse.

London's streets surrounded her, embraced her, as if being a womb soon to give birth. It was. She sensed the birth fluid all around her, actually felt it, as she was bathing in it, as it comforted her, frustrated her.

– You're free, she told people passing her. – You can do what you want.

Some of them hurried on, glaring at her in suspicion and fear. She ran after them, hunted them, until she caught them and shook them, shook them hard.

– You're *free,* she emphasized. – You can do what you *want*. Why don't you? What's *wrong* with you?

– Let GO of me, you crazy BITCH, a woman shouted back at her.

– «Let go of me, you crazy bitch», Lori chided. – Are you out of your mind? Are you well? What possesses you to say such insane things, woman? Are you human or sheep?

And there was fear in the woman's eyes, as Lori left *her,* left her behind.

Lori danced on Trafalgar Square, danced among the pigeons, their wings blowing wind in her hair, her long, unbound hair. Their wind and the water from the fountains mixed in the air around her. People stared at her, and she stared defiant back at them. A lot of people stared at her, and she wondered about her imagination, as she pondered the unbelievable, whether or not one or even more of those watching vibrated sympathetic harmonies.

The dance ended, but to her it really truly didn't. She gasped for air, sweat pouring from her skin, ruining her clothes. She probably smelled and she didn't care.

A boy, a young boy met her stare, flickering on and off her in the busy Square.

– What are you dancing to? He wondered. – There's no music.

– Oh, but there is, she said.

She walked to him, stopped right in front of him, as she kept staring at him.

– What is your name? She asked him.

– J-justin, he replied, turning deep, deep red.

– J-justin, she nodded, grinning. – That's a great name.

She touched his jaw, caressing it softly.

– There is music, she insisted. – You just have to listen. If you don't listen you certainly won't hear anything.

And she gave him her business card. He looked at it, at her, as if she had flipped completely… And perhaps she had. She grinned, a grin quickly spreading to her entire face.

The good mood didn't leave her. Not as she descended the escalators in the Tottenham Court underground station, not as she appeared on Waterloo Station, and she picked a train back south.

All windows were open in the summer heat. The wind… *filled* the coach. She reached out with her hands, in a hopeless attempt to… to touch the wind, and she laughed deliriously.

Hampton Court felt… different. In all ways her eyes could see, it looked exactly the same, but it felt different. And nothing had happened, nothing of substance. The car still stood on the parking lot, of course it did, a lonely horse on an abandoned square of asphalt. She went through the motions the remains of the day, with her family, with them speaking to her, and she replying, not really listening, not really speaking.

The next morning, she stood in front of the bathroom mirror, brushing her hair. Everything looked the same. Nothing had changed. She brushed her hair harder.

She wondered if it was always this way. That the joys of yesterday would fade in the early morning light.

Lori saw her children and husband off, as she always did, every morning. It was time for her to go as well. Simple. Just dress. Fix yourself up, and do your thing. She left her jacket and walked out the door. She could recall her dolling herself up before the mirror, but she couldn't recall that there was any tangible result. Her car was in the driveway, ready for use. She walked past it, and headed for the neighboring house. The loud music inside made the entire house shake.

She rang the bell, heard nothing of it. She stood for a few seconds in front of the door, tripping impatiently, before pushing down the handle. The door was unlocked. She pushed it open and walked inside, closing it behind her almost as an afterthought.

There was a strange, colorless twilight inside. Walls, ceiling and floor were white and gray and dark, no colors, only the flickering twilight. The music filled the house. It was impossible to tell where it came from. She walked from room to room, through one bizarre setup after another. The man was an avid collector of all kinds of stuff. The house was filled with old and exotic items. It raised her eyebrows in all kinds of cheerful ways. She kept walking until she oddly enough found Kelly and Richard in the living room. Kelly crouched nude on the floor, half sitting, half stretching, displaying herself to the man not really looking. He played a guitar, tuning in to the music from the speakers. He had a shirt on his upper body. Aside from that he, too, was nude as a toddler. Lori could easily see his prick, hanging down, still dripping of juices, forming a pond on the carpet below the chair.

They didn't see her at first. She walked to the center of the room, and then they did see her. She moved and her moves turned into a dance. She stopped looking at them with a weird, downright scary face. She found the piece of chalk in her pocket and held it up, drawing their attention to it. And they looked at it, followed its path through the air as she drew a circle, a wide, wide imperfect circle on the floor, and pieces of the chalk were liberated to the air, the twilight surrounding them all. She felt lightheaded, detached from herself, as she waved to them, calling them to her, calling for them to join her in the circle, in her circle.

Marx grinned at her, as he took Kelly's hand and led on across the floor. They were clearly on something, their eyes wide as a field. She saw her own eyes mirrored in theirs, wide as an ocean. They entered the circle. She gestured for them to sit down, to join her on the floor. She sat there with her feet crossed, and a few seconds later, so did they. Her body started swaying. She reached out to them, and they grabbed her hand. Her swaying spread to them, becoming their own. She squeezed their hands, squeezed hard. There were cries of pain, silent, unheard in the inferno of sound surrounding them. Only the masks were heard, the masks cracking open. Lori smiled. She closed her eyes. They did, too. The world was spinning. She sensed it. They weren't actually moving. Nothing was happening, even though she fervently wanted something to happen. They still sat there, sat there crouched in the circle, holding hands, swaying together. Her lips moved. She knew she was speaking, but there was no sound, sound of discord. Something… happened. So subtle at first. She sat there on her ass, swaying, and she felt the first stings of discomfort, and then… in one heartbeat, two… arousal.

She pulled herself towards Richard, pulled him closer to her. Still holding on to his and Kelly's hand she embraced him, crawling onto his lap, kissing his lips hard, noticing as yet another afterthought how her nipples hardened, how the sweet itch changed to pain. Kelly said something, clearly angry.

You're not jealous, are you? Lori said to her.

And she turned to the other woman, embracing her, too, kissing her lips hard, too. Kelly attempted to pull away at first, but Lori held on to her, began caressing her in bold, insistent moves. And Kelly's body softened, and a moan escaped the sore lips. Lori noticed Richard's wandering hands on her, and yelped, almost in surprise. He undressed her in swift, decisive moves. She felt her shirt slip off her shoulders and arms, felt her panties run down her thighs, stop a moment on one heel, and then go away. He buried his head between her breasts, and began sucking a nipple. It was bright sunshine outside, but here there was twilight, and mist, and night. She slipped up and down on Kelly's delicious body, touching her sex, her burning sex. Richard grabbed her hips, lifted them up a bit, and pushed himself inside her. She gasped, a loud, prolonged trumpet sound reverberating throughout the room, the room of mist. For some reason, she stared at the chalk forming the circle. It seemed to rise from the floor, turning into sand. Kelly writhed under her, so sweet so needy. Lori touched her sex, and the writhing body pushed against her hand, her wet hand. They moved, but never outside the circle. The circle turned into a wall, one of sand and mist. And even the room dissipated around the three, the three beasts copulating there in the sand. The lithe body beneath her hardened, as her own did, as she stood on all fours, with the man's hands on her hips, with her face buried in the woman's groin. Hot water flooded Lori's probing tongue. Richard grunted behind her. He began slapping her butt. Shocked, she turned. He kept slapping her, and suddenly her need increased tenfold. She moaned in ecstasy. He wanted her, wanted to come inside her. She wanted to protest, but he kept slapping her butt, and all her protests waned. She wanted him, wanted him to come inside her, wanted his seed.

Moans and grunts, light and heavy, echoed within the confines of the circle. The female on her back cried out. The female on all fours cried louder, as the roar of the male washed over them. Everything turned upside down, inside out, as all three fell to the floor, hitting the soft dunes in the desert night, tangled in sweat and juices, tangled in flesh, and nothing and no one breathed anymore.

Chapter Five

Lori called Julia and told her to come.

– Come *now,* she called in a throaty voice. – Come this instant. No, you won't have any trouble finding it. In fact, you can hardly miss it. Just follow the music.

She paused a bit, before whispering, before calling.

– I felt… something. A… stirring. I've looked for days, now, for centuries, for some sign that it is *real.*

She put the cell phone down, and turned, twisted in Richard's insistent arms, sighing happily, as his hands once again ventured to her swollen parts. She sat in his lap, writhing, as she slowly began to move up and down. Then he pushed inside her, and her face transformed into joy, into lust. Kelly rubbed her body at her back, so eager, desire clouding her eyes.

Julia walked into the living room, as the three of them lay entangled on the floor, a bit outside the circle. They had just had another row of orgasms, and looked at the newcomer with pleasure and contentment and hunger in their eyes.

She stopped just inside the door.

Lori had a book in her lap, reading with a loud, raunchy voice.

– The path to a human being's inner self is reached through the enjoyment of the senses, she read. – There are many paths, but without this crucial link the search for illumination becomes that much harder…

Books were spread all over the floor. Richard had quite a collection of arcane prints.

She and Kelly rose. Julia took one step backwards, but then she stopped. They walked to her and stopped left and right of her. Kelly softly, tenderly and hungrily patted her cheek. And soft, tender and hungry was the kiss. They began undressing her, her feeble protests easily overcome.

– We'll gut you, Lori said fiercely, – as we gut ourselves, as we cut open what obstructs our Self from arising from our depths.

They pushed her in front of the large mirror, and they made her watch as they denuded her, as they exposed her, as they slowly lit her fire. She watched in the mirror as Richard rose, as his cock rose.

– Have you been doing this all the time? She whispered. – How can you… can he still be… *ready?*

– Human sexuality is obstructed, too, Lori told her. – Along with everything else making us human. Tear off the blindfolds, remove the preconceptions…

– And we'll see the world as it is… infinite, Kelly completed seductively.

– Fear not, Richard said drowsily. – You'll catch up to us soon enough. This is just the beginning…

– The beginning of everything, Lori the Demon assured her.

And the spear penetrated the shield. And the spear was sharp for the first time, and the shield no longer shielded anything. Julia's face, like that of her peers, dissolved into intense desire.

It had turned dark outside. It had finally turned dark. The four of them lay entangled by the window, easily exposed to anyone that might pass by. Lori didn't mind. Lori didn't care. Candles lit the room, and nothing else, except the four's fevered minds.

– Everything… she mumbled, clearing her throat. – Everything happened so fast, so *natural.*

The others nodded eagerly, speaking without words. She felt them, felt every touch, every small meeting and parting of skin.

– Richard has... something. It's time now. Time…

Richard nodded, more to himself perhaps, than to her, but to her as well. He jumped to his feet, doing so like a young male in the forest, and she felt the animal pull. His cock dangled from side to side at his thighs. He walked to a drawer, and pulled it open, picking up a small box.

– I have to warn you, he admonished them. – This is Blue Moon Acid, very strong stuff. And probably even more… potent after the day we've had…

– I don't know, Kelly said, clearly worried. – Shouldn't we eat something first?

– We haven't eaten much today, Lori acknowledged. – And that's okay. That's exactly how it's supposed to be. Usually acid is a slow rising tide, but with us tonight, it will be a *deluge*.

The parallel vision revealed it to her, showed what was coming.

– It probably doesn't matter, Kelly shrugged. – It feels like we're dreaming anyway. Everything we've done since Lori entered the premises and started waving the chalk feels like a dream.

– Row, row, row your boat, Julia sang, – roughly down the stream, life is but a dream.

She giggled, hopelessly out of it.

– But in other ways…

– But in other ways, Kelly kept saying, – it feels sharper than any serpent's tooth, and not like a dream at all.

– Do you know what, Richard chuckled. – I just realized we haven't taken anything yet. My goddess.

There were eight pills in the box. They took two each, in rushed, swift moves.

The flame burned. Lori blinked, and that brief moment, that eternity the blink lasted, she could glimpse the fire, one in mist, one in night.

– The shit doesn't work yet, right? It will take at least an hour before it starts working, and probably two before it works in earnest?

– That's right, Richard replied. – Even though it might happen faster since we haven't had any food.

Lori blinked, and after a brief moment, an eternity, she spoke in an indistinct, remote voice.

– I can see the fire. I can see it burn, burn the air.

Julia hit the drum. There was no music from the speakers anymore. Richard played the guitar.

– Perhaps we should eat, Kelly said. – Perhaps we should have eaten.

– No food, Lori stated, Lori repeated. – No food. No food. No food.

The drum and the guitar box, and Richard's fingers, his moving fingers, sent ghostly music into the room, into the bodies of those swaying and humming on the floor.

– The Anti-Social Behavior Act? Lori turned to Richard and spoke to him without any introductory comments.

– Applies only to noise made at night. He grinned, grinned wiiide. – A deliberate concession I've chosen to make… because it's so damn funny.

– Fines for graffiti, Kelly howled. – There are fines for everything these days. If I was to draw or write on a toilet wall, I could be sentenced to prison. Tony and David and Theresa and their like in full blooooom.

Bloooooooooooooooommmmmmmmmmmmm.

Lori thought.

– The noose is tightening, she sang. – The fruit is more than ever dying on the wine. Only stone flowers are growing in the city, in the big, big balloon city.

There were shadows in the room, long shadows from the candles, the candles shadowing the room.

– Open, she sang. – Open to all forces that might find me, might *ravage* me.

Her snarl echoed, echoed, echoed in the big, big room, the big as a hall room with walls fading, fading, fading.

The shadows stretched. She saw it, felt it, a pull in her skin, inside the forehead, the frontal lobe, the frontal lobe, the back, back loooobeeeeeee.

Julia stretched on the floor. She was playing with herself, her eyes far, far away, as she rode the seven horses, as she rode the dragon. Lori kissed her on her lips, and her lips were a fire, the kiss a universe.

– People, she said, swimming in flesh. – People…

– Sssee how they sit there, she said, she spoke, she hisssssed, – day people, in their bright light, pretending there are no shadows, avoiding the night, the joyous and wretched night. But the night, wonderful and terrifying, denied so long, is returning from its long exile.

She swayed, she swayed in shadow.

– And then there are the people thinking, and often not really thinking at all.

Richard played, finger-played the strings, the quivering strings. And she heard his sssong. She heard her voice take flight. She spoke. She thought. She was flying.

– You're right, thinking is not enough - it's just a start. The need to look and seek further doesn't come out in most people - even those who do think. Most just want to feel they're superior because they think a little and are liberal. When they come face to face with anything really disturbing to them, their brainwashing kicks in. Goodbye thought.

He smiled. She almost gasped. It was so strange, so unexpected, compared to her impression of him.

– I just learned something, she stated. – Thank you, thank you.

She walked to him, crawled to him, grabbed his head, and kissed him on the lips, kissed him hard, drawing blood.

And the blood was a riveeeer, and she heard its roar.

The shadows on the floor stretched, and stretched, and the light from the candles flickered and *moved.*

– Red yellow, Yellow red, she incanted. – Shades of orange, of fire, color, no color at all.

There was a sun by her hand. She traveled through infinite Space, and there was a sun in the palm of her hand. She brushed off the deadly solar winds as if they were nothing. There was a universe in her hand. She looked up and swallowing that universe was a vast, vast black hole. And then, in a flash, in a moment shorter than a matchstick flare, she was beyond that, and the vast black hole was only a pinprick in the vast Universe she had become.

She gasped. She breathed. And in that single breath was another universe, another black hole swallowed by her fiery dragon gap. And another. And another. The room… the room had become fireflies dancing in the dark, dark space of reality. She hardly saw the others anymore. Only when she squinted her eyes, she was able to spot them through billions of years of mist, of stardust and ashes.

We are alone, she thought saddened, triumphant. I'm more me than I ever was.

The closeness of touch, of skin against skin and burning desire brought them close again. Fucking brought closeness, brought unity. Skin joined. Mind joined. Two, three, four became one in repeated explosions of pleasure, of joy, of delight. One burst of rampant, uncontrolled sexuality lasted Forever, ongoing, never ending. She stayed with them, even as she walked alone, pushing into the shadows, the deep, deep, deep twilight night.

There was grass, and there was concrete, hot beneath her bare feet. She walked in a garden of shadows. In a narrow alley, she saw a dark shape appear from a fast growing cloud of smoke.

«Beware the dark man. Beware the hooded woman walking through the desert».

There was a voice formed out of the very air itself.

Sometimes there are riders, the voiceless voice whispered.

– Sometimes there are riders.

She looked up, startled.

– He said something, she said. – Sometimes… there are riders.

Voicing it sent another chill through her.

She hummed, hummed to the song of fire and shadow, what was now filling the room, what was now the room. What was now her.

– Open, she hissed. – I am *Open*.

Come and fill me up. Fill me up and turn me upside down. Empty my cup.

Roared the voice calling in the desert.

She laughed giddily, ripping pages from the book in her lap. Sheets turned to paper crumbs, to the pile of paper she was building between them.

– The fire is true, she said. – Is passed from mother to daughter, from father to daughter, from mother to son, from father to son. What is true in one generation doesn't fade in the next. What is true in one generation fades to nothing in the next.

Julia and Richard played, and their ghostly dark frames danced in the ether.

– Fire devourssss, Kelly mumbled. – Fire growssss.

And the children die a little every day, as they grow, as they fall, the voice in the garden of shadows beckoned. Dwindling is the world, dying is the world.

Strike a match did the witch, and the inferno began.

Lori laughed, laughed giddily, hysterically, as she stared like hypnotized at the pile of burning paper on the floor. Dry, withered grass caught fire, caught wildfire. It rose towards the ceiling in one, swift swoop. Its tongue licked the white surface, transforming it. Lori looked like transfixed at the ceiling as it slowly turned brown, turned black.

Looked from the outside, at the four people sitting inside the circle. It seemed like the fire was sucked upwards and didn't touch the four at all, even though the dark flames danced in their faces.

Lori gasped, as air burned in her throat. She rode Richard, rode him hard, and her entire body was on fire, her dark hair dancing around her body. Julia and Kelly played with each other close by. Lori felt them, too, felt their joy. She cried out in her ghostly voice:

– No reward without risssk.

Flames spread on the floor, licked the walls, as they danced and twisted in the mist and shadow in their cave. She reached for them, fascinated, mesmerized and attracted to the powerful, the beyond powerful energies. They pulled her away, away from the beautiful flame. The four of them sat on the lawn. They stumbled outside, as the flames consumed the house. It hissed and roared at them, in its blatant disappointment, and the trickle down their spine, the fear cutting into them felt very real. Lori sat on the lawn and laughed, laughed her heart out. The dark laughter filled the night as the house, the vast structure she imagined behind them disintegrated in an ocean of embers.

The bright light hurt her eyes, and tears obscured her vision. They stung her, stung her eyes, her skin as they hit her thigh, her bare and sticky thigh. Male and female juices still flowed from her cunt. She noticed, absentmindedly, how the waterfall kept flowing, as the pleasant heat inside of her slowly subsided.

– M-mommy?

She looked up. Toni stood a few steps away. A bit further behind were Tom and the two boys.

– Hello, honey, Lori said calmly.

A few minutes later close and distant neighbors, and a bunch of firemen had joined them. Smoke covered the area. Water from the firemen's hoses extinguished the last of the flames in the blackened ruins of the house, still dousing the surrounding structures in order to keep the fire from spreading. Lori Michaels stood there with a blanket covering her body, staring at the patterns endlessly forming in the shifting smoke, light and shadow. She saw a figure dancing in that flickering vision, in the wet inferno the place had become.

She glanced at Richard. He wasn't pleased. She could easily see that.

But when he noticed her glance, he just shrugged and grinned.

As a limo showed up, and he entered it, he laughed to his heart content, so loud that it was heard over all the present engines and noise. He waved to her, a brief greeting, filled with humor, with dark, wonderful joy.

She held out both her hands towards Julia and Kelly. After a brief hesitation, they stepped forward and took her hands. And then, shortly thereafter smaller hands joined those of the other three. Lori smiled to her daughter.

They walked inside, inside the other house that had been Lori's home.

– A bit drastic a way to deal with an estranged neighbor, don't you think? Tom glared at her.

She looked amused at him, wanted to kiss him, but thought that she better not, with her lips and cheeks and hair covered in semen and juices. She couldn't suppress the giggle working its way up her throat. No way!

The three women showered, showered together, giggling and screaming loud. They sensed it, how the LSD slowly waned in their system, even as it lingered. But their excitement didn't truly stem from that, they knew it didn't.

– Real, Julia declared. – It was real.

– Real, Lori whispered.

They washed each other, soaped each other in, with soft hands, so very soft hands. The laughter and almost childish giggle persisted. The burning sensuality, even though waning, didn't fade. They kept caressing each other, but it was done more out of compassion now, than desire or lust. All three enjoyed the closeness of the others, the comforting touches.

– I know you both, Julia said. – During this short, long night I've come to know you better than anyone I've ever met. There are people I've known my entire life I don't know half as well as you.

Lori showed them to the guestroom, and joined them there. She locked the door. There was a large bed at the center of the room. The three of them sat there, on their asses, their feet crossed in front of them, in a circle, knee against knee against knee, touching in the circle, touching hands, touching lips.

– Ah… Lori gasped.

And it was as if the gasp was uttered in a large room, one of sounds and shadows, where the light didn't come from any fixed point but from everywhere, every single point in the very air surrounding them. It was as if they just drifted away, into limitless space, into the giant Void.

When the powerful lamp in the sky returned they couldn't tell how much time had passed. They stared at each other with dark stars in their eyes.

– We slept, Kelly said at the breakfast table the next morning, as the morning light filled the kitchen. – And it was total blackness, as if we had shut down completely. But it wasn't total blackness. There was somewhere in there, where we did dream, somewhere we couldn't reach.

– That does sound so cool, Jeff said, his usual exuberant self.

Even a warning glance from his father didn't get him to pipe down. He blushed as the two unknown women looked approvingly at him. And the loving glance his mother sent him made him soar even higher.

The other two kids looked very brooding and very thoughtful.

Lori brushed her hair in the bathroom. She began setting it up, pinching it with needles, before halting the so very familiar process, before letting her hair be, letting it flow down her shoulders, letting it dance in the jet stream behind her. She did help Tom with his tie and handed him his briefcase, gave him a goodbye kiss on his cheek.

He didn't betray a single emotion. Not in his face. Not even in his eyes. But she could tell his mood by his steps. She always could.

She did go to work. She waved to Julia and Kelly, and drove off. Tires whined as they protested the hazardous turning of a curve. Slow, everything was so slow. She pushed a hand under her skirt and touched her naked cunt, rubbed it slowly and methodically. It was hardly necessary in order to make the fire rise in her, but she enjoyed the sensation, enjoyed skin against skin. More, she wanted more. She stopped in the garage, just about managing that before gasping, before stretching her body in the seat, before the steam covered the windows. The body sagged in the seat. Hair covered her face, swallowed by the wide-open mouth. Her hand kept moving a bit longer, reflexively, echoing the frantic moves of yestersecond, of distant, distant times. Her head rolled back and forth, as she kept gasping for air, as her rapid breathing was slowly, slowly waning.

She crossed the garage «plaza» to the elevator, slightly correcting her dress, her hair. Her dark tresses just kept blowing in her face and she gave up handling it. She laughed throatily, giddily beyond sound. Men and women, employees stared at her. She let them. Let them stare.

The elevator swallowed her, and she let it. It took her up, but in reality it took her down, down, down, to the dark, lower spheres she had dreamt and fantasized about. The executive floor, it seemed dead and silent, in spite of the seemingly hectic activity around her.

– Hello, Paul, she softly greeted him.

He reddened. He actually blushed like a teenage boy hardly out of his diapers.

Her office had been… fixed. Marco was very efficient and his people quite able to handle a great variety of indiscretions. It had been redecorated. Marco had quite correctly assumed she didn't care for the previous décor anymore.

She walked to the window, looking down and out. It was a cloudy day, low clouds, wispy clouds, drifting, changing before her eyes. A cauldron boiling somewhere, and then, in a glimpse, as the clouds momentarily parted, she spotted a mountain, tall and foreboding and mysterious, and she gasped in delight. She put her palms at the window, pushing her head against the cold glass, reaching for the incredible sight in the distance.

It faded, like a mirage, never really there.

She choked, pulling back, sniffing as she headed for her desk (her new and shiny desk). Suddenly the headache returned, with a vengeance. It felt like her head split in two. She rushed to her purse and, reaching inside it without having any recollection of having opened it. Her hand closed around the small bottle.

– No pills, she mumbled. – No pills, no pills, *no pills!*

She threw the bottle across the room, and it broke against the wall, and the dozens small capsules flooded the floor, the floor with the moving, all the moving shadows.

The headache slowly subsided, taking its time, longer than ever before. She fell down in her chair (her new, soft chair), a small tear manifesting at the corner of her left eye.

– The pain is real, she stated, conviction, certainty dawning in her eyes.

She rose from the chair. Pain shot through her entire body. She gasped and moaned, as she stumbled forward on the floor. The shadows, the dancing shadows there. They attracted her, pulled her in, and she let it happen, desired for it to happen.

– Come to me, she mumbled, she called. – COME TO ME!

And imagined that they moved, approaching her, hearing her call.

She bent down and picked up the pills, meticulously, one by one. Her hand full she walked to the bathroom, and dropped them in the toilet bowl. She flushed it all down, and watched as they vanished down the drain.

Uncertain if she had ever left she returned to the other room, and the shadows. But the pills were gone. Now, there were only her… and the shadows. They rose around her, embraced her and invaded her, as she danced with them. There was a forest she glimpsed, at the edge, at the edges of her eyes, and she laughed giddily, and the forest echoed with laughter.

And then the room, the very air turned dark. She turned her head slightly, looking at the window. And in the window-frame, in the open air outside, she saw a raven.

It floated in the air, flapping its wings, easily holding its position there, just outside the window, so skilled, so great. A lump stuck in her throat, and it subsided only slowly as time passed.

She took the elevator down, sensed herself descending, falling, falling down, down, down, to the level beneath the lowest level. The door slid open, and she entered a lush jungle. The smell was so powerful that it made puss flow from her nose. Her nose itched. The jungle breathed. As it breathed in and out she sensed its pulse quicken, its heart beat faster. It whispered… to her. The trees, the animals cried out. To her.

A glimpse, an eternity, then there was ache, dull and far worse and the sharp pain.

The female standing there in the forest glen shook violently, something in the wind, a violation, a horror, assaulting her. She cried out in despair. Everything… dried up around her. Wherever she turned she saw only death. Naked trees, dead long ago. Corpses, both human and otherwise picked half clean, a horrid stench, not of decay, but of corruption, of slow, agonizing demise far worse than death, in a lifeless landscape beyond desolation, beyond ordinary destruction. As she looked up she realized the horrible truth. There was no life here, no life at all, nothing to pick clean the sea of bodies. The sky wasn't blue anymore. There were no clouds. There wasn't any sky, not even any stars, just a putrid gray, endless and everlasting, preserved in this test tube of… Nothing.

She screamed, froze and fell, fell on the hard concrete between all the cars, all the poison-breathing, bad smelling carriages down in the garage. Unconsciousness assaulted her, deep and black.

Beyond deep, beyond black she sensed herself be touched, be lifted, be carried, and be moved in a howling poison-breathing carriage. She smiled, as she kept shaking inside, as the horror stuck within.

She awoke in a hospital bed sometimes in the afternoon. They had drugged her. She noticed that instantly. The pain was gone. The whispers were gone. Her senses dulled. The body heavy and stuck.

Lifting her head a bit, easily enough, she looked at her hands and feet. No handcuffs or restraints. She wasn't considered dangerous then. The grin felt alien. Everything did.

Helen Weaver appeared in the door. Lori wasn't surprised. The grin widened.

– They… notified me, the therapist said. – You're listed as my patient.

– Hello, Helen! Lori greeted her, way too loud and over the top.

There was a sour, unidentifiable stench, not smell in the room. As Lori looked at Helen it seemed to grow and multiply. Helen used perfume, very strong anti-perspiring stuff with a close to strangling «quality», but it wasn't that.

– You smell, Helen. Lori looked seriously at her, with a pointed stare. – It isn't so much a smell as it is something… deeper, beneath the stinking perfume. I suspect nobody but me can detect it.

The room itself was strange, at first, until Lori realized that no one else saw it like she did, until she realized the self-evident, that it was her, her perception.

– Hello, Lori, how do you feel?

The venom in her voice was as strong as ever. Lori despaired of never having noticed that before.

– You didn't bring any recording device. Lori felt good when she saw the thunderstruck look in the other's face. – I can tell, you know, tell now.

She stretched on the bed, stretched pleasantly, a somber look passing over her face.

– I experienced something… extraordinary, Helen. I'm… I'm *becoming*.

– Becoming what exactly? Weaver's voice was as dry as ever.

– I don't know yet… but I will. I know that!

She sat up in bed, swinging her feet outside the bed, removing the blanket.

– You know what, Helen?

Before waiting for an answer she continued, kept going.

– I think everybody should smell their own piss and shit occasionally. It would make for a far better world. What do you say to that, *huh?*

A very small wrinkle manifested on Weaver's forehead.

– You're ill, Lori.

– Ill? Lori's voice rose markedly. – Now, who's delusional? I slipped and fell. It can happen to the best of us, Helen. Not even your best fantasies can prove differently.

– I won't let you go, Lori. Weaver sounded almost in love.

Lori looked at her, and Weaver's lips started quivering.

– And more; Lori spat sweetly. – I realized I've given others, given you power over me. That ends now.

Helen had always seemed mysterious, somewhat deep to her. Now, when looking behind the façade, below the surface, below the waves she realized there was nothing there, and that it bothered Helen horribly.

The doctor entered the room, casually, a face quite impassive.

– Hello, Mrs. Russell, he said pleasantly. – How are we feeling today?

If he had known people using the word «we» in such a context drove her close to homicidal, he would probably reconsider.

But he was okay enough, at least compared to his present colleague.

– We are feeling great, Lori replied sweetly. – I'm okay, am I not?

He began sweating as both women looked at him.

– Except for a few minor bruises, we can find nothing physically wrong with you…

– Then I guess I shouldn't stay here and occupy a bed for someone needing it more.

Lori rose. She had expected to be unsteady on her feet, but she wasn't.

– I'll just be taking a shower, she said, very friendly, – and then I'm out of here. Will you make sure my discharge papers are signed, doctor?

– Certainly, Mrs. Russell, the doctor said, visibly red above his collar.

Lori walked to the closet where she expected her clothes to be, and they were, not really ruined in any visible way. She grabbed them all and headed for the hallway.

She stopped a bit, in front of the doctor, totally ignoring Weaver.

– I almost forgot. Where is…

– Down the hall, the doctor replied hoarsely.

Lori waited until she was well down the hall before checking for her cell phone. It was there. She couldn't help the sense of sickening relief grabbing hold of her.

She called the family lawyer, speaking in a fast, excited manner.

The shower felt good. The trickle of water on the skin cauterized her, strengthened her somehow.

The room was hot, dry, the summer heat flowing through the window. She dressed in slow, languishing moves.

Before she had quite finished dressing Weaver appeared in the room accompanied by an orderly, a very big orderly. Lori felt the pangs of fear in her gut.

– There is a psychiatric ward on this hospital, Lori, Weaver said. – I would like you to go with me there, please.

There were steps in the hall. Lori smiled. Weaver's smile faltered.

A man, impeccably dressed greeted Helen with a tip of his derby hat, and handed her a piece of paper.

– What is this? Helen looked incredulous at Lori, not at the derby hat. As she read it, it practically started shaking in her hand.

– That is a subpoena to appear in court, Lori grinned. – I'm suing you for misconduct, and for breach of patient/therapist confidence. Do you want kidnapping added to that?

The orderly visibly pulled back, several moments before his feet actually began moving.

– As I told you… Helen, Lori said icily. – I've given other people power over me, and that ends, now. I'll have a restraining order ready for you at the end of the day. I'm not willing to even look at you more than I absolutely have to.

And Helen Weaver pulled back, not certain what had happened, where she had gone wrong, where she had failed in her zeal.

It was done. Lori passed her on her way out, leaving the dank room, stopping for a moment to kiss Helen on her cheek, feeling the triumph swell within.

And she knew it was yet another meaningless act.

She entered the cab.

Everything turned dark. Everything was bright outside, but inside it was as if darkness surrounded her like a sponge.

The cab moved slowly through the streets, through darkened, empty streets. There were no other cars, but the cab never seemed to pick up speed. She looked outside. Paper and garbage floated across the street, danced in the air. There was smoke, blowing from a leaking pipe somewhere.

The children rushed to her and embraced her as she walked through the door.

– I'm okay, she assured them.

I'm more than okay, she thought. I feel great!

Tom took her arm and kissed her on the cheek.

– It's a good thing there is a weekend coming up, he nodded. – I presume you don't bring too much work home this time.

– No, not this time, Tom, she replied.

They settled in the living room. As usual all the windows in the house had been closed, but for a different reason than usual. The ash stench from the neighbor ruin was so pervasive that she smelled it even between breaths. She saw it between closed eyes, saw the fire.

She found herself by the dinner table without having any recollection of having walked there.

Pieces. My life is pieces.

I gave other people power over me. That ends now.

She repeated it again and again, like a mantra.

A butterfly flapped its wings outside the window, hovering unsteady in the air stinking of ash. Jeff put on a piece of music, on the low volume he was allowed. She walked out on the floor, and began dancing, dancing to the loud, pouncing music. Her children stared at her. Her husband stared. She didn't care. Her hair blocked her sight, but she saw still, knew exactly where to put her feet.

The loud music faded. She stood there on the floor, still now, breathing happily, moving constantly, eternally, her eyes sparkling.

– I love dancing, she cried. – I just *love* it!

She sat on the bed in the guest bedroom, shaking like a leaf. Slowly, only slowly the surroundings began making sense to her.

– Love it, Trish parroted. – Love it, love it, love it.

Even the parrot's voice sounded sinister in her ears. The squeaking voice from the distant living room didn't sound distant at all.

There was a sound outside. It took a while before she realized it was Mr. Holcomb's lawnmower. It was so loud, such an affront to her ears that it hurt. Louder than it should be, than it used to be. It was easy noticing Mr. Holcomb's frequent glances towards the house. He couldn't see her, but he wanted to, that's for sure.

Mrs. Rutherford walked her dog. Her head was turned constantly towards the house. It was quite funny watching her twist her entire body to be able to look back after she had passed the house. Lori giggled.

There was a sound, a buzz in the air around her. She cocked her head, listening carefully, unable to determine whether it originated inside the room or somewhere outside. It sounded electronic, but at the same time it was something disturbingly… organic about it. She realized that it was the same sound she had first heard minutes ago, the one she had mistaken for Mr. Holcomb's lawnmower. It was…

It was *evolving*.

The door was ajar. Lori spotted a flushed face there in the crack.

– Come here, honey, she told her daughter.

Toni straightened and walked into the bedroom, fervently attempting to hold on to her composure after having been found out.

– Sit! Lori tapped the bed. – Sit with me!

She saw herself at Toni's age, awkward, shy and not sure of anything, pretty much exactly how she felt right now.

Toni sat down, timid and anxious, looking at her mother beneath lowered eyelids.

– What's wrong? She abruptly exclaimed. – Please tell me what's wrong!

– Know that it has nothing to do with you, honey, Lori assured her. – Mommy is just going through a difficult time right now. It happens to everybody at some point in their life.

– Don't «mommy» me. The girl jumped to her feet. – I'm not a little girl anymore.

She rushed out of the room, and closed the door hard behind her, and there was a loud crack shaking Lori's world.

Lori sighed. She rose and left the room, returning to the living room. Toni wasn't there. The television was on. A voice spoke somewhere, probably through the television set, but Lori couldn't identify it or tell what it was saying. Tom sat in his favorite chair. He didn't look at her.

Not much was said, really, the rest of the day. Lori hardly recalled anything before the entire family made their weekly church visit on Sunday. It was a hot and humid day, and everybody was sweating profusely in their fine and thick clothes.

But Lori was *sweating*.

– What are you *doing?* Tom asked her in a voice akin to a whisper.

– I'm not *doing* anything, Tom, she gasped.

– You're sweating, he glared, – sweating beyond reason.

It had to be true. Everything was staring at her, and as the organ music and the priest's chanting voice mixed insanely in her head, it took an evident turn for the worse. She started growing lightheaded and her vision turned blurry and dark.

She vomited violently and loud, right there, kneeling on the aisle carpet, without really recalling how she got there. And everybody stared, stared hard.

The mood on the way home was, if possible even heavier than it had been on their way to the church.

– You should do a complete physical check-up, Tom said lightly, very lightly.

– I've done that, she replied. – There's nothing wrong with me. I just got fed up, that's all.

He held his tongue until they returned home, and the children left the living room.

– Have you any idea how damaging your behavior is to the children? Her husband blurted out.

– Funny you should mention that, she responded icily. – I guess you would claim that the backstabbing and dishonesty and cutthroat environment you take for granted, that I used to take for granted is providing a healthier education?

– What kind of talk is that? He said angrily, with a bitterness she had never before sensed in him. – What will you do next? Join a convent?

– That I'll never do, she grinned, without humor, with grim humor. – I can promise you that much.

– This isn't you talking, he stressed. – Think about what you're saying.

– I do, she insisted, walking to him, grabbing his hand, attempting to reach him, knowing that it would never work. – I've never felt like I thought I felt. I just fooled myself into believing that. This suicide life is beating us down, and I've finally realized that.

She stared into his eyes, holding onto his hands, even as he tried to break free.

– Is it so terrible to realize, at the age of forty you don't know shit about what the world is about, and that you never will? I don't think so. What I feel now, this moment is a good thing: The suspicion, no, the certainty that the life one has built for oneself is a house of cards.

– What do you mean? He spat angrily. – We have a financial secure future.

We had. At least we had.

She just looked at him, shaking her head. He didn't know what she was talking about, not even what he himself was talking about. He would never understand.

There were loud sounds all over the house, one loud sound, impossible to pinpoint. THUMP THUMP THUMP. It kept up for ten, twenty seconds, before it let up, before it faded. His eyes widened. She realized that he was staring at the mirror. He attempted to shake himself free, free from the hands holding on to him.

She let go of his hands, let go of him. He stumbled backwards, distraught and even practically beside himself. She had never seen him even remotely like this. He had never seen her like this. She turned towards the mirror. There was nothing there, nothing but her. She turned back towards him.

– What did you see? She wondered startled. – What are you afraid of?

– Afraid? He gawked.

– You saw something, didn't you? She said excited. – You actually saw something.

– I saw nothing, he stated, visibly clamming up.

– You don't understand, she said softly, her excitement waning. – You don't understand that either, not even that.

They left each other, there, at the center of what had been a cozy living room. Lori hurried to the bedroom, opened the door to the closet, grabbed some clothes there, and went to the guestroom, walked back and forth a few times with a heavy load of clothes, before falling down on the bed, without moving, without thinking, her eyes staring at nothing, dead to the world.

She finally sat up, eons later. It was still day, still bright sunlight outside the chilly twilight of the bedroom. She changed clothes quickly, changed into her training gear and rushed out of the house, setting out on a long, strenuous run.

There was just the run, and nothing else. The buzz in her ears slowly became that of singing birds and the flowing river. She leaned against a tree after having run flat out forever. Lori giggled, laughing happily, darkly, deliriously and didn't know what to think. Her surroundings, the park itself seemed to… shift, to become something completely different, independently of her blurry vision, her eyes filled with burning sweat.

It had become twilight by the time she made her way back to the house, one resounding in her mind like distant thunder. She stopped by the burned-out house. It dominated her vision, her entire perception and she grinned. She stood there for a while, taking in the sight, before heading the last few steps home, and her surroundings shifted from the outside of the nice suburban house and changed into the bathroom. The shower was loud, its water hitting her like needles of fire. She screamed in shock. The force of the water froze her, and she feared she melted under its relentless heat, until a long time passed, and she realized that it wasn't really that hot, and came to enjoy its merciless onslaught. Each time another drop hit her brought another sensation, and there were millions of them, millions of rapid touches pulling her away from there, to a different place she could only glimpse.

The bathroom was filled with steam afterwards, to a point where she could hardly see the walls. There were shapes there in the mist, and they watched her as she dried herself, enjoying the sight of her curves and moves, and it excited her. She felt the heat where the towel or her hands touched her skin, as she spotted her own, indistinct figure in the mirror.

The room seemed much bigger than it usually did. The shapes moving through the steam appeared both close and far away. She gasped, as one suddenly stood right in front of her, and stared at her with its black eyes. The steam looked more like mist, a mist on a moor a warm, warm summer evening, a jungle filled with shapes, shapes initially appearing to be trees, but then they didn't, and the black eyes and eager hands moved in on her and touched her.

The world returned only slowly to her idea of normal, and she gasped in relief, in disappointment, in an arousal that wouldn't let go.

She had opened the window wide, but the steam and heat were still slow to go. Lori sat on a stool at the center of the bathroom, fondling her breasts, playing with herself. She gasped and breathed, and each gasp, each breath embraced her like fire. Her surroundings no longer mattered, not in any way. The curtains no longer covered the windows. Anyone passing by outside would be able to see her, see her in all her glory. The thought excited her, raised her heat further. She gasped and fell over, her neck softly hitting the sink, balancing her right hip on the chair, the rocky chair. Hands moved faster below. She feared she would fall and hit the floor hard, and didn't care, care, care. Movements slowed down and she remained in that position for an indefinite stretch of time, breathing, breathing, breathing. Her hair covered her eyes and she couldn't see. She finally rose and returned to the shower on shaky feet, just as sweaty as she had been upon completing the run, and she used solely the cold water.

She dried herself before the mirror again, fairly cool and collected. It was just a mirror again, nothing extraordinary, no shapes in the mist, no invisible eyes observing her. Her movements were slow, lavish, as she took her time drying her wet and somewhat chilled body.

Her bedroom again, previously the guestroom. It was quiet there, fairly peaceful. She sat there shaking, fully aware of what Helen Weaver, or any therapist, for that matter, would make out of the last days' events.

She dressed and returned to the living room, calm on the outside, not revealing the raging storm within.

Tom and the children were there. They watched television. She joined them, sitting down in the vacant chair, not having or gaining any clue of what was on, on the square box. They sat there in silence, watching nothing.

Lori went to the kitchen. She made a heap of thick slices of bread, making sandwiches topped with ingredients, vegetables, ham and cheese, and all kinds of stuff she found, and began eating the first one before she had finished making the last. Today's run had just made her incredibly hungry. In a very un-English way she filled a large glass with milk and drank almost all of it in one sip. She filled another glass.

She sat there, at the dinner table and fed, while staring at her weak reflection in the window, at the coming night beyond it. Tom entered the kitchen, took one look at all the vegetables, hams and remains covering the desk and floor, and promptly returned to the living room.

There was a pressure at her temples. She shrugged and proceeded to devour the remains on the table. As she looked around it slowly dawned on her that there were crumbs and bits spread unevenly across the entire kitchen. It was like a tornado or something had raged through the room. She found the small broom and began the strenuous task of cleaning up the mess, shaking her head in dazed wonder.

Toni stood in the doorway, staring at her.

– Mommy was hungry, Lori said, – very hungry.

The Hunger at least temporarily abating, she put away the broom and stuff, and finally returned to the living room. It was different, a different living room from what she had known, even though she couldn't pinpoint anything and tell exactly what was different. She imagined she saw a sea of faces in the mirror of the windows. Faces gathered… gathered to…

Watch.

There was that sound again, the sound not being Mr. Holcomb's lawnmower. It was louder already, and rising. A silent cry in the night.

Jeff stood there, not quite calm, his hands shaking. A fever ran through her then. It was the strangest sensation. It just touched her, but wasn't really a part of her.

Jeff faded away before her eyes. She watched it happen. One moment he was there in the room with them. The next he wasn't. She saw his eyes. He didn't truly notice that something, anything was happening until the very last moment. She saw his eyes change, from dullness to perplexity, to horror.

It took some time before it dawned on her that Toni was screaming. The scream was cut off, and the girl just stood there, frozen, staring at the spot where her brother had been standing just a few seconds ago.

Jeff returned. He reappeared on exactly the same spot he had disappeared. It was Jeff… wasn't it? Lori stared at him, the grown man in their midst. He attempted to speak. It took several try-outs until he got it somewhat right.

– Is that you, Mother? Did I make it? Did I finally make it back?

There was such anguish in the man's voice, the man looking more like Jeff's older brother than Jeff. He looked around him, and she realized startled that what he saw wasn't what they saw at all, but something completely different.

– I didn't make it, he cried, – not completely. Listen, mother, listen well.

She attempted to speak, but was unable to.

– Sometimes there are riders. They come at the early morning light. They come at dawn, when you think the darkness has faded, and you're safe. Remember that. *Remember!*

And he vanished again. And this time he didn't reappear. They waited for minutes for him to reappear, but he didn't.

Toni squealed and ran into Lori's arms. Her other son, his name impossible for her to recall, pulled towards his father. Suddenly, just like that, like a snapping of fingers, the stage was set. Lori felt drained, exhausted, the horror and wonder of what had just happened striking her in waves.

Tom went right to the bedroom. She could see him in there, packing his suitcase, the crazed look in his eyes not going away.

She waited for him at the door, making one final attempt.

– Something incredible happened tonight, she said. – You know that. You saw that, as we all did. We should seek the answers together.

– Weaver was right about you, he snarled. – You're crazy as a looooon.

His voice rose to a high-pitched level beyond anything she had ever heard from him. It was he that sounded pretty much like that loon he mentioned.

– Don't you get it? It's this world that's the illusion.

She waved with her hand, including the surroundings, the house, the street, the streets.

– Not in the sense that it doesn't exist, but in its significance.

She looked at him, feeling hollow, feeling alive. Had she ever had any feelings for this man?

His crazed look intensified a bit more, and for a moment she was sore afraid. Then he rushed out the door, with his son and dog in tow, and she released a sigh of relief. The door slammed shut behind him.

She fell to the floor then, collapsing with her hands glued to her face, her body shaking in huge, heartfelt sobs.

Chapter Six

She did the right thing, and bringing Toni, she drove to the closest police station and reported her son Jeff as missing and kidnapped, which she saw as at least a part of the truth.

– We heard him scream, Toni mumbled incoherently to the nice police officer, – but we never actually saw anything. They were like ghosts. Ghosts!

– Has there been any ransom demand? The officer asked Lori.

– None! Lori replied softly.

She waited a bit, stretching it out deliberately.

– You should know that I and my husband no longer live together and that we intend to take out separation. We've had trouble for some time, but this, for some reason was the final straw. You should talk to him, of course.

The detective made a note. Lori made no effort at reading it.

After the «interrogation», they were led out in the hall and made to sit down. Lori held around Toni, preparing them both for a long evening.

She heard whispers, both confident and not that they were real. There were glances. Lori and Toni focused on each other.

– I'm sorry for screaming at you, Toni whimpered, bowing her head.

Her words were more or less incoherent and Lori doubted that anyone else understood what she was saying.

– For what time?

Toni giggled with a sore subtext in her voice and her mother was pleased.

They were called back in and were not separated.

The detective pushed a button on a computer keyboard. Lori heard her husband's choking voice.

– He just… disappeared.

– That was our experience of it, too, she stated.

They heard the entire recording of Tom's statement. There was nothing there contradicting theirs.

– Let me assure you that we take this very serious, he told them both. – We do believe a crime has been committed, and we'll do our best to solve it. We'll get in touch.

Translation: we don't know what the fuck has happened, but we believe you're on the level.

If only they knew, she thought.

On their way out, she spotted the officer that had pulled her aside the other day. He stared at her with his small, small eyes, and she felt the threat emanating from him. It was not something she could misunderstand, even though he made no overt move towards her or anything.

The walk out of the police station felt long as a year, the drive home as well. She kept glancing in the mirrors. The police officer or someone equally suspicious didn't appear.

They returned to the empty house. It didn't appear empty at all to Lori, but filled with shadows. People's voices kept touching her eardrums.

She returned to that special place in the living room where her son had last stood and vanished, vanished and reappeared and vanished again.

There was nothing there, nothing quantifiable, nothing she could put her finger on at all. Her daughter stared at her from the doorway.

– Don't worry, mommy won't disappear. – I promise!

Suddenly she realized what a hollow promise that was. She hurried away from there and rushed to the young girl, embracing her in a fierce hug. The girl was unresponsive and her skin damp and cold. Lori focused an iron-hard will she desperately hoped she possessed on not shaking.

She brought Toni with her to work the next day.

– What happened, mother? Toni asked, finally able to form coherent sentences again, as they drove on the road.

– I don't know, sweetie, but we'll find out. We will find your brother, I'll promise you that. Somehow, we'll find him, no matter what we have to do.

Her eyes briefly closed, and she saw it again, relived it, desperately attempting to make sense of something that didn't make any sense at all.

«Sometimes there are riders». She saw them, saw them ride, and almost drowned in the cold, cold sweat flowing from her skin.

– I don't like this place, Toni said, as the elevator door slid shut, and they ascended the tall building.

– Good! Her mother said. – Very good!

It didn't make sense, not to her limited perception. She was limited, so very limited. Cold and hot showers of sweat continued ravaging her. She knew, knew beyond belief that she smelled, in spite of all the antiperspirant she had applied. The elevator doors slid open, and her smells mingled with that of the people, all the people inside, as she opened up her perception to the large area ahead, the long hallway, all the small cubicles where people worked. She smiled.

– Hi, Paul, she greeted him, in such an intense way that he couldn't help but respond and grin widely himself, and that, in turn made her smile widen even more.

They arrived in her large and spacious office. She closed and locked the door behind them. And then she bolted it by pulling her large desk in front of the door.

Toni stopped, practically froze right inside. She stood there for quite a while, while Lori studied her, and then she raised her left hand, as if probing, towards the whirling dark shadows in the middle of the room.

– You can sense it? Tell mommy you can sense it!

The girl nodded. And when sensing Mother wasn't pleased with the reply she voiced it.

– I can, mother. It's like a Storm embracing me.

And then she walked, or rather stumbled, tentatively towards it. Lori joined her there, and then the storm embraced them both, and it felt so good, so very, very good.

Lori sat down, crossing her legs in front of her, and Toni did, too. Lori grabbed her hands, and the girl grabbed hers.

– Don't let go! Lori admonished her. – Whatever happens never let go!

She glanced around her, at the vortex surrounding them, at what most people walking into the room wouldn't know were there.

– Show us! She cried, both besieging and commanding. – Show us the world beyond.

Lori and Toni sat there clutching each other's arms. She nodded, and Toni nodded, as well. They didn't let go of each other, but one hand from each let go and reached for the plastic bag not far away. Two hands grabbed it. Two hands emptied its content on the floor, the floor of clouds not there.

I want this, Lori thought feverishly. I want this more than anything in the world.

– So, why is it here? Toni wondered, the wonder still not fled from her face. – Why here, of all places?

– I don't know. Lori shook her head, considering it. – Perhaps because I'm here, because we are here, or perhaps it's a random thing, constantly changing, moving from place to place.

Two hands emptied the content of the bag on the floor. The knife, the chalice and the various herbs dropped on the floor. There was no sound. The heavy knife and chalice hit the floor as if it was dropped on a heap of cotton. Lori grabbed the knife, pulling the hand she held closer to her. In one shift move she cut deep into the fleshy side of Toni's hand. There was just a line first, hardly more than a line, until she squeezed, and the red fluid flowed into the upright chalice.

– We pay the price, she called. – We risk it all, pay the piper, in order to reach beyond the mundane world.

She handed the knife to Toni. The girl hesitated a bit, just a bit, before accepting the blade, the sharp tool. She pulled the other's hand to her, and cut, cut deep into the fleshy side of her mother's hand. There was pain, deep pain, as her life flooded the cup and mingled with that of the other.

– Now, say the words, she told her brood.

– I'm not sure I remember it, remember it right, Toni whimpered. – We should have brought the book.

– You remember, Mother said. – You're a bright kid, and you want to remember, want to with all our heart.

She crumbled the various herbs between her fingers, and the dust fell into the fluid, and vanished beneath its boiling surface. She procured a lighter from her pocket, and began heating up the chalice in her hand. A nod and Toni straightened, as she began reciting the strange, ancient words. Lori translated them to English in her mind, as she, too, began speaking them, on the second turn, as her voice joined that of her daughter.

«Many do this ritual, this sacrifice of Self, without succeeding. They're not ready. They don't want it enough, don't crave it in their deepest self. They're not the Earth and sky, day and Night we one day all will be. But we are. We seek the wastelands, the endless fields and forests beyond matter, beyond experience, beyond life. We want to know what's hidden, want to see beyond the thin veil of reality, beyond this pinprick of existence. We know Magick is a true and potent force in the world. We will succeed or die. To all the dwellers in the eternal sea… grant us *access*».

Lori began noticing the heat in the metal she held, she clutched. She knew that Toni did, too, noticing the thin line appearing on her brood's brow. They repeated and kept repeating the words, and after a while they could no longer tell how many times they had done so. It felt sort of self-perpetuating after a certain time, like crossing a threshold, a line in the sand. Lori drank. Toni drank. It slid down their throat, and they felt the first stirrings of strength leaving their muscles. Their grip weakened. The chalice slipped from their hands and fell to the cotton floor and hit it with a loud dump, a sound of thunder. Numb, her tongue felt numb. She kept speaking, kept chanting, and the other inside the circle, the burning circle did, too. Something passed between them, passing from hand to hand, and back again, flowing like blood. Lori looked at her hand, her fingers, at the swollen fingertips, burned and ashen. She kept chanting in a monotonous whisper, her lips in perfect synch with the pair she glimpsed across the vast abyss.

Suddenly there was a sound, a deep bass tone from a distant bell, shaking the ground, the ground no longer a floor. The vortex widened and spread to fill the room. The two of them sat there gasping, while reality turned itself inside out around them.

Lori opened her eyes. She wasn't quite sure how it happened or could happen, fairly sure that they were already open, and had been all the time.

But she did anyway, and she Saw the world. Her open eyes opened further, opened to another level. One more pair of eyelids was pulled from her eyes, and she knew her eyes had always been closed before, except perhaps during times of stress or during dreams. It happened slowly, painfully, as if she was pulling herself from a deep sleep. The room darkened, and the walls were suddenly filled with doors, and they were all opening. No matter where the two of them looked, they saw doors (or portals or gates or doorways) open up and dissolve. They stood on a plaza with many roads. They couldn't tell how many roads there were, only that there were too many of them to count, and new were constantly added. Each was a vortex sucking them in. A man stood before them. At least the creature resembled a man, or a woman, or a many-hooded beast beyond belief.

– Welcome to the Crossroads, he greeted them. – Can I be of service to you? Is there anywhere in particular you want to go?

And there were sounds, and she couldn't tell whether or not «he», he/she/It spoke those words or if he spoke at all.

– We're fine, thank you, she replied with her still numb lips.

And there were only garbled sounds, and she couldn't tell whether or not she spoke coherent words or if she spoke at all. Perhaps intent was enough in this place. Perhaps it was the only thing that mattered.

The next second he was gone, and they were alone again in the vast wasteland surrounding them. She squeezed Toni's hands in desperate panic, and was somewhat comforted by the same response.

Choose, one voice said.

Choose, another voice admonished them.

Choose not to choose, a third, hundredth or thousandth voice bespoke them.

Choose one path, the first voice insisted.

Choose one path, the second voice admonished them.

Choose all paths, the myriad of voices advised them.

They were whispers, insistent and threatening and cooing and everything in-between. Lori and Toni remained on the spot, fearful of moving, fearful of standing still.

The storm kept intensifying around them, tearing them apart. And the storm was like wind, like whispers, like thoughts. And they heard it all, and it assaulted them like a roar, and they were inside its mouth, and it was too much, and they both screamed, and the scream never stopped.

They sat there frozen, with their mouths open, back in the room, the normal, mundane, boring room. The gate had been closed, slammed in their faces, and they couldn't tell if it was deliberate or if it had just happened by itself. Lori focused on breathing, breathing, breathing, while sweat poured from her brow and flooded her eyes.

She focused on meditating on calming down the rampant fear inside, on her daughter, sitting opposite her, shaking like a leaf. Lori grabbed her and pulled the unresisting, paralyzed body to her, rubbing her, comforting her the best she could, knowing it would never be quite enough.

Saliva flowed from Toni's open mouth, her slack lips. Eyes were non-responsive. Skin was cold and dead. Lori shook her. There was no response, none at all. Lori shook her again, harder, hard.

– Look at me, Lori snarled, grabbing the other's head in both her hands. – *Look* at me!

Toni stopped shaking, shook one more time, and a terrible moment Lori was terrified that she would just fade and never regain her faculties… before her eyes refocused and life returned to the skinny body. She yelped and turned limp in her mother's arms.

They sat there for an immeasurable time, while days and nights passed outside their bubble of reality.

Toni stared bewildered at Lori, stared at the room around them, now so normal, so thoroughly mundane.

Lori touched her cheek, made her look at her, conveying a measure of calm to the girl.

– We're new at this. She spoke insistently. – Perhaps not so strange then that we… we failed. We didn't really know more of what we were doing than an infant taking its first, hesitant glances at the world.

She nodded, to the girl, to herself, seeing the confirmation in the eyes so like her own.

– But we will!

She rose, and pulled her daughter up with her. There were no more clouds on the floor. Whatever had been present was gone. The chance, their window of opportunity, had passed.

Lori walked to the door and pulled the desk away from it, put it back in place, a bit, just a bit skewed.

– Now, that looks so much better, doesn't it?

Toni nodded, wide-eyed, with numb lips.

No one rushed through the doors this time. They were probably getting used to or insulated at what they saw as her antics. Every executive had his or her idiosyncrasies. She grinned.

Lori cocked her ears, at least she imagined she did so, and she listened, before turning back towards her daughter.

– Does the room, this place sound silent to you?

– Yes, silent.

The girl sniffed, as she, too, was listening, wondering, reflecting, pondering.

– But it isn't, not really. We're only experiencing it that way, after the onslaught of… of the Crossroads. It is as if I can hear the smallest sound, now, and identify every single one.

Lori looked at her daughter with fondness in her heart, as she listened to her words. A warm trickle of a river broke inside her. She wasn't alone anymore.

Listening to the sounds, she did know them, knew them intimately, even as they disgusted her. Only by listening beyond the everyday sounds of this place, she found one attracting her. She heard a river close by, a tiny trickle of a river, heard its ice break and its water flow.

– It's raining. Toni frowned when looking at the bright sunshine outside. – Is it raining, mother?

– It's always raining, Lori said.

She wanted to smile, to lessen the brunt of the words, but there was no way anything could do that, really.

– Mommy will be quite busy the rest of the day. Will you be okay?

– Yes, mommy, the girl said subdued.

– That's my girl.

She patted the girl's cheek and the girl let her.

– Listen… there's no use crouching in the rain. You will get wet no matter what you do.

– I *know,* mommy, the girl said sullenly, but stubbornly, defiant, giving mommy her best of smiles.

The day passed in a daze. Lori went through the motions, the particulars of her working day, without really being present, and she had to strive to be. In one way it was easy, because of the excited buzz persisting inside, and in another it was hard, precisely because of that.

There was a staff meeting. On the surface, and to the others participating, it probably looked like any other staff meeting they had ever participated in, but to Lori it wasn't. For a lack of a better word she had become… *sensitive,* both concerning the group and to the individuals around the table. She had been for a while, to a degree, because of her extensive experience with the corporate scene, but nothing like this.

When someone spoke up, or was about to speak up, she knew way before they actually did. She knew what they would say, and also their reaction to her comments. It was instinct, but uncanny, unprecedented. And she was calm, collected, and in control, and they were wrapped around her finger, and she smiled.

Toni sat in a chair by the wall, the very image of the perfect, understanding daughter. Paul brought her food and drink, and she gave him her best smile.

Rhonda Lasko approached Lori during a break.

– Is the girl all right?

– She seems to be. Lori shrugged. – It's hard to tell, of course. It always is. But I would say she is in good spirits, even though she clearly wasn't up for school, after what happened. And she couldn't stay home alone or with friends, either. I felt that she needed her mother.

– I think you made the right decision, Rhonda nodded. – You never know with the young these days.

No one stated bluntly exactly what had happened, but Lori was willing to bet that it was a badly hidden secret, and that the entire workforce, Rhonda certainly included knew everything or practically everything.

Not the particulars, of course, but the mundane part of it, the part that average people could or were willing to grasp, the story that Lori had given to the police.

They believed that.

Lori took one and one step forward, spoke word for word, uncertain if there would be another. She kept observing Toni closely, knowing beyond knowing that the girl would have collapsed in horror, if she had been left alone for even the tiniest of moments.

The five people around the table looked at Lori, and she got the funniest feeling somewhere, and somewhere along the line. She kept talking, seemingly unmoved like the sphinx.

– And there you have it people. We have a long way ahead of us before we see any tangible results of this one, but it will surely be worth it. Our goal is no less than world domination, and I, for one am convinced Coleman Enterprise will be up for the task.

Blackwell, Turner, Florie, Brandon and Lasko applauded her and her bold words. Rhonda looked strangely at her. Lori had sensed her distress all day, but had taken it for the famous corporate stress factor Lori and Weaver had had their chat about, but now she wasn't so sure anymore. Rhonda's frown or worry looked suddenly more like fear.

Wilson Florie studied her. She could tell. Wilson was a young man on his way up, one of Marco's newer protégées and acquisitions. There was something deeply troubling by those eyes of his. To Lori it was.

The cell phone rang. Lori shook her head in irritation and pulled it from her pocket.

– Excuse me, she said, rushing out in the hall.

She walked until she could neither hear, nor see the five and her daughter.

Then she finally answered the phone, pushed the «accept» button.

– Russell. Yes, speaking. Yes, she's with me. Of course, she is. As I told the principal… You want to speak to me in private? I'm afraid that's out of the question right now. No, as stated…

The voice in the phone interrupted her, and kept yapping, and the flow of irritation suddenly grew irresistible.

She broke the connection and returned to the office, her office.

– That was Mrs. Higgins, one of my daughter's teachers…

– A matter of bad communication at the school, I take it? Lasko roared with her dark trumpet voice. – That's so typical today's public service.

Lori shook her head in amazement, wondering if someone was tapping her phone, and Lasko had a direct line to it. She sat there, seemingly totally unconcerned with Lori's pointed stare. Lori almost giggled hysterically.

– I'm not sure exactly what was on the woman's mind, whether the principal had spoken to her or not, but she was fucking rude, was what she was.

Nervous laughter echoed through the air. Lori realized that she made them nervous.

Very good.

She nodded to herself.

– As I was saying… She looked at them all, all the five gathered around her table. – Life is a dance, and we will make our own, personal version of it. We will dance to a new and different tune, and the dance will be our very own.

She nodded to herself, noticing how she got to them, reached them, fully aware again of how charming and inspiring she could be.

– «Life is a dance»? Toni mimicked her afterwards, when they were alone again.

– It's pep talk, honey Lori sighed. – Every executive makes such inflated speeches, pretty much like the politicians, I guess.

She noticed startled that her daughter turned the pages of the very secret Rodham-report.

– You shouldn't do that, she scolded the girl softly. – That's very secret stuff. Mommy will be in a lot of trouble if others knew you had read even a single letter of it.

The girl put it back on the table so fast that one would be tempted to think she had burned herself. Lori once again looked at her with more fondness in her heart. She grabbed the folder and put it back in the drawer, immediately turning the key, locking it all, and thereby protecting it from curious eyes.

– Don't be mad, but it's about genetic engineering… isn't it?

The girl asked quietly.

Lori looked at her, staring her down, and the girl shrunk in the chair.
– I'm not mad, honey. She sighed again. – Mommy is just amazed by your ingenuity, that's all.
The bright smile lit up the room.
Lori used the last few hours of the day to get some paperwork done. She had fallen behind lately, and had a lot of catching up to do. The shadows grew longer and longer while she kept signing papers and writing instructions, and her headache grew steadily worse.
Toni sat there, by the wall, reading a book from the shelves, an annual report, if Lori wasn't much mistaken. Suddenly Lori envied her daughter. She was so excited about everything, studying all subjects as if it was the most important thing in the world.
Words and images turned indistinct before Lori's eyes, making it impossible for her to work anymore. She put it all away, and sat back in her chair, closing her eyes.
– Genetic engineering is… a good thing?
Toni finally voiced her concerns.
– It can be honey. It can potentially help a lot of people.
The two of them left the office, left the building when the shadows had grown very long and most people had long since gone home.
– Have a nice evening, Paul, Lori said. – See you tomorrow.
– You, too, Mrs. Russell, he replied. – See you tomorrow.
– Have a nice one, Paul, Toni grinned brightly.
– You, too, Ms. Russell, Paul grinned back, and Lori realized that the poor guy actually had a sense of humor.
Taking the elevator down felt weirder than ever. It was as if Lori's veins were burning on a low, low flame. Even when the doors opened to the garage below the sensation persisted.
Driving home felt… slow, not at all like the short drive it in truth was. Everything seemed the same, seemed… normal or what went for normal. Lori knew it wasn't. They passed trees, the many trees by the roadside, withered, dying, even as they should be blooming.
She turned off from the motorway. Another car took off right afterwards. She frowned.
– Is that car following us, mommy? Toni wondered.
Just when Lori had convinced herself it was a trick of her overactive imagination.
– Possibly, she nodded. – We'll see.
Debating with herself what to do she finally chose, one, two, three seconds later to take the usual route home, to not alert the possible stalker that she

was on to him… or her.

She turned left. The other car, fairly far behind turned right. She exhaled in relief, not really relieved, unable to decide whether or not there was a legitimate reason for concern.

– Remember, mommy, her daughter told her, very serious-minded, – the fact that you are paranoid doesn't mean they are not out to get you.

Lori let out a loud laughter, quickly looking at the smaller form by her side to see if she had hurt her, but Toni was smiling, and then they both laughed, a brittle shaking of the body, the vocal cord and the eardrums.

The house was silent, eerily spooky and felt so very, very empty. The ground trembled under her feet, and the floor continued to do so when they stepped inside. The kitchen looked the same, but wasn't. She frowned as she spotted a few vegetables remains she had missed yesterday.

– It will take some time before dinner is ready, sweetheart, she told her daughter, striving to keep her voice on an even keel, and to pay attention. – Perhaps we should order something?

– No, please, Toni pleaded, – I can wait a little for real food.

They began making dinner. Lori began, and Toni joined her quietly. The fridge was still filled up. In fact, it was fuller than it would normally be, since the household was a lot smaller than it used to be. They would have an abundance of food for days, before it would be necessary to restock supplies.

Lori realized that she heard the music, realized it the moment she heard Toni hum the strange melody.

It wasn't an unpleasant sensation, far from it, even though it clearly still felt unsettling to her. She joined in on the humming, and mother and daughter exchanged brief, sore smiles.

The smell of cooking filled the house, the suddenly overpowering sense of smell joining the sound of the music dancing in their ears.

– Does Jeff hear the music, mommy?

– Yes. Lori nodded grimly. – I would most certainly say he does.

They sat down by the kitchen table, and began helping themselves to the food, far more informally than only yesterday.

– This is good, Toni declared. – Beats prepackaged shit and take away any time.

She looked at her mother, a bit of challenge in her eyes and stance, because of the no-word. Lori cast a reproaching look at her, by old habit, but then she shrugged indifferently, both deliberately and not.

– Beats any shit not made by the amazing mother and daughter team, she acknowledged, and felt a warm trickle of hurt when the uncannily wide smile lip up Toni's face.

It tasted great, but she couldn't really fully enjoy it. Jeff's face and everything else that had happened kept blocking the simple joy of the moment.

The mother and daughter moment, renewed by the shocking recent events couldn't be completely enjoyed either. The two of them kept casting each other awkward glances.

They did the dishes, a far smaller heap than it used to be. Once again, the tender points of the moment almost overwhelmed Lori.

– Mom…

– Yes?

– Will you and Dad ever get back together?

The girl's voice was cracking just a little, no matter how much she attempted to keep it from happening.

– No! Lori shook her head instantly, without having to think about it. – At some point, even before this we parted company, and now life will take us down totally different and diverging paths.

She had wanted to word it carefully, for her daughter's sake, but she had wanted to be honest, too, and honesty had won, and she was glad.

– I… understand.

The girl nodded, attempting to put up a brave front, crumbling in Lori's arms.

– What happened to Jeff, mom? She spat angrily. – Who… took him?

The volatile, conflicting emotions exposed in the face before her both shocked and pleased Lori.

– I don't know, sweetie, or if anyone actually *took* him, or if it, whatever it was just happened. We know so little about this, about ourselves. I know he managed, years after he disappeared, to find himself back here, for a moment. He learned and is learning, and we can and we will, too. I swear this to you, before all the infernal gods there may or may not be.

Her own words shocked and thrilled her.

– Y-years? But he was gone only a moment.

The look of incomprehension overwhelmed the flicker of comprehension Lori knew was there.

– A moment for us, years for him. You saw your brother. He was clearly older, an adult even. He was in another place, living out those years there.

Toni nodded slowly, painfully.

Lori walked to the window, staring at the ruin there.

– Reality is vast, so much bigger than most people give it credit for, or can even imagine.

She turned back in a whirl, grabbing her daughter in the arms, grabbing her hard.

– And we know that, having experienced it first hand, and what we experienced was only a tiny fraction of the infinity out there. You know what I am talking about. We touched it together, you and I.
– Yes, Mommy, Toni whimpered, clearly in pain because of the hard grip, but gritting her teeth, standing her ground.
Mommy let go of her, a little startled, a little sorry. Her features softened, as she brushed a strand of hair from the girl's face.
The bell rang. The two of them looked at each other. Lori gave her a comforting look, a pat on the cheek and walked to the door. She heard the bell ring, one, two, three times.
She opened the door and before her stood Mrs. Higgins, one of Toni's teachers.
– Hello, Mrs. Russell, the woman greeted her sternly.
– Hello, Lori replied, frowning.
An awkward silence rose instantly between the two.
– May I come in?
– You may not, Lori replied, very deliberate.
The woman had already taken the first step forward and was on her way in when Lori gave her the negative reply and blocked her way.
– Both Toni and I have been through a lot the last few days, and we would appreciate some peace and quiet.
– To not send children to school is a very serious matter, Mrs. R...
– EXCUSE me, MRS. Higgins, didn't you hear what I just said? I told your principal in very plain words my and my daughter's feelings in the matter, and I expected that to be the end of it. I know he told you, so why are you here, Mrs. Higgins?
– I'm here on behalf of the child, Mrs. Russell, the older woman said with venom in her voice. – Someone has to speak on behalf of the child, when the mother doesn't.
Lori looked at her, and she was pleased that the look inspired fear in the woman's eyes.
– You're not, of course, she stated calmly, the snarl in the voice not audible, in any overt way, but still very much there. – You're just concerned with your own, overblown vanity.
And the crazed look in the teacher's eyes intensified. Lori kept talking, and kept her from speaking her outrage and hatred.
– I think I will have to speak to your principal, Mrs. Higgins, and also to the board. I want you removed from Toni's class, from your job actually. You shouldn't teach children. Rest assured that your reputation precedes you, and that several other mothers agree with me on this, and that they will indeed

come forward and speak their mind, if you pursue this matter in any shape or form. *Is that clear?*

The woman clearly had trouble breathing. She opened her mouth to speak, to spit out hateful words.

– Is that clear, Mrs. Higgins?

– Yes, Mrs. Russell, the teacher replied faintly.

– Good. Now get off my property before I call the police.

Mrs. Higgins blinked and gasped.

– You would call the police on *me?*

Lori stepped outside, very close to the other's heated body.

– Of course, I would. You're a danger and a menace to everyone you set your sight on, and I certainly won't stand for it. Others might, and have, but I won't, not anymore.

The old lady backed off, never taking her eyes off Lori, looking at her as if she was Satan incarnated, and Lori grinned at her, and was so very pleased with herself, and the childlike joy rising within her.

– You will regret this, you *witch,* the old lady shouted from the gate, as she made her way down the street, her voice rising to an even higher pitch. – You will get what's coming to you. That is my promise, my wow, the wow of any good Christian. «*Thou shall not suffer a witch to live*».

Lori closed the door, breathing rapidly, realizing how shaken she was. Toni stood there, shaking, too.

– Thank you, mother. She's a wicked and bad thing, and has been after me for so long, and I don't think I could have dealt with that right now.

They embraced, shaking in each other's arms, and the shaking slowly, very slowly subsided. The light turned dark behind Lori closed lids, and she opened her eyes. She turned the key in the lock. They returned to the living room, still clinging to each other.

– Popcorn? She said casually.

– Popcorn, Toni confirmed, a gleam in her eyes.

They watched TV. Images flickered before Lori's eyes, but she couldn't tell what they were. It was all just a jumble of nothing. There was a flavor to the popcorn, but she was unable to discern what kind. Time passed, and she knew she should be able to mark its passing, but when she attempted to focus on it, on any given moment, it slipped away.

God Save the Queen began playing on the screen. Lori grabbed the remote control and quickly changed the channel. There was some talk show on. She turned off the television altogether. The living room turned quiet and dark. Toni looked like she was sleeping, slumping in her chair. Lori walked through the house, holding around her arms, sort of embracing herself. It did feel weird, as if she wanted to grab something, and it wasn't there.

Panic gripped her, as the images of her fading son reappeared, and assaulted her anew. She hurried back to the living room, fearing what she would or wouldn't see, but Toni was there, and her eyes had turned clear and aware again.

– Mommy?

– Yes, sweetie? Lori strived to keep her voice even, to not reveal her anxiety.

– I wonder… the girl persisted, – did someone actually pull Jeff away or did he do it himself, without knowing?

– I… don't *know*. Frustration entered the older woman's voice.

– We are all like him, aren't we?

Lori looked at her, undecided whether or not she would or should reply or how to reply.

– We are all the Earth and sky, day and Night… right? You and I, Jeff and Austin? Whatever we are we got it, inherited it from you.

– I would say that is a fair assumption.

Lori looked away for a moment before turning back and looking steady at her so very mature daughter.

– So, will we disappear like him?

Lori knew where this had been heading, and had wanted to avoid it, but had known, beyond knowing that there was no way to do that.

She walked to the girl.

– Stand up! She bid the girl in the chair.

Toni did, clearly anxious, waiting for the other shoe to drop.

– As stated, Lori told her, making sure their eyes met and that the contact held. – We touched the world together you and I. You can be certain of one thing and that is that I won't shit you, won't treat you like a child anymore, won't keep anything from you in order to «protect you», and that I will share everything with you. If nothing else you can be sure of that.

– We don't know? The girl said.

– We don't know. Lori nodded. – We may be exactly like Jeff, or there may be variations. We don't know, but we will find out.

They both exhaled, feeling a little better, a little worse.

Lori remained restless. She paced back and forth ceaselessly. It clearly disturbed Toni, but that fact didn't keep her mother from pacing.

So, she's worried, she thought. Tough!

She needs to grow up, anyway.

It was late, and the neighborhood had turned quiet, and Lori started yawning, but neither the excitement nor the anxiety let go of her. Something was nagging her, and it wouldn't let go. She took another round through the house. Her steps were fast, almost frantic. She stopped in the dark kitchen, hid in the shadow cast by the streetlights, and turned cold all over.

The unknown car was still there, a bit further down the street. And this time she also got a good look at the man behind the wheel. He was out for a walk and a smoke. It was the policeman; the one with an axe to grind that had stopped her during her more or less reckless driving.

In that moment, she didn't consider what he was doing here, only that he was here. She pulled back, retreating into the living room, its far end at the other end of the house.

– Mommy? Toni wondered.

Lori just looked at her, unable to speak.

– Can I sleep with you in your bed tonight? Please?

– Yes, honey, Lori managed to reply, to choke.

She went another round, making sure all the doors had been locked, and that all the windows were closed. She looked under her bed and inside the closet of the bedroom, and knew she would do it one more time before going to bed.

The two of them brushed their teeth. They took their turn on the toilet bowl. She stared at the moving shadows on the pink wall, while doing her best to comfort her distraught daughter. They both returned briefly to the kitchen to fetch the two large knives there. Lori held the knives in front of Toni and gave her one. She didn't say anything. Toni nodded solemnly.

Lori tried to call out with the cell phone. There was no connection. In a place where there was always a connection, there was none, and it didn't surprise her the slightest.

They undressed and went to bed, pulling close together in the middle of the large marital bed. It felt strange to have the young, skinny body next to hers. Lori closed her eyes, but she still kept them on the knife on the night table. Toni eventually fell asleep, moaning in her bad dreams. Lori stayed wide awake. She wanted to sleep, but couldn't. She lay there, staring at the ceiling, at its shifting patterns, convinced she would never be able to sleep. Sounds in the night kept rising her ire. She heard steps in the hall, and formed her hand around the shaft of the distant knife, convinced she would wake up the next morning covered in blood. The door to the closet stood slightly ajar. She glimpsed all kinds of things in there, cold, vicious eyes and what was worse. Her daughter changed behind her back into a horrible monster with long claws and fangs and glaring eyes. Lori fell into a pitiful sleep not long before the early dawn, and awoke not long after that tired and weary with the sun shining in her face through the closed curtains.

Chapter Seven

The first she did was to check the phone. The cover was back on. Breathing a sick sigh of relief, she carefully, in order to not awaken Toni excited the bed, grabbed the knife on the night table, and walked out in the hallway. There was no one there. The house was quiet and empty. After a brief hesitation she called Kelly, called her friend, and told her everything, hating the tension in her own voice.

Kelly told her she would call Julia, and cautioned Lori, told her to be careful and vigilant.

– Yes, cautious, Lori nodded, – vigilant, absolutely.

Mother and daughter made breakfast. They ate in silence. Lori recalled her daughter's face in her sleep, peaceful and yet anxious.

– Mommy?

– Yes?

– Do you think I can ever go back to school?

Lori considered it for a second or two, before speaking.

– Eventually you will have to, I guess, but it won't be until after summer break.

There was a hesitation in the young girl. Lori smiled to herself seeing herself in the skinnier form.

– I don't like it there, young Toni said decisively. – I don't like it there at all. The whole place is the pits. The teachers are cruel and vindictive, the children are totally indifferent to what goes on in the world, and the whole place is… the pits.

Lori closed her eyes briefly, stretching her smile a little.

– I know it was your ticket out of an even worse place… the girl hastily added.

– Yeah, but I still hated it, Lori said promptly, with a passion stunning her.

She rubbed her daughter's cheek in an attempt to take the sting out of the harsh words.

– Besides. She shrugged. – It's good to have you present at the meetings. My… colleagues don't know what to make of you, and it unnerves them.

– It gives you… an edge?

– In a cutthroat world it does precisely that, Lori Russell nodded.

The girl hesitated some more, before shrugging and a way too adult expression came to dominate the still innocent face.

– I like being your edge. I love being Mommy's edge.

And that unnerved Lori more than just a little.

They brushed each other's hair afterwards. It was so pleasant and so peaceful. Lori sat there with her eyes closed and just enjoyed the sensation of having her own maid. And afterwards, when the delicate flower was in her hands: that, too felt good.

Toni Russell had grown up, and even though the process clearly had taken time, it could also be said that it had been defined in a single day in time.

She set the girl's hair up, just like she had done her own. They stood before the mirror, their hair the same, dressed the same. Except for the obvious difference in size, at least at first glance they could pass as twins.

They stepped outside, into the warm summer breeze. Lori made certain that the door was locked. She nodded, and Toni nodded, too. The sky and the air were a whirl of sensations, striking them softly. The car waited for them in the driveway. Lori used the automatic key to open it, and everything looked okay.

The drive seemed almost surreal to her. Usually the entire drive from home to the office passed her in a daze, and afterwards she couldn't really recall any details, but today she noticed or seemed to notice everything. The images in her mind were so sharp and so clearly defined when she parked the car in the garage that she was convinced she was actually able to recount every little incident on their path. In fact, the experience seemed so vivid that she couldn't convince herself with absolute certainty that the drive had truly ended.

The unknown black cat in the neighbor's driveway. The newspaper landing in the bucket of water and making a splash on the concrete stairs. And that was merely the first two houses. It was all there. She could remember all the ragged details of Mr. Holcomb's face while he pulled his lawnmower out on the lawn, his pink little tongue when he wet his lips, staring at her (or Toni's) cleavage.

Everything.

To her he wore his intentions on the outside exactly like a sore thumb. He wanted to take both mother and daughter with him to the woods and satisfy every single impulse he entertained.

– Are you all right, mommy?

Lori realized she was shaking. She wanted to push the button in the elevator, but kept missing because her hand shook so hard.

– You're spooked! Toni stated bewildered.

– Yes, spooked, Lori echoed the girl's words.

The elevator door closed.

– I'm all right, she insisted, desperately attempting to calm both her daughter and herself.

The air touched them as they passed through it, touched their skin and the inside of their nostrils.

Paul sat there, as much a part of the furniture as… the furniture.

They were alone in her office. In one way, it felt so peaceful there. In another it felt totally intolerable.

– Do you want me to brush your hair again? Toni asked, practically begging.

Lori glanced at her watch. Her first appointment was an hour away.

She sat there in her chair, leaning her head backwards, enjoying the sensuous feeling of the brush through her hair.

– You have a few more gray hairs, Toni said softly. – Don't worry. I'll take care of them.

She pulled them out, one by one, with amazing efficiency. Even that seemed pleasant enough, almost otherworldly.

The day passed in a daze, to the point that she could hardly recollect anything about it, except a glimpse she caught of Rhonda's worried glance. She didn't understand that at all.

They returned to the quiet, small house by the burned-down ruin in the afternoon. The neighborhood remained the same. It stared at her, at them.

– Let them stare, mother, Toni said in contempt. – Let them denigrate and shame themselves.

Lori nodded, looking at her independent and aware daughter with fondness in her eyes.

– They shame themselves, not because they're staring, but because the reason for it. They envy us, because we hold our heads high, and they keep bowing their own. They've got no pride, beyond the pat on the head their particular master gives them.

So young and so wise, and Lori understood the anger, even the venom in her voice, understood it so well.

Kelly and Julia sat on the stairs. Lori saw them appear, as if in a mist or through a dream, and a huge grin transformed her face.

It was as if they hadn't been there a moment ago, but now they were, unmistakable, undeniable. They were there, when Lori stepped out of the car with their hugs and support, and Lori had trouble breathing. The interior of the house looked completely different, bright, filled with shadows.

– It's SO great seeing you guys, she exclaimed.

– What, didn't you think we would come, in your time of need? Kelly chided her affectionately, kissing her softly on the cheek.

Lori didn't reply, didn't voice a reply, but just sat down in a chair, and broke down in tears.

There were more hugs, more kisses, and slowly, very slowly she found herself climbing out of the pit she had fallen into.

– Come, Julia whispered in her ears. – Come.

And they were on their way again. They walked to the Hampton Court Railway Station. The air was hot and dry. The huge, salty tears dried on Lori's cheeks.

Kelly stopped her after a minute walk or so.

– We need to save this face, she stated decisively.

Lori looked at the display of the cell phone her friend held up and had to agree. The face on the screen was a smear of makeup and tears and everything.

After spending a few minutes with brushing and painting, it once more looked fairly presentable. Lori nodded to herself, still a bit down. The others, Toni included nodded encouragingly.

The train stank of diesel or whatever, as usual. It was impossible not to notice, even in the tight-knit company of the four. They noticed it easier, really, the stench tearing in their nostrils like blades. It didn't matter that all windows had been opened wide, that the wind filled the compartment and blowing any attempt at keeping hair done.

Lori enjoyed it, enjoyed the air in her face, her black hair blowing all over the place. She heard the whistle in the trees as the wind caressed them. Another smile broke on her face when she studied the birds flying in the slipstream of the train. She saw them in a whirl of motion, of air, and wasn't certain what she saw, a glimpse or more, a shadow in bright sunlight. It shook her gently, the realization…

Among the birds, in-between black and white feathers, she spotted a raven.

Its screeches stayed with her as she walked in the warm afternoon sun through London's busy streets. It made her turn alternately hot and cold. The four women walking side by side did so with an… an attitude. They exchanged secret smiles as if they understood something others didn't. And they did. Lori knew they did.

In their slipstream, there was also something… something she was unable to quantify. She mumbled something.

– What was that, dear? Kelly said.

– I know there's something going on, Lori said aloud.

– There must be. Kelly nodded. – Too much has happened for it to be mere coincidence.

– Sometimes I feel I can grab hold of it, Lori said, gritting her teeth, – but then it once more slips away.

They slipped near Hyde Park, and they heard, increasingly loud the music.

There was a free concert there tonight. Lori realized it had been at the back of her head all the time. She had, without being consciously aware of that fact moved them here since they had stepped out from the Underground station pretty far away.

They had walked for quite some time, walked quite a distance through the enormous central parts of London, but Lori didn't feel tired, didn't feel tired at all. She was sweaty to the point of her clothes being stuck to her skin, but she didn't mind.

– It's *him,* isn't it? Kelly smiled in awe.

– I would say that is a safe bet, Lori nodded graciously.

She had found that Kelly had a thing for Rock stars, young and old.

This one was clearly of the old guard, to the point that he didn't even try to hide his graying hair anymore.

– He's *hot!* Toni grinned.

– He has sold out a long time ago Julia, sniffed critically. – And I *certainly* don't mean the concert.

Kelly looked angrily at her friend. Lori hastened to be the voice of reason.

– Well, he has his bad and good sides. He has done lot of strange or rather conformed things in later years, like many of the «heroes» of the sixties and seventies. He, like the rest of them, should have finished what they started.

– But many of the songs are from a time when they did care, Kelly cried, – when they did think and act, and lived, and rebelled. They just quit, like many of us do, like many of us did, like many of us will never do again…

Lori had, even though she was the oldest of the four been far too young to experience the sixties and seventies, but it and its stories had always resonated within her, and created a longing for something… something *more.*

And then they were inside the festival area, where a lot of bands had played and would play the next few days and nights, and thoughts and considerations and reason mattered no longer.

They began dancing almost immediately, like so many of those present. Toni clapped her hands above her head and moved with a wild, transcendent look in her eyes, and Lori knew that if she had been able to see herself in the mirror (like she did in the young girl's mirrors of the soul) she would have looked similar. It was a wild evening, turning into a wild night in London's central green area. Mind faded and mind grew. The wilder the dance became, the stronger Lori felt, the easier came the thoughts, until they flowed like a river, sharp as a knife.

The lyrics echoed in her mind, stirring her memories of the past and forgotten thoughts, words whispered into her mind like daggers. She danced with a man, a good dancer, danced close, and it excited her to feel his body against hers. Toni danced with a boy, danced tight. Lori knew she should be worried, but she wasn't. The heat of the moment chased all worries away.

The band ended their chore, quite calmly. Everything was an exercise in civility, really, not anything like the wild séances from her youth burning in her memory. She felt the sting of disappointment, felt… cheated.

The next band sucked. There was no way around that, no matter all the wishful thinking in the world. She caught Kelly's eyes, and her friend caught on instantly, which said it all, really. Julia had stopped dancing a bit earlier. Toni stood there with the boy. He was holding her hands, panting like an eager dog. The girl kissed him on the cheek and left him, and returned to her three companions.

– Don't worry. She shrugged proudly and with blushing cheeks to her mother. – He was easily handled. I had him eating off my hand.

She was a girl at the top of the world, and Lori chuckled a bit, just a little worried.

They moved on. The night was still young. Lori felt young, carefree. They sat down on a bench somewhere, a considerable distance away from the concert area. They could still hear the bedlam from there, but it was faint, unimportant. Their hearty laughter submerged most distant sounds.

She studied herself in the pocket mirror again. The mascara had once more spread and decorated her face in all kinds of creative ways. She sighed.

The others didn't look much better.

– It's supposed to stick no matter what, Kelly complained. – The advertising clearly states «sweatproof».

They exchanged glances.

– I guess we sweat a lot more than their test subjects, then, Julia smirked wickedly.

There were more fond smiles.

– Let's just remove the damn stuff, Lori told the others. – All of it.

They began on the painstaking process of cleaning up their faces. Everybody helped each other. It became a sort of catharsis, another small relief in a stressful life. Lori zoned out occasionally, as was her want. She could freeze in the middle of any given task, and just stare at the world with empty eyes, clearly not there.

– What do you see? Julia wondered breathlessly.

– I… Lori hesitated. – I don't know.

She saw nothing, really, except mist drifting through shadow. If she attempted to zone in on the particulars, it slipped away from her.

But out here, in the world, if she focused her attention she was able to glimpse a shadow by the nearest tree, or at the edge of her vision, and she shuddered.

– The Dark Men are coming, she said, very clear and with a voice clearly her own, but markedly altered compared to how she remembered it.

– The… Dark Men? Kelly prompted her.

– The Dark Men are coming, Lori repeated, frowning.

She wanted to say more, she knew she did, but then she got distracted, and whatever she was going to say faded at the tip of her tongue.

She shook her head in bewilderment, in need, but there was nothing more.

– I can't remember, she cried, and struck her hand in the wood beside her.

– Don't worry, Lori, Toni said, very serious minded and intense. – It will come to you. It will come to us all.

The surroundings rushed back into Lori's vision, and in spite of the boundless frustration, she imaged she saw the world in a clearer light than ever before. She looked around her and she saw the world.

The woman on the worn bench caught a glimpse of her face and curious, driven she straightened the phone and its camera. She saw the lines in her face clearer than in years.

Lori rose from the worn bench and straightened, looking humorously at her companions.

– I, for one am sick and tired of not seeing my face, she declared.

The four laughed heartily, and in what was only one more time among many in recent nights they saw each other and themselves with new eyes.

They returned to the streets, to the noisy surroundings. Often it was destructive to Lori's spirit, but not tonight. There was a lot of noise, but mostly from open doors to various establishments. The loud music overwhelmed the sound of engines. Even the smell of gasoline occasionally faded away to insignificance. She released one button, two buttons in her blouse, and laughed off Toni's worried glance.

She stopped outside a noisy establishment. Without thinking twice about it, she walked right up to the large bouncer guarding the entrance, and the others followed her reluctantly.

The tall woman had almost walked past the sentry when he put a fleshy hand on her shoulder, and stopped her cold.

– The girl isn't old enough, he stated firmly.

She gave him a look of contempt making him shrink in his tracks from a roaring lion to a squeaking mouse.

– My *sister* is certainly old enough, she snorted, – and don't you *dare* say otherwise.

They entered the smoky and badly lit locale, grinning in triumph. Toni glanced around her, both wide eyed and with a huge grin on her face. The look she sent her mother was both one of worry and doglike gratitude.

– You handled them so well, Mommy, she said breathlessly. – Like a *queen*.

– I did, didn't I? Lori both frowned and grinned simultaneously.

And just like that, the room turned darker, as if the lights, all the glittering lights in the room didn't quite take.

She studied the people in the room, all of them, not just those visible in the glittering lights, and she nodded to herself. Toni studied her and followed her line of vision, and trembled. The music was loud, deafeningly loud, but mother and daughter walked in a sort of quiet bubble.

– The shadow people, the girl whispered, – they are scary, mommy.

– Only to those scared by them, mommy replied unconcerned.

The people in the room didn't return her pointed stare. Some looked away deliberately, and some ignored her, ignored her by not ignoring her, that is. A thrill shot through her, and she smiled, a smile threatening to crack her mask of unconcern.

Excitement and terror warred within her.

– This was no coincidence. Julia cried accusingly. – You chose this place, chose it deliberately!

Lori met the eyes of Elvo, of elvo465@yahoo.com across the steamy room, scratching her right shoulder, seemingly absentmindedly. He wore the green-painted rose in his breast pocket, and was also instantly recognizable to her in other, less definable ways.

«Let us meet in a public place», she had written in the mail to him, «and not say a word to each other, not even acknowledge each other presence».

He had agreed and suggested this place.

She wowed to keep to her end of the bargain, and hoped he would do the same.

Was there a flicker of acknowledgement in those dark eyes? She suspected there was, but couldn't tell, not conclusively, and she smiled, smiled to Julia, countering her friend's sullen look.

I enjoy this, she thought.

– I *enjoy* this, she cried.

And practically everyone in the room turned and looked at her, as if they heard her through the noise and the music, or at least she imagined they did, and she didn't feel intimidated at all.

They had their drinks by a corner table, the four girls on their night out. Toni got only half of the liquor compared to the other three, but she still had trouble keeping up with them. Lori felt a little bit worried, somewhere deep inside, but it didn't manifest in any visible or tangible manner. The room turned a hazy shade of gray as her ability to sense her surroundings was slowly diminished.

She danced with a man. It wasn't Elvo, even though she spotted him from time to time. Her partner ogled her and she let him. She ogled him back, and as she had more than suspected, he pulled back embarrassed, and looked away, and she left him on the spot, casting him a condescending look, not allowing herself for a moment to let her disappointment show.

They found themselves outside again, the four of them, moving through the streets like the wind. Lori glanced at them all with fondness in her heart.

– This is nice, isn't it?

They looked at her a bit incredulous.

– I mean, really nice. You mean so much to me, all of you. Our friendship is only a few days old, but it doesn't feel new.

– It doesn't feel like that at all, Kelly nodded tenderly.

Toni looked at her mother with shining eyes, grateful over being included.

The streets and the four's surroundings looked unreal to Lori, more so than ever, but the three close to her, in her bubble looked real and well. It was such a pleasant feeling, bathing in the glow of friendship and like-mindedness.

– This, she said, – this is only the beginning.

They nodded and she knew they understood.

– I didn't understand at first, she said, – when Lynn told me, but I think I'm beginning to.

The light flickered on and off on Piccadilly Circus. One moment it turned dark, and the only light was the full moon between the drifting clouds. The next the light turned itself back on. A beastly shriek sounded in the distance, and all four of them shook, shook inevitably.

It did touch them briefly, even in their happiest moments.

– Wild, Kelly whispered, both exalted and anxious. – We are *wild*.

– Four wild women on the prowl, Julia cried, shouted at the depths and the heavens, not caring that everybody in the street and beyond heard her.

None of them did.

Everything was a blur to Lori from then on. Later, when she thought of the coming days she could never quite recall that time in her life properly. It wasn't the alcohol. They drank that night, but not that much. They didn't need to. Toni was intoxicated and even drunk, but not excessively so. She was just… happy.

– So, I told them, she snorted, speaking through her nose, – my revered classmates, what a bunch of snotty bitches they were, and that it was about time they got their act together, and they just *laughed* at me.

The sore undertone in her voice didn't escape the older women and they caressed her and comforted her. They sat around a table somewhere in a room, at some club. Lori couldn't recall its name and didn't give a damn. It was late at night. She knew that much.

And didn't care.

It was a fairly lively place. People danced on the tables without being chastised by the club's supervisors or any employee. Some of the guests took offence, of course, someone always did, but they relented quickly, when they saw that they didn't have any support.

Lori had to pee, just had to. She had been holding back for way too long, and the pressure suddenly rose to an unbearable level. She excused herself with a smile and ran off.

The roar of voices faded abruptly as she closed the door to the lavatory behind her. She was alone in here, amazingly so, with all the empty stalls and toilet bowls. Both emptiness and silence greeted her. She picked one bowl and closed that door behind her, too. Safely boxed in she pulled down her pants and panties and sat down on the bowl, sighing in relief when the waterfall flowed.

The phone rang. She looked at the jacket in her lap, letting it ring, listening to the aggressive tone, sensing the violent shaking touching her right thigh. It stopped. She sat there for a while longer, deliberately relaxing for a bit, enjoying the muddled thoughts the alcohol created.

The phone rang again. She looked irritated at it, at the piece of plastic sticking out from the pocket of her jacket. The sound cut through the pleasant haze of the moment, and she grabbed the phone and raised it to her ear, answering the call, glimpsing the UNKNOWN NUMBER message.

– Yes?

A dark, deep voice sang:

Patty has her home in the sand
The golden sand falling from her shoulders
And she smiles at you with her playful tongue

She frowned a bit, before clarity and determination grabbed hold of her.

– London Bridge is falling down, falling down, falling down, Lori sang, in a caricature of a song, of his song.

The other end fell silent.

– And isn't that supposed to be «her head in the sand»? Lori countered sarcastically.

– I've got your number, the male voice hissed, burning into her mind like a drill.

– Obviously so, honey, Lori said sweetly, – but why don't you come over so we can get better acquainted?

– I will, the totally insane voice swore. – I do. I will come. Fucking eager cunts will get what's coming to them.

Then the line fell silent. The brief «conversation» ended. Lori lowered the hand holding the phone, shaking her head, unable to keep the hand from shaking.

She made an effort, but not too great an effort to remain happy and unaffected when returning to the others, and she reckoned she was successful. Neither of her three companions sent her a concerned look.

They stumbled out of a misty tavern sometimes well beyond midnight. It was too late, way too late to take The Tube or the train. So, they had to search for an available cab, always a strenuous task. They finally managed to call one to them when they actually began feeling their sore feet, a result of them having either stood or walked, with little rest for close to twelve consecutive hours. Lori realized they had walked from one late open pub to the next several times. She shook her head in confusion and attempted to regain her composure through a haze of muddled thoughts.

The cab drove through empty back alleys and shortcuts, where most drivers hardly fared. At least the driver didn't try to cheat them by circling and taking all kinds of strange detours.

The city looked like a ghost town, like ruins not yet ruins. Lori blinked slowly, seeing everything in a weird light. An eerie feeling grabbed hold of her and didn't let go. The streets weren't empty, but were full of ghosts, revenants, semi-transparent beings moving back and forth with no apparent direction or motive.

And then there were the shadow people staring at her, studying her in unrelenting ways she sometimes, right now found quite unnerving.

– Are they here as well? Toni whispered. – Can you see them?

– I can see them, she confirmed, too tired to lie to her daughter.

The cab stopped in front of the nice house, by the burnt-out property, in the nice neighborhood. It happened so fast that Lori didn't quite catch it. Before she had registered anything, Julia had paid the driver (handsomely) and the other three waited while Lori fumbled with the keys. She unlocked and opened the door, and the four of them walked inside. An echo of the phone-conversation with the possible stalker earlier tonight returned to her. She closed the door and made sure it was locked, walked through the house and checked doors and windows. The others glanced at her. It was as if the mere act of returning here had brought back all the bad things. She wanted to tell them about the phone call, but she needed rest, was so tired, too tired to care.

Dreams began minutes before she went to bed, and followed her into sleep.

They slept in the same bed, the marital bed the four of them. Slept like the dead. Lori imagined she saw a man stand above the bed with a knife in his hand. He grinned at her, and she couldn't move, not an inch, and he knew that, knew that she was completely helpless and vulnerable, totally unable to fend off his cruel advances.

I'm coming for you, Lori, sweet, sweet weak Lori. I will cut you open, gut you like I would a fish.

The wicked laughter made her shiver and moan in fear, and it was as if she was shrinking, fading away to Nothing.

Then the quality of the dream changed, subtle at first, then in dramatic ways. Nothing was filled with something. The image and sensations of a windy field grew in her mind. On a small lawn on that vast field, dry red leaves blew slowly up a slope, defying gravity, defying everything. She blew with them, rising like a bird on an upstream flow of air.

She woke in a rut at midday, and in a strangely uplifted condition, not certain, not certain at all how to feel, the extensive drunkenness from last night not really notably present in her body chemistry at all. The giddiness hadn't fled though. On the contrary, her good mood persisted. The others woke up. She gave them smiles, kisses and caresses, and they returned her affection with smiles, kisses and caresses.

In a fit of vigor, she gathered all the used clothes and carried them to the washing machine. She looked behind the door before entering. There was no one there. She walked inside the chilly and pleasant room, and put down the clothes, closed the lid and pushed the button. The hum from the machine interrupted the relative silence.

They sat at the breakfast table, grinning at each other.

– Aren't you guys supposed to be at work? She scowled at her two adult friends.

– Aren't you? Julia shrugged.

– Touché…

Laughter, feeling so good.

It was such a strange sensation to actually have time in the morning, to relax and to think, and to consider one's options.

Tom called, very aggravated, and it didn't truly faze her.

– What do think you are doing? He said without introduction, speaking very loud, so loud that the other three couldn't avoid hearing him.

– I'm not doing anything, Tom, she replied patiently.

– You won't GET AWAY with it, you know. Don't think for a minute you will GET AWAY WITH IT!

He was on an old-fashioned, practically *ancient* analogue phone, another fact creating another strange ambiguity in her. When he slammed down the receiver she *heard* it. It was like someone ringing a dozen big bells simultaneously. At least that was how she experienced it.

The brief, insane «conversation» was over before it had begun.

She couldn't help but cringing, shivering a little. There had been real hostility and antagonism in his voice, his very behavior, not merely anger.

And… more, a kind of irrational hysteria bordering on insanity. It was as if he was accusing her, blaming her for all kinds of malady, all the malady in the world, and she had to wonder if there wasn't more, more than what he had experienced the night he left the house, something he didn't tell her.

She finally drove to work. Toni grinned at her from the passenger seat. The policeman was there, attempting to hide himself and his car behind the bushes and the corner. Was he never on duty? She waved to him, very deliberate and telling. He scowled at her.

– Mommy?

– Yes, honey?

She heard the concern in the girl's face and focused on her, on her concern.

– What does that man want?

– Nothing good, Lori stated and shook her head. – I think that is a safe bet.

– So, is he a *pervert* or something?

Lori felt a bit of relief and had to smile when she heard the anger and the obvious sense of irony and guts in her daughter's voice.

– I don't know, honey. He might be, but most of all I think he, for some reason has chosen me or us to represent his perceived, wounded vanity or something like that.

– But that's *crazy!*

– It isn't *sane,* I'll give you that…

The road seemed different today. It seemed different every day. The route felt totally unfamiliar to her, as if she had never come this way before. She blinked and shook her head. It did her no good. At some intersection, she had no idea what direction to choose, and stopped right there, pearls of sweat suddenly covering her brow.

Two signs appeared in her vision, signs she could swear hadn't been there a few moments ago. She breathed a deep sigh of stark relief, as she turned left and drove on, finally spotting familiar sights, the tall Coleman-building in the distance.

The clouds on the office floor were gone. She fixed her hair and her face in front of the mirror. The mirror didn't look like a mirror at all, but like a window into a room large and deep, not at all like the tiny space behind her. The elevator was going down in her mind, and it had mirrors on all walls, in the ceiling and even on the floor, and she saw herself suspended in an enormous, endless space filled with lights and shadows.

She was called into Marco's office after a couple of hours, not too soon, not too late. Rhonda sent her the same, anxious, indiscernible and puzzling glance when they passed each other in the hall.

The first thing Lori noticed, when she stepped into Marco's office was the moving clouds on the floor.

He sat there, behind his desk, like he always did, every time he had granted her access. She stopped in front of the desk and sat down in the chair without waiting for him to offer it to her. He frowned.

– You were late today, he remarked, perfectly calm, as always.

– Yes, I was, Marco, she reproached him.

He shrugged.

– It's no big deal. As I've restated time and time again your time is your own. I'm just curious, that's all.

– I'm sorry, Marco, she said softly. – It won't happen again. It was just the celebration that got out of hand, that's all.

– Celebration? He inquired, still as unfathomable as a sphinx.

– Of my freedom, she stated proudly.

He rose, and that, too amazed her. She couldn't recall he had ever done that in his office while she had visited it before.

– Then allow me to join in on the congratulations, he grinned. – He was holding you back, keeping you down. Now, you're free… to fly.

Something was… off. She couldn't put her finger on it, but it was there, scratching at her under the surface of reality.

The clouds… they were still here, for him, and she looked startled at him, realizing something in a whiff of a single moment.

She wondered if it was just her, or if he truly looked at her differently.

– Thank you, Marco, she heard herself say.

They parted company, and he grabbed her, giving her a kiss on the cheek. He let go of her and she went on her way.

She returned to her office. Toni waited for her there. The girl sat in Lori's chair behind the desk, lost in the world of her earphones. Lori easily heard the loud music. Toni looked up briefly, and moved to the other chair, soon to once again be lost in the music. Lori sat down and began working. It happened practically automatically. She didn't resist the process. It felt like putting on an old, worn and too small shoe.

Time slowed to a crawl. No matter how many times she looked at her watch time or its measurement didn't move very much. Her experience of time was slow, so very slow. Even the very word time seemed to be stuck in her head on an endless loop, and she feared a headache was coming on, and then, like clockwork, there it was.

Toni sat in her chair, being quite the quiet, polite young girl. She was reading a magazine filled with women with a lot of make up in their faces. Once in a while she rose and walked to the window and looked down at the outside parking lot, the way Lori also often did. No one that didn't know her would suspect that anything was wrong or off in any way.

Mother and daughter left a little later than Lori usually did. They walked casually and in high spirits. The girl was particularly talkative and upbeat. Lori glimpsed Rhonda in her office again. Her old colleague wouldn't look at her.

The elevator ride was spookier than ever. Lori experienced it in a sort of trance where everything was out of whack. The walls and floor and ceiling didn't seem to be there at all, and they seemed to be suspended in and floating through a vast, empty (but not empty) space. There were shapes, what easily could be living beings she would be able to see if she dared squinting her eyes.

One moment the elevator didn't seem to stop on the bottom floor, and panic gripped her.

Mother and daughter sat down in the seats. Lori started the car and drove away from there.

– Are you okay, mom?

How can you ask such a stupid question, you ungrateful brat?

She pulled herself together by an act of will.

– Well, I always feel tired after work, she grinned, – but today I didn't, so I guess someone did something right.

Toni nodded, very, serious-minded.

The girl pulled something from the pocket inside her jacket.

– Rhonda gave these to me, she said in a rushed, embarrassed tone. – She told me to give them to you in stealth and not let anybody else get them.

Lori looked astonished at her. Whatever she had imagined was the reason for her daughter's slightly bizarre behavior it wasn't anything like this.

She recognized the familiar Genesis-logo at the top of the sheets, but the paper was strikingly red, different from other official communiqués. This was a red paper, a «for your eyes only» document, meant for a select few in any given company. She had believed herself to be one of them, and she wondered what dangerous secrets they held for Marco to not include her in them. He had chosen her as his confidante, his loyal and trusted associate long ago, or so she had believed.

Her stomach was acting up again. She had sensed its coming all day, the slow rising of undue pressure and soreness in her ass and lower belly, but the actual, familiar pain practically erupted and the need to shit turned almost overwhelming, and she had to stretch her willpower to the utmost in order to not shit herself. It happened quickly, as it usually did, from one moment to the next, so fast that she experienced it as an assault, as if somebody had jumped out of the shadows and struck her in the belly.

She rushed into the house from the garage, glimpsing a knowing, understanding smile from her spawn, and then she sat there, shit flowing from her ass like a waterfall.

Genesis was about genetic engineering and its implications in the future society. What more? What more could there possibly be? She sat there and skimmed through the sheets Rhonda had given her, given her by proxy to boot. Rhonda had been scared. She was never scared. Rhonda was greedy and ambitious and certainly not prone to any social conscience, not any that Lori had ever witnessed.

The shit in Lori's arse turned cold and hard, while she sat there, skimming and reading.

These sheets contained information about study groups, about lab rats. Batch nine looked promising. Batch fifteen didn't. Lori wasn't a scientist and didn't have any scientific training what so ever. She had never been involved with anything but the business part of Coleman Enterprises, but something made her frown when she began reading, reading thoroughly what was on these pages.

«9b is exhibiting promising signs, far beyond average. So does 9r».

That was a rather large batch. She wasn't surprised, though. Coleman Enterprises had always had considerable resources at its disposal.

She frowned. There was something, something she couldn't quite grasp.

«Subject 100a crossed the shaky bridge easily. The ball floated in front of his eyes during the entire walk without shaking. We've had a breakthrough. It was clearly right to move 100a up a level. It is my recommendation that we move several others up next week».

Suddenly she turned cold all over, as realization hit her.

The subjects were humans, not rats or apes or anything. Human beings!

Someone knocked on the door.

– Are you there, mom?

Lori realized that she had been sitting there for more than half an hour.

– I'm here, she heard herself reply.

– Dinner is ready soon, Toni gracefully enlightened and reminded her.

Stiff as a rock Lori had trouble moving properly when she attempted to rise. She managed somehow, rubbing her sore muscles and stretching until she

regained a modicum of moving ability.
– How long? She spoke through the closed door.
– Ten minutes tops, she heard through the closed door.
– I'll take a shower, she said. – Just a quick one.
– That's okay, mom, Toni said lightly, and Lori could see the shrug, her daughter's kind smile. – I'll just turn down the heat a bit. Just take your time.

A catching swelled in Lori's throat, as she undressed and stepped into the shower, and her tears of happiness drowned in the rain.

The entire house seemed strange. The feel it gave her was so different from before, before, when she had been a completely different person. Mother and daughter sat there and had their dinner in something akin to silence, both lost in thought.

There was no music from the adjacent property anymore, obviously not, but Lori imagined she heard it still. Richard Marx's face flashed before her inner eye. A sigh passed through the house, through them, and they both felt it. Toni moved from her chair at the other side of the table and to Lori's side, seeking close to her. Lori noticed easily the slight shiver in the other, smaller body and put an arm around her in a comforting hug.

Lori looked through the window afterwards, at the ashes of the other house. The window remained dirty, no matter how much Tom had scrubbed it. Soot had settled in the very glass, somehow, creating a strange effect when looked at from a certain angle.

It was the window behind the spot where Jeff had stood when he disappeared.

The experience still felt new to her, raw, like meat. She understood that. Her son, her flesh and blood had been brutally pulled away from her life by unexplainable circumstances. But there was more to it than that. It was the event itself, not merely her emotional attachment to it. Most people missed that, but she didn't, not anymore.

She hesitated a bit, before steeling herself and reaching out and touching the glass with the totality of her palm.

There was a jolt of sorts, but not really that pronounced. Images, sensations didn't exactly assault her, but they were tangible, real. The very idea of this was impossible, but still, here it was. She saw, sensed briefly a remote, alien landscape, with two moons in the sky. But no people. No people anywhere.

«Sometimes there are riders».

She sensed her flesh and blood. Its «scent» was close and far away.

Her smell didn't sense that, but something within far deeper and more powerful did, and she knew that with a certainty that brought her pleasure beyond belief.

The pink sheets had been thrown on the floor in a random pattern. She looked at them, unable to read them with her eyes, but she remembered them, remembered every word.

There was no pattern, none she could discern, no understanding.

– What are you doing, Marco? She mused. – Where are you going with this?

She knew it would bring them at odds with each other. She didn't need any sixth or tenth sense to tell her that, needed only her savvy and business-experience, what he had hammered into her the last twenty years.

The tide was coming, for her, at the very least for her.

She could see, easily, the possible forces converging, ganging up on her, the small pieces uniting into an unaware, directed force. She didn't need any special abilities for that.

The crazed schoolteacher.

The insecure therapist.

The company with its head, the corporate mogul.

The policeman, seeking retribution for an initial imagined slight.

The betrayed husband (who hadn't been betrayed).

And other, yet unrevealed factors and people.

It might all come at once, or as a series of events, building momentum… until it had destroyed her.

But only if she let it…

Slowly, perceptibly she rolled her left hand into a fist. Choosing the left hand felt strangely right. She stood there for a long time, facing the sooty window and the neighboring ruin until the stench of ashes had settled in her nostrils, and she knew, no matter what she did it would never go away.

Chapter Eight

The day began early, like her days usually began. The neighbors began staring the moment they saw movement inside the house. It wasn't hard for her to notice them, no matter how hard she strived to avoid it. She strived, like she did every morning with getting rid of the cobwebs dulling her mind. Splashing water in her face never helped. When she looked into the mirror in the bathroom she saw a sleepwalker.

The person in the mirror didn't have eyes, didn't have a mouth or a nose. Everything was plastered on, unreal, fake and dysfunctional.

Mother and daughter made breakfast together, something that had become a daily routine lately. They mostly did everything together.

The girl smiled to her, with her open and happy smile. Lori sensed no regret there, no detachment.

She closed and opened her eyes, sensing a slight irritation behind the eyelids, sensing the shadows in the bright sunshine. They were there, ever-present, calling to her, displaying themselves, revealing themselves to her.

Revealing truths, awakening all the heat and cold inside her.

– Society wants to… to turn you to stone, Lori said to Toni. – Don't let it. Don't ever let it!

– I won't! The girl stated solemnly, a little shaken. – Not ever!

Mother and daughter had breakfast together. There was no rush. Lori no longer cared whether or not she would be late for work. She stared out of the window, until she once again noticed her daughter's look, and turned back, turning her attention away from the shadows.

– There's something out there, somewhere, she said slowly, – something calling me… that has always been there, and always will be there.

– I think I know what you mean, Toni nodded eagerly. – I feel it, too, a pull, a dark wind in the night.

And the warm sunshine didn't seem quite as warm anymore.

But the lingering sensation persisted and remained.

The grown woman was about to say something, but held her tongue, but couldn't hide her nervous reaction from the very perceptive girl.

– It's coming for *us,* isn't it?

– Yes, Lori admitted. – Inevitably. I think it's coming for everybody.

It has waited, patiently, for millennia, for eons, for someone like us.

And the voice she heard was Lynn's voice. She saw her, as well, at the edge of her vision.

Mother and daughter did the dishes, the taste of the food having long since faded in their mouth. Each and every tiny bubble formed images, sensations in and out of their consciousness. Outside was a beautiful summer day. Lori stood in the driveway and drew breath and sighed deeply. The eyes lingered on her, like they always did. She ignored them. Pearls of sweat quickly grew on her forehead. She stretched her body, letting lawnmower man see a bit more of her.

A chill passed through her. She deliberately ignored it.

Slowly, only slowly she returned to the sanctity of the house. Toni met her there, with her backpack, ready and eager to start the day. They walked to the car. The air inside it was hot and stale. They let its doors stay open for a time, a long time before seating themselves.

– Will you open the window on your side, honey? Lori said.

– You bet! Toni replied.

It was still scalding hot, enough to make sweat pour from their brow. It took close to a minute of driving, until they reached the motorway and the higher speed there creating a constant, powerful flow of wind before they began cooling off. The enduring windblast made a mess of their hair, and that fact alone made Lori grin widely.

– How many are there, mommy? The child asked. – How many of us, of our kind?

Lori considered her impossible question, considered it long and hard.

– I don't know, honey. I just know there are many. The existence of one suggests there are more. The existence of seven more than proves there are many, a number difficult to measure.

She considered it some more.

– We *are* the new order, the Earth and sky, the day and Night.

The ramifications staggered her, and her own admission of it froze her cold in the hot sunshine.

They drove to the small township by the industrial park. Lori parked on an almost full lot after the usual wrangling and maneuvering, and they began their stroll through busy streets.

She felt the pain in her stomach the moment they passed that old Indian restaurant and stared incredulous at herself in the window.

– Are you okay, mom?

– Yes, she replied, smelling her own, cold sweat.

The pain subsided slowly, until it was nothing but a tiny irritation in her consciousness.

She walked the streets with her head tilted, as if she was listening to something, something she couldn't quite hear or perceive.

– I know there is something going on, she mumbled, as she close to delirious stumbled across the street.

She looked at her daughter with eyes sharp as talons, and knew Toni was unable to decide whether or not she was worried or afraid, if she was afraid for her or of her.

Lori smiled, as she was listening to the music rising from beneath.

It led them across the street, into the shadowy alley and through an arch to the modest square by the church. Birds flapped their wings and rose in the air when they crossed the open area. In-between all the white and gray wings she imagined she glimpsed a movement of black.

– Do you feel it, mommy? Toni whispered in excited awe. – Do you feel *life?*

– I do! Lori confirmed. – I *do!*

Experiencing her daughter's unveiled enthusiasm and joy made a catching grow in Lori's throat.

They passed by a row of fashion stores. Toni looked with doglike longing at the clothes being displayed.

– Do you want a new dress for the dance tonight? Lori asked casually.

The teenager frowned at first, studying her mother, fearing she was kidding. Then she realized that the offer was true, and her face cracked in a silly and astounded grin, and she embraced the other, bigger woman with an excited outburst.

– Thank you, mother. THANK YOU!

Lori felt the girl's heart beat against her own and wanted to echo her daughter's excitement.

They did some window shopping for a while, before deciding upon an initial approach. The store had air condition and dark-painted walls and ceiling, a welcome and refreshing contrast to all the other shops where conformity was celebrated.

The woman meeting them looked special, but not outrageous. Lori… liked that. She looked natural, emanating a quiet confidence, as she greeted them and led them into the isolated, smaller room in the back of the building, safe from prying eyes from the street.

Shadows reached far at this place. Lori couldn't tell whether or not that was good or bad, and that worried her a bit.

– I have to say, I enjoy this place, she told the woman in black. – You manage to be both interesting and fairly popular, as I understand it.

– Thank you, we make that extra effort, the woman replied, and Lori sensed how she tried her best not to sound like a trite advertising. – We weren't always on this «High Street» spot, but started out in a less prestigious area.

Every piece of cloth here was black or dark enough to resemble black, which wasn't really that original anymore, but within that limitation was a true variety of form and content. Lori found herself extremely pleased and thrilled just by being here.

Toni danced to the dark, innovative music, trying on a plethora of new clothes. The music whispered to you, not so much screaming. Lori found herself trying on new clothes, too (of course). She sighed in her weakness, dancing like the teenager to the whispering chords.

– You *want* these clothes. The saleswoman grinned wickedly and solemnly. – I can tell. You should indulge yourself, you know.

Lori touched what felt like a second skin. The fabric was so soft, so elegant and alluring. She wanted it, wanted it badly. One day, today was special. She sensed it, as she watched herself in the mirror.

– Mommy, Toni cried, – what do you think, mommy?

The girl made a pirouette before the two women, showing off, betraying her teenage insecurities. Lori felt a touch of irritation, but let it go quickly, faced with her daughter's excitement, mirroring her own.

– You look cute enough to eat, darling, she nodded.

Her daughter grinned.

Lori studied herself in the mirror. This wasn't just a dress, but rather a suit, with a jacket, and a skirt, and boots to match, black and dark blue velvet in a killer combination. She looked dangerous and beautiful and tantalizing, all at once.

Toni did, too, adding her youthful exuberance and obvious innocence.

– We'll take both, Lori heard herself say.

This wasn't indulging herself. This was taking what was hers.

The woman folded the clothes neatly and put them in bags with the store's insignia on each side. Lori paid with her gold card. The woman handed her the receipt and the bags with a professional, polite smile.

– Here you are. I'm confident you will be pleased. Please visit us again.

Mother and daughter left and walked back towards the car on the same route they had come. The traffic surrounded them. The noise from both the humans and the cars invaded them. The arch and the alley gave them only a brief respite from that.

Work felt brief, felt insignificant, even though she kept her eyes wandering, studying people with a deliberately casual look, and kept Toni at her side at all times.

– Something has changed, she told her daughter. – Whether or not it is our perception of it or not remains to be seen. It's difficult to tell, isn't it?

– Yes. Toni nodded. – I believe that's a fair assessment.

She smiled, so pleased to be taken into her mother's confidence.

Lori looked for Rhonda and eventually encountered her, or spotted her in glimpses. The woman was clearly avoiding her. Lori glimpsed a drawn, what she perceived as haunted expression, but didn't want to be obvious about her interest in her colleague, didn't pursue contact aggressively, since Rhonda clearly wanted their strange, clandestine relationship to remain that way. Rhonda looked scared in Lori's eyes.

It was difficult to keep up the appearances. Only decades of playacting saved Lori from revealing her own, nagging…

Doubt, misgivings, fear, apprehension, anxiety?

Paul studied her, or so she feared. She hurried into her office. Toni was right behind her. The girl closed the door quietly, already having reached the first level of professional stealth and subterfuge action.

Lori sat behind her desk, sifting through reports. They were just ordinary, boring information and reactions, letters and numbers turning indistinct through her sore eyes. The teenager listened to music through her headphones, dancing on the middle of the floor to rhythms Lori could only speculate at. Toni's eyes were closed. She was smiling, and dreaming herself away, and Lori found herself dreaming with her.

It started out so casually and innocently. She began visualizing Paul, the hard muscles under the smart dress. It felt natural to picture herself going to him, stepping behind him, and begin rubbing his broad shoulders. He turned and smiled to her, such a pretty smile. She bent forward and kissed him on his upturned lips. His pretty smile invaded her mind. She sat down on his lap and loosened his tie, unbuttoning his shirt, boldly moving between his thighs, seeking the hardening thing down there, and all the time there was the pretty smile invading her, making her giddy and elated.

She found herself gasping aloud, and pulled back to the stark reality behind her desk, with her hand between her thighs, shock carved into her features. The hand, wet and slimy like her panties, pulled back by itself, with minimal contribution from her conscious mind. She stared at Toni, but the girl hadn't even opened her eyes, and kept dancing undisturbed. Relief flooded Lori. She just sat there, frozen like a statue for goddess knows how long. It took at least a couple of minutes before she managed to force herself on her feet and steer herself towards the bathroom.

She splashed her face. The water from the sink seemed ice-cold. She gasped again, looking at herself, her flushed face in the mirror, still shaking her head in disbelief.

Sweat covered every piece of her body and made her clothes sticky and uncomfortable. It took a long time before her breathing returned to normal. She began cleaning her face, rubbing off the ruined makeup with a wet cloth. Then she removed her panties and began washing her stinking… her stinking cunt. She bit her lip while doing so, fearing it would make things (the stench) worse. It itched down there, and burned, and she couldn't believe how out of control she was. She threw the panties in the waste basket, deciding to not give a damn and returned to the office. Toni was still dancing with closed eyes, and didn't seem to have noticed that she had been gone at all.

My, goddess, Lori thought. I'm a wreck.

I don't just look like a wreck. I am one.

She dumped back in her chair, picturing Paul's smile behind her closed eyes.

The day ended eventually, and finally. She had her meetings, convinced at least her two o'clock and the very least her three o'clock saw straight through her. Unfocused and irritated she almost fucked up several times. It ended eventually, finally on a somewhat relaxed note.

The two of them passed Paul on their way out. Lori nodded to him, striving to keep a neutral expression. Toni gave him her best smile.

The day seemed short and sweet, now, in the car, driving home. Lori breathed deeply in and out.

– I think I'll have to find myself a new job, she told her daughter casually.

– I think that would be wise, the child agreed, wise beyond her years.

Lori suddenly realized that children noticed far more than parents and adults would guess. They saw through all the masks, straight to all the inflamed hypocrisy beneath, but kept silent, and their own infections started growing. She rubbed the girl's cheek. Toni pulled back, but given the usual smile of assurance she relented.

– You know you can talk to me about anything, don't you?

– I do, the child assured her.

Julia and Kelly waited for them on the stairs. Four faces cracked in smiles. Lori and Toni could hardly wait to get out of the car. Julia and Kelly met them halfway, and they hugged, two and two and all four together. They walked inside, floating on a cloud of emotion.

The house sounded quiet. Lori couldn't remember it being quite like that before, when a nuclear family had lived here.

She noticed her own restlessness, a constant itching beneath the skin.

The house, no matter how quiet spoke to her, or whispered in her ears, touched her skin in a way no other house could.

Or… was there something more?

The sensation intensified on the spot in the living room where her son had disappeared, where he had faded away like mist.

But only for a moment. When she reached for it, it faded, like her son, her flesh and blood.

– We'll find him, Kelly told her, – … somehow.

– We will, Lori insisted. – The world has changed. At last our perception of it has. What once has been lost can be found again. We just need the right information, and the knowledge and sets of skill making it work for us.

All four of them made dinner. It could have been messy, but wasn't. They worked well together, anticipating each other's moves, easily avoiding what could be the others' obtrusive motion.

– There is clearly something here, between us, Julia stated, – a bond we cannot deny. I get a sense of Deja Vu, of familiarity with every glance we give each other. I dreamt about us last night, and it was the most powerful dream… *vision* I've ever experienced.

Lori frowned, imagining for a moment that she could actually re-experience her friend's fevered dream, before that, too, slipped away.

They sat by the dinner table in the living room, laughing and drinking and eating, enjoying the moment, the fleeting moments of frozen time.

Toni giggled, before putting down her glass, sniffing, choking.

– What is it, honey? Her mother asked, even though she could guess.

– Everything has become so much better lately, hasn't it, mom?

Lori waited patiently.

– But Jeff is gone, mom, plucked from our lives just like *that,* and we sit here enjoying ourselves like hell, and it doesn't feel *right.*

The other three patted her, comforting her the best they were able, and it helped, helped them all a little.

– I believe Jeff would want us to keep living, honey, no matter what, and we *will* find him.

– I know. The girl dried her tears. – But it still doesn't feel right. And it isn't just him either, but everything else that has happened, the certainty that something… *is* coming for us.

You bright girl, Lori thought glumly. You incredibly bright and perceptive girl.

Lori frowned again. The other three looked attentive at her.

– He said something, she mused. – «Sometimes there are riders», and the way he said it made it clear it was a warning.

– *Riders?* Kelly wondered. – People on *horses?*

– Probably not, Lori acknowledged. – Probably a figure of speech hiding something far more sinister. He didn't have time to explain it properly.

– He was old, Toni practically shouted, before catching herself, reddening. – Well, not really *old* old, but an adult. Years had passed for him in the seconds he had been gone.

Julia and Kelly looked at them both with sympathy and horror in their eyes.

– What I saw, Lori said with a hollow voice, – in the few seconds he stayed, was an experienced man, with scars to prove it, both on the outside and the inside, one who knew what he was talking about. Toni is correct. He wasn't old, probably not more than a few years older than when he disappeared, but during those years he had endured hardship we can only imagine.

More images, sensations danced behind her half-closed eyelids.

They did the dishes together, too, and it worked like the preparation to the dinner had done, equally like a joy and a catharsis. Lori felt she desperately needed both.

She and Toni showered, and then they took on the quite pleasing task of dressing up in the clothes they had purchased earlier. They stood there, like two twins before the mirror, a perfect match.

– You didn't say anything about upgrading your wardrobe, dear Lori, Kelly said. – Or I would have taken steps to match you.

Lori was pleased to notice the jealousy and sense of menace in her friend's voice.

Hair was groomed, and groomed again, until mother and daughter finally found mercy in Julia and Kelly's eyes, and they were able to move on.

– It's turning dark, mom, Toni said.

It didn't, really, and wouldn't for some time yet, at least not in ways average citizens would notice. Lori speculated that Toni was able to notice minor changes in the air, in her surroundings, with senses considerably keener than what most people enjoyed. There had been other instances as well when she had noticed this about her daughter. It worried and pleased her.

They fitted their high-heels around their poor feet, and were ready to go. Lori locked the door behind them and they walked down the stairs and down the driveway. The community house where the party was arranged was only a few blocks away. So they walked, like several other neighbors, even though there were those driving, taking the car with them wherever they went. Mr. Thompson and spouse would drive the fifty meters from their house to the community house's parking lot, like they did every year, and they were in no way unique, only excessive.

It was a hot and dry summer evening, and they began perspiring after less than a minute outside. They took frequent breaks and didn't make haste in any way, but in spite of this their skin was quickly covered by a thin layer of sweat.

People stared at them, like they always did. Lori didn't mind, for her own sake, but she noticed that Toni glanced nervously around, and that made her very angry at her curious neighbors.

It wasn't hard to know that their senses were growing keener. All four of them looked in wonder at the world, so much more astute than just weeks ago… or yesterday.

– What is it? Toni wondered.

– What is what? Mother asked casually, very casually.

– I thought *my* eyes were constantly moving, but that was before I noticed yours. You look almost… spooked.

Lori caught herself, an added layer of sweat itching at her brow.

– I don't know. There is something… something in the air, but it keeps slipping away from me.

The memory of her disturbing dream was suddenly clear and vivid in her mind.

The music had started up. They heard it long before they turned the last corner and caught the sight of the giant, ugly and square building in front of them.

– I guess we're fashionably late, Julia shrugged.

– Very good, Lori scowled. – We're spared all the introductory bullshit.

– Not to mention all the talk about sponsors and advertising, Toni contributed brightly.

Lori looked at her with fondness in her heart.

They entered a dark and murky world with occasional spots of warm light, and were pleasantly surprised by that, smiling to each other as they made their way to the dance floor. It covered a significant part of the interior, but then again, the building, its entire interior was so big that there was room to spare for practically anything.

The four coconspirators were dancing with dozens of others, mostly teenagers and youths. Lori looked envious at Toni and the other chicks. They didn't seem to have any trouble jumping around with the high heels.

She forgot the flash of despair the moment it appeared and threw herself into the art of letting go. In the flashes of the blinking light and composite shadows Lori glimpsed her friends and daughter and yet another smile crossed her lips.

A few boys courted Toni, and Lori allowed it, graciously.

The first bout of dancing ended. The mother made sure the daughter followed her older friends to the table section, but she didn't have to try that hard. Toni wasn't that interested in the bungling boys.

Lori, Toni and Kelly sat by their table about halfway between the dance floor and the bar, while Julia fetched their beer. There was quite a bit of space between the tables and it was possible to hear oneself think (and engage in a meaningful conversation without screaming).

– There is a vitality here tonight I can't quite recall from earlier annuals, Lori noted, pondering the froth at the top of her Guinness.

– I just think everybody has a sense of impending doom, Kelly grinned wolfishly. – They want to get their licks in before everything goes boom.

– I think they feel that they *have* to make it livelier compared to last year, Toni stated without doubt in her voice. – That was quite simply too boring to be true.

– And then they have overcompensated and allowed too much? Julia chuckled. – I can believe that. These local arrangements are usually filled with hypocrisy and sexual angst.

– Cheers! Kelly cried, raising her glass.

Four glasses met and parted. They sat there rocking on their chairs a bit, to the drums and energetic guitar playing.

Julia kept turning her head, though, until the others had enough and prompted her to spit out what was… what was bothering her.

The thought dawned on Lori like sudden rain.

– There's a lowlife by the bar, Julia said. – He's surrounded by a worshipping cult of women.

They had, briefly between all the people passing back and forth a direct line of sight to the group of people Julia was talking about and took a look. The man sitting at the end of the bar did seem to have the ears of the five rather pretty women keeping him company.

– Am I wrong or are the chicks eating up every word he says? Julia wondered with a clear subtext of anger in her voice.

– It sure looks that way, Lori remarked.

There was something… unsettling about the whole scene. It bothered her, and she didn't know why.

– I guess he is the evening's smooth talker, drawing to him all the dumb chicks at the party, she shrugged. – There are lots of those.

– Aye! Kelly hissed.

All four shrugged, deliberately and proceeded to drink more Guinness.

The alcohol, at least its initial stages worked quickly on Lori, as it usually did. The physical numbness in the lips and mouth and the beginnings of a slurring speech was noticeable, she knew, to those listening to her profound musings. A huge, happy grin appeared on Toni's face, very much a mirror of Lori's own, Lori suspected.

She wondered briefly if she should do something about Toni's consumption, if she should caution her, but then the thought slipped her mind and she forgot about it.

They played jazz during the more formal parts of the festivities because it was the correct, conservative thing to do, making sure people fell further asleep.

Most of those present were well into the celebration and actually ignored the dismal attempt at slowing down the excess.

Lori danced with a guy at some point. She could neither recall his face nor the name of the song played afterwards, but that was all right. It was still fun.

The girl across her table said something, and for one horrible moment Lori couldn't recall her daughter's name.

– This is so fun, Toni said happily.

She was drinking lemonade and that was so mature and responsible of her that it made her mother almost speechless with pride.

– It's a good thing you're focusing on controlling yourself a little, Lori told the girl during a brief mother/daughter moment.

– I can always celebrate to excess at a later date, Toni grinned, clearly more than a little tipsy.

But not mindlessly so, not a helpless victim of all the predatory young males in attendance. Lori relaxed some more. When a predatory young male asked her for a dance, she accepted. She was very conscious of the fact that she had rejected his advances against the not so mindless young daughter, but he was very charming and she relented, waving apologetically to her three companions. They returned the wave with wide grins and told her to go for it.

The dance floor had been filled up occasionally during the evening, but was now about half full. The lights glowed and pulsed as the handsome young stud took the seasoned woman for a spin. The mood was fun and light. She giggled darkly, meeting his eyes fiercely and unafraid.

He was young, but not so young that she had to worry about his mother showing up and hammer her. A handsome, devil-may-care fucker, if she had ever seen one. She sighed happily.

While they danced she found herself in the room in a completely new way. She giggled again.

– What? He asked.

She dried a bit of saliva from around her mouth, looking at him with her dark eyes.

– I just had an epiphany, and realized, for the first time in my life what three-dimensional space truly is.

He pulled her close and kissed her on the lips. She resisted briefly, before responding. The silver moonlight reached the hall through the large ceiling window and mixed with the artificial, modern brightness. He was bold when he touched her, when he pushed her at one of the pillars. She released a pleased sound.

Something buzzed in her ear, an irritation, a coincidence making her turn her head. She saw three men charm her friends and daughter. Her smile gained a sarcastic touch.

– Ah, you guys planned a two-in-one, or rather a four in one, she noted. – Or you wanted to run away with the young chick while her mother was distracted. Anyway, I've never favored such approaches much.

She freed herself from his grip. He didn't really attempt to hold onto her.

– Come back in a few hundred years, kid.

She returned to the table.

– These gentlemen are leaving, she said icily.

They did. Toni looked at her, wondering, a little hurt.

– They planned on gangbanging you in some remote and rather bland place, she enlightened her daughter.

– So, this was a well coordinated operation? Kelly said incredulous.

– It was indeed, Lori confirmed.

– Those *creeps!*

Julia expressed her contempt in a loud voice, easily reaching across the hall.

Toni had turned pale and very angry. Lori's heart went out to her, but she held herself in check. Sometimes the best way to support or comfort somebody was to keep your distance.

Lori looked around for the four boys, but didn't see them.

She looked again a couple of minutes later. This time she made a sweep across the entire populated area of the building and outside, but they were nowhere to be seen.

– My stomach is acting up again, she replied to the others' inquiring looks.

And it was.

They had more to drink, but she drank more cautious, now, checking the beer for any foul, suspicious taste, and the three others, very astute as they were couldn't avoid noticing.

– My stomach is acting up, she said defensively, – that wasn't bullshit, but not enough to spend half an hour on the john.

She paused a bit, before deciding to commit herself fully.

– I feel shitty, or at least strange, stranger than usual, and I have the entire day.

She felt silly.

– A stomach acting up is often a sign from the subconscious mind, Julia said, – and since we're closer to the subconscious than most people it isn't too farfetched that you may have noticed something without being fully aware of it.

– You noticed the boys, Toni said, a subtext of spite evident in her voice, – even if you had your lips buried in the boy's face.

Lori decided to let that, too pass. Teenage girls were fond of carrying grudges.

There is something going on, she thought.

A shimmer in the air wasn't quite a shimmer, wasn't quite what her eyes saw.

The lights came on, flooded the hall. One formal part of the festivities remained: the dinner. Fanfares went off in her head. Everybody or most of the people present gathered around the large table in the next hall. There were a few speeches, blissfully short, a lot of bullshit, especially about the greatness of the local community, and more jazz.

– You'll get used to it, kiddo, she joked with her daughter. – It's an acquired taste, that's all. There are a few of those around.

– Not so loud, mom, Toni whispered, glancing embarrassed around her, fearing all the accusing looks.

Lori cackled aloud, hitting her thigh and pointed a finger at her daughter.

– You're good with her, Julia said later, when they were both in the lavatories, washing their hands after peeing. – You made her forget, at least to a point the recent unpleasantness.

– Thank you, Lori said, a little somber, – I believe I've improved with her lately, at least, after years of neglect, of wrong priorities.

She took her time back, deliberately. Toni and Kelly sat by the table, and weren't surrounded by a pack of hungry two-legged wolves. Lori relaxed again.

– I've felt more than shitty all night, she admitted to her friend. – I can't relax, can't enjoy myself.

– Waiting for the impending doom, huh? Her friend said. – Well, believe me, I know how that is. And you have clearly reason to be paranoid.

She wanted to say more, but instead the two women held and squeezed each other's hand.

It had turned dark, turned twilight again, and in another strange way Lori imagined they were outdoors, sitting around the campfire, a giant fire, many people sitting in a wide circle. She saw it, through what felt very much like a true experience, but there was more. A man sat by the fire. He was practically burning, or so she imagined. She also heard the sound of hooves growing louder, of riders approaching.

Lori almost jumped in her chair, as she was shaken back to the here and now, and met the eyes of her three companions and they seemed so very far away. Even when she grabbed their hands and held on for dear life, they seemed distant and lost to her.

There was more dancing. She lost herself in it, except for the tiny scratch irritating the back of her neck. It kept asserting itself, and she did keep her eyes on her surroundings, both letting herself go and staying on her guard.

It seemed impossible, but she did it, feeling so astute and alive and anxious beyond words.

She spotted the youth that had been dancing with her earlier, one in the gang going for her daughter, spotted him outside the window, between the trees. He stared in, and she feared, at her.

Distracted, she was so distracted. She…

They sat together around the table again. She looked at her watch. Time didn't really seem to be passing at all. It just stood still there, dancing at the edge of the precipice.

– … and so he walked to me, Toni mused. – He just stood there, attempting to vocalize his thoughts. I guess he wanted to ask me for a dance or something, but I was saved by the bell.

Hearty laughter. Lori heard herself, as if from the outside, as if the laughter wasn't actually her own at all, but someone else's.

The boy was no longer outside the window, and she didn't see him anywhere else either.

She sensed someone behind her, and turned, but there was no one there. Studying all the people in her sight did her no good. If any of them was planning mischief she couldn't see through their mask of indifference.

– Okay, Toni spoke up cheerfully, – who wants more beer?

– Not I, Lori replied, glancing at the remains in her glass.

– Not I, Julia shook her head.

– Not I, Kelly confirmed with a glee in her eyes.

– Good, the girl noted, – then I can buy the next round without being looked at with suspicious eyes.

She was off in a rush, conveniently snapping a bill from Lori's wallet.

Lori looked at the almost empty glass again. She was full. The last sip she had consumed had felt very trying. There had been a resistance, as if the fluid no longer wanted to flow down her throat. It was her seventh or eighth glass for the evening and clearly the last.

– I'm drunk, she sighed with a sad face.

– We all are, honey, Kelly grinned.

– I didn't think I would be tonight, you know, Lori said. – I felt so astute during the first few glasses, like I would be drinking forever, and I know every single drunk says some stupid thing like that, insisting how alcohol cannot touch them, but I *still* felt like that.

Kelly and Julia exchanged looks. Lori saw it, or believed she saw it through the haze of her vision.

Her bladder was full again, and she stumbled to the lavatories. There were a few cubicles available. She chose the second on her right, and sat down on the cold seat. Then she realized that she hadn't pulled up her dress, and pulled down her panties, and rose to do both, before sitting down again. Then, finally the powerful beam of piss hit the water far below.

Indecipherable patterns revealed themselves to her on the door. No matter how hard she strived, she couldn't make sense of them.

She glimpsed what she knew positively was her own eyes in there, a slow flash of revelation, of obscurity, but there was nothing else, no matter how hard she strived for another disclosure.

The toilet paper was soft, easily torn. She had to stay careful while she rolled it out. Her sore ass whimpered while she dried herself. She pulled up her panties and pulled down her dress, flushed the toilet and opened the door. The mirror at the other end of the room seemed misty, covered by a film of moisture. She walked to it and touched it with her palm. It was completely dry and felt hot to her skin, not at all like glass usually felt. She rubbed her palm back and forth. What had seemed like misty steam remained. She touched her palm with the fingers on the other hand just to make sure. The skin remained dry.

The noise in the hall only slowly returned to her as she stepped outside. Music sounded muted, distant. Kelly waved to her. Lori returned the wave, as she returned to the table.

– Where is my wayward daughter? She asked lightly. – I'm thirsty.

– It seems like she, too has developed a case of puppy love, Julia sighed.

Lori looked towards the bar, where she expected to find the girl, and then not spotting her there, shifted her attention to the table a bit to the side, at the end of the bar. Toni had joined the girls standing around the smooth talker. Their number had increased to eight. All eight looked at the man at the center of their attention with evident admiration in their wet eyes.

– I'll go and *fetch* her, Julia said, – break the enchantment and expose the prince for the beggar he is.

Lori's headache took a turn for the worse, as her friend faded from her view. She rubbed her forehead with a pained, impossible-to-hide expression.

– Jesus, Kelly shook her head, – perhaps you should really consider having your head examined.

Behind the light banter there was real concern. Lori swallowed hard and sent her a grateful look.

– The pain has grown progressively worse, she acknowledged, – and never been worse than tonight.

– Headache is supposed to come the morning after the drinking, Kelly nodded softly.

For some reason Lori caught an image of a computer. It was on, and working on full capacity, sighing in pain, threatening to break down. The blinking light blinked fast enough to gasp.

Two teenagers really went at it on the floor, dancing as if the world was about to end, drawing critical looks from adults and the family crowd. Lori's attention was drawn to them, to their exuberance. A sting of envy rose with the smile.

The lights began flickering everywhere, or so it seemed. She felt a hand on the shoulder.

– Your eyes, Kelly said. – They blink so rapidly.

– Am I sleeping? Lori wondered. – Am I dreaming?

Kelly studied her with a bit of concern in her eyes.

– It feels like I am, as if everything is moving incredibly fast… or has slowed down to a crawl.

– You're experiencing something akin to hyper-reality, her friend said. – There are tales of such events among… among powerful adepts.

Her friend smiled and relief flooded Lori briefly. Kelly was okay with it. She was really okay with it.

Worry returned with a slam dunk of thunder.

– Now, I'm actually becoming thirsty, Kelly said exasperated. – What's happening?

They both turned their attention to the table at the end of the bar. The smooth talker had now gathered nine eager listeners around him. Julia looked just as… as mesmerized as the rest.

– I'll go to put a stop to that asshole, Kelly swore. – We'll be right back.

Lori wanted to tell her to stay put, to warn her, but she was frozen with indecision within and without. Nothing worked, except her racing, overworked mind.

She watched, helplessly, while Kelly strode towards the hell at the edge of the bar, saw her cross an invisible boundary to join the other females. The nine and the male turned to her smiling. Her first few words were angry, but then she stopped, and it reminded Lori very much of something like a fly being caught in amber, or in a spider's web, or any other cliché she had ever heard.

The man was in his early thirties, with light brown hair, perfectly ordinary features, except for a pair of bushy brows stealing the attention from the rest of his features.

Lori heard him speak, as clearly as if he had been standing right in front of her, but it didn't affect her, not like it did her daughter and friends and the other women. He was talking all the time. It was as if there was some pattern to it. It was weird, weird, weird. He spoke a lot, spoke mainly about inconsequential subjects, but…

What was he *saying?*

To others listening in it probably didn't sound strange at all, and before they knew it they were helplessly mesmerized with something that certainly wasn't his winning personality.

Suddenly she could hear his words, what he truly said, and it made her blood turn cold.

Lay now your mind to rest. Rejoice in the eager service of the Service. You are mine, mine to command and rule. My bidding will be the only thing on your little mind.

It went on and on, like there was end to it.

This *was* hyper-reality, this horror slamming her a thousand times a second, driving ice-cold spikes through every cell and nerve-ending of her body and mind. Now, time did slow down to a crawl. She saw herself rise, saw herself go to him, join his other eager and weak-willed dolls, saw it happen many times, while she stood frozen on her eternal spot.

He clearly had some control over it, since he could decide who would be affected and who wouldn't. She watched him turn away those he didn't desire, knew he wanted those he had, knew he wanted her.

And then she could finally move, and she *moved.* Her feet fled of their own volition. She walked with fast, fluttering steps towards the exit, very aware of what was happening, of what she was doing, of what kind of cruel decision she was making.

The cold night air outside struck her on the second step from above, and she stopped, wild, mindless panic crawling through her veins while she scoured every part of her surroundings.

– No, not home, she mumbled, – they'll find me there, find me everywhere they'll know I'll go.

She ran, ran flat out, breathing so hard that her lungs threatened to burst. At some point, it dawned on her that she had lost her shoes, her high heels, but she felt nothing but relief and kept running. People she encountered on her way didn't look threatening, but she kept her distance still. They weren't that many and increasingly fewer as she removed herself from the community house's immediate vicinity.

Hampton Court Station appeared in her cloudy vision. For a second or two she was terrified that they would anticipate this, too, but a cold, hard and strangely calm voice inside told her that if that was true nothing she would do would matter. She kept taking one more step in front of the other.

The train waited for her, clothed in mist and shadow. She didn't buy a ticket, but jumped right on the closest coach. There were no other people there. She desperately wanted there to be, but was also terrified by the very thought. The seat by the door pointed to itself. A shrill laughter erupted from her sore throat. She sat down and crawled as far into the corner she could possibly come.

The train began its journey to nowhere. She shook as it shook, very aware of how she appeared. Anyone entering the coach would instantly recognize a woman that was scared to death.

There had been no thought beyond the rudimentary during her escape, and there still wasn't, really. The queue of rampant, unpleasant thoughts was instantly and constantly delegated to a currently useless part of her brain.

The dark landscape flowed past her outside the envelope of the train. She didn't see it, didn't see anything. Empty eyes stared at nothing. The train stopped at a few stations on its way. She wasn't reacting one way or another.

Slowly, only slowly the train moved away from Hampton Court and the nightmare it had left behind. The woman sitting in the corner didn't move, didn't blink. She kept ignoring, locking out thoughts of yesterday, the present, tomorrow and everything that could have been. The rhythm of the slow-moving train comforted her feeble mind somehow. The clouds looked so bright and the land below so dark. It comforted her. The electric light turned itself off and on in an impossible to determine pattern.

She threw up, hard and painful. The vomit decorated a large area from the edge of her dress to across the room. Her head fell back, hitting the wall, hurting so much, adding to the tears filling her eyes.

The journey to the end station of Waterloo lasted only twenty minutes. It went on forever, repeating itself endlessly. She sat there, half asleep, half astute and awake, her empty eyes huge as planets, re-experiencing countless versions of yesterday and tomorrow.

Part two: Realization

«The bond that links your true family is not one of blood, but of respect and joy in each other's life. Rarely do members of the same family grow up under the same roof».
Richard Bach

Chapter Nine

She had shit herself. That thought persisted at the back of her mind, no matter what others that might be roaming her battered consciousness.

Streets and details were just a blur to her. She kept rushing forward, kept putting one foot in front of the other, and that was all there was.

She crouched in a port-room, trembling. There was a lot of food in the trashcans. Starving as she was, she devoured it without looking at it. She crouched in the port-room, trembling. Between moments there was nothing, no recall, no life or even existence. She heard singing. The toilet was old, derelict, a twisted mirror image of the front, the perfect facade. She dried herself. The sore spot between her thighs seemed to have grown and multiplied in terms of both reach and pain level.

Her panties were gone. She faintly recalled having thrown the filthy stuff into a trashcan, but wasn't sure. The mirror was dirty, and didn't show more than pieces of a dissolved face, one with stricken features, an eye there, lips elsewhere, a part of something that might be a nose, a fistful of hair hiding what might lurk beneath. She washed herself, or at least she tried to, rubbing soap and paper dipped in hot water between her thighs.

There were other people there, but they didn't seem real, somehow, no more than ghosts, revenants walking the edge between this world and the other.

It was raining. Lori was running. She didn't know why, but she ran flat out and didn't stop, but kept charging forward. A large, woolen hole had taken the place of her thoughts, of her reason. She ran and couldn't stop running. Something had scared her, scared her badly, she knew that, but couldn't recall what.

Red light shone in her eyes, illuminating her mind, but blinding her to her surroundings. She glimpsed in her fever a dark spire and building against a less dark sky.

The red light formed patterns in the rain, in the chaos her mind had become. She leaned against a brick wall somewhere. Reality split into the thousand raindrops before her. She whimpered in her ongoing terror. It squeezed her in its grip and wouldn't let go. She stumbled on, oblivious to everything, except the rain.

The dark Hyde Park loomed before her. She recognized it somewhat, even in the bottomless hole her mind had become, the stupor she had fallen into.

It opened up to her before she entered it. It was no problem climbing the low fence. Obedience and fear kept most people out after dark.

And she saw herself beyond both such trifles.

She wasn't completely sure it was dark, though. Sometimes, in her memory she imagined there had been daylight or at least twilight when she had walked through the gate, and it hadn't been raining. The gates closed at dusk, she seemed to recall that.

It was raining, now, pouring down heavy showers. Hyde Park was huge. She had no idea where she was, or where she had been. An impenetrable gray wall made her blind and deaf and mute.

«Follow the breadcrumbs», a young man told her.

She wanted to scream at him, spit on him, and tell him how completely disgusting she saw his obscurity, but her voice just didn't work.

The lights from the city seemed so incredibly far away. The park looked unimaginably huge, like a jungle with a labyrinth of paths and gates, not at all like she remembered it.

She walked past the building in Kensington Gardens, but even though it was easily recognizable it didn't look anything like she remembered. Everything in the park had changed, even though it stayed the same. Her two eyes saw nothing strange.

Around the corner in the hedge labyrinth an old man sat on a red-painted bench. He looked straight ahead, seeing nothing at all, not moving even the smallest body part.

She stood still and didn't move a single body part, studying him.

A lot of people passed by, and stopped, and stared at her.

– What is she staring at, daddy? One with a boy's voice asked someone she couldn't see.

She wondered what he meant. Everybody could see the old man on the red bench… couldn't they? Suddenly she caught herself wondering what he was looking at. She walked behind him, staring in the direction he was staring.

There was nothing there, really, nothing standing out in her eyes.

Another man stared at her, or rather at the place she had been standing when staring at the old man on the bench. Goosebumps broke all over her body.

A red light illuminated a fountain in front of her. This was later. She had no idea how long time had passed.

It didn't really turn dark in this seemingly eternal twilight summer. The ever-present moon didn't cast such a strong light on the fairly bright night sky, the summer twilight.

She stared at the unknown woman in the mirror, convinced this wasn't her face. It was younger, for one, markedly different from hers under the well-known thick black hair. She wondered briefly if this was Toni, an older Toni, but caught herself shaking her head. This was Lori, a younger-looking Lori, and she shook her head in bewilderment.

The mirror was not a mirror, but mist forming in the air. The image she studied in the fluid surface was identical in every aspect to how it was supposed to be or rather had been. The landscape behind her, the clothes the woman wore, how the hair fell. Only the face itself was different from how she remembered it before entering the park.

– Do you know my name? She and the girl in the mirror asked.

Her voice sounded shockingly loud in the silence that had been.

Thick smoke rolled slowly in from the right and front, staying close to the ground, hardly even rising in the air at all. It eventually surrounded her. She was alone again. No more other woman in the mirror.

She ran again, or at least walked in a fast pace. Stark terror drove her forward, into the gathering mist.

Water still flowed in the streets the upcoming gray morning. She heard people pass by, back and forth from the port-room where she was crouching. Indistinct shapes moved far away from her position. They didn't look at her, most of them, and those doing so didn't act on their visual input, didn't dare approach the fearsome and unsettling strange creature disturbing their ill at ease stroll.

Then, something changed. Shapes entered the port-room, rocking her relative tranquility. She didn't move, not even an eyelash or a finger. It was no use, she knew that. She knew they would find her, that they had already done so.

Their voices buzzed in her ears, like through a quiet roar of distant waves. She felt their hands on her, felt them touch her, cautiously, not invasive, but it still made her crouch and shiver in fright and paralysis.

– New, expensive clothes… but *look* at her. She has experienced something *bad* this one.

Female touch, more a breaking of boundary, more an invasion of personal space.

– She isn't injured, isn't hurt, at least not physically.

– No panties. Has she been…

– Her clothes are truly the latest and hottest. That dress wasn't on sale a month ago.

– Sell them! I don't care. She heard her own voice, harsh, even and without modulation. – But know that you should be… cautious while doing so. And I would not use the credit cards if I were you.

They stared at her, even more timid than usual.

She still didn't see them, except as indistinct shapes. Their voices sounded far more distinct than the features and faces.

– Let us help you, the boy said. – Please come with us.

There was a nod, imagined or real. They grabbed her and helped her up.

– No hospital, she mumbled. – No police, no registration.

– Don't worry, the boy grinned somberly. – That isn't an option.

There was a face, or a glimpse of one, depicted in stark color. Pale hues blinded her once again.

The people on the street outside, the street outside itself imposed on her, still far away flashed in and out of her consciousness. She walked, stumbled forward, one foot in front of the other, aided by the perceived kind strangers.

The surroundings and sounds changed, somewhat. Names, scenery failed completely to appear in her conscious mind. It was all touches, breathing and the scent of wet and dirty clothes. They moved away from the main road, from Bayswater Road (she remembered), to a quieter area north of Hyde Park (she remembered). She whimpered. One of the girls brushed a hand at her cheek, attempting to comfort her, to calm her distress.

– She has been through a bad one, this one.

The words still didn't register, didn't make sense to her wet, feverish mind.

Black and gray supplanted the bright gray and white image in her open, unseeing eyes. The last remaining strength left her feet, and she fell, or would have fallen if they hadn't grabbed her, grabbed her and held on.

The sound of traffic faded to almost nothing, to what it sounded like inside a building.

– We'll take care of her, one of the girls said.

Male scents faded from her nostrils.

– No one will harm you here, the other girl told her, assured her. – We will not allow it. Do you understand?

Lori nodded with numb lips.

The girls undressed her, gently but persistent.

She felt them… spread her thighs, inspecting her, gently, cautiously.

– There's no… no semen, no visual signs of hard penetration, but I guess she could still be...

The two glanced at each other.

– Have you been raped, honey?

The words made sense to her only slowly, their meaning dawning on her through painful realization.

– No. She shook her head and chuckled darkly. – At least not in the conventional sense.

Then she went away again. She knew they were speaking to her, or attempting to, but it was nothing more than meaningless babble to her.

They put her in a bathtub, in scolding hot water, and rubbed and washed her. It felt pleasant, not invasive at all. She didn't close her eyes, but enjoyed the relative blindness, as it slowly faded, and the room revealed itself to her.

It wasn't a bathroom, at least not in the traditional, modern sense. The tub stood at the center of the room. There were no tubes. They used buckets to bring water to it and from it. It was pleasant in a way, simple and pleasant. She enjoyed being coddled, not needing to think or respond, in any way, to anything.

– This is a church?

– It used to be, the tall blonde grinned.

Lori noticed the painted glass, the various remaining ornaments in the room. This had been the sacristy, the priest's room below the altar.

– I followed the breadcrumbs, she whimpered, – but they didn't lead anywhere.

They comforted her, as they dried her with a huge towel, with kisses and touches and kind words in her ears, as the violent shivering slowly ceased.

They dressed her. The clothes were worn but clean and felt good to the touch.

One of the girls reached out a hand.

– Hi, she grinned solemnly, – I'm Caitlin Everheart. This is Adriana Morris. Welcome to Castle Rayon.

The name made sense to her, somehow.

– What's the significance?

– Perhaps none, Adriana said. – Perhaps we wanted to name it after a building neither synthetic nor natural?

The new arrival looked at them with eyes like wounds.

– I'm Lori, she said. – …

She didn't say more. They looked her with sympathetic eyes.

– I want you to understand something, she said, glaring at them. – My worst, unimaginable fear wasn't that you would throw me into a dark and dank dungeon, but that you would take me back to my starting point… to *him*.

They nodded solemnly, grabbing her hands, holding on to her, as if they were drowning and not her.

– Come, Caitlin said softly. – Dinner will be ready soon.

And just like that the new arrival smelled the scent of spices and food.

And just like that, not that much later she sat by the dinner table with quite a few other females and males. She hesitated a bit, before starting on her feeding.

– We're all strangers here, Caitlin said gently, – strangers to ourselves, each other, and the world.

Lori grabbed a piece of meat and wolfed it down. She quickly lost count of pieces, minutes and all. Memories slipped away and everything was here, now.

She moved her eyes constantly, fearing she would glimpse the face from her nightmares, hear the horrible and enticing voice. Her right hand and then her left began shivering, and shivered harder as time went by, until she could no longer feed herself, and they had to do it. It spread to her entire body. They had to hold her, whisper comforting words in her ears. It didn't stop the shaking, but kept it at a manageable level.

– Goddess, a boy said with chill in his voice, – I've never witnessed such fear.

– I feel so cold, she whispered.

They looked apprehensive at each other, her terror inevitably affecting them.

– She has been cast out of her world, one said. – Everything that was precious to her is gone.

Someone hushed her up, but the damage was already done.

Lori nodded slowly. They saw it, how the last remaining light in her eyes died.

She went to bed. How she actually reached it remained a great mystery to her. She saw nothing on her way. There were no conventional beds, but a room filled with mats. She chose the one in the deepest part of the room and pulled the blanket over herself without undressing.

Sleep blessed her eventually, she believed, even though she wasn't certain. It all felt the same to her, the same horrible oneness.

The next days and nights passed in a blur. They fed her, most of the time, like they would a baby. On the few occasions she fed on her own it was just mechanical, with no conscious thought. Aside from her obvious size, her adult body, it did indeed seem like she had just been born.

There came a day or a night at a distinct future moment she could suddenly reason again, where she regained her sense of self again. She was unable to tell how long time she had spent in obscure surroundings, but her eyes cleared, and she grabbed the spoon from the stranger's hand and put it in her own mouth.

She burst into tears. It went on for the rest of the night and most of the day, the rest of the day and most of the night. They touched her, caressed her, whispered words in her ears and were able to give her comfort, some small comfort. She began revealing the beyond extraordinary and shocking to them, forced herself to repeat it all in her mind and through the sounds her lips formed.

– I suspected, she said in a dazed voice, speaking evenly, daring them with her eyes to express their distrust, – yearned for it to be true, but I didn't know beyond knowing before that horrible moment… that Magick is real. He took everything that was my daughter and my friends and twisted it beyond recognition, in order to fit his own purpose.

– But there must be something to be… done about it? Caitlin shuddered. – It must be possible to reverse the process?

– Of course, Lori shrugged.

We just have to find it, to approach something we hardly know anything about… from scratch.

The shadows and the steam and mist in the room pulled closer to the human beings present from all possible and impossible sides.

– Not only did he twist beyond recognition the three I held most dear in the world, she said after a while, – but me as well. I knew, in that very moment what the score was, knew I was leaving everything valuable left in my life behind and I fled beyond reason, in order to escape the fate of the others, and I knew, by so doing that I was dooming those I left behind and saving myself.

Just a little taste of the incredible and horrible world beyond what had been their ken she gave them, before backing into the shadows, away from them, very much like a wounded beast.

It was enough. The little more than a minute, the few sentences she had spoken had given them an insight stunning them. She saw the dancing shadow flames her eyes had become in theirs.

The rain outside fell hard and relentless, in their eyes reflecting the stranger in their midst.

She stood in the doorless entrance a while later, staring at the rain. Its scent rocked her world as much as the sight of it did. She heard a sound of someone approaching and crouched in sweat and distress.

– Is that you, Slater?

– It's me, he said cautiously.

They called him only Slater. She didn't know if it was his last or first name and didn't care.

He touched her on the left shoulder, rubbing it gently. She let him.

– I still can't see anything clearly more than a few steps away, she said. – Why do you think that is?

He didn't reply. He held her. She allowed it.

– They call it heavy showers on the weather services, Slater said. – I guess that's accurate.

It was like a storm to her senses, but muted, distant, like everything else.

She could hardly smell him, even though his hand on her shoulder was close to her nose.

They stood there for a while and time just went away, and she enjoyed that somewhat, instead of all the ants leaving their piss in her veins.

– We're all outcasts here, he said, – driftwood on life's garbage heap.

– That's so poetic, she whispered, just before her expression hardened anew.

She shook off the hand on her shoulder, the itching pain crawling through her veins instantly returning.

– You'll come around, he said. – Everybody does, when they realize there's nothing left to return to.

Sometimes later he had left her. She didn't turn to look, but knew he had.

It had stopped raining. She was alone. Looking at the dry ground and feeling the warm air against the skin, it was like it hadn't been raining at all.

She stood before the cracked mirror and the sink a day or two or three later, rubbing the bright color into her hair. The result was very striking. And she realized that it wasn't only the color of the hair either, the change being more than skin deep. She looked at a skinnier woman, unknown in both movement and telltale signs.

– You look good, Caitlin said, – younger, somehow. The difference between you and us is no longer apparent. You look... good.

When she once again had refitted her new clothes, and stood side by side with Caitlin and Adriana, and the other women, the difference was even less noticeable.

– I don't think anyone that used to know you will recognize you, Adriana said. – In fact I think they could look straight at you and still don't realize it's the person they once knew.

– That person no longer exists, Lori said.

She nodded to herself, nodding some more.

– Those we encounter today won't notice you much either, Caitlin instructed her. – People are coming and going all the time here. You're merely one more lost bird among many.

Lost, Lori thought.

The sleeves were a bit short. She pulled them down with a determined pose. They stayed put, at least for the time being.

She was still big, and taller than any other female here. It felt strange looking at herself like this, this stranger.

– You need to be strong and fierce, honey, Adriana said, – and I feel confident that you are.

– I am! She stated, holding her head high.

– I knew you were, the very first time I say you, beneath the shaking exterior.

– It's a good thing, too, Arthur said. – We aren't exactly popular.

– I don't care. – Popular is for mediocre people.

The delighted laughter warmed her, encouraged her.

– I learned that long before I came here, before… this, she sniffed.

Streets passed by, as she put one foot in front of the other. The whispers and stares started almost immediately. People glared at them, looked at them with unkind eyes. The surroundings pounded her. She began shivering. It didn't turn worse, but kept going at a low-keyed level. The streets remained unfamiliar, outside her realm of reference for a while, but then, as they passed the pub and turned a corner and began ascending Queensway, a very public place, she knew where she was.

Queensway was the tourist trap of the Bayswater area, and she hadn't visited it that many times, but she recognized it. She began shaking. That didn't turn worse either, but kept going on a noticeable level. She squeezed Adriana's hand, squeezing it hard. Adriana kissed her cheek and comforted her the best she was able.

– Can you guys hear it? Lori wondered. – Can you hear the piano?

They cocked their heads and listened, shaking their head.

– I can't hear it, Slater said.

– I do, Lori insisted. – A melody so poignant, so deep. It was there all the time, when I was distracted, but now, as I'm focusing on it, attempting to home in on it, it's fading away.

– Reality is fickle, Caitlin said. – Heisenberg said it's an accident waiting to happen.

They passed doors, several stores playing various types of music. Lori listened carefully, but nowhere did she hear her melody poignant and deep.

– Heisenberg was correct, Adriana stated, her attention locked at a point upstream in the stream of people.

They all froze slightly in their tracks, even as they kept moving the moment they spotted the pair of police constables ahead.

The coppers zoomed in on them in what was practically an instant. They waited patiently, with anticipation in their eyes, while the group made its way to their position.

– We have to endure this, Arthur told Lori. – If we attempt to evade them, they'll just crack down on us that much harder.

The unpleasant memory of the Hampton Court policeman briefly resurfaced in her mind.

And that was the trigger. Suddenly the world assaulted her. Her surroundings pushed at her from all sides.

An old man with a huge belly had his dinner by the sidewalk table. He sat a moment enjoying the moment when the chewed piece of food slipped down his throat, leaving the fork on his platter. It slipped a bit, threatening to fall off the edge.

He grabbed it. The metal felt cold against his skin. Lori opened her mouth, exhaling, releasing all the air in her lungs, and had trouble breathing.

And there were others. She sensed them and their actions in beyond poignant ways. The entire street seemed to become a part of her immediate surroundings, every point of reference and angle something she could reach out and touch, actually touch.

A girl had her chocolate ice cream. The chocolate tasted sweet on Lori's tongue. Another old man, one hardly more than skin and bones walking with a stick. She felt the stick in his hand. A baby whimpering from a stroller his mother pushed, looking at the world from his narrow cavern chinks, learning early what life was about.

As she studied the two coppers, she watched them in immaculate detail, seeing their ugliness exposed as the pale shadows played on their shifting features.

– They're just another set of bullies, she shrugged. – Nothing special at all.

The group caught up to the two's spot on the sidewalk, where they surveyed their domain.

– They are our enemies, she told her companions. – Don't think for a minute that they aren't.

– The fine lady has a history with cops, has she? Caitlin stated.

– She has, Lori replied.

The group's laughter was not unkind.

The man and woman in uniform, further irked by the kind laughter took one single step forward just as the group reached them.

– Ah, a new fish in the pond, the male cried out for all to hear.

– And she's cute, too, the female said, her features looking even slightly crueler in Lori's eyes.

The female grabbed her around the jaw, deliberately patronizing, holding it there for a while, twisting the head back and forth.

– How old are you, honey?

– Forty, Lori replied, with just the expected touch of defiance in her voice.

– Another joker, the male said exasperated. – Where do you guys *find* these people?

The female let her hand fall.

– Will that be all? Lori asked calmly, striving to get the dialect right, to not speak with her usual, cultivated voice.

The female stared at her, angry and with a touch of fear, but not enough of either to make her act on it.

– For now, she snarled, – but we'll talk more, honey.

The two of them dissolved into the general background and the group continued on their way.

– Any time, Lori told her to her back, making her turn briefly.

Two, three steps felt timeless, felt like she touched the very fabric beneath her feet.

– What was that? Caitlin wondered.

– It was like I could see right through them both, Lori said.

– Well, whatever it was, it was damn impressive.

They looked at her with new eyes, no longer as a victim, and that made her feel twice good.

The sense of hyper-reality faded, and perceived normality reasserted itself.

The warm wind touching her skin persisted.

– You know, Caitlin said, frowning, – you don't really look like forty at all. If you hadn't told me, I would have said with conviction you weren't a day over thirty… or something.

– I have gray hairs.

– Who hasn't, Slater commented unconcerned.

And there was more generous laughter.

And the horrible, persistent choking in her throat let up a little more.

They walked through, to her unknown streets, moving away from the tourist traps. She saw that her companions knew the area well. They moved with quick, confident steps. She followed them, moving with them, still outside the group, apart from it.

In her heightened state of consciousness, it was more apparent, not less.

The light from the burning disk above seemed to be coming from everywhere, from every angle around her, not just from that single point above.

– What is it, honey? Adriana wondered.

– It's the sun, Lori replied. – It's… so warm and fills me with such a good heat. I've never noticed it in quite that way before.

They touched her and fondled her and hugged her, and they, too were warm.

It lasted for a minute or so, but its lingering effects still made her feel good about it much longer than that.

They turned a corner and she noticed that their smiles turned visibly dull and strained. It would have been noticeable even without her sharper senses.

– That ugly building over there houses a «food bank», Caitlin said and made Lori aware of a place across the street. – We don't go to those places often, but sometimes we have to.

– It's only open an hour each week, anyway, Adriana snorted.

Everyone's mood fell considerably by the sight of that place and its closed doors. All kinds of unpleasant thoughts, dim possibilities she hadn't considered since childhood roamed Lori's mind.

They walked on, a little faster, a little less relaxed.

The buildings seemed to be fading around them, and she blinked, and realized, somewhat startled that they actually were. Lori and her new companions reached a downtrodden, or rather even more downtrodden, open area.

– Welcome to our private junkyard, Arthur said.

It obviously was a junkyard, with tall heaps of junk on a large property.

– But is there anything for… us here? Lori wondered. – It must be picked clean for valuables pretty fast.

– Professionals come here, searching for things to sell, Slater shrugged. – We come here, searching for things to use. Items are left to rot at this scrap cemetery every day. There seems to be an endless supply of things people no longer need.

It brought Lori further back into her childhood, where she and her siblings had done similar acts in order to grab hold of more cash, in an often-wasted effort to put more much needed food in their skinny bodies.

Her current companions changed into scrawny children and she glimpsed a scrawny, smaller version of herself in the rusty more or less metal surface of the heaps of junk surrounding them.

She studied Slater without studying him, in the effective ways she had taught herself in the boardrooms. He was fairly young, at least ten years younger than her, perhaps more, reminding her in many ways more of a young boy than a man. She stifled a rise of contempt by an act of will, scolding herself.

Most of them were around Slater's age or younger. They looked so carefree, in spite of their grim circumstances.

She excelled in the hard work of pulling and coaxing stuff free from its chains of junk and time. It brought her thoughts away from what was lurking below the surface of her consciousness. She couldn't help herself. It stayed there and would never leave her.

A couple of kettles had been stuck between pipes. She aided Adriana's efforts in pulling them free. They glanced at each other at first, but then they looked, the awkwardness slowly fading.

– So, what happened to you? Adriana asked cautiously. – What made everything go… sour? It wasn't just that one creep, right, but… more? Did people seek you out or was it all a coincidence?

Lori pondered the question.

– I still don't know, know whether or not it was only him or if he was part of something bigger. She shook her head in distress. – There was certainly no lack of… of enemies or potential enemies. But one day everything was fine, the next it wasn't. It was a slow thing, I guess, hardly noticeable by the initial rumblings, a fist in the face not visible until it struck, both sudden and not.

She hesitated and shook her head once.

– No, that isn't completely true or properly describing what happened. It was slow and the fist was on its way long before it hit, but I wasn't really fine before either. I just pretended that I was. In truth, I was so fed up with my old existence that I could hardly function at all.

– I've heard that, all that a lot, Adriana nodded solemnly.

– I made the first, initial steps on a possible new life for me and my daughter and friends, Lori stated calmly, numbly, – and then it was all suddenly taken away, just like that, as if this man just waved a magic wand and wished for it to happen and everything I knew about life, all that I believed to be true vanished like steam.

Her knuckles whitened as she pulled loose one of the kettles.

– I will tell you guys what happened, when I'm ready. You deserve it and I might have placed you in jeopardy by joining you.

– All of us already are, Adriana stated softly. – Every fucking human being on the planet.

Lori pondered that, pondered it again and nodded.

– My mind is so open, she said incredulous.

– «You only live twice», Adriana stated passionately, – «once when you are born, and once when you look death in the face».

– That… feels so right, Lori acknowledged. – It truly felt like I was dying, like my daughter and friends… died, and in that very moment I knew, knew I had to flee. It felt like death or something worse than death was chasing me. It still does…

From the edge of her vision she saw something move. When she turned and looked at it, there wasn't anything there. She shivered, a shiver growing steadily worse.

– The shadows, she mumbled.

– What's that, sweetie?

– A friend of mine said they were spirits, curious alive and dead spirits come to pay their respects… to the coming *Power,* to the…

She shook her head.

They kept working, kept pulling shiny and not so shiny objects from the garbage heaps surrounding them. Lori began sweating. She welcomed the hard work, its forgetfulness and physical prowess.

It was subtle at first, hardly noticeable. She worked with them, with the people around her, men and women she hardly knew. It dawned on her slowly, like a pleasant touch. They touched her, body and mind, comforting the haunted spirit she had become.

She smiled to them, returning their kindness, their comfort, frowning distraught, knowing there would be no comfort to enjoy anywhere.

They carried their heavy load back, back to the derelict old church.

– There is something… something right beyond my reach…

They smiled at her, didn't ridicule her. She wanted to go to them, hug them affectionately, but she held back, stayed her hand, her shaking hand.

– I know it will come to me, I just *know*.

Everybody looked at her. They couldn't help it, as if they were drawn to her intensity, the almost visible fire and emotional turmoil she projected.

And her sensitivity to their emotions and thoughts and desires grew yet another notch.

– I've been opened beyond measure. There's nothing in me that hasn't been opened. I must just learn to access it, to interpret it all.

The others studied her. She knew that, and studied them, too, did it without looking at them.

And it wasn't just them. There were her surroundings, wherever she walked.

They entered a quiet street. A car approached from far away. The scene looked so familiar, so eerie.

– It's getting dark, she mumbled.

The burning disk up there still hovered high in the sky. Air turned dark around her.

– I'm so *sensitive*, she marveled, – and it is nothing compared to what I'll become. I can feel it growing, filling me up like I'm a sponge.

Everything came crashing down on her, abruptly, brutally. She practically fell on a bench and crouched and crumbled there, her eyes flooding with tears.

They sat down with her. She pushed herself at those who did, sobbing hysterically, shaking violently.

Toni, Kelly and Julia's faces danced behind her closed eyelids, and all the various funny and heartbreaking faces of theirs she recalled. Jeff's face, both as a boy and the brief glimpse of him as a young man lingered and burned. The hatred in Austin and Tom's eyes scolded her anew.

– My daughter, she gasped, – she was so beautiful and proud, and he took her, and my friends and crushed them, turned them into nothing... with a snap of his fingers.

– There must be something we can do, Arthur said.

– *No,* she said, suddenly absolutely terrified again, – there's nothing, not yet, not before...

She just went away again. She made sure they listened to her, took a good, hard look at her beyond spooked expression, before letting go of Arthur's collar, letting go of Adriana's hand and drifting away and losing herself in the vast, gray space of her own mind.

They supported her. She had a sense of walking, but knew it could just as well be her imagination.

– Such fear, Caitlin mumbled. – I didn't know terror like that could exist within a person without that person being...

Her voice trailed off, just faded away with Lori's awareness.

A beastly shriek sounded in the distance. Everybody in Lori's company shook in the cold draft the air had become.

Lori didn't.

All the possible divergent paths before her were cloaked in shadow. She could see it all clear as day.

– Let's go home, Adriana said.

– Home, Lori echoed.

Lori followed her, followed them back to the old church. It took a while. At least it felt like it did. She noticed every single detail on the walls and streets and swaying trees caught in her vision.

A car horn honked aloud. The hand of the man doing the honking had a mole by the index finger. A woman carrying a baby shook imperceptibly. A group of tourists chatted excitedly and pointed at objects of interest. They didn't speak English or anything she was able to understand, but she imagined she could still understand what they were saying.

The meaning of the silent chatter in her surroundings kept eluding her.

Every time she attempted to focus on the transparent shadows, they faded away that much faster.

The baby howled in her ears and made her cringe in a sudden headache.

The old church appeared in her vision and she sighed content when noise faded and silence seemed to reach for them and surround them in a protective bubble.

It seemed to her that the entire building was cast in shadow and special colors. It tingled so pleasantly in her gut.

When she crossed the threshold, it tingled in her toes and her frontal lobe.

She helped out in the kitchen, making dinner. They worked with several ovens and kettles, a meal far more extensive than she was used to, but the sting of sadness and despair kept haunting her. The sight of the girl with the open, cheerful face burned her eyes. She crouched in pain.

– You're thinking about your loss, Caitlin mused.

Lori nodded with huge wet and weary eyes.

– We all do, almost all the time.

There was a lot of touching and fondling. Lori pulled back, awkward at first, slowly becoming a part of it, relenting and returning the comforting touches.

They gathered around the dinner table. It wasn't like any dinner she had ever enjoyed, but an orgy of scent and taste and sound and impressions.

– I'm so very vulnerable right now, am I not? She stated. – I would fall for anything.

– On the other hand, you're *open,* Adriana countered. – You would know in an instant if we were set to subdue and corrupt you. The question is if you will let yourself be ruined by your past or if you've grown strong enough to embrace your new life.

Lori nodded, setting her jaw at a determined angle. She looked at everyone around the table, the new and only slowly familiar faces and the even more unknown texture beneath them.

There was hesitation and then more of it, and then she relented.

It erupted like a floodgate within her, in rage and chokes, a rainbow of emotion. She told them everything, all that she had left out earlier, every single detail about what she had recently experienced, a bit hesitant at first, as she feared their scorn, their contempt, but then she didn't care anymore. The scarred woman opened up like the less delicate of flowers.

She told them about the first alarums, the first stirrings in what had seemed like a well-ordered existence, about her own growing dissatisfaction with the life she led. They listened to the sound of wind, the growing breeze in her voice. She related the experience she and her two new friends had had with the infamous musician, and several of the people in the group grew visibly excited, rubbing themselves in sensitive places. They nodded in sadness and interest when she described her brief, all too brief meeting with Lynn Jenny the Witch, and gasped in horror when the story ended with the man she was mindlessly fleeing from.

– Nothing is added or left out, Lori stated, somewhat calm. – Now, you know as much as I do.

It had taken the better part of an hour. The room turned quiet. They stared at her and averted their eyes, and she couldn't tell which was which.

– He clearly has some kind of persuasion power, Arthur mused. – It is quite fascinating, really, or it would be, if he wasn't such an asshole.

– I would guess there are a few rotten eggs in every basket, Adriana shrugged, deliberately.

– Looking at history, witches are, in general clearly the victims, Slater said, – victims of massive persecution, of what is practically genocide.

Lori looked at him with endearing eyes. She actually felt it, how her entire attention seemed to be locked on him.

– We are modern pagans, Caitlin declared, – the legacy of the ancients, before the city and religion.

The gathering grinned a little in jest, but nodded in acknowledgement.

Arthur rose abruptly and ran off. Everybody looked incredulous at him. He returned with a book in his hand.

– The Burning Times by Frode Johansen, a Norwegian born world traveler and declared witch, Arthur said.

He flipped the pages, but it didn't take him long. He knew where he was headed.

– «Sometimes there are riders», he began.

Lori's heart jumped in her chest.

– «They come at the early morning light. They come at dawn, when you think the darkness has faded, and you're safe».

She mouthed his early words and then she spoke the last part of the sentence with him, sensing how the choir shook the room and everyone in it.

There was more flipping of pages.

– «Modern «scholars» tend to play down The Burning Times», Arthur kept reading. – «They set the number of burnings and executions of witches at «only» 60 000, while the real number is at the very least ten times that. They also ignore the fact that many killings didn't go through the courts, but were performed in silence and stealth. Entire villages and towns and valleys of people following the old ways were exterminated and it began long before the «Dark Middle Ages» and took off with the Christians taking power almost 2000 years ago».

A chill and exhilaration both started at a deep level within Lori and spread, making her shake and throb. The catching in her throat hurt.

– I…

She crouched. Sounds seemed to fill her ears, her consciousness.

– I hear something, she frowned. – I hear the sounds of hooves against the ground, but also hands striking drums, not in the way of any given army, but what would be played around a campfire, in a circle of… of witches.

She rose abruptly and rushed off into the other room, cold and hot sweat pouring from clammy skin. Slater caught up with her and held her, and also

some of the others, once again comforting her with touches and soft words.
– I should leave, she sniffed. – I'm endangering all of you just be being here.
– It's your choice, Slater shrugged.
She shrunk upon hearing the contempt in his voice.
– But don't act like you're being noble, Adriana said pointedly. – If you leave it will be because you're afraid of letting go, not because you're doing us any favors.
She saw herself leave, saw herself walk all the long way to the exit and continue through the city, leaving death and destruction in her wake.
And something was waiting for her, out there, in here.
– It doesn't matter where I go, she stated calmly.
And with that realization both peace and further upheaval coursed through her.
She saw herself return to them, saw herself undress and join the swirling mass on the floor, saw them squirm and moan and wail in the grip of her boundless passion.
– It works the other way around as well, she stated solemnly. – If I stay I will become one of you and you will become a part of my destiny.
A beyond powerful sanity burned in her eyes, as she looked at them.
She slipped into Slater's embrace, kissing him hard on the lips, turning to all of them, making contact, turning up the heat, until they were all, herself included gasping in beyond fervent heat.
They returned to the other room. She returned to them all, joining them, becoming them, becoming herself. They were like a gauntlet, an honor guard greeting her, singing her praise, and she felt loved and powerful. She undressed as she walked, as she caressed them with hands and eyes and lips and burning skin.
Clothes slipped off them, all of them. Beyond hot skin touched and glowed.
Flashes of unpleasantness, glimpses of her old life haunted her briefly, before the beyond pleasant surrender ravaged her. She kissed a boy, mending wounds and scars and making everything better. He stared at her with dedication and affection and a desire sufficient to melt all the ice there was, touching her in beyond invasive ways and making her gasp in need. When a girl kissed her lips, it felt just as pleasant, just as casual. Her eyes turned hazy, her eyes cleared. When she turned and looked at everybody with her big eyes, her pointed stare, she turned slowly, rotating in the gathering circle, making sure she had everybody's attention, a few seconds later confident that that was indeed the case.

– Sometimes the forest people, the dark ravens leave the forest, in order to consort with mortal men, she said with a loud laughter both carefree and dark, as she let go, as she fell on a heap of warm, eager bodies. – That time is now, and not all the riders in the world can stop their flight.

Arthur grabbed her from behind, kissing her neck. She caressed his cheek and reached down to grab him and pet him, and he began shaking in desire.

She began humming, the eerie song rising from her throat filling the space, all the space there was between the people gathered in the old church.

The others joined her, one by one, pulled into her dark glow until it surrounded them all, until everybody was humming, chuckling and moaning and growling together, doing together, not becoming one being, but certainly one intent, their passion suddenly riding them that much harder, like a pulse hitting them all over the skin, a potent and magnificent force.

Chapter Ten

Both the nightmares and the pleasures followed her into a confused and brittle dormancy. It didn't even resemble ordinary sleep, as she had experienced it the first forty years of her life, of her *existence*.

A woman beat a slow bass drum on a field of young trees. Her features began dissolving, flowing like mercury pretending to be flesh. She was changing, changing into Jenny.

Lori entered a forest, one old, with tall and thick trees.

By a pond in a glen, two women, two witches greeted her.

– We've been waiting for you for so long, one said.

– We've been waiting for you for so long, the other echoed.

She sat on the worn, rusty bench outside and studied a girl rolling a black bike on the other, far side of the street.

When she woke up she did so in a heap of nude and warm bodies and a happy, happy smile spreading slowly on her face, as she and others started stretching and moving and touching and fondling each other, and the sense of familiarity flowed through her with an almost overpowering certainty.

In a glimpse lasting an eternity she witnessed a man being filled with bullets. He fell backwards, shot asunder and crouched on his back with dead, unmoving eyes. Two girls found him. Paramedics entered the room, the garage complex and took him away. They found the occasional faint heartbeat by a sheer coincidence when one of them accidentally touched his neck. In the ambulance they started reviving him, in vain. They reached the hospital, continuing the efforts on an operating table, finally shaking their heads and pulling back. The body is still, unmoving, full of holes, soaked in blood.

Minutes passed by. The surgeon and her staff removed the masks covering their mouths, retreating from the operating room one by one. An orderly arrived for the body, pulling it from the table to the stretcher.

A loud gasp erupted from his open mouth as his body started jerking. He sat up, soaked in sweat. Everybody still present in the room stared at him in horror.

She walked outside in the warm and pleasant summer morning. There was no bench there. She placed herself with her back to the wall and closed her eyes, and let the sun caress her skin.

They gathered around the table for breakfast, smiling and chuckling and touching, the powerful sense of familiarity strengthening itself further in Lori's mind.

She stood by the window, looking at the street, the square and the distant people.
– I feel the wrongness, she mumbled.
Than, catching herself she straightened herself and opened her eyes wide.
– I CAN FEEL THE WRONGNESS, she shouted. – IT'S SCREAMING AT ME WITH ALL ITS PERVERTED DISCORD
And people far away turned and glared at her in fear and putrid hatred. She returned the stare and made them back away in shock and fear. It wasn't just her imagination. It happened!
They waited for her inside.
– Our sleeping tiger, Slater greeted her.
She kissed him on the lips, and when the two females appeared she kissed them, too.
– There is something inside of me… pushing to get out, she frowned.
A hand rubbed her back, comforting her some more.
She drifted back inside, to the comforting depths of the building, to her shoes and clothes.
– I need to go to the library, she said. – Do any of you happen to have a library lending card at the London Library?
– I have, fair maiden, and I will accompany you on your journey.
Arthur stepped forward quickly, before any of the others could react. She smiled radiantly to him.
– My hero…
She pushed her body close to his and pulled him with her, and they were off.
It felt strange to leave the church, what had quickly become a home again, not surrounded by her many new companions. Being with Arthur alone felt… different.
– I need to access the internet as well, she said, – and I don't feel confident doing that at the library.
– That's no trouble either, he said.
– Good, she whispered, for a moment unable to meet his direct, penetrating stare, – very good.
They walked, walked all the way, crossing Hyde Park in the seething hot sunshine, taking their time.
– I enjoy this, she told him. – It's quite the different pace from what I was accustomed to. And it isn't just because I want to avoid underground stations either. I feel… good. Walking, too, makes me feel… good.
They sat on a bench in Green Park, snuggling a bit, enjoying the closeness of the other.

– This closeness is new to me, she stated, striving with the words. – This is, too.

She enjoyed his touch, enjoyed touching him, her desire burning on a low flame. The birds sang to them from the trees. It hardly seemed like sound at all, but something quieter, deeper. It would rattle her if she acknowledged it, but she didn't.

Time slipped away, but she didn't care.

She tasted his lips again. They lingered on hers. He fondled her breasts and it felt so very, very pleasant.

– Look at us, she giggled, – making out like two young lovers to be.

– Have you always been this cynical?

She pondered his question, but not too long.

– I have to say yes, I'm afraid…

They walked on, leaving the large park area, entering London's more elegant region, where much of the town's accumulated wealth was gathered.

– I know this area well, she said, nodding to herself. – I've been attending quite a few lavish parties here.

There was another bench, more fondling, more relaxing right outside the library. It was right across the street from where they sat.

– This place is rumored to have the largest collection of arcane knowledge outside private homes, she finally said casually, very casually, deliberately breaking the delicate mood.

There was a cold draft, or they imagined there was. The eyes looking at him were steady and calm.

– I need to find out… what's going on, she said quietly, with an intensity burning him, – need to find out as much as I possibly *can,* in order to prepare, prepare for whatever is coming. We all need to do that, in order to thrive and for our very survival. I'm sorry you guys have become involved in it, but you are, and you probably would have been, one way or another even if you hadn't accidentally hooked up with me.

He found himself nodding, staring into what seemed like huge, black eyes.

The library held a modest, pleasant temperature. Arthur walked to the reception desk with her in tow. He showed his card to the man sitting behind it. Lori studied the man, but found nothing in his expression, no reason to be more anxious than recent events had already made her.

They were led into the inner sanctum of the library and it truly looked like one, far removed and isolated from the world outside. She held Arthur's hand, as if they were boyfriend and girlfriend, excitement visible in her very stance.

– We seek books and scriptures of arcane knowledge, Arthur conveyed to

the librarian.
– Any in particular? The man asked.
– We're practically novices at this point, Lori said sweetly, unable and unwilling to hide the dark glow in her eyes. – That is certainly how you should consider us.
The man hardly reacted to her feminine wiles. He seemed non-descriptive, anonymous, the perfect, mythical librarian.
The three of them entered an enclosed room, one where fans hummed in the background and the temperature obviously was rigidly controlled.
– Many of the books and manuscripts here are original editions and you won't be allowed to take them off the premises, but you will be allowed to read them, provided you're able to use extreme caution.
Lori could hardly contain herself. She reached out with a hand, attempting to touch the air itself.
And for just a second, expanding to eternity she imagined she did.
And what was best about all of it: she saw, or at least glimpsed understanding in Arthur's eyes.
– Look at this. Crowley, Blavatsky, Cagliostro… and countless known and unknown and infamous magicians. I love it, I just love it!
– They even have Crowley, Arthur mused and nodded, – «the wickedest man in the world». Perhaps the world *is* moving forward…
The librarian had left the room. They sat there with a stack of books, practically forgetting time and place.
She found her notebook, her stitches-bound notebook and began taking notes and doing her first, rather simplistic drawings.
There were lots of pages turning, revealing nothing, nothing except more useless and mundane information. Lori kept going. She made sure to read everything Arthur had read, while he only read what she didn't downright discard.
– When do they close? She asked a very long time later.
– I haven't the faintest idea, he admitted, shaking his head in wonder.
He studied her, she knew he did.
– What? She wondered, as gentle as she could.
– Just looking at you, he shrugged.
She smiled and returned her attention to the books.
It was raining outside. They noticed that much.
She shook her head at one point, dizziness almost overwhelming her. She shook her head again and kept going.
It was no longer raining. Texts, images and uncanny sensations began hurling through Lori's consciousness.

She wondered if it had turned dark outside, if twilight had started just a little.

– I guess we can return tomorrow, he said casually.

– Hush!

She raised a finger to him, not really to him, giving him a sweet, disarming smile. The room turned quiet. He looked astonished at her.

> «Greetings neophyte sorcerer (she read) - a word to the wise: you won't find what you're looking for here, wherever here is, or in this book even, but you will find it, because what you're looking for is no place, but inside you».
>
> Alan Rachine 1904 AD

– The letters…

He didn't say anything this time, but was content with waiting.

– They're glowing.

– Glow…

– When you look at them at a certain angle, she insisted excited. – He knew that I, or someone like me, would come here, to look for his treasure.

Her intensity was almost more than he could bear. He didn't speak.

– «We are Shadow», she read, – «a power within ourselves and there are dark rivers we pass through during our lives we may draw strength from».

She met his eyes without turning. He saw her eyes even when blinking. She saw more than that, saw the entire him, and herself and their place in the room.

– «There are basics you may study, mighty sorcerer, in order to increase your chances of breaking through, breaking through to the other side, where your unlimited power dwells. You will find them here and other places, where I and others point to, but never be content with that. Seek with a Hunger burning you and you will find, find everything you desire and more».

She heard his voice, the sorcerer's voice, saw him sit at this table, writing his message across time and space.

She scanned and copied the pages she was allowed to scan and copy. The others she copied by hand. She realized startled, when the librarian came to inform them that the place was about to close for the day that she had filled almost an entire notebook with text and illustrations.

– I can't draw, she insisted, looking at the elaborate drawings with awe in her eyes. – I've never been any good at it.

They walked through the summer twilight, and stopped by the neon glow in order to study her notebook.

– A witch scribes her Grimoire, her Book of Shadows in inspired moments, he stated slowly.

She took his head in her hands and kissed him on the lips, kissed him again.

They walked through the twilight night.

– The streets seem so different, now, she mused. – As if someone has removed everything here and exchanged it with something eerily familiar.

She felt… high. There was hardly any other word for it. She turned around and around, and didn't get dizzy, didn't experience any dizzying spell.

A chuckle rose from her throat. She stared at him with speculative eyes, and he didn't look away.

He led and she followed, through dark and narrow alleys. It was yet another part of town she had never frequented much as an adult. She felt young again and reckless.

People looked at them or she imagined they did, but she shrugged them off.

Arthur knocked quietly, cautiously on a door at a start of a mews somewhere. She noticed he didn't ring the bell. Nothing happened at first, but he didn't seem impatient or anything. She fought to curtail her boiling impatience.

Then, she heard it, the faint sound of someone moving, of feet touching stairs.

A dodgy character (if she had ever seen one) opened the door. Except for the staring eyes, a wild-growing beard covered most of his face. He cast a quick glance at her, as if she wasn't there at all.

– Hi, Nastrade, Arthur greeted him cheerfully, but clearly muted, – this is… Terri. She needs secure web-access.

Terri, I'm Terri, Lori thought.

– And with secure I reckon you mean *secure,* Nastrade grumbled, his voice sounding like rusty saw-blades rubbed together.

He had clearly noticed the other man's slight hesitation when naming the woman, but didn't comment on it.

– Indeed, Arthur gawked.

Nastrade retreated inside and they followed him. The door closed behind them. The stench emanating from the man almost made Lori faint on the spot. They followed him down narrow stairs. She heard music from somewhere, somewhere distant, but couldn't pinpoint any direction. There were no windows in the hallway they walked through. She imagined they had descended deep below the ground.

It was hot down here. She began sweating almost the instant she stepped into the sizzling air. Their host led on, into a fairly large room filled with computers and equipment.

She saw no windows here either. The notion of being underground just grew.

The dodgy man pulled out a chair to her. She sat down in it.

– This is ready to go, he told her. – You can do anything with it, probably far more things than you know about.

She began typing and clicking, ignoring his patronizing voice and manners. It was indeed a classic setup, intuitive, beyond easy to use.

– Listen, and this is crucial, Nastrade instructed Lori. – If the alarm sounds, you will leave your chair and leave this place as fast as you can. Understand?

– Y-yes.

– That means they've broken through my first line of defense and that means that they will probably be able to break through the second, third and fourth if they set their minds to it and are given sufficient time and opportunity.

She nodded eagerly, in order to convey her understanding to him. He ignored her and left her.

Arthur sat down by her side and shook his head at the door where Nastrade had vanished. She shook her head in return and after giving him a sweet smile, she focused her attention on the screen in front of her.

Her email account was first priority, her secret or at least secretive email account. She opened secretwitch@gmail.com with a smile, still amazed that she had managed to get hold of it before anyone else.

And there it was, finally, an email from mark247@yahoo.com

She opened that first, seeing it, for some unfathomable reason as the most important.

Sorry about not responding earlier, it said, I agree, we should meet.

That was all.

Its sending date was yesterday, long after she had sent him hers.

Where and when? ☺ She wrote and pushed the send button.

There were a few other emails. She checked them out, too, but it was like she had surmised and expected. They weren't really that interesting, at least not anymore, not to the person she had become.

Then she saw it: his quick response. He had clearly been sitting in front of the computer. She opened the email.

What about at Large Bucks coffee shop in New Oxford Street exactly one week from now? I will be wearing a green cap. ☺

Such a well-known public place is probably not such a good idea, she replied. I should warn you that I am in some serious trouble and that you might be caught in it.

That sounds ominous, but I am not easily put off, my dear.

She began responding with a strange urgency.

We may be monitored right now, she typed fast, very fast, and then the alarm sounded loud and shocking. FUCK, WE ARE. Watch out for yourself.

Nastrade charged forward. She pushed send with a shaking hand and jumped up from the chair.

– So soon? Nastrade said incredulous. – Boy, you must be caught in some *serious* shit.

She backed off. Arthur grabbed her hand and they hurried out of the room and the seemingly endless path up the stairs from the heated underground. Out in the streets she realized that she had trouble breathing again.

– He's right, she gasped. – I am, and a danger to everyone around me.

– We knew that the moment we found you, he said. – We're through taking shit from anybody, you know that.

She nodded, pulling herself together.

A shaky, defiant laughter pushed up her throat as they hurried off.

– How many «lines of defense» does he have?

– I have no idea.

They stuck to the shadows and dark areas as they advanced through the city. The darkness didn't scare them. Any bright spot made them jumpy and apprehensive.

– We belong in the darkness, don't we? She whispered. – In the dank and narrow alleys and spaces of the world.

He didn't reply or comment on it.

– I guess we always did. We just didn't know it.

She took his shaking hand and squeezed it with her smaller, far more powerful grip.

– That means we also fit well in this cloak and dagger game someone is playing with us, of course.

They rushed through the unknown London streets, fading into the deeper shadows of their path.

People were still up when they returned to the church, returned home. They noticed immediately that something had happened, something affecting her and her companion in profound ways, catching easily the twin look of disquiet and excitement in Lori's eyes.

Lori and Arthur told their friends and fellow rebels everything, every single troubling and exciting detail.

The others embraced and comforted them, and Lori felt embraced and comforted, felt a great lump grow and multiply in her throat.

She was very conscious of how it continued doing so, as she joined the others in bed, as she faded and grew in their heat, as she glowed in hers, as night turned to dawn and to morning, and to dusk and night again, and she rose with the airwaves into the great basement of herself.

They stayed on their guard, on high alert the next day and night, days and nights, studying carefully people walking by and especially those stopping outside and staying for a prolonged time.

Slater and others reached out to their contacts sending what was practically coded text messages and stuff.

IT'S A SUNNY DAY IN IRELAND

And the response could be:

IT'S RAINING HERE AS WELL

– There is increased «activity» everywhere, Slater said. – They all enjoy added attention. It is noticeable, even though not necessarily overt or obvious.

– It would be presumptuous of me to take credit for all that, wouldn't it? She joked.

– It would. He nodded serious minded, good humored. – But you're clearly a part of it, whatever «it» is.

– We all are, she said, suddenly feeling very astute and aware. – My fate became yours the moment we met. And perhaps it would have been even if we hadn't met. Perhaps there is no way of avoiding what's coming, no matter what hole you hide in?

He grabbed her and kissed her on the lips in a swift and furious move, in an attempt to grab the wild ride that had caught him, but she just dissolved in his arms, fading away until she stood two steps off.

– You're sweet, she said and a light touch of his cheek accompanied her words.

She stepped close to him and kissed him, and he crumbled in her ruthless grip.

Weeks flowed like days. Lori and her new companions partook in a bigger meeting of squatters and disfranchised people a few nights later. Lori, fearing she wouldn't be able to blend in, was surprised at how easy she did. There was a large, dirty wall mirror at the industrial site in Hackney, and when she studied the crowd's mirror image there, she easily recognized the tall, fair-haired young woman, but she was hardly distinguishable from the rest.

A boy, a late teenager, high-strung and still defiant spoke up.

– We've grown *used to* government and corporate harassment, but this is still something new.

Angry and defiant shouts of agreement met his words.

– We need to step up our game, he shouted. – Playtime is OVER, people.

– Look out for provocateurs and spies, Adriana cautioned her.

That startled her. She had forgotten. For a tiny moment she had actually forgotten.

– Take that fellow over there, her friend and sister said. – He's fairly well known in our circles. But new people join the various houses and gatherings and get-togethers all the time. It's impossible to expose everybody. He's an obvious decoy, one designed to make us lax and overconfident, diverting our attention from the rest.

She studied the young man. There was nothing obvious or overt distinguishing him from the rest. Perhaps he strived a bit too hard to fit in, blend in, but that could just as well be due to youthful insecurity.

– There are also several kinds, Adriana continued. – The agitator, sent to stir up trouble, the quiet observer type, those here on a specific mission and more. Many don't even know about each other. It's a goddamn *horserace*...

Lori smiled. Adriana was funny, in a kind of non-funny way.

The palpable energy here coursed through her, almost as if she could digest it, use it for personal purposes. The anger and passion of those gathered moved the air, making it something alive, animated, something she could almost... no, something she *could* taste, a warm piece of meat, a delicious ice-cream a warm summer day.

– It feels so good to be in disguise, to be disguised, she told Arthur. – It is as if I'm invisible, that I can move among everybody I encounter without them noticing or even see me.

She squeezed his hand with an excited gleam in her eyes.

– So, the corporate queen finds pleasure in the company of us lowly mortals? He teased her quietly, ambiguously.

– She does, she responded promptly, blasting at her own doubt. – The former corporate whore goes where she wants, does what she pleases.

A chill passed through her and she knew it wasn't her imagination. She pulled closer to him and he held her.

– Are you alright?

– It's nothing, she replied, giving him a beguiling smile, – nothing I can put into words.

The site sort of immersed itself on her, not only the people close to her or her immediate surroundings, but the entire block, wall to wall, brick to brick, flesh to flesh. One moment the sensations were hardly more than suspicion and innuendo, the next full-blown certainty, unmistakable vibrations swarming her.

Evening ended, night ended, somehow, even as she slept through the next day, and the next and all the next after that. The Night welcomed her and her new friends. They sat around the table, in the light of the candles and exchanged thoughts and dreams and anger and hopes.

Her speech and demeanor slowly returned to what it had been during her childhood in Brixton, a change evident and pleasing in so many ways. It was strange watching it happen, being aware of it all, both consciously and subconsciously.

– It feels like I've never lived anywhere else. This is my life, now.

She told them with both a catching in her throat and determination in her eyes right after midnight, at the darkest hour, summer twilight hardly reaching them through what they perceived as far away windows.

– I recall vividly I and Arthur's return that night, even more so than I do everything in this our new age, remember your anxiety and grim determination, the amazement over how much a single work of fate had changed your lives. And then you accepted me, fully, completely and unconditionally. I felt a great lump in my throat, felt it grow in the nights and weeks to come, to a point that it no longer mattered, and as the time passed by, and we floated down the currents of the Dark River, I knew that it did matter more than ever.

Her words and passion… penetrated them. There was something about her, not immediately evident that they couldn't help but respond to.

– I have changed, and I am changing, she stated proudly, – but you have and you are as well. The stranger brought irrevocable change to this place, this fellowship, a quality that wasn't present before her arrival.

– You speak about yourself in third person, Adriana pointed out. – Not all the time, but you just did.

– I did? The dark woman shook her head. – I wasn't aware of that.

She paused a bit.

– Doesn't everybody?

– You know what? Slater chuckled. – That makes sense. That makes *perfect* sense!

The words followed them, and her, into the night, into the dreamscape of the old church.

The others slept. She wouldn't quite fall asleep, not even after the extensive fucking. Naked skin pushed gently at her from all sides. She couldn't quite connect to her closed eyes, and they remained open, or so she imagined. The sweaty, slowly cooling body writhed on its back under the blanket. The eyes stared at the tall ceiling above.

She slept, she was fairly confident she did, but her eyes stayed open, and seemed to move of their own volition, making her able to see herself and her brethren from many different angles. It felt easy for her to imagine that those big, big eyes levitated without the body, moving around from the lowest floor to the highest ceiling in the building.

The need to pee grew overwhelming and she opened her eyes and disengaged herself from the other sweaty bodies. She crossed the cold floor to the lavatories and still her eyes seemed to follow her around and not stay attached to her body. When she sat on the toilet bowl and peed, she stayed with those still sleeping in the hall outside, felt their warm bodies against her skin.

She returned to her office, where she and her wayward daughter had made magick together, returned to the chaotic reality of the Crossroads they had accessed in the room filled with shadows.

You found this place, said one of the figures they had encountered in the language she hadn't been able to understand then, that she understood so well now. Congratulations! Once you've found it once, you'll always be able to return to it and it will never let you go.

The smile resembled much more a snarl. Lori moaned in her sleep.

She moaned both content and fearful simultaneously while opening her eyes to the bright light the next morning, still not convinced she had actually awakened.

The others opened their eyes with her, the building itself coming alive around them, as they once more spread through it and made it theirs.

She noticed her own urgency through the senses of the others. They shared breakfast, shared themselves, as they always did, but her thoughts were clearly elsewhere. Caitlin glanced at her with anxious eyes. Lori returned a comforting smile.

Breakfast was done, devoured in a rush. While the others prepared to do their daily excursion, she sat on the floor with her books and potions and candles.

– Are you certain you won't accompany us? Caitlin asked.

– No, I will be casting a divination spell, she smiled, – in an attempt to cast the day in light and the night in darkness. You go, I will be fine.

They did, with a little regret, looking beyond curious at their resident witch. She was alone, except for Tanya and Henry that was on guard duty, and ready to act and call the others back at a moment's notice, if trouble was brewing. Tanya stood by the entrance and he between the opening and the clock in the attic, scouting the world outside their domain.

Lori sat on the floor, in what resembled far more twilight than day. Everything was cast in a dim fire light, the illumination from the outside hardly present at all. She saw it through the mist in her eyes. There were quite a few candles, many different kinds, quite the makeshift collection. There was a knife, and even a sword. She spotted a human skull, a demon mask, and lots of witchcraft paraphernalia like pentacles and necklaces and charms, saw a lot she knew wasn't there.

She lit incense. It spread in the air, invading her through her vibrating nostrils and open eyes. She focused on breathing, breathing evenly. Minutes passed as she sat there, as she made the final preparations.

– DORDUS TARDAS! She cried out with a loud voice, and continuing with a glance at the open Grimoire by her left hand: – TASDAS ASELARDE MASEVETI.

The words, even their initially hesitant pronunciation made a certain obscure sense to her, even if she couldn't interpret it. There was a rhythm there, in the chain of discord. She repeated the words, like the text suggested that she did, and continued from there. Ten, fifteen seconds passed and confidence entered her voice. She turned the page and the rhythm of her delivery improved, her pronunciation changed to a point that it seemed flawless, and once again the words seemed to gain meaning in her mind, her suddenly so astute awareness. Her eyes turned distant. The words kept flowing from her mouth. She heard a whooshing sound, as if something moved in the room, moved very fast. Her attention didn't waver, but stayed on the task, on the spell, but her eyes still saw without moving, saw the room. It didn't change in any obvious way, but she easily imagined it did.

The movement slowed down, shadowing the room, her immediate surroundings. The room turned around her. She knew she sat still, but the entire room displayed itself to the eyes both in front and at the back of her head. First it was as if her eyes became a fish-eye lens, but then… then it was as if her entire head had become eyes.

She blinked, and even in the darkness of the blink she spotted shapes and movement and an eerie, all-encompassing painting that didn't look like her physical surroundings or what had felt like her physical surroundings at all. Shadows surrounded her. She sat and they stood, but she still imagined that she had been elevated above them.

Her blink ended. She opened her eyes. Two women, the two witches stood before her.

– Do you remember us, sister? They choired.

They stood on ground that looked like, felt like and Lori was convinced had to be forest bed.

– Welcome to the Temple of Symbols, one of the witches greeted her.

Lori realized startled that only one of them was speaking. When she studied them, they gained individual characteristics for the first time. They suddenly looked startlingly different from each other.

There were trees all around them, trees making out a forest, one vast without end. It was the same here. She was nowhere and everywhere simultaneously.

– Symbols…? She wondered.

– You think you can't see them, right?

She turned and there was the other witch.

– But you can.

She turned and there was the other other witch.

– You just have to learn to unfocus, unstuck yourself.

– It's easy, a matter of angle.

– If you succumb to the rigors of the Crossroads, you will lose yourself.

She heard it all simultaneously, all of it garbled, beyond chaotic. She drew breath, even though she no longer needed to breathe.

– The first is the last, she heard herself say and felt silly. – That isn't that claim from the Christian bible, is it?

– Don't be silly, she heard, and realized that she had replied to herself.

It made sense to her, now.

She stopped before a tree. It had looked like an ordinary tree, but no longer.

– That is a tree, she marveled, – is the…

– The Temple of Symbols.

– A tree, the witch said.

It all made sense to her, now. Suddenly it all made *sense*.

– The forest is our home, she said startled. – It's a part of ourselves from ancient times we've never truly left behind.

The symbols on trees changed before her eyes, becoming letters with the same meaning, even though the letters could never properly convey the true meaning.

The words, the voices, the very language played in her ears, in the deepest mush of her brain.

– Understanding has found you, a witch said.

– You have found understanding, another witch stated. – Have found wisdom hidden beyond words, beyond crutches and crystal balls.

– Understanding eludes you, a witch said.

– But it won't keep doing it, the other witch stated.

One breath of wind and everything was blasted away. She was elsewhere, drawn there in an instant. There was a revenant howling where the crossroads met. Dizzy and nauseous she blinked the sweat and pain from her eyes. A bony hand touched her, did it before she could do anything to avoid it. It burned and chilled her both.

The bony hand pulled back and suddenly it was as if it had never been there at all. Footprints faded, didn't appear in the sand. The creature not there backed away.

The whispers began, cajoling, seductive and reaching very, very deep in her self.

Silent people
Spoke to her
Like invisible figures
Appeared to her

– Choose all paths, the choir told her.

Choose one path, the second voice admonished her.

Choose one path, the first voice insisted.

Choose not to choose, a third, hundredth or thousandth voice bespoke her.

Choose, another voice admonished them.

Choose, one voice said.

The vast wasteland imposed itself on them. A man, or someone or something she imagined being a man appeared before her, and there were garbled sounds.

– I am fine, thank you, she heard herself speak.

Her lips felt numb beyond numb, as if they weren't there at all.

There were sounds. Whether or not they were words or something else she couldn't tell.

– Is there anywhere in particular you want to go? He asked her. – Can I be of service to you? Allow me to welcome you to the Crossroads.

She stared at a many-hooded beast beyond belief, one that briefly resembled a woman or a man or something completely different.

Each path was a vortex sucking her in. Paths revealed themselves to her. They stood on a plaza with many roads, countless intersections. She gazed and couldn't stop gazing at portals that kept closing as she watched. The room brightened, suddenly blinding in its brilliance. A horrible fatigue grabbed her. Slowly, painfully she imagined the world. Lori closed her eyes. She sat there gasping, realizing startled that everything happened backwards. The vortex shrunk from filling the room, to be hardly more than a tiny whirlwind by her hand. The ground turned solid, turned to a floor once more.

A bell sounded distant and deep. Chanting and monotonous whisper faded in her throat. Her fingers, the swollen fingertips burned and ashen healed as she watched. Toni flashed before her, and then she was gone.

Lori's lips, tongue and larynx kept moving, kept speaking the spells, the dark words transforming the world. They faded only slowly, relentlessly slowly. Lori sat there, sat still on the cold floor, her eyes so open that they hurt.

She reached, as strength returned to her limbs for the chalice. It seemed to flow into her hand. She pulled its tip to her lips and drank greedily the water it offered her. The vomit flowed from her mouth, countless heavy drops flooding the cup in her hand. The metal pushed at her skin turned cold, cold as ice.

– I thank you, she called, – all the dwellers in the eternal sea for granting this witch access, a success beyond life and death. Thank you for showing her the hidden beyond the thin veil of reality. Magick is a true and potent force in the world. She found the wastelands, the endless fields and forest beyond matter and she thanks you. She and her fellow seekers are the Earth and sky, day and Night and we crave all this in our deepest self.

There was more than one voice, the others more than distinct in her ears.

Dust, resembling dusted herbs covered her fingers. They looked like fluid, like fire in her crimson vision.

Disorientation left her. Her vision cleared.

– The book, she mumbled. – The book is here.

She licked the blood from her hands. Its taste was rich and salt.

Her hand, her strong hand put the knife away. The world whooshed around her, sounds coming from everywhere and nowhere. The triumphant smile broke on her face. She sensed how the world returned around her. It shook her and strengthened her violently. The book rested by her hand, her left hand. Tanya and Henry appeared before her. She sat there, sweating hard, grinning what she knew to be a savage, a beyond savage grin.

– Is everything alright? He asked, clearly concerned.

– Everything is great! She replied giddily and chuckled aloud, loud enough for the laughter to echo through the entire building.

The Crossroads… lingered in her consciousness. It kept revealing itself to her in slow flashes. The old church was no longer only the building it had been to her. She grinned some more. Tanya and Henry studied her with anxious eyes.

There was some tiny voice inside of her that wanted to alleviate their fears, but she easily silenced it. She knew she appeared intoxicated to them, but didn't care.

– I glimpsed a slice of eternity, she stated calmly. – I gained knowledge. Knowledge is power.

She rose, a little unsteady on her feet. They rushed forward and supported her.

– Thank you, she mumbled, kissing both pair of lips presented to her. – Thank you so much!

The tree, the temple of symbols faded in and out five steps away. She gained more of its secrets.

– I twisted myself inside out, she cried excited. – I dived inwards, inverted my vision, looked at and experienced myself through my own eyes and senses. I twisted the world, making my own thoughts *real.* Such is magick. Do you understand what that means, what it *signifies?*

She responded unconcerned to their concerned glances. If they spoke she didn't hear anything.

– The roar of silence overwhelms the world, she chuckled brazen and loud.

Her euphoria, though clearly fading in strength by the minute didn't leave her. It kept burning on a low flame and charged through her as bursts of excitement long after the others had returned.

She observed while they carried a fairly well-kept, fairly recently painted bench to the spot by the entrance. The moment lingered in her consciousness, never truly leaving it. It made her shake her head in wonder and apprehension.

The smile stayed on her sweaty face. Enthusiasm kept filling her. They saw it. She imagined they could see everything, also what she didn't share with them.

– You look so pleased with yourself, Caitlin said.

– I am, she replied smug and enigmatic. – I am!

She wanted to tell them, tell them everything, but she held back.

– I have to stress that I haven't truly proven anything, she told them. – Everything I experienced can just as well be ascribed to fever fantasies.

– But..? Arthur asked her like an eager kid.

– But that being said, I feel like I am close now. It feels like it is truly just beyond my reach, *our* reach and no more.

She showed them the tiny distance between the thumb and the index finger, no more, and she imagined they touched and entwined.

The draft blew a tune. They heard it, but didn't quite get it.

The rest of the day fell from her eyes like a stone. The evening brought more of the same, more elation and giddiness. Her newfound friends gathered around her. Close and far didn't matter. She could always reach out and touch them.

– You came to us like a lost soul, Slater said, – but you've become so much more than that.

Saying it with flowers, she thought distracted, lots of flowers.

She stood by the bench right outside the door and stared into the London night. The very moment he grabbed her hand, she returned his affection. It was a reflex, practically an automatic response. When two hands squeezed it happened simultaneously.

The two smiles felt like one.

– You guys saved me, she breathed. – I was less than driftwood, totally at the mercy of the cruel forces of the world. With your help I regained my confidence and even added to it.

More words, more inspired thoughts came to her. They flooded her.

– And now I'll help you accomplish wonders…

The words themselves brought more water flooding her shores.

She found herself seeking more solitude later. There was a staircase up into the tower. Some of it had decayed to the point of being a danger to anyone walking on it. She held on to the banister and walked on the side, maneuvering herself upwards.

The alarmingly loud creaks made her shrink in her tracks. She pressed on.

There was something up here, something up here, too.

While she imagined she rose on warm air like a balloon and climbing the derelict staircase was hardly any effort at all, it, whatever it was… entered her or filled her up from somewhere within.

It felt good using her strength. She practically dragged herself up on the banister. It was almost as hard as climbing a rope vertically, but she managed.

She stumbled onto the floor where the bell hung, almost falling. She stood bowed, breathless, supporting herself on her thighs, her conquest bringing a wide grin to her sweaty face.

The bell hung there, slightly vibrating, unnoticeable to most eyes, but not to hers. She stepped close to it and struck it lightly with a knuckle. There was a sound, resembling that coming from a tuning fork, but lower, a deeper octave. The waves from the sound hit her slowly, almost like something tangible. She blinked a number of times, in a series, a sequence, and in each blink was another image or sensation. The gasp released itself, independently of her. She bit her lip, bit harder and hardly felt it, and feared she would harm herself. The tongue reached out and touched her lips. There was no blood, or if there was, it had no taste, nothing making her notice it.

She stood in the opening and watched the city, the city below, its thousand lights and million shadows. It changed with each blink, each new sensation into something new and different and unknown.

The smile grew slowly on her lips, as she stood in her tower watching the changing city below.

She drew breath, drew it hard. The sound behind her made her turn around. She saw no one there. Confusion rattled her.

The dark voice reached her from an echo in a hole in the air.

– There's a sound, a cry in the dark, a rumble in the ground. There's a change in the Earth and the sky.

– Jenny? Lori said to the air.

Another draft touched her, and another, and another. Whispers reached her from all the open portals.

The indistinct image in front of her, in the opening where she had beheld the city solidified, turned steady.

She looked at an unknown room, looked at her daughter, at Toni.

The girl looked at her as well with a fixed stare, with cruel features Lori hardly recognized.

– Hello, mommy.

Lori attempted to speak, but failed.

– I've searched long and hard for you, and have finally succeeded finding you.

Lori wanted to speak, but held her tongue. There was something… a frown within, a growing… *suspicion* holding her back. Toni didn't look at her, but just at the point where she was supposed to be. Her eyes clearly focused all wrong.

– The Master has made me powerful, Mommy, strengthened all my natural gifts to an uncanny degree, made me strong enough to find you no matter which rat-hole you hide in. Speak up or step forward and I will take you to him.

You can't see me. You just pretend to do so, in order to lure me into your master's clutches.

She wanted to speak up, to rush forward and hug the young girl, but kept herself from doing so with an iron-hard control she had never imagined she possessed.

There was something resigned about the young and cruel face, a fatigue she fought hard to conceal, in vain from the sore eyes of her mother.

– I will tell the Master that I've encountered you, of course, and he will come and fetch you, and you will be reunited with Julia and Kelly, and we will all once more be happy together.

The image, the overwhelming presence faded, and once more Lori stared at the distant city with blind eyes.

She fell to her knees, coated in sweat, nauseous to her core.

Chapter Eleven

Lori felt jittery, felt high anxiety for days afterwards.

She impressed upon them the need for caution, for vigilance, and didn't back down until they started acting upon her concern.

– If you observe anything out of the ordinary, no matter how small or seemingly insignificant, please take note and tell the rest of us, she implored them.

– You're seriously spooked, Slater said, speaking to her as if being an old friend, as if he had known her for years and not just a fairly short time.

– Yes, she said. – Yes, I am.

– That's good enough reason for us, he said. – If you're spooked, we believe you have every reason to be.

They turned to walk away.

– I encountered my daughter, she said quietly. They turned back and kept giving her their full attention. – I saw her in a kind of magickal vision, as clear as I see you now. There was little or nothing left of the girl I knew. She has become a dedicated servant of… of the bad man, of the Wicked Poet. I believe she used some kind of locator spell. I don't think she was quite successful, but I can't be certain. I guess they would have been here by now if she had struck gold, but…

– There's no way to be certain, Caitlin said.

And if they had been on their guard before, that was nothing compared to their level of alertness now. They posted permanent sentries in the tower. There were, at any time two present, often more, scanning all directions.

Lori drew the face of the man she had only seen in glimpses that faraway night in time. She drew several copies and they grew more accurate at every new attempt. There was actually a smile, or a near-smile on her face when she distributed them among her newfound friends and allies.

– This feels amazing, she sniffed, – absolutely amazing.

Her artistic talent had bloomed and kept improving, showing no sign of going away.

They looked at him, at bushy brows and pleasant, cruel features.

– If you see him, run, she bid them. – Don't try to speak to him or even go near him. He can enthrall you with his voice. At least that's what I presume he's doing.

– We need guns, Slater said, desperation notable in his expression and voice, – so we can kill him, so we can defend ourselves if the worst kind of enemy is making a visit.

There was shock among them, but not as much, Lori suspected as there once would have been.

– Perhaps we do, she acknowledged. – Perhaps we need to *be* weapons as well.

That shook them, she saw that it did, but she ignored it, shrugging it off.

– I feel something, she stated, – feel something awakening.

She shook her head, frowning at her own statement.

– I've felt it for a long time. My friend Jenny told me, but I wouldn't listen, not then.

– Was she among…

– No! Lori shook her head. – She disappeared before that, disappeared without a trace. I only knew her for a short time, but it was like there was a connection between us. I felt it the very moment we met.

She drew more images in a frenzy, of Jenny, Toni, Kelly and Julia.

And Jeff, not the least Jeff.

And her former husband, her other son, her therapist, the stalker policeman, of William Synos, his boss, her former boss and colleagues, of anyone she could think of that could be significant to their future.

– I lived my adult life as a delusion, she stated, – but now I'm awake.

She climbed the tower again, still in the frenzy, standing before the bell, looking at the city below. Her hands moved. They drew the city. Time passed again, as she kept drawing and forgot herself.

They placed a plate of sandwiches before her and she munched them, hardly taking her attention from the drawing. She drew on a large canvas, one meter across, a little more than half that high. Pencils and color pencils spread across the floor in what almost looked like a pattern. She crawled back and forth as she chose one, discarded another.

Obsessed, I'm obsessed.

The thought dawned on her slowly, abruptly, a brief flash of insight among thousands of others rising within.

She hardly saw anything but the canvas and the occasional color pencil glowing in her mind.

It was some time later, night, day, neither when she realized she was chewing on one of the pencils, that she was actually chewing it to pieces, swallowing its dusty remains.

The canvas had been placed by the wall, presumably by her hand. She stared at the drawing, unable to take her eyes off it.

The point of view was from the tower, through the opening where she had faced her estranged daughter, towards the east. It was extremely detailed, almost like a photo.

It made her gasp startled and excited. She marveled as she traced the lines with her fingers, her so very sensitive skin.

She eventually climbed back down and showed it to the others. They stared at it openmouthed.

– It's so… detailed, Caitlin gasped. – I've never seen anything like it. A cursory glance may convince you that you're looking at a photo. Stare at it long enough and you might imagine that it's far more detailed than any photography.

Lori looked at it, too. She kept looking at it, immersing herself in it.

– There are… vines on those buildings, right? Adriana wondered. – And moss and grass and soil all over the ground, on the streets and the sidewalks?

The buildings were hardly buildings at all, but ruins, pale remains of what they would see if they walked outside and watched them right now.

– They, all the drawings are so life-like, Caitlin said. – I feel like I'm drowning in them.

– Perhaps we should consider displaying them? Arthur offered. – At least those not so personal.

Lori looked fondly at him.

Then, then her mind started working overtime again, bringing thoughts, a different type of creation.

She caught everyone's eyes, just like that. When she spoke, it was with a low-keyed intensity taking their breath away.

– We… *have* power. Our… our very presence creates a ripple in reality. Witchcraft is a state of mind, not flashy powers. We don't need any of that in order to reach out and touch the world, to change it into something more to our liking. We will hide, if we in truth are hiding in full sight of the world.

Slowly, slowly they all began smiling, practically grinning from ear to ear.

– Life is a dance, and we will make our own, personal version of it. We will dance to a new and different tune, and the dance will be our very own… not the puppet-waltz most people willingly and mindlessly dance today. People exist in silent despair. Even rebels, revolutionaries live mostly alone, desperately seeking likeminded people, seeking their long-lost tribe.

She paused, paused for effect, building the expectation in those around her, like a politician, feeling a faint shame, shame no more.

– Well, they need look *no* further.

And they rejoiced, shouted their joy, silent and loud through the room.

– That's poetry, Adriana breathed.

They walked close to Lori, more than signaling their agreement, their support.

Urgent activity overtook them, rose within them, vital and irresistible.

– Are you sure? Arthur asked uncertain, while the two of them stood by themselves later.

– I'm sure, she said. – I'm confident in my conviction that the right thing to do is to challenge the world head on, not hide in a rabbit hole and hope the bad men won't find you.

Those around her nodded, first slowly, then with greater conviction.

They spread a sheet on message boards and walls across London and on the Internet, one page with a brief text:

> **Visit the Dark Lodge, where free men and women gather, gather for the misty night, where anything is possible.**
>
> **It's a «club», an esoteric, eclectic «society» of rebels and witches and independent people. If you are two of the three you qualify... ;)**
>
> **Watch this space for further information.**

They found an old, abandoned warehouse west of Portobello Road, the best of several great choices of venue.

– Correct me if I'm wrong, but there have been more of these lately? Lori wondered.

Her words echoed through the vast, empty halls.

– Sure have, Slater confirmed. – Available space becomes increasingly available for free use these days.

– I heard about it, Lori said, – and when I could do that, at the top of the ivory tower where I lived, it must be pronounced indeed.

– I'm certain you heard about them as potential investment objects, Adriana said, more than a little naughty.

– Poor little rich girl, right? Lori grinned.

And they all laughed aloud, and the echo turned into something resembling thunder.

The laughter, the mad laughter stayed with her and encouraged and empowered her.

– The future, she mused, she cried. – The future is NOW!

The place grew on them, as more and more details fell into place, as the central big hall was filled with big and small objects, as the emptiness ended and something else replaced it.

They hung long, shredded curtains and twisted sheets of paper from the ceiling, obscuring the view and the room, making it into something it was not. The decorations changed the place, until they hardly seemed like decorations at all. The finished result created a sense of mystery and more than inspired the imagination. She marveled as she walked the paths of something resembling a labyrinth, pieces of the various realities she had glimpsed in her dreams and visions.

People filled it up in high numbers. They filed through the invisible gates from all the four corners of London and the Earth. Lori watched them, studied them, from spots unseen. It was easy. The building had been used for techno trance dance parties a few years back. They had made vantage points to scout for the police.

– He is an informer, Adriana stated with confidence.

Lori knew which of the males approaching from the west she meant. He walked a certain way, and tried too hard to be inconspicuous.

– She is one, too.

The woman clung to a young man, making a production of it.

Lori marveled how much her power of observation had grown, how easy it was to see straight through most people. She marveled at the energy emanating from many of those entering the main hall. They practically glowed in her mind, even as those entering under false pretenses and some others emitted a sick, subdued radiance.

The gathering settled somewhat, even as it kept seething with restless vigor.

– Thank you for coming here, she spoke into the microphone, broadcasting her voice through the hall.

They could see her, but not her face. She didn't even look like she had done since a time after she had moved into the church. She still feared everybody could look straight through her disguise, her double disguise.

Her voice had been altered, been distorted so that they couldn't recognize it, but she still feared that her friends had done something wrong so they would anyway.

Everybody studied her, and glanced around the hall at the others gathered there in bewilderment and curiosity.

– Have you ever asked yourself why they can rule us so easily, how they can manage us to the point that we seem to ourselves and others like hardly more than two-legged sheep?

Unrest grew. She sensed it, had no trouble sensing it.

– It's because they have developed the old divide and conquer tactics to an uncanny degree, she shouted. – Together with distract and divert, with the stick and the carrot they've created a system where we're all wearing chains without noticing. We're divided and marginalized. We make it easy for them, unable as we are to speak up about unpopular subjects in public.

The sea of faces grew indistinguishable before her, as if there was one, giant face with eyes, nose and mouth and ears, turning distinct, appearing with clarity beyond reality.

– In case you didn't notice: I'm not excluding myself from all this. I was, until recently only yet another mindless drone unaware of the deeper issues challenging current humanity. I was too proud, too busy, preoccupied with the distraction of modern existence, but No More.

She wondered whether or not she imagined a few of those standing closest to the stage voicing those two words with her.

– I've found a new, better path. It isn't easy or in any way straightforward and brings with it its own set of problems. It's a bigger picture, filled with intensity and passion and frail with previously unseen dangers.

She paused, hesitated, even though she imagined that her audience didn't notice that.

– I will talk a bit about the path of a Witch.

And now she did pause, deliberately, looking at them with a steady stare. She couldn't believe how steady it was. The occasional laughter and scorn didn't find her wanting.

– There's a long stretch of gray, a Long Walk, a winding road, where all witches, perhaps all that want to be human beings must walk, a never-ending path where boundless fire rises from the ground and burns the very air itself, where you can see the trees for the forest.

The faces shimmered before her in ever-shifting light and shadow.

– Big words, big mama, a black man said aloud.

– Not at all, she replied in an instant, – you ain't heard nothing yet…

She raised her hand in a fist.

– Words are not unimportant, she stated, she cried with passion, – but they need to be backed up by action. This city, this world belongs to us, not the liars and pretenders. They can only rule as long as we *allow* it.

She… stirred them, she knew she did. It wasn't wishful thinking.

– Homelessness in London has grown with ninety percent since Boris Johnson became major many years ago and is rising rapidly. Everything is going from bad to worse here, like in almost every single place or area on the planet. We allow yet another intolerable situation to continue. We have a habit of doing that. Our impasse and blatant cowardice must end.

Quite a few others held up their fist, mirroring hers. There was a humming in the hall, one easily noted. She felt the stirring within. It burned and boiled and hurt as it spread and multiplied.

She thought of Jenny again, but this time it strengthened her.

– We will UNITE, she shouted, – and vanquish our common enemy.

And the cry became a roar.

And the roar persisted as she walked among them later, as she mingled and burned in their company.

She walked among the decorations of paper and cardboard and ancient furniture making paths and enclosing space in the hall, flanked by her «bodyguards» Slater and Arthur, projecting strength and confidence, followed by glances of interest, hope, rejection and disdain.

The various groups and factions sat in their circles, talking excited among themselves. The talk turned quiet when she approached each one. A group had actually made a fire in the hall by the exit. Most of the smoke was pulled outside by a powerful draft. There was very little coughing. The flames danced in the air, flickering like constantly shifting eyes.

She stopped by the group.

– Hi, she greeted them.

– Hi, a girl said, giving her a hostile stare that Lori had no trouble recognizing from her own adolescence.

Lori smiled, making an effort to not make the smile patronizing. She sat down among them, in one of the few available slots in the circle. Their obvious interest burned pleasantly in her gut.

– Nice speech, the same girl said pointedly. – You actually sounded like you knew what you were talking about, but can you back it up?

– I just did, Lori shrugged. – I have, for quite some time, now experienced shit you hobby radicals can't even imagine.

The girl and a few of the others looked hurt and bewildered at her.

The rest, however, Lori noticed didn't take her words as a personal insult.

– So, where have you been all this time? Another girl asked respectfully, clearly wanting an answer to her question.

– I've been hiding myself, Lori replied, – like most of you.

– You grew up in Brixton, right? A boy stated. – But you haven't lived there for a while. Your accent wasn't quite right, not all the time, at least.

– You're quite perceptive.

– And you talk fast, the first, persistent girl stated.

– And act fast as well, Lori said unconcerned.

– How so?

– That's enough, Lisl, another girl said.

The others now looked a little embarrassed at the girl.

– I don't mind, Lori said.

– You don't? Lisl said nonplussed.

– Not at all. You speak your mind. Should I object to people speaking their mind? Isn't it to encourage free speech, truly free speech one reason we gather here tonight?

Lisl looked at her with sudden approval, taken aback. Lori grabbed her hand.

– Don't you see? Getting the lot of you to show up tonight is already a win. This isn't a party, an indifferent gathering, but a political meeting, free of most of the bullshit usually frequenting such gatherings, filled with radical and aware people.

– And witches, Lisl said naughty.

But there was no conviction in her naughtiness.

– And witches, Lori agreed, – adding one more level to an already multi-level congregation.

She rose.

– Come with me, she bid the girl and reached out a hand.

The girl reached out a hand, too, and Lori grabbed it and pulled her on her feet. When Lori let go of the hand and walked away, the girl followed her.

– Where are you taking me? She asked sullenly.

– To wherever you want to go.

– Are you always so irritating?

Lori didn't voice a reply.

– And if I want to go back to my friends?

– You will go back to your friends.

Lisl froze. Lori stopped, too, and faced her, stared at her with penetrating eyes.

– When you've spent some time at your new home, you will go back to your friends and share your experiences with them. You will do so with enthusiasm and in extensive detail.

She walked on with casual steps. Lisl rushed to catch up with her. She glanced around her with wide eyes.

– You gather one representative from each table or at least each grouping, she said with the beginning of amazement in her voice. – You pick the most outspoken, those initially most critical towards you, and you gather them in the palm of your hand. We will all become your emissaries, your dedicated spokesmen, and our words will have special significance precisely because of our initial reluctance. That's… that's… such a simple, straightforward and downright brilliant strategy.

This time, when the girl looked at the older woman there was a taint of awe in her eyes.

– You're a bright girl, Lori conceded willingly, more than willingly, Lisl realized.

And there was that ambiguity and sense of menace again Lisl couldn't help but notice.

Not all, but most of those from the old church brought one uneasy individual of obviously various inclinations and age with them to the exit.

– Welcome, Lori stated. – Know that we're pleased you're here and that you've decided to make this notable change in your life.

They didn't stay there for long. When Slater brought the last follower only a few seconds later, they immediately took their leave, charging into the street at a casual pace.

There was the very familiar echo of sirens in the distance. Doubt turned quickly to certainty. The sirens grew loud and alarming.

The meeting had been over for a while and people knew that. They had filed out well before the first close sirens were heard. Most of them had long experience in avoiding the police. Some of them would still be picked up at random, including several people that hadn't even been at the meeting. The police, as usual arrested people quite indiscriminately.

The crowd led by Lori and Slater didn't encounter them or even came close to encounter them.

– Where are we going? A boy wondered.

– To your new home, Arthur told them.

– It isn't much, Andrea said, – but it's a home, our home.

They walked through streets where everything seemingly solid seemed to move around them, just as much as the people.

– This, all this seems like a mirage, an illusion, the boy said stunned.

– Current society *is* an illusion, Lori nodded, – not in the sense that it doesn't exist, but in its significance.

Lisl kept looking at her with awe in her eyes. Lori allowed that.

– The true reality is so much more, Lori added.

They avoided the nearest underground station, and the next after that, and the next and the next, steering clear of all of them that night, not even venturing close to any of them.

– It's far to walk? Ethan queried.

– It is, Slater confirmed the boy's strong suspicion.

– I enjoy walking, Ethan sniffed.

They sat down at some sidewalk cafeteria at some point, very relaxed and good humored. It was obvious to the newcomers in the group that even though their new companions were tense to a point, did study their surroundings more than most people would, they couldn't be described as nervous.

– We're not… in a hurry? Lisl asked Lori, as they sat there, drinking coffee, passing around the entire pot.

It was free. This place was clearly an alternative venue, where inexpensive and also healthy food was served. Lisl drank another sip of the hot, tasty coffee. It looked like she had never had coffee before.

– We're on… a quest, Lori replied, looking a little distant, pondering the issue, – travelers not weary, in any way, on our way home.

– Where is… home? One asked.

– Where the heart is, another snickered.

– No, Lori said quietly, – where the heart belongs.

Her own words or their echoes moved her, touched her beyond reason, propelling her onward.

– Our wild heart, she added, – our fire, what is worth anything to keep burning. It goes with us everywhere, of course, but thrives in spots and moments of variety and passion.

She rose, leaving her not yet empty cup of coffee on the table.

– We should leave. If they *are* looking for us tonight, this is one of the places they will look.

They did, heeding her words with a sudden haste. The grown and growing group moved through the streets. Lori had a sense of flowing instead of walking. The buildings they passed appeared… organic to her, the light in the windows like dark, dancing fire. She imagined that the gargoyles in the gothic landscape flapped their wings.

The streets had turned quiet when they turned the corner and the old church displayed itself to them, as sinister and inviting as Lori had ever felt it.

There were no people, no watching eyes she or her friends could detect. They recognized those standing outside the building as the sentries they had left behind earlier this evening.

Everybody walked inside. The newcomers looked around with big eyes.

– Home, Lisl breathed.

– It's a simpler life than you're used to, Arthur cautioned her.

– I don't care!

She sent him an open and excited smile.

– Welcome to Castle Rayon, to the Dark Lodge in the wilderness.

– I feel it, Ethan said bewildered, – feel so very welcome.

The sleeping mats on the floor also made an impression on them. The entire room seemed to Lori to be illuminated strangely, different from what she had known.

– Welcome to the world of the *Stranger*.

The newcomers looked at her again. It didn't faze her. She didn't shrug it off, but pulled it all to herself, devouring it from her surroundings, like a… like a vampire.

That made a chill trickle twice down her spine.

Weary but not tired travelers returning from their venture went to bed, lying there under the blankets in the sizzling summer night and talking excited in the darkness.

– This was a great and inventive idea on your part, Lori, Caitlin said with practically visible blushing cheeks. – It may even lead somewhere.

– Somewhere, Lori acknowledged.

The thoughts just kept churning in her head, turning into images, sounds and sensations, into visions. She could not tell if she was awake or sleeping. Words and phrases, speech and slices of conversation kept repeating itself in her mind. She stood upright at the center of the circle gathering on the church floor. Moonlight saturated air, flesh and stone.

And that was all she could recall the next morning. Cries of both crows and ravens echoed pleasantly in her ears. She sat on the bench outside and started drawing. It quickly turned into the scene of the inside of the church bathing in moonlight.

The light from the sun didn't reach her and she could see the emerging image with immense clarity.

Lisl joined her, sat down by her side.

– You… draw?

– I draw, Lori acknowledged.

– It's… beautiful, Lisl whispered, – so intense and *real*. It is as if it's pulling me in, as if I can't resist its lure.

The girl's red hair looked darker, like blood in the weak light of Lori's vision.

– So, what happens now?

Lori turned to her and froze her with her intense stare. The blackish eyes drowned her.

– I'm your designated guide. We made the decision of doing it like that before we picked you guys at the meeting. Look at me as a teacher of sorts, but please do me a favor and don't apply any authority to that position. We're equal in our search for the secrets, for the knowledge and wisdom of the world and beyond.

The girl was drawn in, drawn into her picture. Lori knew she was already there. The young and curious face stared at her with open admiration.

– That is so… so wise, the innocent creature marveled.

Lisl looked at her with a sudden pained expression in her eyes.

– You're so self-assured, she whimpered.

– I'm not, Lori assured her.

– You are, Lisl insisted. – Take it from me. You're practically glowing with confidence.

– I'll take your word for it, Lori said kindly.

– What *happened* to you? You come from nowhere… with answers.

The cries of crows and ravens mixed in sore ears, becoming interchangeable.

Lori closed and opened her eyes.

– I saw the Abyss, and it kept staring back at me in a thousand ways I could not possibly endure. In one giant sweep of insight I saw the world, saw beyond our current circumstances, and knew, at least to a point what to do.

The young girl got it. She shivered in the warm sunshine.

– You remind me of my daughter, Lori said spontaneously.

– That's a great compliment, Lisl said shyly, – thank you so much.

– Come, Lori bid her.

Lori rose and walked inside, and Lisl followed her. They climbed the stairs to the attic together.

– Shit, this is hard, the girl gasped. – I thought I was in great shape, but you beat me soundly.

Lori nodded. Her physical prowess had also been vastly improved lately.

They emerged into the attic. Lisl's eyes turned wide and filled with wonder. She stared at all the drawings, unable to look away.

– This is you? You've made all this… recently?

– I couldn't draw, Lori stated. – I just couldn't draw. Now, suddenly, it's like I can't stop doing it.

– That's amazing, Lisl said, – in more ways than one.

– It's connected, somehow to my talent and life as a witch, Lori mused. – After I had acknowledged that part of myself, so many other things followed.

– You opened up yourself to infinite possibilities, Lisl said, – and you inspire others doing so.

She looked at the drawing depicting the view through the eastern opening, tracing its lines with her fingers.

– What does it mean?

Lori didn't voice a reply, but just looked at her.

– Its meaning seems pretty straightforward, the girl replied to herself.

She looked at one of the others. It depicted people coated in shadow. They walked in an alley lit by streetlights, but darkness surrounded them. They walked straight forward, as if they were headed for the observer, actually growing out of the image. This was more a stylish, impressionistic drawing without details. The figures had few discernible features, and could be both sexes. It was named. The inscription in the right corner below said «Dark

Men coming».

– Even my handwriting has changed, Lori said subdued. – It's like everything I was before is going away, and something new and unknown is taking its place.

– I bet that scares you, the girl said with more of her old naughtiness.

Lori didn't comment on that either. Her face spoke volumes.

– But it excites you as well, the girl continued softly, – and you should never allow yourself to forget that. They say that being born hurts.

Lori nodded to herself, but the girl had turned her back to her and didn't notice.

She walked among the drawings, pulled to each and every one of them, unable to keep her attention on one, before being drawn to the next.

– Look at this! She cried. – It will cause a sensation if you ever display it in public.

She faltered, even before she saw Lori's telling expression.

– But I guess that you will never do that.

Then she smirked, going from one extreme emotion to another.

– This isn't another test, is it, to see if I'm easily fooled?

This time Lori chuckled. The spontaneity of the laughter felt good to her.

– If it is, it's more than good enough to fool me. Then I bow to your clever ruse, magician.

Lori frowned and couldn't keep herself from doing so.

– What is it? The girl wondered anxiously. – Is it something I said?

Lori shook her head.

– No, nothing you said.

– You doubt yourself, don't you?

The girl stepped forward and closer to the woman, her newfound companion.

– I guess it's healthy to suffer some doubt. She nodded to herself. – Yes, I definitely think that is a good thing when you experience powerful visions, the kind demanding equally powerful expressions. My guess is that it is hard to tell what's real and not.

She hesitated a bit before touching the other's cheek.

– But I think you should lighten up a little, go easier on yourself, she remarked. – Your speech and performance at the gathering was quite something, you know. At least it was different and honest, and it did impress quite a few.

– Thank you, I think, Lori grinned.

And the girl returned the grin.

– You picked me because you wanted to convince a cynic, right? So, even though I want to kneel before your highness in nosedive admiration, I can't do that.

She was indeed bright and intelligent and spunky, like Toni had been. Lori fought with herself to keep a stoic expression.

– Another observation not that far out, Lori said in the same light tone. – Listen, this has been a very invigorating conversation, but I guess breakfast is ready soon, and you should go down there and help out with its preparations, young lady.

– Yes, mother, Lisl joked.

She waved as she made her way back down. Lori returned the wave, clearly distracted.

Eyes, independent of her body or at least her conscious mind sought the open view to the east. Her attention switched back and forth between that and the drawing, blending together like night and fire. It made no difference that it was full daylight outside. She struck the left fist at the wall, silent snarls erupting from her twisted mouth.

The hollow voice in her head, not really a voice at all.

You have always been afraid to scratch the surface, to go deep.

– I've always been afraid… she mumbled.

She looked down the practically broken staircase. There was no one there, no one close. She walked to the far wall. The drawings still looked pretty much the same from there. They were mostly various scenes from London. She looked at her own face and figure and two other unknown women, at least two with distinct features she didn't recognize. She recognized Hyde Park in moonlight.

Another was from Newcastle and depicted a man with dark flames dancing on part of his body. Newcastle was a pretty unique city. She had visited it several times and was pretty confident that she recognized the area around the central police station. She even remembered it clearly, now, when staring at the image her hand had made, the angles, the people and the surrounding buildings.

All the pictures were fairly descriptive and self-explanatory, like Lisl had pointed out or rather hinted at, but aside from Lori's big canvas Cinerama drawing, they didn't really say much, not without a proper, currently lacking, very lacking context.

The full moon rose over Hyde Park. She saw it. One brief blink did that. When her eyes opened a moment later, that moonlight still lingered in the room. She saw herself draw the moonlight, draw one night in Hyde Park. That had happened several nights ago. She studied her handiwork right now.

Then she realized stunned that her headache had returned, and as she instantly recognized its context, cold fear mixed with the rising anger.

Her feet and hands brought her down the ladder. She joined the others in breakfast around the table. They touched her in thousand small and big ways, and she touched them. Their bright, shiny faces warmed her. She raised her glass with orange juice in a greeting to them all.

– To all the ravens flying in from the forest, she said quietly.

– TO THE RAVENS, they echoed as one being.

They all started eating, started feeding, and it was pleasant. Her keen taste felt each flavor on her tongue, and as it slipped down her throat and hit the stomach. She studied each person present, not giving away anything of her inner life, or the fact that she studied them, she knew she didn't.

– This has an absolutely phenomenal taste, Ethan explained. – I can hardly believe it.

It was an easygoing, euphoric mood around the table, exactly as they had planned and hoped. The catching in Lori's throat didn't keep her low-burning anger away.

– I guess it's connected to the setting as well, he added, after clearly having pondered the issue a bit. – But lots of good things can be said about natural food. Where do you get it?

His enjoyment didn't seem in any way lessened.

– It's getting increasingly harder to get hold of, often tainted with pollution as it is no matter where it comes from, Adriana said sadly, – but still possible, if you make that extra effort, even for poor slobs like us.

– You can say that our poverty makes our inventive, Caitlin said. – Necessity breeds invention.

The meal passed slowly to Lori, but to the others it clearly flowed easily from one moment to another. Her perceived juxtaposition, the different viewpoint separating her from the others made her even jitterier. They noticed, of course, like they had to, and made a continuous effort at bringing her into the fold, to alleviate her mood swings.

The clouds moved across the sky outside. They gathered by the entrance afterwards, looking attentive and excited at the lone figure standing before them, the woman that had, in such a short time come to mean so much to them all.

– Good morning, she greeted them, as if she hadn't actually spent most of the morning with them already, – and well met.

– WELL MET, LORI!

She smiled, or rather gave them the ironic grin they had learned to know so well.

– This is the second day of our new quest together. You say goodbye to your old life and welcome the new. It's an initiation as old as the ages.

– The ages, Arthur breathed and nodded.

She looked at him with stronger fondness in the blackish eyes.

The steady stare penetrated them all.

– Speaking for myself I've recently experienced changes, paradigm shifts to last a lifetime. Sometimes, during that transition, long before one single brutal change was forced upon me, I realized that I had never fit in, never belonged in the society so hostile to life I had strongly believed to be my home. Today, if not before I'm making that ongoing process a conscious, deliberate decision.

She drew breath. They looked at her. She looked at them.

– I'm emptying myself, throwing away the old me, embracing the new. The past is prologue. I'm Lori no longer, or at least not only Lori.

– Who are you then? Lisl asked her, with her open, innocent face.

Lori pondered the issue briefly, before replying.

– Call me… Genesis, she said. – Yes, I am Genesis.

The name, designation, ramifications echoed in the Void. She heard it, tasted it on her tongue for every kiss she received. They approached and acknowledged the Stranger in their midst in ways she definitely enjoyed.

– Hail, Genesis, Lisl greeted her.

– HAIL, GENESIS! The rest choired.

Everybody walked to her, hugged her and caressed her, enthusiastically embracing her and her decision, and she felt good about it.

More time she couldn't quite calculate passed around her and in the big world outside the old building. It practically passed through the flesh and the mind and the spirit making Lori what she was. She didn't mind wasting time. She didn't think like that anymore.

She made a conscious effort at separating herself from the group, and it happened. Once again, she stood before them, making her presence, her individuality known. Their attention stayed on their Genesis and hardly anything else.

– We go out into the world two and two, she stated with a playful smile, – and return when we return, with knowledge and perhaps even wisdom to the tribe. It's risky, but that's the entire point. Without true risk, no true gain.

– We make our initiation like witches did in a time long past, Arthur said, adding his voice to hers. – We share the sweet rewards.

Excitement and enthusiasm and apprehension surged through them. Genesis spotted that in every shiny face she glimpsed.

A sudden gasp pushed itself from her mouth.

– What is it?

Arthur was by her side in a second. She looked amazed at him.
– I sensed it… a release…
– Something you can't identify?
He grabbed her hand.
– No, that's just it. I *can!*
The two of them seemed to be all alone in the crowded hall. She looked at him in dark excitement, the others being hardly more than ghosts around them.
– I did it! I opened myself and grabbed one single grain of sand and kept it from slipping through my fingers.
She grabbed him and kissed him on the lips, kissed him hard, breaking skin and making blood flow. He saw her lick her lips. She saw her triumphant grin through his eyes.
Lisl stepped forward. The world rejoined the two at its center.
– Two and two? The young, insecure girl queried.
– Two and two, Lori chuckled. – Partners in crime and life.
She looked different, in both behavior and appearance. That became quite evident to her, when she once again looked at herself through the others' eyes.
The inhabitants of the derelict Castle Rayon nodded to each other, cast each other one final encouraging smile, before the both sweet and apprehensive parting. Lori approached the entrance and Lisl followed her.
They walked through the open door.

Chapter Twelve

The bright light and seething heat embraced her, casting both of them in shadow.

They walked through the streets. Lori moved through them, hardly touching the ground.

– You move your eyes like… like a hawk! The girl mumbled.

– I do, don't I…

She turned north. They didn't see any of the other pairs. After a while they moved up Craven Road. Lori studied the young girl by her side to such a degree that Lisl got visibly embarrassed.

– Can you hear the music? Lori asked her abruptly.

Lisl frowned, clearly concentrating, pondering the question.

– There was a man playing a fiddle a while back, wasn't there?

– No, no. Lori shook her head. – I'm not talking about the music your ears hear, but what you can sense with your mind, what's playing beyond all the noise and makes the ground beneath your feet shiver and heave.

The girl shook her head timidly.

– No, nothing like that.

– Not now, Genesis declared, her black eyes twinkling, – but one day you will!

– You're scary, do you know that? Lisl mumbled.

The dark laughter shook her again.

Well before Craven Road changed into Praed Street they turned right and not long after that found themselves heading up Sussex Gardens. It truly felt like a garden of sorts to Lori's senses. It hardly mattered that her eyes and ears saw and heard a broad and heavily trafficked road.

She closed her eyes while moving, and she grew more aware of her surroundings, not less. The annoying noise grew to a pleasant hum in her ears.

– What is this? Lisl wondered. – What is our objective here?

– No objective, Lori shrugged. – We're on a quest of self-discovery, of painting our life, and London is our canvas. London is such a great canvas.

It felt so right saying that. She felt the mixed thrill and chill again the moment she uttered the words.

And right then, it was as if their surroundings came to life to her. A man, a fairly young man, wearing an old-fashioned hat seemed to change before her eyes, turning old and disheveled. A woman looked even worse, looked dead, like walking rot.

Not everybody in her line of vision had changed. Most of them had vanished altogether during the moment she blinked, but those still there had transformed into a lesser version of themselves.

The surroundings themselves had changed as well, but that, in itself didn't surprise her much. She was beyond astonishment. The road, the ground, really was covered in green, and trees had grown everywhere. The buildings, those still left were practically ruins.

– What do you see? Lisl wondered.

Lori turned. Lisl was changed, too, but not that much. Her clothes were different and worn. The face had a few wrinkles. She still looked fairly young and vital.

– You zoned out completely for a moment there, Lisl insisted. – You kept walking, but it was like you weren't here at all.

Everything had returned to the way it had been, as if the long, long moment of her blink hadn't happened.

– I do that, sometimes, Lori said slowly, as if she feared she wasn't able to speak. – Don't worry about it.

She kept walking, hardly even breaking her pace. That made pride course through her.

– I felt like I was going insane for a while, she said calmly. – I don't anymore.

The somewhat cryptic comment did make the girl frown and grin,

– I don't think you're going insane or are insane, the girl said shyly. – I remain unconvinced on the matter of what you are, but I know for sure you're completely different from anyone I've ever met, a searcher and clearly experienced both. I suspect, strongly suspect I can learn a lot from you.

– I suspect that, too…

– You're making fun of me.

– Yes, I am.

They both chuckled and that made both slow down briefly and ponder their own feelings.

– There's such truth and honesty between us, the girl declared. – I like that!

– I like truth and honesty as well, Lori stated. – I've been fed up with falsehood and dishonesty for a long time.

That statement made the other give her a closer look.

– I know the feeling, she eventually said. – People suck sometimes.

The singing was heard by both, by all. Lori noticed how people listened to it and knew it wasn't just her. Lisl tilted her head a bit before smiling. A little further up the street, at an open area to the right young adults moved like children in a circle, choiring, singing, chanting. The circle turned and turned and turned, becoming partly indistinct in Lori's vision.

A woman stood at the center of the ring of people, casually directing, conducting them, like others might do an orchestra. It made Lori frown, made at least the beginning of a chill touch her.

– These are children's rhymes, the woman said. – Do you know why children enjoy them so much?

A boy replied. Lori didn't quite catch his words.

The woman grinned wickedly, or so Lori feared or imagined.

The moment passed. She and her charge walked on.

A man crossed the road ahead. He glared at them. Lori felt it as if those staring eyes touched her. Lisl visibly reacted to his presence as well. He disappeared around the corner.

– Did you see that guy? The girl said. – What a creep!

She was clearly shaken.

– I saw him…

– He was creepy as hell.

Five, seven ten seconds later, when they reached the intersection, Lori cast a casual glance down the street where the man still should have been easily spotted. He wasn't, was nowhere to be seen.

A bunch of giggling teenage girls dressed in what were clearly school-uniforms ran on the zebra stripes across the street. It felt like such a precious moment to Lori and she wished she had carried a camera in order to capture the moment for posterity. The sight burned into her retina, stayed in her mind, as she and her companion reached the end of Sussex Gardens and crossed Edgware Road.

Many images almost identical, but not quite kept crossing her vision. The powerful impressions turned themselves on and off, but when they were on their presence felt like an unending flow burning in her gut.

They searched for a place to stop, to settle down, not really looking at their watch while doing so. They took their time and enjoyed the walk.

– This is a walkabout of sorts, isn't it? Lisl stated.

– It is, Lori replied without pondering.

– Walking is such an underestimated pleasure, Lisl said brightly. – And you see so much more of the city when you're not riding the Tube or the train, or driving a fucking *car*.

The warm, pleasant breeze seemed to surround them, caress them. Lori tried not to enjoy it all too much. She kept looking out for dangers. She didn't spot any. There was the woman with the baby stroller on the corner, the teenager walking in the same direction as they did at the other sidewalk. He turned a corner and faded from her view. Lori shook her head.

They found a quiet, inexpensive vegetarian place, with modest interior, used chairs and tables and design parts Lori more than suspected had been found at a garbage disposal facility. It looked quite appealing to her, and that in itself made her feel even better about it.

The worn furniture was echoed by the place itself. The sight of the scratches and missing painting on the walls, the pervasive signs of decay the entire building emanated echoed pleasantly within Lori. Lisl studied Lori and Lori studied Lisl. The girl tilted her head.

They sat there, with their spicy dinner and cool, pleasant drinks. They were talking between bites and shallows, talking all the time.

– I love the way you named yourself, Lisl said empathically, – and I love what you named yourself. It's both great symbolism and significant for the reality where you've grounded yourself.

It was both a spontaneous and well-thought-of statement at the same time. Lori sensed that, somehow, and that acknowledgment, *admission* strengthened her further in her resolve.

– I love that you say that, and the way you say it, she said. – It makes it all… worthwhile, somehow.

The words echoed in her thoughts. The thoughts echoed in her consciousness, extending it beyond, well beyond ordinary. It was like a well of emotion, a pressure cooker in there. It had to express itself, one way or another.

The meal… ended, but seemed to go on. They cherished the toasting, the devouring of the drinks, the long, pleasant afterglow of the dining.

She found her pen and paper and began drawing not long after that. The running teenage girls quickly came to life on the paper resting in her lap. Lisl moved over to her side of the table and watched mesmerized as the figures and forms appeared.

– It looks so lifelike, the girl whispered. – It is as if I am actually reliving it, as if it's actually happening right now.

Lori drew the woman, the teacher, the instructor. She frowned. There was something about that face making her react, somehow. She drew it in more detail, in an effort to better understand what, in vain.

– She looks spooky, Lisl said. – Is that how you see her?

Lori found herself nodding, unable to offer a further explanation for her unrest.

A bunch of young girls at a nearby table had a conversation. Squeaking, almost unnatural voices hurt Lori's ears. It sounded more like bad recordings and not like humans having a conversation at all. Their faces reminded Lori about harpies. She drew them as well, in short bursts of movements, her fingers turning numb in the bargain.

One of the girls had a pimple on her nose. It had cracked and lots of puss flowed from it. To Lori it seemed like there was no end to it. The girls weren't exactly quarreling, but they were yapping endlessly.

– I use Quextran, the dominant among them said patronizingly. – It succeeds where everything else fails.

– That isn't exactly true, another girl objected. – You shouldn't buy *all* the hype, you know…

The others glared at her. Their accusing stares made her shrink in her tracks and shut up for the rest of the conversation.

– I bought this *great* jacket, a third girl said excited. – Personally, I think *everybody* should buy one.

Lori felt how a major headache was coming on. Lisl looked at her with sympathetic eyes.

Unpleasant voices and faces eventually and finally faded in Lori's mind and in the reality surrounding her.

The two of them remained there, long after they had finished their meal. Most of the others had left. Only a few tables were still taken. Hectic activity had given way to a more pleasant setting, one akin to silence.

The vortex within Lori persisted in its… its motion. The hand holding the pencil kept moving, seemingly of its own accord.

She eventually put it away. She didn't want Lisl to sit there by herself. Her hands kept tingling. The buzz in her frontal lobe kept rearing its insistent head.

– May I see it?

The girl didn't look bored at all, but had the same flush of excitement burning beneath her skin.

– Of course.

Lori handed over the drawing book.

– That's… us, isn't it?

– It is! Lori nodded.

It is and it isn't, she thought.

– But they don't look exactly like us, do they?

Lori didn't voice a reply. Lisl flipped the pages.

– The girls, she giggled. – They truly look like harpies, don't they?

Lori shook slightly, before regaining control of herself.

– You will become famous one day, the girl declared. – I know you will!

Lori smiled, enjoying the girl's youthful enthusiasm.

– You're so young and idealistic, she remarked.

– While you're old and cynical? Lisl countered lightly.

Taken aback, Lori pondered her words.

– I don't know. I certainly used to be and existed without a second thought about my surroundings and the world. I was… dead, I think, even though I walked and breathed.

The girl took her hands and didn't say anything.

They rose, virtually simultaneously, as if by unspoken agreement and returned to the streets. Once again everything moved around them. Their walk was slow, their posture relaxed. They leaned on a wall somewhere, facing the sun with closed eyes, enjoying the heat on their skin.

– It's so nice walking around and not have to actually do anything, Lisl mused. – I used to be such a busybody. Something happened and had to happen all the time.

– When the human being is free its mind is less burdened with unnecessary thoughts.

Lori stated casually.

It was such an obvious, downright ridiculously obvious conclusion, but it still made her feel even more uplifted.

Darkness swept across the sunny street.

– Or perhaps it makes all thoughts flow, and everything hidden or misplaced return to us. Nothing is concealed anymore.

The chuckle sounded loud in her ears, sounded dark and free.

– I cast a spell, she cried. – I cast a spell unbinding the illusion of the world.

Lisl nodded and smiled some more, and then, as she turned to Lori to offer her solemn concurrence something caught her eye.

Lori opened her hand. A dark shimmer, a… whirl floated above it. Lisl gasped in astonishment.

– The progress is… slow, Lori said. – There might be one confirmation of progress one given day, and then weeks may pass until the next, but I am getting there.

The shimmer faded slowly, until it had completely disappeared and a less confident or driven person could persuade herself or himself that nothing extraordinary had happened.

– It's like a dream, Lisl whispered.

– My friend Lynn Jenny knew, and she practically told me, but I didn't listen. I wish she was here, now, when I'm open, opening like a flower.

She paused a bit, frowning.

– I realized some time ago that I really wanted to be able to do something like this and that I've always wanted it. Do you understand?

– Y-yes, the girl stuttered.

– I think you do. Lori nodded to herself. – I think you always have. You may not have been consciously aware of it, but it has always been there, deep down, and I can assure you that awareness will come.

The sound of someone blowing a horn interrupted the deep, long silence between them.

Lori imagined the silence had lasted forever.

They walked on, in the area north of Oxford Street, where there were quite a few alternative venues. Lori nodded to herself. The prevalent mood echoed within her.

The stench of spices played pleasantly in their nostrils. They walked through a dark alley, a narrow passage. Lori sniffed the air without even thinking about it. It made her smile. She glimpsed her moves in the windows. The chuckle rose easy in her throat. She was fast and sure and light on her feet. Lisl studied her and Lori knew she got it, got that it wasn't only her mind that was opening like a flower, but her body as well.

A car pulled over right in front of them. Lori noticed a bit before it happened. The smile kept playing on her lips. Two young men sat in the front seats of the car, looking at them with interest and hunger in their eyes.

– Greetings on this fine day to you pretty girls, the driver called to them.

The two girls didn't look very concerned or timid when they returned the close scrutiny.

– Greetings, Lisl replied casually, playing along.

– We're tourists, the driver said, – visiting this great city. We're on our way to a hostel in… Camden, but London is so damn big and we seemed to be lost. We're clearly in need of guides.

– Is that so? Lori said pointedly.

– That is so, the man in the passenger seat nodded. – There's also an excellent pub on the premises. We've heard high praise about the parties held there.

Both men cackled. A burst of irritation surged through Lori. She suppressed the urge to act on it. Her emotions had also grown in potency lately. Everything about her had.

– They are pretty boys, aren't they? She turned towards Lisl.

– I suppose they are, the girl snorted in contempt. – I very much doubt they have anything substantial between their ears, though…

They turned as one their attention back at the two in the car. Both men had lost their cocky attitude. She had snapped her fingers and made it so.

– We have some time to kill, she shrugged. – I guess we will take you up on your kind offer.

– Hop in, then, the driver said, exhibiting a stubborn streak, quelling the frown.

Lisl ran to the other side of the car. The two wanderers opened a door on each side and hopped inside.

The car accelerated from its position by the sidewalk on whining tires. Lori and Lisl were pushed back in the seat.

– I'm Ronny, this is Dave, the guy in the front passenger seat said.

– I'm Lori, this is Lisl, Lori said.

– Nice to meet you both, Ronny said, reaching out a hand.

Lori did, too, and they shook hands. She didn't flinch when he studied her, but Lisl did, when he did the same to her. She was blushing, making the man grin.

– You need to turn left at the next corner, Lori instructed the driver, making the frown grow deeper, making her display a patronizing grin.

She turned towards Lisl and grabbed her head, pulling her close, kissing her on her lips. Lisl froze momentarily, before turning soft and accepting, returning the increasingly invasive caresses. They made out for a considerable time, before pulling back and sending sweet smiles to the two in front.

Ronny made another abrupt turn on whining tires. It didn't feel rough at all to Lori. She enjoyed what she perceived as the slow flow of the streets through the windows.

– You're zoning out again…

The girl's soft voice brought her back from whatever place her mind wandered, but not quite. A part of her remained there, in a realm of constantly shifting impressions and sensations.

– What do you see? A hand touched her forehead, rubbed it in comforting strokes. – Anything *exciting?*

– It's hard to put into words…

She found her pen and paper and began drawing. A flask hit a white brick wall a hot summer day and broke, and its water splashed everywhere on the wall and on the ground below.

– What is she doing? She heard a male voice she could not quite connect with anything. – She looks totally out of it.

– She's an *artist,* Lisl chastised him. – She's entitled.

What Lori saw on the paper was a far cry from what she did in her mind, in that never-settling realm. It made her frown in anguish.

– I need to do more brushes and colors, she mumbled.

– You're doing fine, Lisl insisted. – Fine!

Lori finished the drawing and began on another almost before she had turned the page. There was the usual urgency, the need to finish it quickly. She hardly glimpsed the pen and paper in her vision and almost exclusively the image forming in her mind.

Dave waved a hand in front of her eyes. She was aware of him doing it, on one level, but it brought neither irritation nor distraction. Even bumps in the road and Ronny's reckless driving didn't deter or disturb her art. She and her moves seemed to be flowing in an ether where kinetic energy didn't matter.

Giddy excitement touched her briefly.

She showed Dave the result, a lone building in a quiet street and yard. A sign over the door said:

SAVAGE HOSTEL

Please leave your (need for) calm at the door

Dave grinned. Then he frowned, unable to pinpoint the reason for his apprehension.

– You know the place from before, I take it?

– I've never set my foot there or heard about it before, in any way, she told him with a patronizing snarl.

And his unease deepened.

And that pleased her beyond words.

The car made a turn and the drawing became true in her vision. The two images merged into one. The colors were the same as well, though not so visually powerful. They didn't even approach the potency they had in that shifting realm roaming her expanding mind.

The scenery in front of her began shifting in her vision, a jigsaw puzzle constantly setting and resetting itself.

They found a parking lot, or at least a large, unused and open space not that far away. Dust blew across what was obviously an old construction site, with walls still remaining here and there.

Other cars were covered in dust. They had clearly stood there for a while.

– An abandoned and potential urban renewal area, Ronny said pleased. – The car can definitely rest its wheels here for a while, at least until we bother locating a suitable parking house.

They approached the hostel from the back, but she still saw the front. When they stepped inside she experienced two hallways simultaneously, and the reception area from two different angles.

– You wait right here, ladies, while we secure our rooms, Dave said in a horrible attempt at being charming.

Lori returned a gloriously fake smile.

– Is this our path? Lisl asked, casting a glance full of doubt at Ronny waving to her with a silly grin painted on his mug.

– It's on our path, Lori sighed, – and as the lore tells us: we must stay on the path, or all is lost.

She saw the path ahead of her, its pleasant turns and ugly twists. A shaking passed through her.

The woman behind the desk smiled to the two men stopping before her, greeting them in a friendly and easy-going manner. Lori didn't actually hear the three speak, at least not verbally, but their language was still pretty plain to her. Every being she encountered had started speaking to her. Everyone in the room did so right now. A fly buzzed by the window. She noticed how Lisl studied her. The floor seemed to move beneath itching feet, somewhat attached to shaking legs. The buzz and whisper burrowed into aching ears. Angry, insistent voices drowned the excited voices in the hall.

Dave and Ronny did their best to charm the girl behind the counter, but they were clearly struggling, even though the welcoming smile never wavered on the receptionist's face.

– They're not getting anywhere with her, are they? Lisl giggled.

A man stood outside in a pocket of darkness. He held up a burning hand making the skin of half his face glow. The skin on that side of the face seemed to fade and only the naked skull remained.

Lori blinked and he was gone.

Lisl studied her closer, but Lori showed nothing of herself, her inner turmoil.

The girl had evidently not seen anything.

A man, a young man shock visibly no more than five steps away. He stared at the same spot outside where the man with the burning hand and partly bare skull had briefly stood.

She walked to him, rushed to him. She caught his eyes, and he turned towards her.

– Do I know you?

Her voice sounded weak in her ears. She looked puzzled at him.

He stared at her. Sweat covered his forehead, as he, like her kept glancing at the empty space outside where the man with the burning hand and exposed skull had stood only seconds earlier.

– Probably not, I'm afraid. He shook his head and smiled. – Since I don't know you. I've never seen you before in my life.

– My bad, she said casually. – Sorry about that.

– That's alright. He smiled some more. – We all have a twin somewhere, right?

She wanted to ask him about the vision, if he had in truth seen what she had seen, but she held her tongue.

They slipped away from each other. To her it seemed like it happened in slow motion, as if they moved through water.

She returned to Lisl. Dave and Ronny returned from their less than satisfying encounter with the receptionist.

– We've got great rooms, Dave grinned. – We only need to share it with five others.

– There is no need to include us in your «we», Lori informed him, a distinct chill in her voice.

That did take him down a peg or two, but he still didn't seem to get it. It was like he didn't listen to her at all, but kept pushing in order to get her to submit to his charm.

– The pub at the house is open, Dave grinned. – We've heard many great things about the wild parties held there. You gals may go there and wait. We will just put away our luggage and be with you shortly.

He touched Lisl's cheek briefly and then raced off with his pal.

– They paid the beds for us, Lisl whispered. – They do expect something in return for that, don't they?

– They might, but you shouldn't let them push you into doing anything you don't want to do, Lori impressed upon her.

– I know that, the girl said aloud, smiling to her. – You don't need to protect me, you know. I can take care of myself.

They walked the short distance to the pub. It was about half full, with quite a few available seats. The two of them sat down in a deep corner, far from the bright windows. Lisl glanced at Lori again, noticing how her eyes wandered all over the place.

– You are very astute, Lori remarked casually. – And yes, there is reason to be concerned.

– I do feel like we're being followed, Lisl whispered. – I've felt it a long time, long before I joined up with you guys.

– That was one of the first things I noticed about you. You looked haunted. It wasn't hard to spot at all.

The girl crumbled a bit in the chair, but didn't comment on it directly. Lori watched how her eyes were drawn to the open door. The older woman turned and saw Dave and Ronny enter the room.

They walked straight to the bar. Dave waved to the girls. Lori and Lisl returned the wave, not very enthusiastic.

– Should we really be doing this? Lisl wondered. – It doesn't look like it will be much fun.

– It might be, Lori said, pondering the subject. – This looks like a fun place, with quite a few possibilities for enjoyment, for a successful evening.

– And it's our path, Lisl added, a little pointed.

– It's our path, Lori nodded.

She leaned back in the chair, closing and opening her eyes.

– I can practically feel it, you know. The familiarity of everything happening around us here is so strong, so powerful that I keep wondering if it just has to be my imagination running wild, that I suffer from projection of my desires and am deceiving myself royally, believing my wishes, my yearnings for an interesting life have become reality.

The choke entered her voice unbidden. She couldn't keep it away.

Lisl didn't say anything, but studied her even closer. The girl had quite the penetrating stare as well.

Lori pretended she didn't notice.

She had a hard time concentrating, keeping herself on a somewhat even keel and welcomed the two men to the table, even smiled to them. Four pints of Guinness were put on the table. Her boiling insides threatened to take control of her lips, her hands and her eyes. She grabbed the glass and devoured a considerable amount of beer without tasting it.

– I can see you're thirsty, Dave grinned.

He was always grinning, it seemed.

She returned the grin. It didn't cost her anything. She drank some more. The women had a toast, smiling pretty to the two guys.

– To tonight, Dave cheered.

– TO TONIGHT! The four toasted.

Glasses met and parted with the special sound resembling that of a tuning fork. It echoed pleasantly within Lori. She found herself smiling earnestly to Dave.

The music began, low-keyed from invisible speakers, a backdrop to the conversation, but there. That, too, resonated within her. Everything did, really, a constant flow she pulled to her or pushed away.

She watched as the foam in her glass became a part of that. It looked like a tide to her. She worked a bit with controlling it, but it took only a minute or two before she got the hang of it. A smile broke on her face. More dark beer pushed itself into her mouth and down her throat.

Dave frowned, wondering what he had seen, if he had in fact seen anything extraordinary at all.

Lori kept listening to the conversation, observing the people around her, not really caring if the two men noticed her absentmindedness. She did multitask, like she had always done to some degree or another.

Her ability to do that had picked up recently, like so many others of her previously nascent abilities.

Two boys, two students had a conversation about their life at a given university. She heard them easily.

– There are many small tricks you can use in order to improve your grades, one of them insisted. – It isn't really that hard and there's no excuse for not making that extra effort.

– You're absolutely correct, the other practically echoed his solemn behavior. – Studying is a waste of time if you don't.

The serious, self-righteous conversation made Lori break in laughter.

There was no… content in their conversation, none what so ever, nothing beyond empty trivialities.

– Please share, Dave encouraged her. – Spill!

She glanced over at the two boys, and he caught it.

– Ah, you're listening in, he said.

– It just makes my funny bone twitch. She shrugged. – The two of them sounds like studying is a high calling, the highest possible calling in human life. I attended the university and called bullshit early on. The most eager students and most teachers and lecturers are overzealous solemn pricks.

She didn't exactly speak loud, but loud enough for the two men to hear her and cast angry glances at her.

– Cheers! Lori cried.

Glasses met and parted.

Lisl enjoyed the beer, studying the glass and its content with keen interest.

– I dropped out of school early, she said with a pleased grin on her face. – I was bored out of my skull.

A bunch of girls, old enough to drink, but not much more than that sat on the opposite side of the boys, a little farther off. Lori still heard them without effort.

– I use Quextran, the dominant among them said patronizingly. – It succeeds where everything else fails.

The other girls gathered around the table nodded awestruck.

– I will try it, the girl on her left said. – I will do so as soon as the stores open tomorrow.

They sat there humming and buzzing and drinking, with little more than that on their minds. Lori tried to keep herself from getting agitated, but failed miserably. She just couldn't lock the mindless chatter out.

– My jacket feels so pleasant to wear, another girl said. – It is the latest from Savile. A friend recommended it to me and I'm glad she did.

Lori and Lisl exchanged glances, equally vexed.

– You should do it, Lori told Lisl. – You're of the same age and it doesn't come off as the patronizing talk of the older generation.

The girl jumped to her feet with a wide grin. It was quite evident to Lori that she looked forward to what was ahead of her.

She marched off to that other table.

– What are you mindless hens yapping about?
They looked stunned at her, not even managing to give her an indignant stare.
– Me? I wonder if you have anything sensible to say, anything at all.
She stopped right in front of them, allowing them to watch her, study her. Still unable to utter a single syllable they did.
– You are aware of what a useful tool you are to those in charge, the rich and powerful, right? You do know that modern advertising is about word of mouth, of picking the most popular and influential girl or boy in a given group and make him or her buy a certain product, state a certain mindless «opinion» and given political outlook, and thus make all in his or her circle of friends adopt that?
– What is she doing? Dave gaped.
– Look at her and feel joy in your heart, Lori told him. – She's good, and she's standing up for herself.
– What are you saying? One of the girls asked, actually asked.
She and several others sent suspicious glances at the girl using Quextran, and also at the other girl with the pleasant to wear jacket. A wedge had been struck in their armor of perceived superiority.
Lisl picked a chair from a neighboring table and sat down with them.
– It's pretty well-known material, actually, she grinned, grinned darkly, showing off her fangs, the fangs those gathered around the table suddenly perceived. – The point of advertising isn't really about making people buy a given product, but about selling a particular way of life. By making it all about people's need to be successful or safe or about belonging, advertising is more than anything promoting consumerism itself and the superficial, uncaring society it creates.
– We are not tools, the girl using Quextran attempted to regain the initiative.
These youths were not stupid. They knew the meaning of the word and also its slightly different, even more patronizing urban slang significance.
– You are, Lisl said decisively. – It's pretty self-evident, even.
Lori watched it all. She saw how it drew attention from the neighboring tables and from the room at large. She was one of the first, but not the first that rose and turned her chair around and joined the table that was suddenly the center of attention.
– The people in charge know and have known for some time that traditional advertising doesn't work, so they have devised a new strategy that has shown itself to be quite successful. Selective word of mouth is definitely the new commercial wonder. They use any trick in order to trick you into

buying stuff you don't really need and you aid them in their deception, helping them into fooling you.

– Every English child grows up with their school uniforms, Lori spat, – becoming good, little soldiers and servants.

To verify that beyond doubt the two girls providing free advertising rose from their chairs and left. Several of those accompanying them hesitated to follow them on their retreat. Five of them didn't. Lori's heart started beating faster in happiness.

Others quickly made use of the empty chairs. The conversation continued.

– That was so brave of you, one of the girls said to Lisl. – Thank you!

And Lori knew that Lisl felt good about it, that she had to fight hard with herself in order to present an indifferent facade.

They kept participating in the discussion, turned conversation. Lisl continued to stand up for herself. Lori watched it as it occurred and a warm, treacherous feeling rose within.

Time flowed. More beer was consumed. The warm lamps lit themselves or seemed to. Lori didn't see anyone turning them on. Daylight faded, both inside and outside. The world changed in independent minds, at least ever so little.

– It's such a great thing every time established truths are challenged, a boy said. – I want to experience that often. I would want to make it a daily, ongoing occurrence in my life.

– There is certainly a great need for that, Lori said, showing her agreement by giving him an appreciative smile.

Everyone looked at her. He certainly did.

– Current human society sucks on all levels. We need to be better, much better than that.

She shrugged, deliberately. They didn't feel at all like she was shrugging.

There was more toasting and even more drinking. Lori felt her body turning numb, but her mind remained as astute as ever. She knew it did, watching the reaction of the others, all the others around the table and nearby tables.

– That was very… elegant, all of it, Dave told her, very appreciative.

– Thank you, she said solemnly, flippantly. – I think so, too.

In a fit of silliness, she toasted with him and gave him the look, the one making his throat turn paper dry.

– THE BASEMENT WILL OPEN IN TEN MINUTES, one of the staff announced.

A mumble of expectation was heard throughout the room.

A guy shook his head in bewilderment.

– What's the big deal? He said sourly.
– The basement is a more… interesting place, a guy sitting next to him informed the uninformed sourpuss.
– At least it can be, a girl said, with notable expectation in her voice and face. – Its moody atmosphere and special setting alone makes it worth it.
People glanced at their watch, some bored, others marking time. Time suddenly passed slowly. Quite a few present glanced repeatedly at the wall clock. Its hands hardly moved, didn't seem to be moving at all.
They walked downstairs, following the girl with previous experience or/and their own burning curiosity. The basement, the dungeon revealed itself to them. Torches burned on the walls. The furniture and general elaborate, but fairly simple design was clearly meant to convey something different, and to generate unusual notions in those venturing here.
– Look at this setup, Lisl whistled and turned to the girl. – You didn't shit us. It is something special.
Lori's fingertips tingled. They were practically itching. She rubbed them against each other, in an effort to make it stop, in vain. A pentacle hung on each wall. A sweet type of incense nipped at her nostrils. Something down here, deliberate or not affected her. She could not help but react to it.
It affected others as well. She watched how a boy twisted his head in hard pulls. He had obviously no control over it. It continued for several seconds until he, with an effort made it stop.
Her eyes turned huge and strange as she made a further study of the room.
The girl, Harmony studied her with anxious glances.
The bar was a half circle at the center of the room. Behind it a huge fireplace brightened the backroom, a dance floor otherwise cast in shadow.
A huge painting, Children of the Midnight Fire hung prominently displayed on the opposite wall. She felt drawn to it, an impossible mirage in a dark night.
The itch to start drawing burned within, but nothing happened.
Her hands didn't move. The images still drew themselves in her head.
Lisl touched her arm gently, noticing that something… that something was wrong.
– Are you alright?
– I am, thank you, Lori replied, as casually as she could make it.
A film of sweat suddenly, without warning covered her forehead. Her mask stayed on.
The music began flowing from hidden speakers. The lights were lit in the bar, where people had already lined up for more drinks.
Lori, Lisl, Harmony and those in their group found a table and sat down.

There were still lots of available seats in the basement as a whole, but they were disappearing fast.

Lisl and Harmony rose from their chairs again, clearly appointing themselves as maids. They held out hands. Ronny and Dave and some of the others, both men and women put bills in their open palms. The two of them rushed to the bar to fetch more drinks for themselves and their tablemates. They joined the queue with optimistic mugs and fierce behavior.

Ronny grabbed Lori's hand, demanding her attention. She allowed it and turned in her chair to face him.

– You're cute enough to devour, he slurred.

She didn't reply to him. He frowned, but didn't let go of her hand.

– It's hard to get a handle on you, he droned on. – When I first saw I couldn't tell if you were young or old, experienced or not. You're an enigma, my dear and I can't say I enjoy riddles coated in flesh that much. You're hiding something and rest assured that I will find out what that is…

She let him prattle on. His voice faded to a somewhat unpleasant chatter in the background, joining the general buzz of voices. She used the first opportunity, when his grip weakened to pull back her hand and began taking in the room and its current populace.

It wasn't that hard spotting the pile of dust in a corner, the stain on the far wall and other immaculate details. A man on the neighboring table devoured the drink of his half unconscious drinking buddy. No one else seemed to notice. She kept noticing big and small things in an uneven flow. Her intoxicated mind didn't seem to be intoxicated at all. Her power of perception persisted in conveying bits and loads of information to her still soaring consciousness. The smile spread slowly on her face.

– That's my girl, Ronny grinned.

Her attention returned to him, her smile staying in place, the frown never quite manifesting in her features.

He pulled her to him, pulled her close, making her sit in his lap.

– You're not naturally blonde, are you?

He grabbed her hair, playing with it a little, before pulling her face close to his. His alcohol breath mixed with hers. He kissed her on the lips. She found herself responding. He chuckled triumphant. The patronizing laughter kept echoing in her inebriated thoughts.

The two girls returned, their hands filled with glasses filled with liquor.

– The prodigal daughters return, Harmony cried.

They began administrating their load generously around the table. There was more than enough to go around, more than one for each and every one of them. They had used all the money handed to them. It pleased Lori to notice the frown on Ronny and Dave's faces. She giggled and had her first basement shot.

They had toasts (countless toasts). Liquor flooded thirsty throats and splashed already soaked tables. Candles flickered and grew, their ghostly flames echoing beyond pleasant in Lori's soaring mind. She kissed Ronny hard on the lips in pure, undiluted excitement, just for the thrill of it.

She moved her ass over on the table, sitting down on its soaked surface, her ass getting wet in an instant. She hardly noticed.

The woman crouched there on the table, like a cat, effortlessly maneuvering on the limited space available to her. Her face and eyes brightened, as she seemingly included them all in her sphere. She called attention to herself without trying.

– The world is so much more than most people pretend it is, she began. – It isn't even close to what those with limited awareness perceive or think they perceive.

With just a few moves and words she had them in the palm of the hand she held up, even Ronny and Dave, and she giggled darkly.

She held out the hand, and Lisl reached out and took it, as Lori knew she would do.

– We, the two of us are on a quest, a path of discovery and realization.

The shadow emerged from her hand, a little shaky, a little drunk, but still twisting the air, still making a dramatic appearance. Lisl gasped. Harmony's eyes lit in interest.

– We started walking early this morning, Lisl said in a dreamy voice, – and ended up here, exactly where we were supposed to be. It feels so good to walk, to move. Each step brings about a new, fresh thought or notion.

Lori shifted position slightly, a move sufficient to draw attention back to her.

– Some of us have been on a Journey for a long time. It's never ending, really.

The twirling shadow above her palm seemed to expand, to spread up her sleeveless arm.

– When I was four a voice spoke to me. It came out of nowhere, in an empty playground. I've never forgotten its words. It told me I was a dark goddess and would bring untold great and terrible things to mankind. It told me I was one of the emerging Earth and sky, day and Night and many times besides making no sense to me then. My mother, when I ran frightened to her and told her convinced me, the child it was total bullshit at first, of course, even though I knew deep down it was not. Now, it has begun making sense. Now, I understand more and more for each passing day and night.

And even as she spoke about it, shared it with those around her, understanding improved in jumps and bursts.

She glimpsed Jenny. Even in the alcohol-induced fog of her mind, her brief friend appeared clearer than ever.

The witch in their midst raised a hand and the surroundings seemed to fade away, to fall silent.

– Listen, she said, – behold, open up and you will hear what everyday noise keeps you from hearing.

They sat there, perhaps more attentive than ever before in their lives. She shared herself with them, making a real effort at it, and she imagined that they did hear it, or at least its faint echo.

Lisl did, she knew that much. The girl practically shook in her seat.

The sound of the room returned to them. A new song began, flowing from the speakers and people flowed to the dance floor. Lori slipped down from the table. She began dancing long before she reached the open floor filled with jumping and writhing bodies.

The slow song and its rhythm imposed itself on them, on everyone following her. She sort-of registered that about half of the people from her table, sensibly enough stayed behind, before forgetting about it.

They kept dancing without break, or so it felt. Sweat soaked her clothes and she hardly noticed. Happy screams rose from sore throats and it hardly seemed to matter. She felt the heat from the fireplace from far away, and when she stepped close to it, it was as if her body burned, burned for real. In the mirror of the dancing flames she saw shadows flicker on her wet skin. She felt their touch.

A dark humming rose from her throat, slowly forming a chant and a repetitive phrase. She wouldn't exactly call them words. They were far more primal than that.

She watched how Harmony reacted to it, how she clearly knew their significance, how she attempted to conceal her reaction, but failing completely under Lori's ruthless scrutiny, her x-ray vision.

Lori smirked, a snarl shaking the very room.

A dark green light grew out of the shadows. She saw it, even though perhaps no one else did, even though both Harmony and Lisl and several of the others frowned briefly, before shaking their heads in denial. The light existed in the room. It did not.

It… spoke to her, communicated with her beyond sound, beyond words, but she couldn't fathom its meaning or intent, what it attempted to convey to her, if it in truth attempted anything and had any will of its own.

The music created a poignancy within her, an empowerment of rage and sadness she could hardly cope with.

She studied Harmony and Lisl without studying them, without being noticed, without even looking at them. She knew she could do that, now. It wasn't like she had just the experience necessary to do it, but a terrible and vast confidence. The green light, the shadow and countless other manifestations of what shivered and burned her frame and self, told her so much of what she needed to know.

Then she did look at the girl, deliberately, a direct stare drilling holes in the girl. Harmony looked very guilty then. She masked it well, but Lori saw how her lower lip trembled and her eyes flickered.

She was blushing, and when that dawned on her, she blushed even more. Lori watched her, as she pulled back and headed for the lavatories. Lori followed her, while Lisl was chasing Lori.

– What's with her? The girl wondered.

– She's just a little girl pretending to be big, Lori explained casually.

They entered the lavatories, with the large, misty mirrors. Lori suspected that they didn't appear to the others that way, but she saw them like that. Faces in the mirror looked indistinct, as they looked half at them, half directly at each other.

Harmony looked down, clearly embarrassed, bordering on ashamed. She finally managed to speak aloud what she had carried with her the entire evening since they had first met her, since she had lured them into the basement. Lori looked at her with something resembling gratitude.

– I have a confession to make. The owners don't pay me, but give me some props to promote the place.

Lori and Lisl both turned to her and stared at her with their huge, opaque eyes. Lori spoke with her spooky voice.

– We know. At least you're honest in your dishonesty.

– You… know? She said nonplussed.

– Indeed, Lisl shrugged. – You were pretty transparent.

– But we forgive you, Lori said.

Harmony blinked.

– You do?

– Sure, Lisl deliberately shrugged some more. – You shouldn't worry too much about it, you know. We know that a girl sometimes must do worse stuff in order to get by. And it isn't like you've committed murder or anything.

Harmony read confirmation in their eyes. She was very astute, even though she attempted to hide it.

Her face cracked in a grateful smile. She rushed to Lori and embraced her.

– I'm so happy about that, she sniffed, – so very, very happy.

And Lori had no trouble whatsoever spotting what hid behind, beneath her excellent acting, beneath her first layer of deception.

One Harmony showed a piece of herself. But it wasn't truly her, and neither was what hid beneath that mask. The other Harmony showed nothing of herself, and Lori knew that, knew it beyond certainty.

She returned to the dance floor in a kind of daze, but still aware, burning with what hid beneath.

Her earlier table buddies greeted her. They had all long since abandoned that table and spread across the room. She felt them, and knew where most of them were located. Especially five of them stood out from the rest. She felt them hard, as if they were actually touching her.

Her body, her mind began swaying, swaying. It moved on the dance floor of its own accord. She let it. Ronny approached her. He walked right to her and began kissing her. She resisted halfhearted at first, before halfhearted returning his demanding caresses.

The rhythm struck her. She felt each beat. The other dancers turned to shapes she hardly noticed and back to creatures of flesh and blood threatening to overwhelm her. Their blood, their flesh, their loud fever shook her hard.

He was wearing her down. His constant fondling and persistence made her hot and queasy.

His greater physical strength pushed her backwards, pushed her at the nearest wall. She gasped, and increasingly returned his affections.

– Let's get back to the room, he panted.

He kissed her some more, kissed her hard on the lips. She responded promptly and eagerly. He grabbed her arm and pulled her with him, keeping up the incessant fondling. It felt pleasant, so very pleasant. She clung to him, pushing herself at him, as they climbed the stairs, constantly in danger of falling, either collapsing while stumbling forwards or falling backwards, down the stairs again.

They finally reached the end of the stairs and the brighter light. Her vision remained hazy, the distant furniture coated in mist. She felt his lips on her, his stubs of facial hair.

– Hurry, she mumbled, – hurry up.

She pushed him at the wall, knocking over a table and a few chairs in the bargain. People stared at them and chuckled in anticipation, but she didn't care. She began fumbling with his belt and sipper.

The mumbles of his protest eventually reached her delirious mind.

She stopped and stepped back, her fervor fading, though still lingering.

He noticed, she saw that he did. She shook her head. He stepped close to her and grabbed her again.

– I'm sorry, she said, – I don't feel like it.

He tried kissing her. She turned her lips away, and made herself generally unavailable to him, the way long years of marriage had taught her.

– I don't want to.

– Ah, c'mon, love, of course you will.

– NO!

She liberated herself from him, and there was something in her eyes making him stop his advances.

– You weren't exactly unfeeling half a minute ago…

She smiled, her lips a thin, thin line.

– You won't claim I was leading you on, will you? You're not such a little boy, are you?

– But I paid for your drinks, he grumbled.

– You gave me drinks as payment for future services? I'm not that cheap, you know.

She turned and walked away. He didn't follow her.

– I knew he was an asshole, she mumbled, – damn me!

The wind rushed her from all sides as she charged through abandoned hallways.

She sat on the toilet bowl. She was done shitting and peeing, but kept sitting there, shaking with emotion, tears flowing down her cheeks.

A hand struck the wall. It didn't feel like hers at all. The wall almost broke. She imagined that the entire building shook, that they felt it outside, on the parking lot, that lights blacked out for a second and that the second lasted an eternity.

A trembling hand fumbled a bit in the left big pocket of her jacket. She pulled out folded pieces of paper, unfolding them in quick, nervous moves.

There were three sheets, each with drawings of a face. One was of Harmony. Below the portrait was a word.

ENEMY

The other two had the same face, Lisl's face. One said

TRAITOR, INFORMER

The other said

DEVOTED FRIEND AND WITCH

She recalled drawing them in the attic long before she had met either of the women, how she had recognized them both the moment she had first seen them in the flesh.

The pale smile touched her face again. She folded the sheets and put them away.

Everything suddenly seemed so clear, so very, clear to her.

She dried herself, pulled up her panties and pants and walked back out.

The wall to wall mirror seemed to suck her in. Her mirror image filled the room. She studied her face carefully, frowning, tilting her head.

It took her a few seconds to realize that her hair was black, that it was black in the mirror, and now she saw easily that this change wasn't the only one.

She saw that her disguise, all of her disguise had been removed. She made a closer study, inspection of herself. The eyes, the eyes pulled her in, like the gravity well of a black hole.

When she blinked and looked into the mirror only the woman with blonde hair and outlandish makeup and clothes remained.

She hurried out of there, almost colliding with a woman on her way in. The reception had turned very quiet compared to the rush earlier on the day. She headed straight for the basement.

The very act of walking felt easy, effortless. She had been moving around a lot recently, walking more than she had done in years, but not really been running or exercising more than before. Her recent physical prowess just couldn't be a result of mere training.

The heavy music reached her long before she reached the stairs, but the moment she did it struck her hard and soft like a wave.

Smoke lingered in the air down below. It seemed to be condensing and gather in the air above the candles. The flames looked cold to her, not warm. She began shivering and couldn't stop it.

– Where are Lisl and the guys? She asked a girl that had been a part of their party all night.

– They went outside for a while, the girl replied. – I think some of them wanted a smoke.

Lori rushed off, ran back up.

She spotted them the moment she looked outside, at the far side of the parking lot. They stood there and laughed together, clearly having a good time. Nothing seemed to be wrong.

Anxiety lingered in her throat like moisture after rain.

She walked outside. It was as if the terrain rolled at her, like a wave.

A flag pole rope struck repeatedly at the metal shaft, making a rhythmic, repetitive sound.

A car stood with running engine at another corner of the lot.

Its engine sounded loud and threatening in her ears.

Breathless and agitated she made her way across the open space. Lisl spotted her and waved. Lori didn't wave back. She watched Harmony intently, hardly even blinking.

But still, during a blink it was as if a cloud of smoke spread from Harmony and engulfed everyone standing close to her. They coughed and fell to the ground. Bodies and heads hit the hard surface. The gas, whatever it might be didn't affect Harmony at all.

The girl, the suddenly far more mature woman turned her head and looked at Lori with a triumphant grin.

– I fooled you, didn't I?

She held a syringe in her hand and advanced quickly towards Lori. Lori kept advancing towards her. Before Lori had drawn breath, or so she experienced it, they had moved close. Harmony kicked out with a foot, in a seemingly totally unexpected strike. Lori raised a hand. The foot appeared to be… scratching against hard air and pulled violently away. Harmony yelped in pain. She could not stand on the foot and attempted to stab Lori with the syringe. A shadowy vortex surrounded the hand. She shouted in pain and lost the syringe. It hit the asphalt, but didn't break. Lori imagined she heard the sound of the car as it grew to a roar in her ears, but her attention remained fixed on Harmony. Lori felt like a steel spool, more than willing and able to defend herself again.

– You are remarkable, Harmony said exalted, – but then again, we suspected that you would be.

Lori frowned, even as a cold chill and a loud, loud alarm went through her sweat-soaked body and agitated mind.

The car hit her from behind, pushing her a considerable distance forward. She collapsed on the pavement, amazingly so still conscious.

– You idiots! She heard Harmony spit at those disembarking the car. – If you have damaged her…

Lori felt herself be touched and examined.

– She's okay, a man said incredulous, – only stunned. I don't think the car actually touched her, but some kind of hard air protection around her body. You're correct. She is an amazing specimen.

Lori tried to make something, anything work, but nothing did. There was a sting on her calf, and a horrible weakness quickly overwhelmed her. The last image she saw before everything turned black was Harmony's ecstatic smile.

Chapter Thirteen

They crouched by the wall long afterwards, unable to measure time, impressions of the hellish room burned into their consciousness forever. Everything had fallen silent. They sat there, staring at nothing.

The entire room was filled to the brim with bodies and body parts, bloody and cold.

She walked through a landscape of mist and shadow. Other details of her surroundings revealed themselves to her in glimpses, a worn, faded green bench on the left, a wild-growing hedge on her right and the full, full moon above. She realized she had returned to the park, to the night, that night in Hyde Park.

– I wish to welcome you all to this research facility, the woman in the white coat greeted them. – My name is Harmony Coates, and I'm in charge of operations here.

She looked so different compared to the young woman Lori had met in the pub, so much more confident and menacing. Lori and her fellow captives crowded the floor, everyone frozen in fear.

Five, they were five holding hands, clutching each other so hard that it hurt.

«Follow the breadcrumbs», the young man on the red bench told her.

She didn't hear him the first time and he repeated himself.

– FOLLOW THE BREADCRUMBS, YOU STUPID CUNT, he shouted.

The building marking the western end of Kensington Gardens loomed ominous to her right, hardly looking like itself at all.

«Follow the huge pieces of carved up, bloody flesh», a grown man chuckled viciously.

Two women faced her, staring intently at her, probing her as she probed them.

They were far more then five at first, in the building where lots of people in uniform roamed. She realized that those weren't military uniforms, but belonging to a somewhat private outfit. A pad with a symbol, a bird's head had been sown on their arms. Scared and stunned people surrounded her in the big room, everyone drugged out of their minds and unable to offer any resistance to the treatment they were given by their kidnappers.

They had baptized these quarters the pens, because this was where they were returned between assignments, training and torture.

The violent storm replayed itself endlessly in Lori's mind.

– Wakey, wakey, a distorted voice told her.

A wretched stench, light slaps on her cheeks made her raise heavy eyelids.

She sat in a chair in a sparsely furnished room. Harmony Coates sat on a stool in front of her, smiling her excited smile.

– I was wrong, she said, shaking her head in wonder. – I did not fool you. You were on to me, even though there was no way you could be, not in ways acknowledged by mainstream science.

She held up the three drawings.

Lori didn't say anything. She turned her heavy head, striving to work through the drugs sapping her strength and awareness, glimpsing two big bruisers standing behind her.

– I imagine you've drawn more than these?

It was clearly a rhetorical question, but one demanding an answer. Lori didn't reply.

Harmony slapped her.

– Naughty girl, don't you remember what happens to naughty girls?

Lori did, recalled the electric needle on her skin and other instruments of torture she had been submitted to. Her horrible scream and sore, sore throat remained at the upper level of her consciousness.

– Yes, she choked. – I remember and I have drawn more.

This time a kind hand touched her cheek.

– That's a good girl. You didn't try to get smart. Know that that is certainly appreciated.

Harmony studied her with her large, cruel eyes.

– I would imagine that the moments of revelation are mostly involuntary and that you strive with provoking them deliberately.

– That is a fair assessment, Lori sniffed with lowered eyes.

– Don't worry, Harmony said, – you're one of our stars, and you will be treated accordingly. You will never lack pen or paper, or anything else that will help you progress. We expect big things from you. You have such a versatile and wondrous array of gifts.

She found herself once again in the darkened room, just after all the light had vanished there from one moment to the next, as if someone had turned a switch.

But the truth of the matter was that all the light-bulbs had failed simultaneously.

Then she was in yet another place, one equally familiar by now, where they were brought to be trained and probed.

– Tell me the first thought on your mind, subject 940, Harmony said brightly.

– I can hear music, Lori said puzzled. – Do I hear music?

Harmony didn't reply, but Lori's words clearly excited her, and she made a note, a rather extensive note on her digital writing pad. Lori looked confused and miserable at the woman.

– Move the statue, subject 940, Harmony commanded her curtly, encouragingly.

Lori, wearing a full body suit, one very similar to a prison uniform stood in a rather large, bright-lit room, staring at its center, at the small statue on the pedestal with desperate intent on her mind. Fear and boundless anxiety and queasiness warred within her, reducing her to a jumble of angst. Harmony's face had been burned into her retinas and she did not need to look at her in order to see her, obey her explicitly.

You will be a nice and eager girl or there will be *hell to pay,* Harmony's cruel words kept repeating themselves in her befuddled mind.

– C'mon, Harmony coaxed her, with a pleasant voice laced with implied threats, – you've done it before.

That was a feather, Lori wanted to object, with the voice of a sullen, young girl, but she stayed silent, desperate to avoid punishment.

The feather rose in the air. The statue stayed put.

– And when you fought me at the parking lot.

I was angry then, Lori whimpered scared and timid.

Harmony stamped her foot in impatience. Lori shook.

Something… happened, something inexplicable. Wind picked up inside the room, wind turning into shadow, like the one she had manifested in her palm, turning into a vortex, like the one forming in her mind, one opening a hole to nowhere. The statue shook a few times, before falling off the pedestal.

Lori fell and collapsed on the floor.

– YES!

Harmony jumped up and down in excitement.

– Yes, my sweet pet, you have indeed earned your reward.

She walked to the creature crouching on the floor, bent down and gave her a sweet. Lori opened her mouth. Harmony put it on her tongue. Lori closed her mouth and began sucking, a distant, content expression growing on her indistinct features.

The sweet had become such a great comfort, a joyous reward.

– The treatment is working, Harmony made a fist and cried in ecstasy, – *working!*

She made more notes, hardly able to contain her excitement. Then she raised a hand, signaling the guards outside. They entered the room and came and fetched a whimpering Lori.

– Fear and pain is indeed the key, Harmony chuckled, as she walked just behind Lori and the two big bruisers squeezing long since bruised arms.

It wasn't a long trip through the darkened hallways. They reached another room, one dressed like a laboratory before Lori could blink too many times. Two men in white coats received the package from the guards. They grabbed Lori and put her on her back on the examination table, and used the leather straps to secure her.

Lori could hardly move. Harmony stood above her with the needle, the electric needle in her hand.

– No, Lori sobbed and shook and sniveled incoherently, – I was good, wasn't I? I was good!

Harmony rubbed her cheek, like she would pet a cat.

– You were good, she said softly to the woman on the examination table. – Don't look at this as punishment, sweet thing, but as a *reward.*

– Reward? Lori blinked.

– Precisely, one that will make you improve your exciting skills even more, one that will enable you to go beyond your own silly limitations to a level unheard of.

The electric needle was pushed at Lori's unprotected skin. She screamed her throat raw. And that was just the first time. It continued for something that to her felt like an entire *age* and not only a few minutes.

They carried her back to the pens afterwards. The walk through the dark hallways seemed endless. They opened the door and returned her to the others.

Lisl crawled to her and others did as well. All of them attempted to comfort her, in vain, and they knew that. The knowledge of their failure made them shake and sob even harder. They sat there with their backs to the wall, shaking like leaves. All the bright lights made their sore eyes hurt even more.

She kept shaking, having completely lost control of her body. The equally uncontrollable sobs made snot flow from her nostrils.

Once more she walked through the landscape of mist and shadow. It looked different this time, appeared much more distinct in her inner vision. Clarity burned her ever open, unblinking eyes

Lisl, Cathy, Violet and Zachary walked with her. They held hands. They walked through dimly familiar streets. She recognized Oxford Street, even though its buildings were derelict and practically ruins and grass and growth covered both them and the ground. They saw few signs of outright destruction, even though there was that as well. Most of all what confronted them was… time.

Time!

Faces clearly looked older, withered by age.

Time!

With a start, she was back in the white room, so well-lit it was hard to see. They held hands. The pen and paper rested in her lap. She blinked. They no longer held hands. The pen and paper didn't rest in her lap.

Lights, dim lights turning into shadowy shapes began forming behind her eyelids. They moved and danced. Bright, penetrating lights turned dark, bluish, even more penetrating.

The familiar panic grabbed her. She reached for the pen and paper, unable to resist the impulse, the dominion of the sensations accosting her.

The pen raced back and forth across the paper, forming images, even the illusion of movement. She glimpsed them before they appeared on paper and the usual confusion riddled her. Reality blinked out, blinked in. The drawings became reality.

Eyes met eyes, wide open eyes. She reached Lisl, reached for Zachary, Cathy and Violet or they crawled to her. Uncertainty ran her over, the raw panic making her senses sharp as razorblades. They cut her. She felt them, the incisions, all the way to her bones.

Lisl looked at the paper sheets spread out on the floor. The others did as well, when they saw her skin turn pale.

Hand reached for hand for hand for hand for hand.

Blood stained the wall. Machineguns being fired made a horrible noise in her sore ears.

The room remained clean and deadly still. The bright light kept blinding her.

Strengthening certainty, crippling doubt, empowering rage and numbing terror ravaged her.

Harmony walked through the door, as always accompanied by her two bruisers.

– What have we here, sweetie? Harmony said with her eager honey voice. – You have been so good, haven't you? Your last reward has *spurred* you on in unprecedented ways, it seems.

She picked up a sheet, looking eagerly at the drawing filling the paper.

The frown was hardly visible. Lori would probably not have spotted it if she hadn't drawn it only a few minutes ago. In that face, when the two faces mingled and turned interchangeable it was very visible.

Harmony picked up another sheet, one showing the blank side. She turned it over. Her hand shook ever so little. This time Lori didn't need a drawing to see it. Lori knew that Harmony would stick a hand into her pocket in a few seconds and trigger the silent alarm. A few seconds later it happened, just as the drawing had shown her. Harmony kept looking at the drawings with a calm outside demeanor, but with a hidden fear making it increasingly difficult to hide the growing panic.

The door opened and a plethora of guards with guns, big, ugly guns filled the room.

Lori imagined she raised a hand, fully aware of the fact that she couldn't possibly do that, while clutching Lisl and Zachary's hands.

She found herself once again in the darkened room, just after all the light had vanished there from one moment to the next, as if someone had turned a switch.

But the truth of the matter was that all the light-bulbs had failed simultaneously.

A... charge erupted from five connected bodies, five people of one mind and intent. The five saw everything in a bluish light, saw it clearer than anything else they had ever seen. Harmony was pulled into the air... and practically ripped apart. Body parts decorated the walls. She hardly had time to scream. The others, however, had. A fresh supply of body parts kept decorating the wall. The screams filled the room, filled the entire building and the streets of London outside. Lori stood on the moon and watched the Earth, and she still heard them.

She stood on Mars, half naked and saw everything.

They crouched by the wall long afterwards. Their sense of time had been completely eradicated from their mind. They had no way of knowing how long time had passed, if it was just a few seconds or days, weeks and years. Blood and body parts covered every single point of the room. Warm bodies and body parts had started cooling all over the place.

Everyone else, except the five had died and died violently. Everything had fallen silent. No sound broke the silence. They sat there, with their backs to the wall, staring at nothing.

A man's chest had been split in two, as if an alien face-hugger had erupted from beneath his skin. Another had no head. Most body parts had no body, but were just unevenly distributed on the floor, the walls and the ceiling.

Violet rose first. The spot where her back had covered the wall was shockingly free of blood, bone or body parts. The others rose as well. They looked around the room with a chilling calm they didn't understand, eventually directing their attention at the open door, or the hole in the wall where there once had been a door.

The showers were nearby, just right down the hall. They moved there. Feet hardly touched the floor or seemed to do so. They cleaned themselves in a hurry, removing the worst and most visible blood and stain. The hot water hardly reached already burning hot, ice cold skin.

It took several more minutes, but they found the room where everyone's clothes had been stored. Locating their own proved difficult. Everything had been stored indiscriminately in cardboard boxes. They tried on and were somewhat content with various badly fitted garments. It proved easier to find and utilize cans of gasoline. The stench from the garage drew them to their target. They distributed it evenly all over the place, doing so more generously where they found more ripped-apart bodies, found them in all parts of the building. There was more than enough combustive fuel to go around. They opened all the windows, letting in all available oxygen, opening all doors within the building, unblocking all potentially blocking a fire.

Zachary lit a match as they stepped outside into the chilling heat of the London night. Cathy made certain the door stayed open with a chair. He dropped the burning match on the soaked floor. The flames rose to the ceiling quickly. They watched as it spread down the hallway and from window to window in both directions. The entire building seemed surrounded by flames in seconds.

Hand reached for hand for hand for hand for hand.

They walked, stumbling through darkened streets.

Five, they were five holding hands, clutching each other so hard that it hurt.

Lisl shook by her side.

– What was that? What *was* that?

No one replied to her. They just kept staring straight ahead, while they put one foot in front of the other.

A woman had tried to escape through the distant, distant door. She had dissolved to a heap of flesh and bones in seconds. A few weapons had been fired. No bullets came even close to hitting the intended targets. The sound of the guns, the visuals and the sensations echoed a bit in their heads. The silence kept dominating their consciousness.

– That was the music, Lori said unprompted.

Birds flew up and down the streets they walked through. Beaks opened and closed, closed and opened. The five didn't hear the cries, the loud, loud screeches. They walked and kept walking, while the night turned darker and darker and darker around their still shaking forms.

No one spoke. Lori's words and Lisl's outburst remained the only words they had uttered since the forever they only dimly remembered. Eyes closed. Eyes stayed open, open, open. They slept while walking, dreaming everything they would never forget. It just went on and on and on.

Until everything had turned dark, and the only thing their senses registered was the sound of steps, only slowly, slowly, slowly fading.

They woke up in a cemetery, under a tree, in an area without graves. The birds stood in a circle around them. They had mostly stopped screeching. A single occasional screech reached the five's ears well enough. Muted, distant sounds of cars mixed with the sound mix close by.

The sun had come up some time ago. They couldn't tell how long time had passed since they had first seen it, if it was the first, second or hundredth time since they had walked out of the «research facility».

– The sun is burning my face, Lisl complained.

– I see only the moon, Lori said and yet another chill passed through her.

The memory of the time she had spent in that cold, cold building would always be dim, but those key moments wouldn't. They would always be burned into her consciousness like a brand.

– Harmony was correct, she mumbled, – the Goddess bless her tiny, black heart.

The other four looked at her with blind eyes.

This time the chill entered her and stayed.

The birds flew away, one by one. The flapping of wings echoed endlessly in their chaotic thoughts.

– It is as if they were *protecting* us, Violet said, – and now, when they're no longer needed, they leave us in peace.

Her very words seemed to wake them up further. Their eyes visibly brightened. Lori kept seeing them in moonlight, or something closely resembling it.

– We… connected somehow, Zachary said, pondering his own pondering, – and we became greater, more powerful than the sum of the parts.

Lori felt hand touch hand touch hand touch hand touch hand and what resembled an electric charge, re-experiencing the moment the immense power had been created. In that moment, they had been of one mind and a single intent.

– We did good! She stated, holding up both her fists just below and in front of her jaw.

She did so with a shaking voice, but with conviction.

Then she looked at each and every one of the others.

They nodded, one by one.

Lisl stepped forward, stepped close to her and grabbed her hands, clutching them hard. She let go and stepped back. The others repeated her act, one by one.

– We lost control after ripping apart the first few we *wanted* to kill, Violet mumbled, looking down, – but I'm not sorry. I regret only that we killed a few of our… our brethren in the process.

That word… it lingered and kept lingering between them. The others showed their agreement in a thousand small and big ways.
They started walking again. That, like everything felt difficult to do, as if they only recently had been infants appearing from their mother's womb.
Mist and shadow faded constantly in and out of their surroundings and consciousness.
– I'm hungry, Cathy said.
Those words echoed within them endlessly, like everything did.
– The world seems totally... off, Zachary noted, – changed completely from how I remember it.
– We have changed, Lisl said. – The world hasn't. The world is exactly the same.
She looked proud at Lori, proud of herself by the way she was handling herself, clearly out to prove herself to the older woman.
Lori felt brief heat, warmth subjected to that look.
– I'm hungry, Cathy insisted, practically whining.
– We all are, honey, Lori soothed her, – but we have no money and I don't recognize this part of town at all.
– We can be in another city, for all we know, Violet said enraged. – They could have taken us anywhere.
Lori shook her head.
– No, we are in London. I… know we are. It still looks familiar to me, even though these streets aren't.
So very familiar. She hesitated briefly, before speaking again.
– London is our city. It always will be.
It felt so right saying that, so beyond right.
She looked at a corner and two street names. They didn't ring a bell, but it didn't matter. She realized startled that it didn't matter.
– I keep trying to use… to use my power, Violet said in anguish, – but I can't.
They all did, in vain. Nothing, absolutely nothing happened.
– I would guess we are… burned out, Lori said. – We expended a huge amount of energy and that's also why we are so ravenously hungry. We need to... to recharge.
– I can smell food, Cathy said, still visibly suffering, – warm food.
– Perhaps there's a food bank nearby? Lisl brightened.
– A food bank? Violet looked disgusted.
– Precisely. Lisl said, both subdued and brightening simultaneously. – There are tons of those all over London, all over everywhere these days.
– I can just go home, Violet snorted, – and then I wouldn't need such shit.

– You can't go home, Lori said quietly. – You know that, right?

Violet looked like she was struck by lightning, and then, abruptly she burst into tears and practically crumbled before their eyes.

The others embraced her and comforted her the best they could as they walked.

Lori grabbed her jaw gently and held it hard.

– We are the Earth and sky, day and Night, she said with a low, intense voice. – We are the *same!*

She let go.

Violet sniffed and nodded, and nodded again. She dried her tears in swift strokes.

They turned a corner. Lisl's face brightened some more.

– I recognize this street. We're in Hackney. I lived here briefly. They served free meals in St. Marten's church nearby. I used to come there with my parents and siblings.

Her voice and expression turned more than a little subdued and defensive, but relaxing and brightening again when the others hardly reacted to her perceived dramatic revelation.

Lisl ran ahead to the tall doors. She pushed down the handle and proceeded to push the door open. It didn't budge.

– It's locked, she said incredulous.

She hammered the hard wood. The act hardly swayed it at all.

Cathy stopped in front of the tablet to the left of the stairs.

– «Opening time Tuesday 9 to 10 AM», she read. – You got to be kidding me…

A frown, a very deep frown dug itself on Zachary's brow.

– I would guess there's a long queue here every Tuesday morning.

Dismay and despair, overwhelming and loathsome grabbed them and doubled and tripled within, until sizzling and dying like a wet match.

They heard the steps, heard the sound in the eerie silence still surrounding them.

A man approached them. They tensed, still feeling antsy, apprehensive and the paranoid suspicion. The hooks of their ordeal kept pulling at their sore skin.

– There's another place, Moxie's Maw down the street, the man said. – They serve truly hot meals, a real dinner. The place is half decent and interesting in other ways as well. They're even open all days, including Sunday.

He looked and sounded… unthreatening. They allowed themselves to relax a little, just a little.

– Thank you for telling us, sir, Lori said. – That's most kind of you.

– It's the least I can do, he mumbled, – the least anyone can do.

He turned and walked away. Lori opened her mouth to call out to him, but failed to do so.

She attempted to… get a sense of him, to get beneath the… the shell of normalcy, in vain.

They followed his directions and headed down the street. She watched as he turned a corner, watched the corner for quite a while after that, with nothing significant happening.

Moxie's Maw was open. They saw that much at first glance. In a shadow cast by a cloud covering the sun lots of people walked in and out of what was clearly a decaying old building.

They entered a fairly bright and not too shabby hall. Most of its light came from the windows in the ceiling. Dust still floated in the air and in their minds.

There was a queue before the desk where the food was served. They joined it, slipped into it without really noticing that it happened.

Lisl bowed her head in despair. It was palatable. Lori did her best to comfort the girl, without being obvious about it. Lisl, in her dark valley of shame and insecurity clasped the older woman's hands and looked at her with gratitude and adulation in her ashen eyes.

– Those who have wronged you don't matter, Lori stated calmly. – The opinion of others is immaterial. Especially those being an eager part of the herd deserve no respect.

Lisl nodded empathically, drying her dry tears. The burning and awe in her eyes added even more to itself.

She is yours, now. A voiceless voice spoke in Lori's head. Yours to use and mold like clay. Congratulations!

The five helped themselves from the modest, but not meager table of food and drink. They, like many others did begin feeding well before they reached the tables lined up for them, putting pieces of burning hot meat in their mouth.

It was like they could not, could never get enough. They had spiced dishes, spiced soup and everything burned up within them, hardly even leaving ashes.

Lori cast the occasional glance at the others present. They didn't merit more than that, more than a casual glance.

Everyone else glanced at the five, doing so with flickering eyes, as if they could notice something beyond what the instant five senses could tell them.

Their hunger, their profound Hunger finally subsided. By that time the table and the floor around them had long since been covered by remains of their gluttony. They sat there with a stomach that felt many numbers too big and impossible to lift from the seat. Lori burped aloud. The other four echoed her not that long afterwards. Everyone else or almost everyone else in the hall stared accusingly at them.

The five waited patiently, allowing the digestion of the over the top meal to take place in its own time, before even considering moving from their seats and leaving the unpleasant place.

They walked through seemingly endless streets again.

– London is so big, Zachary said brightly. – It's a walker's paradise.

– And we need to walk, to run, Lori said. – We will always be more at risk at Tube stations and on buses.

A screech reached her ears or her mind. She saw no signs that the others heard it.

– And it's *good* for us, Lisl exclaimed.

They all felt her excitement, sharing it evenly between them.

The five of them stopped and looked at each other, sensed each other. Five hearts beat as one.

– We have woken up, Lori stated empathically, – and we will never fall asleep again.

Five nodded and smiled in concert. They were alone in the street. All the other people moving back and forth on both sidewalks didn't seem present at all.

They walked west, taking their time. The sun changed position in the sky, changed the shadows on the ground.

The *shadows,* Lori thought.

– The surveillance cameras will pick us up, Violet said. – If interested parties have control of and access to a considerable number of those, and a way of accessing them all in real time…

– … we'll know soon enough, Lori said.

– Perhaps we should… Lisl said hesitatingly. – Perhaps we should stay away from the others? They are… vulnerable. We are powerful just the five of us, so powerful that no one can mess with us.

– No! Lori shook her head. – Our fate is with the others.

– You know that, Cathy wondered, – know that for a fact?

– I do. There are lots of things I don't know, but I know that!

They looked at her with the usual awe in their eyes. She nodded, as if something had just dawned on her.

The big hotel, with its tall tower was on their right. They walked past it, as if it was no longer there. A few minutes' walk and they would be home.

They walked down Praed Street, going west, further west, through the

Paddington area and into Bayswater.

– How… does it make you feel? Violet asked.

– You know, Lori said.

– That was a few heartbeats of forever, Violet said. – You've been aware of your abilities for quite some time, and have had time to explore them.

– It feels like being high, Lori said slowly, – like existing on a constantly higher and different level of consciousness.

The words came easy to her, as if she had spoken them before she had formulated them.

A raven screeched from a tree nearby, a loud sound penetrating everything. Lori practically saw how it did that, how flesh, mortar and stone dissolved under its power. A deep-felt chill charged through her.

They reached their broad street, with its open space and no longer abandoned church. Lori spotted Arthur and Caitlin in front of the entrance. She saw how their faces lit up and cracked in big smiles. Caitlin rushed inside. Arthur, beyond excited and happy rushed forward towards Lori.

She heard the drums, as his feet touched the ground. They hammered in her ears.

He embraced her and lifted her up, high up in his surprisingly strong arms.

She chuckled pleased. He put her down, very embarrassed.

The others emerged from the church with happy smiles and relief. There were more hugging and kissing.

– We feared the worst had happened, Slater said.

– It did, Lori said.

They knew her subtle wording, her body language well.

She watched them as she spoke and afterwards.

They retreated inside, relief and happiness staying on everyone's glowing faces.

– So, what happened? Slater asked, clearly anxious.

– We were captured. We escaped and left heaps of dead bodies in our wake.

The laughter was loud and callous.

Arthur looked concerned as well.

– All… five of you?

– All of us, Lori confirmed.

Everyone heard her. She had made certain they would. They looked at her in disbelief and apprehension and compassion, all of the above.

Walking inside was a strange experience to her, yet one more such. The place felt so different, even though it had not changed at all. The shadows, the falling of light, how it fell on walls, ceiling, floor and faces, everything and everyone appeared changed in her vision.

She noticed with a glance that everyone was still here, and also the new faces others had brought back. They all had their eyes on her, gathering in a half moon around her, eagerly anticipating her word.

– The Walkabout was a success, she said aloud. – We have all changed, changed again, become more than we were, both as individuals and as a group. I salute you!

She still spotted shock and horror, at least its faint cousins, in some faces, but they were all with her. She smiled.

– We've only been back for such a short time, but it still feels like we've never been away. We've taken one more step on the path we've chosen, and it's only the modest beginning.

She spoke at some length, with a confidence that would have felt alien to her not that long ago. It wasn't that hard for her to imagine her own features as she did. She saw excitement, exhilaration and a hard expression, a suggestion of wickedness that certainly had not been there earlier.

Images, sensations from the slaughter revisited her consciousness, her burning awareness. She once again re-experienced it all, or imagined that she did.

– I'm not sorry that our keepers are dead, she stated calmly, – but I regret that we lost control and killed many of the victims along with them. The… communal mind we experienced caught us completely by surprise. It… ran away with us, making us spectators, passengers in our own bodies. We must exercise and hone our abilities, so that never happens again.

She ended her speech. Silence reigned in the old church.

One by one they stepped forward and embraced her. Skin touched skin. Hands caressed sore limbs and heads. Soft kisses calmed her turbulent insides. A kind of peace entered her and lingered.

She choked, and there was no way she could hide it from them, and she didn't want to.

– The feast… is that still on?

– Of course, it is, silly girl, Slater said. – We postponed it, all of us convinced you would return.

– That isn't entirely true, a girl Lori hadn't met, one of the recent arrivals giggled. – Some of us, also those who knew you, were very impatient and wanted it to start on time, convinced you and the other chick had left, but Bron would hear none of it and made us wait.

Slater reddened. He turned red all over.

Lori looked good-humored at him.

– Bron? She giggled incredulous. – Your name is *Bron?*

– He has hated that name since fourth grade, the girl snickered. – He insisted that we used his family name.

Something hard within Lori softened just a little.

The evening, the summer twilight, with the candles and torches came fast, like a breath. The unsteady long table was covered with cutlery, pans and kettles and culinary delights playing with their nostrils. They gathered around it and sat down on benches and chairs and stools. The dots of pale shadows in the ceiling, on surfaces and people's faces imposed themselves on her. They mostly had water, to the spicy vegan dish.

– This is great, Violet said. – I actually prefer drinking only water to certain dishes. It doesn't twist or diminish the taste like sweet drinks usually do.

She clearly more than enjoyed her new circumstances and company, even though still visibly upset by her recent ordeal and perceived fall in stature.

The gathering had a toast and drank more water, devouring the tasty dish on their hot plates.

Lori noticed easily everyone's stares and glances. She didn't mind anymore. A calm mind returned a calm look to everyone in her company. The storm within remained undiminished.

– A true new age is upon us, she told them sometime later, in a quiet moment between moments. – London will change before our very eyes, into something strange and wonderfully alien, both due to our actions and seemingly unrelated circumstances. It's already here, its initial signs long since manifested and spread

They nodded. Lisl nodded hard and excited. Violet, Cathy, Zachary and Arthur as well. Lori shook her head mentally. They were all more or less on the same page, now, even the newcomers. They had seen a lot already and knew more was on its way. Strange notions and yearnings ruled them all.

– I know it won't be altogether pleasant all the time, Lisl said, – but I'm still looking forward to it. I'm doing that so much that I can *taste* it. Those knowing of our existence, the servants of the old order, have not and will not treat us well. They see our very existence as a threat or an opportunity, which are equally bad. We need to be prepared for the inevitable backlash.

One path, one fork in the road closed before the girl, the well trained and dangerous former agent of the establishment, and in Lori's mind she embraced the other opening up before her, rushing forward with breathless anticipation.

Much of the talk was held in quiet, empathic voices.

– Bron, *Slater* stopped before our house, Emily related. – He just stood there, unmoving, with his head tilted, as if he was listening to something within himself, or at the very least outside any known frame of reference. It was eerie and strangely compelling. We ended up leaving with him. It would have sounded completely insane to us just before he showed up.

Lori did not look at him. She did not need to do that in order to study him. She did not need to study him more than she had already done, had done since she first met him.

– It was the strangest thing, Slater said. – I had walked around for hours, or perhaps days. It certainly felt that long. Suddenly, I heard thunder, felt a pull. I thought I had walked for days, but my true walk started that very moment…

– We live, lived in Luton, Emily said.

A warm, warm flow, a deep profound heat passed down Lori's spine.

– The rest of us didn't have such interesting experiences, Arthur said, – but we all felt an awakening of sorts, a given point in time where our minds started working at an elevated level, kind of like with a coffee rush, but far stronger.

– I dreamt about you, Caitlin choked. – You were screaming in raw, all-consuming pain, and did not exactly enjoy yourself. It sounded so real.

Her voice was even, dull. She sounded distant, not really present in this room at all.

– You sent us on the Walkabout, Adriana said accusingly. – You knew!

– I did! Lori acknowledged.

She showed them a drawing. It was of them leaving the church. She showed them another. They returned to the church in droves, in far greater numbers than they had left it.

– It had to be spontaneous, she stated firmly. – You couldn't know. A Walkabout is about achieving a dream state, becoming wide open to new and strange notions and sensations. You were ready, and you started on your Long Walk, and your life's main path revealed itself.

– We saw you in Slater's eyes, Emily said incredulous. – He was looking at you, at you screaming and suffering. We practically fucking *heard you!*

Lori felt icepicks of pain and joy stabbing her.

Emily took photographs, lots of them with her fairly expensive SLR camera, not holding back the slightest, but like the rest of them embracing the mood prevalent among those gathered at this place time forgot. The others didn't mind, and after a while they hardly noticed the camera and its uneven, more or less constant clicking at all.

Time just went away for them. They didn't grow tired. Night passed and day arrived and they hardly noticed. There seemed to be a kind of twilight within the old church, isolating them from the outside world. They gathered outside in the burning sun at a given point in time and hardly noticed the change in scenery.

– Many live a lie of their own choosing, Caitlin said subdued and exhilarated both, – an existence of silent despair. *We* do not, not anymore.

All the others looked at her with fondness in their eyes.

Emily took more photographs. It was as if she was filled with energy, as if it erupted from a deep, never empty well within her.

Lori felt like that as well. They all felt like that to her.

She sensed the palatable energy in the air, from them, between them. She studied the other four and Slater and everyone else she suspected of being… like her.

– Look at them, Lisl said as she stopped by her side. – There are surprisingly many promising candidates, aren't there?

Lori nodded to her, to herself.

– And they're all excited, practically battle-ready, the girl said. – Even those clearly being reluctant before we left have gained a new attitude and fighting spirit.

– Something has clearly changed, Lori mused. – That's either due to the Walkabout… or the new arrivals. One of those may possess an ability we both lack, one to excite people nearby.

It was still palatable, present in the very air around them and showed no sign of diminishing.

– I will train them, Lisl said, – share my considerable fighting skills with all of you, making us even stronger as individuals and as a group.

Silence descended momentarily between them, still speaking and whispering beyond intensity.

Action followed words. Lisl focused, very determined to make something happen. Lori knew, without thinking twice what she was attempting, struggling with.

– Our abilities have not returned, she said after a while, noticeably hesitant.

– Neither has mine, Lori acknowledged.

– I've tried, Lisl said, clearly frustrated, – tried hard to make whatever worked before work again, but have had no success.

– So have I, Lori said, – with the same lack of result. We're still exhausted, even though it doesn't feel like we are.

– We need to master that, too, the girl cried, – master everything about ourselves in order to thrive in the glorious and horrible days and nights to come.

Lori tried again, tried focusing whatever rested within her, tried forcing the need to draw, in vain.

– Fear and pain is the key, she heard Harmony say.

And fear once more touched her.

She focused on holding on to that feeling, the sense of terror and desolation, and managed to do so somewhat, but nothing came out of it.

– You are our star, Harmony said.

Her voice sounded so real, as if she spoke right now, at Lori's side.

– It… scared me before, Lisl said, – but it doesn't anymore. I used to feel like a freak by the very thought of being… special, but now it excites me. There, in that hall, when we slaughtered friends and foes alike, it felt like a long-lost piece of my puzzle had finally been returned or identified. We are what you, what your lost friend said we are. We are exactly that. Hearing you say that felt so right, so beyond right and wrong.

Hearing the girl speak, her words and intonation made the warm, warm feeling return. She (and Lisl) roamed the church. People had spread all over the place, chosen to join small groups sitting on the floor. An easy-going informality ruled.

The literal euphoria persisted. It made the two of them smile to each other in mutual understanding.

– We need more space, Lisl stated solemnly.

– Fortunately, we have it at our disposal already, Lori said unconcerned.

– Of course! Enlightened, the girl brightened and cracked another excited smile.

She had become so immediate, almost childish in her nosedive admiration of the older woman.

Lori knew, just knew it wasn't pretend, not anymore.

Zachary, Violet and Cathy enjoyed themselves with a group sitting in a circle by the large western window. They looked up in happiness when Lori and Lisl approached and eagerly made room for them. Lori sensed it without trying, had sensed it well before moving closer. Happiness and passion ruled here as well, but more tinged with the underlying prevailing terror that wouldn't let go.

Lori and Lisl sat down. They embraced the three, and were embraced in turn. The five would always share something unsubstantial, they knew that. It would always be there, in good and bad ways, in good and bad days and nights.

– Violet was sharing her thoughts with us about your horrible experience in that building, Emily said, – the terror and desolation, how you all saw yourself beyond rescue and escape, and felt beyond certainty that this, this would be your life from then on, and until you died, and that death would be a blessing.

– It's impossible to imagine such horror, Lisl said, a deep chill in her voice, – unless you experience it firsthand. No words can properly describe or convey it, what it does to you. Our keepers had no compassion. They didn't care about us at all, not beyond the lab rats we had become. We were just a means to an end to them.

– We shouldn't really be surprised, Slater said, seething with emotion and rage. – We know such people exist. They've been exposed, both historically and recently many times. They are the current masters of the world.

– Most people forget such facts, Lori stated darkly, – but we never will!

– You're so brave! A boy said subdued. – I don't know if I could have experienced something like that, and not crumbled like a castle of sand hit by a mighty wave.

– You can! Lisl stated. – You don't know what you're capable of until you face an ultimate horror like that.

– We sat there, in our beyond cruel captivity, Zachary said, – and all hope had fled. Then, suddenly, in a burst of fire, life returned, and everything we had suffered felt inconsequential, like the very worst night terror, perhaps, but one still fading away, turning immaterial after awakening, and this was an awakening beggaring belief, one beyond peer. *We* became the wave, and *they* the crumbling castle of sand.

He reached out with his hands, and the other four grabbed them. They felt it, like they did every time they touched, the contact that would never be broken.

– You as well, Lori told everyone in the circle.

Wide-eyed and hesitatingly they did as she encouraged them to do. Hand touched hand, touched skin, touched mind, and the very core of their being, or so it felt.

She rose, and everyone rose with her, eventually the rest of the gathering as well. They began forming a much wider and bigger circle, where everyone present joined in. It started a little awkward, but it grew into one single, fluid movement.

A… sound reached her ears. It made her frown. A sudden awestruck smile touched her face. Lisl inquired without speaking with her probing eyes.

– I hear the sound of bells, Lori said puzzled. – At least it sounds like bells, but no bells I've ever heard.

The circle formed. She studied it as it did. There was a screeching sound and something… shifted.

– *Shifting,* she mumbled/stated.

She grabbed Lisl and looked at her with urgency on her mind, and opened her mouth to speak, but no sound came out of it.

The girl seemed to get it, get that, and returned alarmed the older woman's attention.

– What is it? What are you trying to tell me?
I am telling you, Lori said.
– I must tell you, now, before…
– Before, what? Lisl whimpered.
The circle was complete, seemed to complete itself on its own, with seemingly no one actively doing anything, but she knew that wasn't correct. She watched it from above, watched how it changed from a circle to a burning wheel turning itself.
She sat in the large, large circle in the old church with the tower looming above them, and spoke to the gathering.
– The silent language is all around us, she told them with her very first words. – We just struggle to understand it, that's all.
– That's all… Arthur joked.
She looked at him with fondness in her deep, dark eyes.
– I've always heard the music, and it has grown increasingly louder and distinct and sophisticated in my head, but what if it isn't really music?
They listened intensively. She sensed it. The need to draw returned. She resisted it, even as it became an urge. The drawings grew stronger, more powerful in her vision, seemingly drawing themselves in the very air surrounding her.
– Our stay at that research facility was very educational. They didn't know that much, really, but they shared generously with their subjects the little they did. In their desire to intimidate us, train us in their service, they told us that whatever rested within us could be measured with their machines, that it had a physical, tangible reality. They were so kind to us, assured us we were not insane, and that we could be a part of something that could be «of immeasurable value to humanity», and in spite of their narrow interpretation of reality… they were basically correct. It corresponds pretty much with my own preliminary conclusions and the hints and innuendos my friend Jenny granted me before she vanished. I read a book a few years back, by a Norwegian mystic by the name of Frode Johansen. In that book, he first described newer research about how infants experience the world. The human brain isn't fully developed that early in a person's life. One of several results of that is that smells may be interpreted as sounds and similar. As they grow older their brains are sufficiently developed, the pathways are connected, and the world makes sense. Then, in the second half of the book he speculated further upon that and gave his thoughts on the next possible step of human evolution. His conclusion is that it is like that with adults as well; that we are not fully developed; that there is a vast, untapped potential in our brain; that there are still wiring yet unconnected; that some of us may

be able to take it to that third level, and that, brothers and sisters is what my brief friend Jenny was talking about…

She heard it, the silent mumble from unmoving lips.

– We do not see the whole picture, Violet cried excited. – We don't see the Other World, the world Beyond, what's right in front of us, don't see the trees for the forest.

– We will free ourselves from the shackles of the oppressive society, Lori stated, – doing so one piece of the time… sometimes many pieces simultaneously, in pushes and pulls, and when that process, that sometimes incredibly trying process is well established, the acts of the world's tyrants, those currently in charge will no longer be of any consequence to us.

I feel it.

She recalled what she had felt before. There had been terror and desolation, but also…

Confidence and triumph, a sense of power undiminished.

– It cannot be stopped, the voice in her head said, she choired, spoke aloud. – It will take care of itself, like a dam breaking.

She blinked and shook her head in wonder and awe and joy-filled terror.

– My Goddess, it *is* happening!

Moonlight flowed through the windows, even though they were confident there was no moon tonight. There was still some remaining daylight outside, but not inside. The pale moon shone on everyone's skin.

She felt light, light as a feather, heavy as a rock. It did not matter. She realized she was standing, and then that her feet were no longer attached to the floor.

They pointed and stared at her, powerful emotions charging through them like slow lightning.

She rose into the air, and not because it happened to her without her consent, but because she wanted to do it, wanted to make it happen. Everyone had their attention locked on her. She watched herself through them, through their wide-open eyes, saw seething energy surround her body, her face lit up in an eerie dark shine.

– Genesis! Lisl cried, Lisl gasped.

The others repeated it, in unease and apprehension and awe. Lips formed the sounds, and feverish minds repeated them. And the name echoed through the hall forever.

The world changed around them, changed in waves. One wave brought one more astounding change. They were outside, in a garden where the grass and the leaves on the strange trees had turned red.

– Such is hyper-reality, Lori said softly, with a beyond powerful voice. –

Such is mankind unleashed.

She heard a bell ring, one, two, ten times.

Then she heard a heavy bell ring one single time, and it sounded like thunder, and the sound wasn't sound, but movement, as if the mind itself took one, two, ten steps from every single angle simultaneously and every single one made her end up on a different spot, all equally true.

Green grass grew on the moon, changing its surface dramatically. The snow on Titan melted during one single violent spring, where the ice broke on a thousand rivers.

The realities of the Crossroads shifted around her, painting and repainting themselves a thousand times each second, and she watched it happen in a slow squeal of delight.

London changed under the onslaught of her pen.

Lori drew the world.

Chapter Fourteen

Twilight descended on London. It started as a chipping of the walls. What seemed slow and hardly noticeable at first became tangible, visible, a living, observable process.

For most of her life she had lived ignorant of what was hiding in the shadows and within her own deep self, but now she was awake beyond awake. Her eyes had opened and stayed open. Just a few months ago, she had been unaware. Now, awareness spiked and burned every single piece of her body, her awakened mind.

It was impossible to say what had set it off, if anything. Perhaps she would never know.

The newcomers settled in well, and continued to do so. It wasn't just those first few days of hospitality, but something far more and lasting. That, too, was easy to discern. Those who had stayed a while had become even more open and hospitable. They had looked at the world with curious eyes for quite some time. Now, those eyes had widened even more.

She roamed the streets in an endless fast and slow walk. There was no distinction between those, not to her, not anymore. She heard her name be whispered and spoken aloud in reverence and fear. They started spreading out in the neighborhood, moving into and not leaving other empty buildings. Some of them also visited those ordinary apartments where people lived.

Caitlin and Andrea knocked on a newly painted door. The paint was dry. They didn't get anything on their knuckles. The hall had also been renovated lately.

Sounds reached them from the inside. Steps turned louder. A hand grabbed the handle. The door opened.

A frown instantly appeared on the woman's brow when she realized who they were and where they came from.

– Hi, Caitlin greeted her brightly, – we're your neighbors, and we realized that we've been terribly amiss in our neighborly duties…

The frown on the woman's forehead grew deep and distinct.

In the brightest sunlight Lori walked in moonlight. The day remained only a pale reflection of what she saw through her expanded senses. The rich texture surrounded her, practically embraced her, as she embraced it, a living thing breathing within. The air reaching her lungs was merely one thing among many giving her life.

She saw all her brethren. It needed no effort on her part, only a slight shift of focus.

Caitlin and Andrea stepped across the neighbor's threshold, imposing on her hospitality. Slater and Justin entered another apartment, where a man and a woman looked bewildered at each other. Genesis watched it all unfold, come to life.

– Look at us, Lisl said with terror-mixed joy, – we used to be the neighborhood's badly concealed secret, but not anymore.

Smiles played on both pair of lips, on all lips in the daring and happy campers moving through the neighborhood with impunity.

– This is such a great day, Andrea said to the woman in front of her. – Isn't it a great day?

– I guess, the woman mumbled.

– What's your name, sweetie? Caitlin asked kindly.

They had seen the name on the door, but forgotten it in a flash.

– Karen, the woman mumbled.

– Greetings, Karen, Caitlin said and grabbed her hands. – It's so great to meet you.

– Erin, another woman replied.

– Peter, a man mumbled shyly.

– You're a Peter, huh? Cathy said with huge, opaque eyes. – I love that, just love that!

It happened all over the square, all day. Everyone had a visit or two or three from the nice men and women from the squatted church. One man slammed the door in their face. Violet and Zachary rang the bell again, to no avail.

– You're a *disgrace!* A woman shouted from the opposite side of the hall. – Cut your hair and get a job like *decent* people. Do you know that your very *presence* here lowers the real estate value?

Zachary started laughing spontaneously. It was loud and wild. The woman turned absolutely frantic with embarrassment and rage.

– Do you know you sound absolutely ridiculous when you spout mainstream propaganda like that?

He told her gently.

She didn't appreciate his wit. She turned around abruptly and slammed the door even harder than the other guy.

Lori and Lisl stood in the middle of the street, bathing in the bright, hot sunshine. They held hands, and shadows grew vast and powerful around them.

– Layers of complexity surround us, Lisl said, the excitement notable in her voice, visible in her constantly changing expression. – The more we discover, the more veiled secrets we brush aside.

Their eyes opened and met.

– You *are* my daughter, Lori said softly. – You, I will never lose.

She stared into the young one's deep pools. She saw acceptance there, and so much more.

Emily walked around snapping photos like crazy. She had a huge, excited smile painted on her face.

Twilight, darkness, when it came this day brought even more awareness and power. Lori felt it, and knew the others felt it as well. The next day and next night did as well, and a variety and quality of life they had only dreamed of earlier in their existence.

She stopped dyeing her hair. It returned slowly to its natural color. The artificial faded and the natural reappeared, practically doing so as she watched.

Lisl combed it. Lori sat on a stool in front of the mirror with her eyes half closed and enjoyed the gentle sensation, both the purely physical and the joy it gave her.

The sounds from both within and without the church reached her ears. Her attention spread, her five «ordinary» senses flowing like water, whatever others there were dancing and jumping in sizzling air.

– Hey, didn't you use to have some gray hairs? I can't find any.

– But all adults have some gray hairs, Lori frowned.

– You haven't. I've looked and looked, and haven't found any.

A smile grew slowly on Lori's face, as insight softly hit her.

– I used to have, she mused, – more and more every time I checked.

Lisl studied her.

– It's difficult to be certain, but I would say you even look younger.

Lori studied herself in the mirror.

– I guess it is hard to tell. If there is a change, it's slow, gradual, difficult to notice from day to day, but I think you're right.

– It is as if your ageing process is…

– … reversing, they choired.

The young girl's face practically burst with excitement, yet another layer of exhilaration and also depth.

– It is yet another aspect of the onset of your power, she cried. – I'm certain of it!

Then it was as if she… caught herself. She lowered her eyes and bowed her head.

– Genesis is powerful beyond words, she declared. – I suspect she has yet to show her full potential. There may not be limits to her might.

Lori grabbed her jaw and pushed her head back up.

– Genesis is not a Goddess, she said, striving to keep her voice gentle, – and she would not appreciate being seen as one, as something to be worshiped.

The girl's eyes cleared. She nodded, and nodded again.

They joined with the others around the long and big table. It had become an eager, dynamic process making the catching in Lori's throat grow further. She sat down. Everyone had their eyes on her. She accepted it. They looked at her with awe and respect. She accepted it.

– Many things are wrong with modern human society, she said softly, – but what almost all of it boils down to is this: People are not independent. They do not think for themselves and lack even the most basic awareness of the world and humanity, what we are, what we truly are, beneath the bluster and pretense and hypocrisy and propaganda. A society with a justified respect for itself and its work, wouldn't merely accept true variety, independence and critical thought, but *encourage* it. We're going to give everyone that, give them basic self-awareness and true freedom… whether they want to or not…

Smiles and excitement lit up their faces. They were with her. They were enthusiastically with her.

– We've made a good start, Violet said, – but even though it feels like we've been at it forever, there's still so far to go, so many… delights ahead of us.

Her enthusiasm was palatable, pervasive beyond words. Joy shook Lori like a leaf.

They had breakfast, they ate, they fed, and every piece of food felt marvelous, both on their tongue and as it spread through their body.

– Food… tastes so much better, Cathy marveled. – It is as if I'm able to perceive every single flavor as it touches my tongue. At least, that's how it feels like.

Many of those present nodded, acknowledging the truth of her words.

– I also feel strongly that this is just the modest beginning, that we have merely scratched the surface of what's to come.

Everyone nodded again, nodded in anxious anticipation.

They sat there, finishing the meal, enjoying even that, enjoying each other's company, every smile and every lucid expression in everyone's eyes.

Lori heard the sound of an engine growing louder. It interfered slowly on her peace. She saw the police van almost as clearly as the anxiety in everyone's eyes. They rose and headed for the entrance.

– There's no immediate danger, Genesis soothed them.

– If there was, it wouldn't be just one car, Slater said. – They would have come at us with howling sirens and an army of burned wheels.

There was remarkably little fear, in a situation where at least the anxiety once would have been abundant.

He and Violet went outside to greet the four constables, ready before the van had pulled to a stop.

– Greetings, Violet said brightly, her big eyes even bigger than usual.

The two men and two women climbing out of the van glanced uncertain at each other.

– We've received complains about you people, one of the women said curtly, cutting to the chase, dispensing any doubt concerning the sinister reason for the visit.

– I can't imagine why, Violet said just as brightly. – If you research the matter, and I strongly encourage you to do so, you will find that we have an excellent relationship with most of our neighbors. It can't possibly come as a surprise to you that we don't have an excellent relationship with *all* our neighbors. Who has?

The four coppers frowned and kept glancing uncertain at each other.

– Look at them, Caitlin said triumphant to the rest gathered inside the church. – They usually come here with total control of the situation, or the very least the illusion of it, but now they're struggling, truly struggling to fathom what's happening. They know something has changed, but the brutes don't have the imagination necessary to grasp its significance.

The four made the usual round in the neighborhood, gathering statements, but success kept eluding them. They did get the desired complaints against the squatters, but also lots of people contradicting that.

– I admit I was skeptical towards those youngsters, a woman said, – but after having actually talked to them, I must admit I was doing them a grave injustice. I was misjudging them completely, and feel very bad about it.

She pondered the matter a bit further, before adding, looking slightly caustic at the constables:

– I would be willing to repeat that in a court of law, if necessary…

The four coppers, as always out to make mischief, had to leave practically empty-handed. They took the statements of those complaining, and only them, but didn't look happy.

Genesis and a few of her guard walked through the streets afterwards, and it felt as if they owned them. They didn't hide anymore. It was a visible, tangible transformation. The way they saw themselves and the world had changed dramatically. Aware eyes and minds cast their attention in all directions with impunity.

– This is… Adriana mused. – This is…

Aware eyes brightened in excitement and enthusiasm.

– We were always so quiet in public, she finally said, – in the hope that we wouldn't be noticed. We still don't take the Tube, but now it's a preference, not something we're compelled and even forced to do.

They walked east on Bayswater Road. It felt like dawn, even if the sun danced high on the sky.

But it was dancing, dancing like the moon, and Lori, and also others present in her surroundings noticed and felt it, felt the strange quality present in Genesis's path.

Other things happened as well, adding to the sideshow of their walk. Crows had started following them almost from the start, squeaking and flapping their wings. They sat on branches on both sides of the road, and flew back and forth in the air.

– I recall drawing this, she mused. – I could never imagine it would become real.

– Your imagination is the limit, Lisl said, over the top excited.

Lori frowned at that statement, even as the excitement inevitably affected her.

They reached Oxford Street. She half expected the crows (and the ravens) to keep following them, but they didn't. They stayed behind on the many branches at Marble Arch, covering the arch itself, the sound of their screech reaching far and following the human beings as they walked the busy shopping street.

Everyone, even the most mundane inclined woman or man noticed something, an unrest, a shaking at the base of their being.

A few of the birds stayed with them, on the roofs and ledges of the city, their distant, occasional screeches more than loud enough for all people to notice.

– It's funny, Zachary said. – We do stand out from the crowd, but not enough to justify all the staring…

He was grinning, not really bothered with the attention at all.

– It is funny, Violet mused. – I must have walked through these street a thousand times, and they didn't look even remotely like this.

Lori glanced around.

– They don't look that much different… do they? She said hesitant.

– They most certainly don't! Lisl snorted. – It's the same quaint stores, the same sickening «high street» consumer bullshit.

Lori observed while people walked in and out of those stores, as they walked inside and outside. Inside, outside, it didn't matter, they were just as distinct to her. They were all being born and reborn in her mind every single moment.

– We are different, she stated firmly. – The streets and its people aren't, not really, not yet.

It pleased her when they all were nodding vigorously, she couldn't deny that.

She spotted a man wearing an old, worn hat by the fruit stall close to Bond Street.

– He does indeed stick out, doesn't he? Violet nodded affirmatively. – But I guess people like him aren't really new here. We just didn't notice them before.

– Perhaps we didn't even notice the crows, the ravens and everything else we should have noticed? Zachary mused. – If we are honest with ourselves we hardly noticed anything beyond the ordinary.

– I know I didn't, Violet bristled. – I also know that the fact that we can now easily admit that to ourselves speaks in our favor.

The words and emotions coming from those close to her, the members of her tribe mingled and joined in Lori's constantly boiling mind. It made her smile some more, even as she continued examining the distant outer parts of her surroundings.

Her circle kept spreading, very much like rings in the water. She felt it and kept feeling it as it happened.

She noticed how they approached the crossroads of Oxford Circus before she was consciously aware of it. People flowed north and south, west and east in a constant, uneven flow. She noticed that she noticed, as an afterthought. It was… unsettling, and turning even more so for each new step forward. The smile stayed in place.

They approached the intersection where Oxford Street changed into New Oxford Street and Tottenham Court Road headed north and Charing Cross Road headed south. She looked at Center Point. The tall, newly renovated building loomed in the landscape… and in one blink it had changed into a ruin where most of the upper floors were gone and what remained was hardly more than a skeleton of the once mighty construction. She rubbed her forehead. The new Tottenham Court Road Link Station appeared to her right. It was covered in green, broken by tall trees. One more blink, two more blinks and nothing had changed.

Then it slowly, very slowly returned to what everyone else was seeing.

It lingered in her vision this time. She watched cracks appear on various spots of the walls. Small areas of moss spread and became imposing growth. It was as if years passed in seconds.

She Shared without trying, and the others looked at her, overwhelmed by the tiny snippets of extended reality her presence provided.

Others passing her on the streets also caught some of it, and they grew visibly distressed and weary.

They walked south, on Charing Cross Road.

– It speaks to me. Every inch of it speaks to me and tells me stories.

– I know, Lisl said, looking at her eagerly, anxiously, – but what is it saying?

Lori frowned, pondered and frowned again.

– Hello… welcome… beware… rejoice…

And a thousand things besides.

– I don't see the future, she stated slowly, – but probabilities. Some of them become certainties, while others remain a mud of constantly conflicting realities, a constantly changing mosaic.

And a thousand things besides.

They passed the old bookstore, the only place still selling new books in the once so traditional bookstore street.

Time unfolded before her eyes.

They passed Palace Theater, in the junction between Charing Cross Road and Shaftesbury Avenue, the traditional pub close by. This intersection brought more activity, more whirling images and sensations. A woman hesitated a bit, missing the green light, and had to wait in order to cross the street. Lori saw her reach the light and cross the street far sooner, bringing about a slew of other changes.

Lori suddenly got busy and moved in a whirl motion, catching up with the woman.

– Call your son, she insisted. – Do it right now.

She saw him leave the small suburb house and cross the street outside, and be run over by a car slinging from side to side on the road.

The woman looked at her as if she was insane, of course, but not for long. Soon, as she became immersed in Lori's sphere, her eyes widened and turned wet with wonder and emotion. She made the call.

Her son's departure from the house was delayed, and the car raced past the house well before the boy walked outside.

– Thank you, the woman said stunned and grateful, awareness of the moment filling her to the brim, – thank you so much.

Later that day, or the next or the next, or a few minutes from then, Lori stood before the Charing Cross Station, the concrete building to the south and east. It looked fine and restored and new one moment. The next its walls were covered with cracks and age.

– It is as if I'm experiencing a lifetime's worth of memories every day or every hour even.

She shook her head in frustration.

– And it still isn't enough.

She walked up and down the street, picking up all the stories she could. She walked up and down the street, and then she did it again, and again and again.

They, she and her siblings in spirit sat inside, in a forlorn, inexpensive coffee bar somewhere, with a large ceiling window bathing the room in its brilliance. A chill from the open door reached them on a warm summer day.

– This is the third long trip we've undertaken lately, right, or am I totally off? Slater mused and shook his head in wonder and bewilderment. – Sometimes I imagine we've done this far more times, often several times *a day*.

Lori nodded to herself. Violet was there, one moment, gone the next. Faces changed, but the Walk remained. One day became many.

– Yes, Lori said. – We've undertaken this trip repeatedly lately, basically walking the same route over and over again. It has become one, single uninterrupted walk.

– An ongoing dreamtime, Violet said excitedly, suddenly there again. – The Other World is so much closer these days and nights, isn't it?

A waken dream.

They walked through Covent Garden, heading east. They walked through Leicester Square, heading west, strolled on the wide sidewalk on Coventry Street towards Piccadilly Circus. They headed down Piccadilly without hurry, without a care in the world.

The Other World stayed close, right outside her reach, occasionally touching her sore fingertips, as she formed them like claws, and briefly extended their reach.

As they reached Green Park, the birds returned in force.

– It's like coming home, she said, a huge grin spreading on her face.

The familiar frown formed on her brow, but it never managed to properly manifest itself.

A dark cloud shadowed the sun. A deep chill passed slowly down her spine.

– Slo-wly, she said.

She looked at the others, even as she continued to look straight ahead.

– They speak, she said slowly. – They speak to me.

– They speak to you? Lisl said. – What are they saying?

Lori shook her head, not exactly in frustration, but close.

– I can't tell. One moment it feels like I can understand them. The next I can't.

Speak to me, gibberish…

– Speak to me gibberish, she mumbled, – speak nothing at all, and reveal to me the language of the world.

A door slammed open. The many black birds made forms, human forms, made Dark Men staring at her. The image shifted and shifted again, until it settled in a new form, a symbol.

The symbol of the raven.

A form flowed forward, like a wave, the flock of dark birds, flapping their wings. Cracks grew on the many walls of man. One, two, three ravens flapped their wings, and whipped up a storm.

– With one decisive act I destroy myself, liberate myself. I make all words dead and void.

She stepped close to the man of words, into his gap, and the dark light turned blinding bright and burned away everything she had been.

She staggered and Lisl and Violet had to support her.

– The man of words, the Wicked Poet speaks to me, she said, – saying nothing at all.

– He will capture you and snare you in his spell? Lisl said distraught. – Is that it?

Lori shook her head in frustration. The moment was lost, and she could see no more. She practically turned blind in the bright sunshine.

Green Park grew to include the city and swallowed them whole. Grass grew on the pavement. Plants covered the concrete walls. London was devoured in growth and decay.

She sat on a bench. They were drying her forehead with paper towels. She kept sweating and gasping, as the visions progressed.

They wet her forehead with paper towels dipped in water. It hardly affected her, one way or another.

A man died in a hail of bullets. He fell on a cold floor and stared at the ceiling with cold, frozen eyes. They drove him to the hospital, calling his death. He sat up on the slab and everyone stared at him in shock and terror.

A woman stared at herself in a mirror, not quite seeing herself, but a distorted, strangely compelling version of her face. She kept staring at it for hours in the eternity of the few seconds it revealed itself to her. Even as it was fading, it was changing further from the original.

It was gone, but still there.

The sky changed above them. On one day, one walk it had been cloudy, threatening rain. Now, it was bright sunshine. The clouds raced across the sky.

She… exhaled. The loud noise and stench of the modern city imposed itself on them once again, and everything she had sensed and experienced seemed like nothing, like a mirage, a pipe dream.

Her pen kept moving across the paper, drawing the dead man, the distorted face, another man standing in a dark room surrounded by fire.

Her hand finally stayed itself. She returned to a calmer state, and sat there breathing evenly.

– I don't really need the pen and paper anymore, she mused, – but it still helps me, helps me *deal.*

– And it helps us, Arthur said softly, – helps us see what you see.

Violet looked stricken at the drawings.

– I've seen this, Violet said stricken, – seen it all before.

– It transcends time and space, Lisl stated. – Of course, you have!

They returned home and were welcomed back by those staying behind that particular day. The dreamtime-walk through London had become a daily occurrence, an important, even crucial ritual in their lives.

They walked through Green Park, crossing into Hyde Park, crossing Bayswater Road, and returned to the derelict church in the quiet street where only ravens, crows and other birds broke the silence.

– It feels good to be home, Lisl nodded. – It feels good to walk the path, the labyrinth.

– It feels great beyond imagining. Violet stated low-keyed, practically glowing with excitement.

The building, the very walls seemed to welcome them, more so every time they returned.

Lori saw it all in moonlight again, saw the tall bonfire and its flames reach high enough to touch the ceiling.

– We need to use the space better, she heard herself say.

– We could use the available space by the windows, I guess, Slater mused. We haven't done so before because there's a chilly draft when the summer ends, but we could use tents, I guess.

All the pieces in the puzzle were slowly put in the right place. She nodded in acknowledgement and granted him her best smile.

– An excellent idea!

She ignored his penetrating gaze.

Climbing the tower did not represent any effort to her anymore. It felt more like she was actually floating on an upward draft than actually climbing. She stood there, not that long later, looking through the large opening to the east.

Lisl followed her up, using far more time and effort in order to accomplish it. She joined her by the large opening, looking at the vast city stretched out to the east.

Events kept repeating themselves in her mind, and she couldn't quite connect to the present.

– Tourists may see it from above, from hotel rooms and planes, Lori mused. – Most Londoners don't. I've seen it like this for a very long time, even before I was aware I was doing it.

Lisl looked at her with the same nosedive admiration that had been her habit lately. Lori turned and touched the girl's cheeks. Lisl understood, to a point the comforting touch. She grabbed the hand and wet it with kisses.

– It can't be easy having that stuff in your head all the time, she said abruptly. – We, the rest of us can only follow you on part of your path.

– There are two others walking it with me, Lori said, with the usual distant look in her eyes. – I can see one of them, Janice very clearly in my mind. She's a foreigner and hasn't arrived in London yet. I can sense her nowhere, except in my visions.

She frowned, and that tiny movement alone brought more awareness, more information to her conscious mind.

– The other is equally imposing, but I can't make out her features. I know she's a woman, but her face is blurry and her nature equally so. Both of them make me shiver at night, in my sleep, and now, in bright daylight.

– I would wager that you make them shiver as well, Genesis, Lisl declared, very loyal and passionate.

Lori smiled and touched the other's face again. A shadow passed over both faces. Lori's features changed again, her eyes turning bigger again, making the girl shiver.

– I want you to submit to me, to focus on nothing but that and on probing the city, scanning it, scouring it from one end to another and back again. Can you do that, sweetie?

– I can, Genesis, Lisl assured her. – I'm both able and willing to follow your lead.

She reached out her hands. Lori grabbed them and squeezed. Lisl gasped in pain and devotion.

Their contact was even more intimate and powerful than before, and this time they could savor the process, notice its step by step progress.

– The dead man not dead died, they choired, – and dreamt his resurrection dreams.

They were only two, and it was less volatile. At least they imagined it was, even as their combined powers pulled them in all directions simultaneously.

Then, with a slight focus of will, they were able to direct their efforts. They followed their path, their physical walk up Bayswater Road, except that this time they viewed it from the air. The sound of flapping wings echoed in their ears. Loud screeches erupted from their mouths, their gaps. The pleasant shock they felt erupted from their minds and created ripples in the steaming water the air had become, spreading, spreading across the pond and from one pond to another, until it reached the sea, and spread across the world.

Even beyond it, into the dark, dark void.

They floated through the ether, up the long road east towards the Marble Arch monument. They saw themselves down there, from behind, from above, screeching, and crying messages to themselves they knew they didn't understand.

Lori saw her face up close, heard herself listen to the cry of the raven. Something… happened. It was almost as if she walked the path a second time, on the same day, the same hour and the same minute, and abject clarity filled her mind, her very consciousness.

A door slammed shut. It sounded that way at least, and the same sense of finality accompanied the sound. They no longer looked east, but into the same room where Toni had been standing when she…

– Break contact, Lori hissed. – Break…

Separating the two hands and interconnecting minds seemed hard at first. Then, one moment or an eternity later it seemed fairly easy. The sinister sight of the dark, empty room blinked out, and they could once again look east, but only with their eyes.

– Everything bad comes from the east? Lisl wondered.

– Several very bad things might and probably will! The west is our stronghold, our fairly safe territory. The east is where our enemies thrive.

They climbed back down. It was not as easy as the going up had been. She felt as if there were actually more hurdles in her path, like she bumped into stuff all the way down.

There was nothing there but air, but the air was full of bumps and hard edges. She shivered down her spine again, not able to tell why.

They welcomed her, welcomed both of them with a thousand glances and kind eyes. She felt it stronger than ever. Lisl looked at everybody with the same excited smile, and they returned it. Violet's evident curiosity was accompanied with conviction. Practically everyone suspected that something had happened, but she knew.

Lori stopped and turned and suddenly had everyone in front of her. All voices faded to silence. She didn't have to tell them to be quiet or anything. They accomplished that on their own. She spoke without raising her voice.

– I thought I was crazy, that I was downright insane, at least briefly, at some point during this eventful year, but I no longer do. It has gone far beyond that, now, far beyond that possibility. We've seen tangible, empirical evidence beyond evidence that all of this is real. Even if we still don't know exactly what's coming, we know that it is. I guess the most «passionate» professed rationalist and «skeptic» would still be in denial, would still deny the blatant reality we have witnessed, but we, being far more sensible than such a beast don't have that problem…

They granted her their laughter and she appreciated it.

She rose into the air, to the height of her kneecaps and stayed there. It was an easy, grateful task, hardly an effort. But that minor use of her power, the tiny show of force was sufficient to bring more visions, more casual revelations.

– We've taken the first steps on the blurry path revealed to us, the one we will stay on for the rest of our lives and beyond. It's not our task to be cautious here, but to be bold and brave, both because we must and because we should. We will keep claiming true freedom, both for ourselves and everyone else, no matter what they throw at us. Once a witch has entered a path in the invisible labyrinth she or he must follow it to the end and so must the witch's companions. Other autonomous groups and individuals will join in, with us or independent of us. Events, both positive and negative will keep piling up. We're only a small part of that, like everybody else. The signs are clear and they have their undeniable mirror image in the «real world», in physical reality. A true new age, partly great, partly sinister beyond words is coming upon mankind, whether mankind wants to or not.

The words flowed freely and she had to shake her head in amazement, and they nodded and understood, and the catching in her throat grew hard and painful and right.

The buzz rose from her, from them, to her, to them, to the streets outside and beyond. They spread out in bright day, and even more in the darkest night.

They climbed the fence long after closing hours and entered Hyde Park. Lori noticed the qualitative difference the moment she stepped across the fence, crossing its borders. She experienced some kind of double vision, both normal, what others saw and what occasionally showed her something distinctively different.

She saw a bush on her right. In one way, there was only the bush there. In another a man stood there, a man seemingly burning, a seemingly burning man not harmed by the flames.

– There is something there, isn't it? Violet stated.

Lori nodded, clearly distracted.

– I don't think he's actually there, but I do see him and sense and feel him from toenail to hair. I can't stop doing it.

They moved further into the park. The path turned narrow in front of them, as if they were moving through an enclosed tunnel. Lori kept seeing slow flashes of events and people, dark shapes just standing there, watching, or moving way too fast to catch with the naked eye.

Her naked eye attempted to match their speed, but didn't quite make it, except in glimpses and flashes. She saw one world with her two eyes, one distinctly different with that glowing on her forehead.

Fear shook some of those following her. She looked at them, looked through them, knowing them fully in one single glance.

Her Third Eye, visible to everyone saw so much more than her other two. She experienced little or no confusion. There had been some initial discomfort, but that faded quickly, as her newfound reality presented and represented itself. She was drawing in the air in front of her, far better than with any physical pen. The many-dimensional «imagery» looked so much more real than what her two eyes saw.

Arthur stepped up by her side, grabbing her hand, her left hand, feeling its power, staring stubbornly at her stark visage. He kissed the hand, mouthing words she couldn't hear.

Her third eye had appeared the first time the other day, while she stood in front of the mirror. It had caused her neither shock nor surprise. There had been no forewarning, nothing her drawings or visions had revealed to her. They had revealed thousands of small and big things, but not that.

She re-experienced it, as if it was in truth happening right now. The air became her mirror, her scroll.

The garden, the wild garden kept revealing itself to her.

– The park is so different at night, isn't it? Adriana breathed.

– So different! Lori nodded.

They walked to The Long Water. It seethed and burned in the silver light of the full moon. The birds were out in force tonight as well, singing their loud and piercing wail. It was a silent night, but beyond the silence she heard sounds, lots of distinct sounds from every direction. She saw and heard a stone hit the water, but not the person or entity throwing it. There was motion, blurry images wherever she turned her attention. Buildings looked like shapes, not buildings. They towered above those walking the night like giants. The water in the fountain they had passed long ago turned red, resembling thick, thick blood. It was not bluish, lacking color, as one would expect in moonlight, but full, deep red. Every other color looked pale, but not the red.

The already powerful impression added to itself in her mind, becoming just as difficult to handle as all the others surrounding her.

The shore of the Long Water and eventually the Serpentine on their right twinkled less than the singing grass on their left. The others noticed invariably how the moonlight walk shook and kept shaking her. They made an effort at comforting her in a thousand small and big ways. It worked. Their touch and smiles and gentle heat did comfort her.

Her two physical eyes told her that she and her companions walked along a quiet water, in a green area constructed by human beings, but her more powerful senses conveyed a different story.

They passed through a dark tunnel. When she cast her third eye ahead, she did spot its end, but even though it didn't seem that far off, the exit didn't appear to be any closer a few minutes later, not even close to ten minutes later.

They walked through a dark tunnel, and while doing so, they were surrounded by a world even more different, even more a step away from the normality they had taken for granted not that long ago. The walls were not walls, but flashes of another reality, or at the very least a vastly different part of this one. Everyone accompanying Lori saw, or at least glimpsed the ghostly images, the powerful sensations imposing on them all.

There was daylight outside those transparent walls, but not one very bright. The short grass on the lawn had grown long. The place looked more like a wilderness than a park. All the buildings had become ruins. There was hardly anything about it resembling a park.

Glimpses, only glimpses burned into their mind and stayed there.

The tunnel faded away. They re-entered the night, and the park. Lori glanced left and saw the buildings along Bayswater Road. They could hardly be said to be even ruins. Thick growth covered what was left of them. One blink and the stark imagery faded away.

She experienced the park during the day, when people filled the place. She didn't need any tunnel in order to see better. The color of the moon filled the empty landscape. Genesis and her tribe walked through a place filled with ghosts. Distant screams reached her across the water

– I imagined myself to become something else, and I did, she marveled. – I never imagined this!

– I guess no one ever does, Arthur said, – never quite knows what will happen once you let go of your old and stale existence and embrace the change.

They reached a spot, an invisible line on the ground. The others made a circle and she stepped into it, placing herself at its center. She sat down, crossing her legs in front of her. They lay down on their backs, stretching out on the dry grass, in the warm, warm night.

– This came to me in a dream, she said, – in countless dreams overlapping each other, forming one or two or five cohesive narratives. We come here, where we are at risk, away from our cozy, somewhat safe haven.

Her words imagined became real to them.

– Look at the sky, she bid them.

They did and looked into, fell into the vast space above and below.

– Close your eyes.

Everything turned black.

– Listen to my voice. Do what it tells you to do. This is a relaxation exercise. You will feel wonderfully relaxed and comfortable.

It… swelled in their mind, filling it to the brim, expanding it, expanding them.

– Focus on your left foot. Let all your thoughts center on it. Feel it turn heavy. Let it fall.

The foot did turn heavy and felt like it fell and kept falling for an eternity.

– Focus on your left thigh - repeat!

She moved all over their body with words and passion, focusing, making them focus on each limb. The entire left side turned heavy and light, then the head and right side, and the middle, and the entire body.

They lay still, feeling like they were floating in a dry, warm darkness without pressure or gravity.

– Relax, Lori whispered. – Relax… You're nothing but a leaf floating pleasantly in the wind, slowly descending into the vast, deep darkness below.

They did. A slight case of anxiety touched them, as they felt her words becoming true. But then the wonderful sense of relaxation imposed itself on them. They became that leaf and also the very darkness it descended.

– Picture yourself rising, walking on two feet on a road through that great darkness, walking down a slope, to the deep forest below. There's a trail, there are stairs. You walk alone, even though you feel the others close by, feel their powerful presence in your ever-expanding mind.

She appeared in front of Lisl, by her side, by both her sides.

Greetings, little one!

Lisl looked at a Lori she had never seen before, one far more imposing than even the demigoddess she had learned to know.

I can't travel with you. There must be a Guide. Someone must stay behind, as a precaution. So I must latch onto you, travel with you wherever you travel.

Lori the spirit reached out a hand, offering it to her. Lisl hesitated only briefly before reaching out and grabbing it. Her entire body started tingling simultaneously. Lisl, Lisl, the wandering spirit gasped. The gasp echoed in the space where she found herself.

– Enter the forest.

They did. They flowed into it, instead of walking, even as they felt the pressure on their soles. Everyone waited anxiously for further instructions, but none was forthcoming.

Lisl reached a clearing with a large tree. She frowned. There was something there, something…

She looked past the tree, beyond it, to what was hidden to her eyes, or would have been hidden to her eyes if she had been corporal, had been flesh. She spotted a door.

What… what should I *do?*

Walk through the door, of course.

– We will Travel, Lori told them, – Travel through infinity times eternity squared, in space/time and its vast beyond. We will meet on the mountain, in a room without walls. The Universe has no boundaries. It's ours to explore and learn from, but never to conquer.

The door opened by itself. They walked to the opening… and stepped through.

Lisl became Lori, becoming Lisl. Lori looked at her hands, her glowing hands. Gossamer threads flowed from her fingers as they moved, flowed from her hair, as it danced around her body.

She/they still walked through the forest, or one forest. There was an opening ahead, and she/they appeared on a vast field, one that didn't seem to have any end.

The full moon brightened the entire sky, the very existence itself. Clouds stark black and white burned and danced, shifting in an infinite pattern, one lasting forever.

A bench and a table appeared in front of her. On a table rested a book, an open book. She read it like that, and it flooded her mind, her fertile mind.

She spotted words and drawings. Both the drawings and words let go of the paper, and floated/rose into the air, becoming tangible, becoming real, speaking to her, her ears, to all her senses, to her burning mind.

They heard the cry of the raven, all of them did. It echoed through the air. Reality split in a thousand pieces around them, and each piece split in a thousand other pieces. One drawing grew to full size, turning into a full-form painting. They faced themselves, faced a Lori and Lisl so very different from how they had previously perceived themselves. They hardly recognized the two forms, the beyond alluring creatures, the mirror images facing them, grinning at them with snarls echoing a million times in their ears and minds and wandering spirits.

The full moon blinded them, soaking the landscape in white, in a whiteout impossible to imagine.

Then, looking down a little, to the left, they spotted a glowing star. They reached out a hand and grabbed it, and suddenly they were floating through Space, and stars were mere grains of dust flowing through their fingers.

They moved. Their feet touched the ground. The ground felt just as solid as it usually did. They were light on their feet, as they walked down a street, one where people faded constantly in and out of their attention.

One second… one second was an eternity.

They moved through a world beyond where being immersed felt easy, like a second skin, one filled with impressions, where each moment brought yet another distraction. The low music seemed to be coming from everywhere simultaneously. One song became many, a choir of multitudes.

A flow reached them from the very air surrounding them.

They caught themselves wondering if this was indeed air… or something completely different. One breath… one breath energized them beyond reason.

One blink and they were somewhere else.

The man with the dull eyes and big belly, the pregnant man, pregnant with dullness, with a misery deeper than words presented himself to them from the center of the town square. They shuddered in their non-existing bones.

One blink and they were somewhere else.

The man with the guitar and burning eyes played for them at the country fair and evoked fear and joy, and a thousand nuances of emotion. Each chord, each new touch of the strings brought yet another emotional response. They both listened and played, played their own strings, played themselves, their skin and bones and flesh and blood.

The other people at the fair heard him, too. Lori watched them, immersing herself in them, in everything.

– BIG! She breathed. – It's all so big!

There were a million tongues reaching their ears they didn't understand, but a billion they easily comprehended. They were pulled away, in a thousand different directions.

They moved, moved through air and across the land revealed to them.

A shape formed out of nothing, not from air, not from soil, but the very ether surrounding them. Lori recognized Jeff long before he quickly faded away, before she could cry out to him or reach for him.

The mountain drew them, as they drew the mountain. They landed there, reaching its peak after having walked for ages, sweating, sweating, sweating in the unrelenting sun, the pleasant, cool moonlight. There was a structure of sorts in front of them, only a few steps away. They didn't walk there, or even flowed there, but appeared… inside. The room… the non-existing room embraced them. They gathered in a room that wasn't there. Another group, several other groups manifested within simultaneously.

They sat down, joining a circle that was already there, even as they sat down first, even as they sat down last.

Lori faced a man at the opposite side of the circle, met his eyes. One casual glance told her everything about him, about everything. A prevailing haze drifted through the room, all its spots and angles, angles, angles. There were no details here, nothing to focus on, except faces and eyes and hands and feet gathered in the circle. She shook her head and kept shaking it. She sat still, observing, participating, drawn with ever stronger pulls away from her flesh and bones form sitting on its ass in Hyde Park, London, the pull threatening to break contact with it, break contact with it forever. She shifted in fear, torn between anxiety and joy.

You are the Guide, she told herself. You are the Guide, guide, guide…

– I work in an office with five thousand other people.

The man said with a sad voice.

– I came here by accident, a woman said puzzled. – I ended up in that old house so long ago, with all those beyond interesting people by random acts.

A series of random coincidences is the Universe, a voice spoke in Lori's mind, her expanded beyond measure mind.

– Ten, the man across the abyss said, – there are ten times ten of us. Sometimes there is less, sometimes more, as reality keeps shifting, as the people involved keeps shifting, but our number is ten times ten.

– The Hundred, Lori stated startled. – We are…

She lost the thread. It was impossible to hold onto it in a place where distraction was a constant, and only its intensity varied.

A ghostly, colorless flame burned in the shadowy room that was not a room. Lori blinked a million times.

And then… there was a distinct, qualitative change. Everything, everyone faded away around her. She gasped distraught, but still burning with hunger. And then…

In one breath that was the Universe a figure appeared right in front of her. The sight startled her, making her blink a million times more. She saw herself, or rather her Shadow, a representation of her eternal Self.

– You… are… me?

They choired.

It was impossible to mistake it(It) for something else, as a threat or a blessing. It was her, no more, no less, so much more.

She was fed an endless and infinite row of sensations, of cold information, of burning thoughts and secrets and truths, and everything below and above

the moon.
She watched and studied with endless curiosity the limited form she had been, what she could hardly recall. It was only a tiny piece of the vast entity she had become.
The voice of Lori from Hyde Park reached her as if through a thick mist.
– The time is up. Your guide is calling you home. Wake up from your slumber, your extreme awareness. Your time is up. Please return to me, to yourself.
She resisted, she did, for many agonizing eternities. Slowly, agonizingly slowly she was drawn to the distant voice. It felt like an endless journey to a distant surface she felt she would never reach.
Lori opened her eyes. All the impressions of her surroundings assaulted her pleasantly, as the memory of her experience rose up and filled her to the brim.
The rest opened their eyes and sat up around her. A deep, unmitigated smile filled their features.
Lisl stared at her, drowning in her beyond powerful presence.
– I feel so relaxed, Caitlin mused. – I feel like I've never felt more relaxed in my life, even though excitement keeps rising in me like a *storm*.
The storm… Lori looked up. It wasn't ending. What they had learned and experienced couldn't be undone, unlearned or returned to the box. Their minds, their very selves, kept working at a higher level of consciousness.
– It is all of us, Adriana said startled. – Not only…
It dawned on them all. Lori saw it, in every little glance and relaxed pose how they realized their own might, what they, in truth truly were.
They looked out at the Serpentine - so lifeless by day - in the shadows of night, so full of life.
– I *saw* you! Cathy said, – saw you stand, hover above the water, both you and not you.
– I opened my eyes for a moment and spotted you by the tree over there, Slater said. – You stood by a bonfire, one burning with light blue flames, looking just as solid, as real as you do now.
They all rose, more or less simultaneously, and made their way out of the park, taking their time, their dreamy eyes and relaxed pose not really leaving them, and if it did, for a moment or two, it returned fast, not really going away at all.
They kept speaking, kept sharing with excited chatter their individual experiences during their Journey, the excitement never quite fading from their eyes.
A loud explosion thundered through the air, rocking the ground, disrupting

their pleasant thoughts. It was far away, they knew it was, but it sounded close, sounded like it happened only a few steps away. Lori saw it, saw the thick, black smoke rise from the city south of the park in the first stronger light of summer dawn. The sound hit them hard, making their ears bleed and eyes flooding with tears. It shook them, shook them awake, wide awake, lulling them back to sleep.

They left the park, jumping across the old iron fence and crossed the street, hurrying back to their sanctuary, fearing no more sanctuary existed anywhere.

Chapter Fifteen

A man stalks through a dark, foggy alley at night. He's a Shadow, turning solid. The air and light twist and change around him, and it's hard to make out his features.

A cloaked, hooded female figure walks on a lonely highway during twilight. There is sunlight. Yet, there's no sun. She carries a walking stick, with a small skull on top. In her other hand she carries a sword, and blood flows from its blade. Her face is Shadow, and it's impossible to make out her features.

And there's Jenny, Jenny looking like a vagrant shouting and gesturing, as flames burn on every side of her, but there's no sound coming from her widely parted lips, her mouth resembling a snout or a gap.

Lori woke up, soaked in sweat.

– Little girl lost, come to me and be found, the Wicked Poet, the man with the enchanted voice said in her head, a remnant of her dream, the dream hardly fading with her awakening at all.

She shook her head in distress, blinking against the bright morning light in her eyes.

He was there. In her still prevalent dream he sat by the bar exactly like she remembered, once again right there in her line of sight.

This time he spoke to her, and she heard him, heard his mesmerizing words. They burrowed into her ears, her mind and froze her, froze her in place. Her eyes turned distant, empty and she joined her friends and daughter as his loyal slave.

She recalled the night before. They had finally been able to sleep, to slumber, in their excitement, in their shaken self, caused by both the Journey and what had slapped their face and made their skin burn not long afterwards.

Lori woke up (woke up again) to the rare sound of a computer laptop humming. She recognized the voice of a BBC (Biased Brainwashing Corporation) news presenter. Everyone around her was drawn to the kitchen, to the beyond dramatic images and sounds. She was drawn there with them.

They watched the screen, and wasn't exactly unaffected by what they saw and heard there.

There had been an explosion, a bomb. The entire New Scotland Yard headquarters had been reduced to ruins. Soldiers still carried body bags out of the ruins. Those gathered in the church listened to the voices and watched the footage with stark fascination.

– It happened while we were leaving the park last night, Cathy said. – I could feel it, practically *feel* it…

A big crowd of broadcasting crews stood posted outside the iron ring that had been raised around the ruin. They all looked alike and hardly deviated from each other and their «reporting» at all.

– Look at them! Arthur said with disgust in his voice. – The parrots of propaganda!

– They overrate this, of course, Lisl said passionately. – One bomb can hardly compete with the many thousands UK, US and NATO in unison agreement have dropped on foreign soil. A reckoning should hardly come as any surprise, and I don't think it does either.

Lori smiled. Her guess would be that the girl would hardly recognize herself and her views from only a month or so ago. She had been radicalized beyond words.

– Or this could be yet another false flag operation designed to help those in charge to tighten the noose domestically and ease the transition to even more oppressive laws and to an even more oppressive regime, Arthur shrugged.

– It could! Lisl agreed passionately. – There have certainly been enough of those as well.

Lori studied the others and she sensed how they basically agreed with the two. She nodded pleased to them, to herself.

– We were all taken in by the general deception, she stated, – but no longer!

The reality of the night kept imposing itself on the day, making that day shrink in importance. The ripples kept building, not fading, as the distant roar of the streets reached her ears.

The quakes erupted every time she took a step.

She clutched Lisl's hand, taking her in a soft lap. The girl shook like a leaf, again and again and again, and smiled, while drifting down the river, the endless Dark River.

The two of them joined a protest sit-down somewhere. They wore big scarves and caps covering most of their heads. They sat there, singing with everyone in the sit-down before the massive military presence.

Parliament Square, a place where protest was illegal was filled with protesters protesting the massive military presence.

The Prime Minister showed herself on the television, the public broadcasts, her face showing an ever-deeper shade of red.

– We will bomb, rest assured of that, the prime minister scowled, spitting saliva during her speech broadcast to the nation. – We will no longer stand for the cowardly terrorist attacks on our cities.

– Why the wig? Lisl asked curiously. – Why today?

Lori wore a big, blonde wig, very much concealing the growing jungle of dark hair below. She wore big, black glasses mirroring everyone looking at her, giving nothing but reflection in return.

– It just felt right, Lori shrugged. – Why not?

The two of them felt like an island in the vast sea of angry and happy voices forever buzzing in her temporal lobe. They lived in a tent in the park. Drumbeat surrounded her. Lisl wet her brow with a cloth, lessening her anxiety.

The government, «as a response to the terrorist threat» imposed new, strict laws of surveillance and control. Most people accepted that, like they accepted everything, but there was a considerable minority that didn't. Many of them were present here today.

Hyde Park was filled with tents and people for as far as the eye could see, and her eye could see farther than any other she knew of. The steady, unsteady beating of drums reached just as far.

She once again revisited her dream about an almost empty Hyde Park in moonlight. A slight shift of focus, and she was there.

One second, an eternity later she returned to the sit-down.

Soldiers dressed in heavy body armor formed thick lines at the edge of the massive crowd. The drums clearly affected the soldiers, unbalancing them. The marching soldiers became a common sight in London, but so did the massive number of protesters.

– NO MORE BOMBING, NO MORE WAR, NO MORE BOMBING, NO MORE WAR, echoed through protest sites and streets alike. – NO MORE SURVEILLANCE. NO MORE BIG BROTHER AND 1984

A folk-rock group played dark, haunting chords at the center between the tents. Other people joined in with both singing and playing, creating a synthesis echoing across the park and beyond.

– UK out of NATO, the protesters shouted. – Kick NATO out of THE WORLD. NO MORE PERPETUAL WAR

Lori and the others made soup and served everyone passing by. A few looked with suspicion at the content in the paper cups.

– It is a nasty looking soup, isn't it? Adriana said sweetly.

Some people appreciated her wit. Others… didn't.

The extended group from the old church sat down in a circle, taking a break, having a taste of their own brew, their Witch's Soup.

Lori sat there, humming and rocking with the others, feeling very much a part of them. A warm, warm feeling persisted within her.

– Listen to all the foreign tongues, she mused. – There are more of them lately, I suspect. People are coming here, drawn here by a notion they don't understand.

She heard the music, its chords and intricate pattern moving within her.

– I've always felt that London is… special, Arthur said eagerly. – I've never been able to put my finger on *why*, but that feeling has always been there.

– I never did, Lori said, – not until recently, until now, but now that feeling has become a conviction, become like a deluge.

She felt it, tasted it in the very air she breathed. Each breath had become a universe of thought and emotion.

Each breath of those around her became a library of impressions.

Then she sensed it. It assaulted her from nowhere, a massive chill from everywhere.

She recognized the tall and skinny middle-aged man standing only a few steps away, recognized William Synos from another life, from a lifetime ago.

She heard voices from a walkie-talkie. He held one in his left hand. Someone called him. He responded with a few words she couldn't hear. She studied him dispassionately, the panic threatening to overwhelm her only a distant, unimportant voice in her busy head.

The mist, growing from nowhere, thickened in the air.

The rate of her heartbeat picked up just a little, sufficient for her to notice. She studied Synos. She didn't need to look at him with her eyes in order to do that. He didn't notice. She knew he didn't, but the fluttering of wings, the anxiety at the back of the neck persisted.

He moved on, turned away and left, without ever taking a closer look at the woman with the blonde wig and heathen clothing.

Lori discovered startled that she was shaking, and couldn't stop it, not for minutes, only calming its display.

Lisl looked closer at her, puzzled and slightly alarmed, clearly aware of her turmoil. Lori took care of that with a light touch of her cheek.

She saw Synos, saw his back as he walked away and disappeared in the crowd. To her he remained. Her perception insisted that he stood right in front of her and that a light of recognition lit his eyes.

That mirage faded only slowly, very slowly from her vision.

The particular point on her forehead was itching. She rubbed it with her hand. It did her no good.

They revisited the hangout in Portobello Road. It was just as filled with people as the other occupied buildings. They were as usual received with full honors, with burning enthusiasm and open, happy smiles.

Hands clutched hands. Lori felt them. Everyone kept their eyes on her. Their support empowered her. She knew they could sense it, sense her. The energy she emitted was noticed by all. It had grown that powerful.

She and Lisl and the others returned to the old church in an upbeat mood.

Lori, and thereby the others were alert, on their guard, as they were greeted by those who had stayed behind during the day. They received a welcome making them feel like they had stayed away forever.

Lori removed the wig and the excessive clothing making her sweat hard in the hot summer, and she felt like she could breathe again for the first time that day.

Nothing much happened beyond that. There was no trap, no sinister people waiting for them in the corners and shadows of the church. The evening remained uneventful and pleasant, and inspiring beyond words.

They gathered around the long table, filled with energy, with fire.

– It feels so great and inspiring, Violet said between the mouthfuls of wine. – Every place we visit is packed with people, with aware and angry people. London is waking up and its people with it.

– They can't arrest the entire country! Lisl cried passionately. – The perpetual war *will* end!

Loud, empathic cries of agreement rose from the gathering.

Lori felt it like a living thing, practically saw its manifestation in the air before her, and the pleasant catching in her throat grew.

The evening ended. The night never did. When the sunlight brightened the shower room the next morning, it was still there as something she could touch and hold in every drop of water slipping through her fingers.

Lisl made Lori's dark, dark shadow hair, tying it into two thick braids, two dancing pigtails.

– I wish I had hair like yours, so thick and beautiful!

The woman rocked on a fragile chair to music only she could hear. The girl stood behind her, making the pigtails, humming a happy tune. Lori pictured one of the early drawings she had made of her. The girl resembled very much that image, now.

– An entire new *fashion* is emerging in the wake of the protests, Lisl said excitedly, – one reminiscent of the Sixties. It's truly a wonder to behold, isn't it?

– It is, Lori agreed.

– We won't be co-opted like they were, though, Lisl declared, – won't be fooled into joining the consumer society we *abhor*.

They found fabrics everywhere, in garbage cans, at markets and outlets, cheap outlets and re-arranged them to fit their random interest, their current heart's desire. *Now,* when Lori studied the strange woman in the mirror, she hardly recognized herself.

Lisl waved a piece of clothing she had just found in a garbage can in the air, doing so with a visible, contagious enthusiasm affecting everybody present.

Lori and Slater, standing at the other side of the street returned the wave.
– Look at her! He remarked. – It's hard to tell that she started out as an infiltrator.
Lori studied him, a little startled.
– You knew, too, huh? She said.
– She was good, but not that good. I saw her doubt, her increasing willingness to put her past behind her. At some point she crossed a threshold, and now, I bet she's hardly able to recall her old life as a government tool. You made quite an impression on her. You, more than anyone made her turn, irreversibly and completely. She will remain loyal to you, beyond death.
Lori felt the ambiguity, the double layer in his wording and voice.
He sounded different, crueler, more cynical, as if something previously unexposed had revealed itself.
– It's a sight of beauty.
She felt a little uneasy, but disregarded it with a shrug.
Lisl's open, childish smile affected her as well, and she loved that it did.
The girl charged them with her catch, her full basket. Others also approached.
– Good work! Lori declared. – Let's call it a day.
They had cleaned the place of all possible valuables, and headed home.
Their home… it appeared different, subtly changed every time they returned. There seemed to be ever more furniture and tents placed along the walls, around the large, open center space, and also other things removing it from what it had once been. All the physical changes were still minuscule compared to the inner transformation of those occupying the premises.
It was tangible, almost visible to her, as she studied them. They had become something completely different compared to what they had been when she had first encountered them, when she had been out of her mind, hardly present in herself at all.
– The Dark River is flowing, Lori mused. – I can feel it rise and flood all shores and fields.
She paused before speaking again.
– The new world is ascending, but the old won't let go quite yet.
– I imagine it will be quite persistent, Adriana said with a chill in her voice.
– I imagine so as well, Lori agreed.
Time flew like the wind, slowing down to a crawl. Lisl and others as nervous as her gathered at the center of the main floor. Their peers looked good humored at them.
– Tomorrow is the big day, huh? Lisl said, both excited and apprehensive.
– Tomorrow is a big day, Lori acknowledged.

Everyone that had been recruited on the same day as Lisl, at the no longer abandoned building west of Portobello Road looked both anxious and nervous at each other and the rest.

– All will be well! Adriana declared, more than a little ironic.

The next morning Lisl and Ethan and the others returned to the circle of friends they had left what felt like an eternity ago. Lori and a few others escorted Lisl there, clearly guarded. Lisl couldn't avoid noticing it.

– I get a bigger entourage? The girl grinned softly. – What an honor!

– There are concerns with you that Ethan and the others don't have to worry about, Arthur said gently, – about your former masters.

Lisl lowered her gaze.

– I guess everyone guessed it, she said subdued, unable to look at them, at Lori. – I'm just glad that the secret is out, that I don't have to be alone with my fears anymore. My masters, as you put it have probably realized by now that I'm not loyal to them anymore, and they don't care much for you when you turn Indian, don't care much for you at all.

Her loyalties had changed… forever.

Lori was no longer in doubt concerning what drawing of the girl that showed the future.

Lisl sought her.

– You knew, too?

Lori didn't voice a reply, but replied nonetheless.

– Why didn't you say anything? You should have told me!

She did look and did sound hurt.

– Why would I do that? You were no longer the girl you had been. You will never be her again. The only reason it is brought up now is for purely practical purposes, the pure necessity of your potentially dire circumstances.

Lisl sniffed and nodded.

– I'm sorry, Genesis, the girl sniffed. – I will make it up to you. I'm yours, yours, *forever!*

Even more than she had been.

Lori touched her cheek briefly, and that was that.

They visited Lisl's old neighborhood, where many of her old friends and fellow local club members had gathered in yet another abandoned derelict building. She and those accompanying her were well received. Everyone was eager to hear about her experience in a now well-known setting.

She was introduced to those that didn't know her, all those who had joined the community since her departure from it and given the floor.

She stood before them with her head held high. There was a qualitative change everyone that had known her noticed.

– So much has happened, she began. – Both good and bad. Words can only begin to describe it. I hardly remember myself from the time before we all visited that particular Dark Lodge.

There were now many dark lodges in and around London and elsewhere, all over the world.

She paused a bit, before continuing, before beginning her passionate account.

– I, as some of you know well, was skeptical at first, to say it the least. I didn't treat Lori and the others with much respect. I'm now glad that I didn't, since that was why Lori picked me. The dwellers of the Dark Lodge value true independence. She picked my obnoxiousness off me, of course, but encouraged my other qualities. I've come to value her as a friend and teacher. We've shared horrors and joys and companionship beyond measure and I can say now that I will never return to what I now see as my old, pallid existence.

– Rest assured that she remains a pain in the butt, though, Lori snarled.

There was laughter, hearty laughter, a necessary counterpoint to the girl's seriousness.

Lisl spoke at some length. She strived to keep it light, to some degree, but what began as passionate only turned more intense as she approached the end. The new, intense Lisl unnerved them a bit, but it also made them *listen*.

– I've learned so much, most of all things I never imagined existed or was available in the first place. It hasn't been just pleasant. We've had people after us you won't *believe,* unpleasant assholes making the average police officer bully a rather pleasant character, but that only made us grow closer and more determined to succeed, to see it all through, and we have. *We have!* We've been smack in the middle of everyone and everything you've heard about out there, of many of the great and disturbing events you've heard about, and I wouldn't want to miss any of it for a second. Even the bad stuff has been good in a backwards kind of way, because it has encouraged us to push ourselves even further on the vast scale of Change. I hear the music. I feel every single second the possibility of that vast Change, of true, uncompromising Freedom.

They looked at the stranger, the mature girl they hardly recognized and couldn't quite decide how they felt about it, about her. She looked at them, giving everyone a radiant smile melting their doubts and reluctance.

– It's so great being back here, with you, she cried with joy and passion and laughter, and now, they recognized her, the smile and the thousand big and small details making her her.

She walked around and embraced them all again, like a young girl at a birthday party. It touched Lori, touched them all. There was something so very beguiling about her enthusiasm. Only a small, cynical part of Lori nodded with approval to herself concerning the girl's performance.

The two groups didn't part for hours, but stayed together and would stay together also after having parted company. It was all so very satisfying. Everything was coming together. Lori felt it in her gut.

– So, do we come with you? A boy, clearly not faking it, emulating the younger, overly skeptical Lisl wondered.

– That's up to you, Lisl said. – We're many autonomous groups and «branches» making out this new wave of relentless, inevitable rebellion, and that's one of our strengths. It doesn't really matter where you are, where you make your stand, not anymore. Rebellion, true and wild is everywhere these days and nights and will find you no matter where you go, and so will its irredeemable enemies.

She kept speaking with the same, quiet conviction.

Several of those present felt the hard trickle down their spine.

They left the building and walked outside. Those squatting there followed their guests out in the yard.

The volatile mix of anxious and excited mood prevailed.

Five people appeared from the gate leading to the street. They looked ordinary at first sight, but they moved with a sinister purpose most of those in the yard had seen before and easily recognized.

– Liselle Forester? The woman in a black suit said.

– That's me! Lisl stated calmly.

– You need to come with us, need to come in for questioning.

– Questioning for what? Who are you to think you can just come here and tell me to go anywhere?

– We're the government, sweetie. We come and go as we please.

– No, you don't!

Once more the girl spoke quietly and with conviction.

– Excuse me?

The woman's smug smile didn't quite go away.

– You heard me. I won't come with you, even if you could have proven to me that you belong to some kind of government organization with the official or unofficial «authorization» necessary to come and fetch people without them giving their true consent.

The evident danger made Lori feel her surroundings like never before. It felt like a light weight at her fingertips, one tilted with the slightest of applied force. She felt flesh and mind alike dancing on the edge of her extended self.

Two of the men took one step, two forward. Lisl slapped her palms together. The subsequent force was far more powerful, created far more kinetic energy than it was supposed to do. She directed it at the two, pushing them backward far stronger than a gust of wind. They were pushed off their feet and fell hard and gasped in pain.

The three other clandestine agents froze.

– You're thinking of drawing your weapons, Lori stated casually, – still confident that you're the resident power of the land.

She didn't move, making no threatening gestures.

It made them hesitate a few more moments, before going for it.

All five screamed in insane pain. The other three fell to the ground as well. All five collapsed, crumbling, hardly more than bags of flesh and bones, looking at the two women towering above them with bewildered, fearful stares.

– Look at you, Lisl giggled, – not a mark on you and you scream like little children being punished.

– You are! Lori snarled. – Now, we'll allow you to return to mommy and daddy before the punishment starts in earnest, and know that if we should ever see you again, no matter the occasion we won't be so lenient.

They took her words to heart. They ran off, fleeing as fast they were able, no longer perceiving themselves as representatives of a dominant power.

Lori and Lisl turned around, returning to the stunned, startled recruits they had never left. Their friends weren't shocked, but their potentially new tribe members were.

– The Dark Men, the dancing shadows are coming, Lisl stated proudly. – *We* are coming!

It slowly dawned on the young boys and girls what they had seen, dawned on them that it was real. They responded with both shock and awe.

– The world hasn't changed or changed that much, not yet, Lori said, – but we have. We're changing beyond anything we might have imagined!

They didn't pull away, but grew even more interested, willing to follow the path their old friend had outlined for them. Both Lori and Lisl smiled.

Another branch of squatters joined the extended network centered at the derelict Bayswater church. Some of its members stayed put, while others followed Lori and Lisl and the others back.

A poster was put on walls all over London and also spread to surrounding areas, across the country and abroad.

Visit the Dark Lodge, where free men and women gather, gather for the misty night, where anything is possible.

It's a «club», an esoteric, eclectic «society» of rebels and witches and independent thinkers. If you are two of the three you qualify... ;)

The Dark Lodge is everywhere, on every corner, in every crossroad and in every building in London and Beyond. Visit it and set yourself free. Stay there and remain so... Forever!

September ended and October began. The heat persisted, both figuratively and literally. The Prime Minister and her ilk kept dropping bombs on foreign soil and uniformed bullies kept beating up and killing domestic protesters. Mainstream media, loyal to the bone to those in charge as usual blamed the protesters. The civil unrest picked up even more.

– Biased Brainwashing Corporation strikes again, a protester shouted.

Two seconds before a police club crushed his skull.

It was all recorded by local photographers and shared en masse on social media all over the world.

Nothing was shown on established media. The angle of all major national broadcasts was that the protesters were to blame, for everything.

– Of course, the protesters attacked the police, Lori snarled. – Of course, a bunch of basically defenseless people attacks uniformed people wearing armor and carrying shields and clubs and arms.

She felt all the rage, the raging emotions. It empowered her.

– You're not a proper police officer until brain mush covers your uniform or armor, Lisl swore.

Ever more truly autonomous groups basically rejecting local, national and global government were formed. Informal networks rose with and between them. Alternative channels of communication, physical and deep web structures were created and used.

– It's so exciting! Violet marveled. – Everything is up for grabs.

Arthur, with a little effort got hold of his old computer hacker pal and others. Several independent lines were maintained. A new world formed, where the old hardly existed at all, at least not as anything but a distant echo or ghost of what was becoming reality.

Lori sat in her tower, her sanctum with Lisl and eight more people, Violet, Cathy, Zachary, Slater, Arthur, Jasper, Charlie and Stanley. Hands joined hands. The imagery and sensations came to Lori almost instantly.

She saw the streets soaked in blood the day after the police had executed a particularly violent attack on the protesters. Those cleaning it up had quite the hard job. No matter how much they brushed the ground, the blood remained. The ten re-experienced the violence, its ghosts and revenants. The vile stench of the old world kept ripping into their nostrils.

The old world remained when they took to the streets and saw long rows of soldiers roaming sidewalks and roads.

The new world persisted in Lori's vision.

– What is it? Lisl whispered. – What do you see?

– I see them burn! Lori said offhand.

Excited gasps sounded all around her.

Her vision showed hot and cold flames lick the uniformed men and women at the other side of the street. The hot flames turned ascendant and almost real. She knew they would be. Hissing embers and whispering flames danced in the air both day and night.

The soldiers and police officers were screaming. They were no longer beating up on and killing defenseless protesters, but were running for their lives, and their wicked laughter had ceased. Eyes in drawn faces looked in misery at the changed world.

The fire and shadows seemed to be everywhere. Houses, people, the very ground, everything and everyone burned.

Lori glimpsed the Burning Man, herself, Janice and others in her vision, a glimpse only slowly fading.

There was no lightning bolt out of the blue, no hidden knowledge or understanding in her mind coming to her involuntarily, instinctively, just a slow trickle of confusing imageries and sensations.

She shook her head in distress, in excitement.

– Everyone senses it, even feels the deep chill in their gut, as their eyes are opening. We're all awakening to the dream. The moon is becoming ascendant. It can't be held back anymore. The dam is breaking. The river will always reach the sea.

Her voice echoed in the void, bouncing off the staring shadows.

She caught a slow glimpse of Toni clear as day, with colors strong as blood, an adult woman staring at her with hatred in her eyes.

A charge flowed from hand to hand until the entire circle burned with it. They sat there gasping, struggling to achieve a modicum of control. The power surged when ten people, a full circle gathered. It ran wild, but they kept it together.

A girl played a fiddle in front of Palace Theater in the intersection of Shaftesbury Avenue and Charing Cross Road on a day with dark clouds above. A younger Lori and Toni walked on the beach. The little girl laughed full of life. She rolled in the dry sand, and dust rose and covered excited eyes.

Genesis rolled her hands into fists, making the two on her side shout in pain. She heard the loud sounds of bones snapping.

Contact was broken. The moment was lost. All ten woke like from a dream.

She had held the hands of Violet and Stanley. She had broken several bones.

– I'm sorry! Lori said.

They looked at her with sympathy and reverence, not anger or regret. A warm, warm feeling filled her, briefly overwhelming the chill in her bones.

– I could have hurt you far worse, she said. – We need to… suspend this, until we learn more, mastering it better, at least.

They still looked at her with understanding, but now it was mixed with bitter disappointment and even resentment.

I could have killed you, she thought venomously.

She shuddered, and it wouldn't stop, no matter how hard she fought to end it.

It kept up hours later. The distant memory stayed at the front of her attention.

She and Lisl held hands, demonstratively. They stood in the sacristy. There was no one else present.

– You can let go, now, Lori told her gently.

Lisl did, reluctantly and took steps away from her older friend.

– I need to do this, Lori stated, – need to exercise control and handle power. When I'm able to master it alone, I will also be able to master it with others.

She reached out with her power, imposing herself on the room, allowing it to impose itself on her. She touched it, touched the fabric of the walls and ceiling and floor, the very air itself.

It took only a moment's concentration. She rose into the air and stayed there, hovering with her feet about half her own length above the floor.

Her power charged the air around her, reaching out to Lisl, but not touching her. Lori doubled her efforts, sensing how her power grew. Lisl felt it and took a step back.

– No, Lori snapped. – Stay your ground!

Lisl gritted her teeth and took one step forward again.

The power hurt her, but she rolled her hands into fists and held out.

Lori pulled her power back, or attempted to, one, two times before succeeding, but that also made it harder for her to stay in the air.

– If I let go, the power grows to immense proportions, she mused. – I will test that out, too, but not now.

She hovered, staying afloat, visibly straining herself, looking at her watch without that distracting her too much.

One minute passed.

The power started spreading again. She saw energy, *energy* bouncing off the walls. She pulled it back, back into herself, and it started growing, festering there.

Two minutes…

Suddenly, sweat covered her brow. Suddenly, it was as if all the power… left her, doing so from one moment to the next.

She fell to the floor and landed somewhat dignified on her feet, not quite in control.

Lisl took two steps forward, stepped close to her, in order to support her, but there was no need for that.

– Something is clearly amiss, a crucial piece. It is as if I can't properly focus sometimes. I could have stayed in the air longer, but not without expending far more power and with less control of it, with the risk of…

She cut off, shrugging.

– No matter, it's sufficient, for now. If I need to strain myself, I'm positive I can rise to the challenge, but until we learn to combine our efforts in a somewhat safe manner, we will suspend group efforts. We will all keep exploring our talents, our individual power, and we will no longer hide ourselves, in any way. It's time to show the world, or at least some selective parts of it what we can do.

The dark shadows danced in her eyes. Lisl felt how expectation rose within, encouraging her own talent, her gift of genetics and circumstances.

The scenery shifted like mercury again. Lori had no sense of moving. She compared it with her visions, the urges leading to the drawings. They sat on the long bench on Leicester Square, catching bits of the people staying and passing through, as the long minutes crawled to midnight.

The people, the many faces on the long marble-like bench flashed before her eyes, in and out of her consciousness. People kept coming and leaving and staying. Four young teenagers passed through, and they evidently felt very safe. No one bothered with them or batted an eye about their appearance. They seemed to fit in just as much as anyone else present.

– I hear countless tongues, Lori said with her distant voice. – They're coming, coming from near and far, very far.

– Can you see them, Lisl prompted her, – see the people?

– I see only shadows,

– You'll be *sorry*. You will want to find me, but I'm nowhere to be found.

The voice spat at her from the air, from the very air itself.

She winced as she watched herself and Lynn Jenny sit in the dark, dark restaurant. When Jenny split under a dark cloud, Lori didn't stay with herself, but followed Jennie, as she rushed to a car on a parking lot not far away. She sat down in the passenger seat. Marc, *Marc* was driving.

Lori and the others crossed the river Thames, walking on the western Hungerford footbridge above the river rising rapidly, visible to the naked eye. Children ran back and forth, sometimes behind them, sometimes in front. It was bright or rather a dismal, twilight daylight, even though Lori knew positively that it was supposed to be night.

The October darkness had become something transparent. She could see for miles and miles from her position on the bridge. A twilight sun accompanied all the other eerie sights imposing themselves on her. It didn't look like the moon, didn't look like the moon at all.

A man dressed in rags and covered by only a thin blanket crouched at the center of the bridge. There were several other sleeping arrangements there, some of them soaked in blood. The man looked completely out of it, like he wasn't there at all.

– You see people «sleeping and living rough» everywhere these days and nights. What a fucked up local, national and global society we have.

Violet's voice sounded strangely emotional. She had matured quite a bit since Lori had first learned to know her. The «cultivated» upper class speech had long since given way to the rougher cut spoken in the streets.

Someone had lit a fire, an actual giant bonfire on the South Bank. It reached for the heavens and seemed to actually dwarf the London Eye. The wheel seemed like a toy in comparison. The flames, the dancing flames whispered to Lori, telling her secrets, misplaced knowledge and horrors beyond imagining.

The wanderers walked through a long and broad dark corridor. Dirt covered the floor and walls. Dirt seemed to dominate the place. They spotted both dry and fresh blood everywhere.

A vision of a cemetery filled with bodies formed behind her eyelids.

She kept drawing in the dark. It didn't really matter. It didn't impede on her ability or anything. Her hand was just as sure. Her hand saw everything it needed to see.

She realized the obvious: that she wasn't actually experiencing the here and now, but events yet to come. It was the clearest, most confusing vision, or series of visions yet. She couldn't quite focus, and even the sense of her feet touching the ground didn't make her feel connected, didn't make the experience true.

Parallel lines interacting… sucked her in, sucked her into a maw she couldn't escape. An onslaught of sensations assaulted her. She could not escape them or make sense of them, of any of it. They pulled her in every direction simultaneously, ripping piece by piece off her body, her mind and self.

The unmistakable sound of the tip of the pencil breaking pulled her out of her trance, bringing some kind of relief, something resembling it at least, and the darkness around her was just darkness, no matter how much it was breathing in her ears and staring into her eyes and imposing its foul stench in her nostrils. She felt the abrupt need to puke because of the foul, foul taste in her mouth. Her skin felt tender, like it was actually burning. She spotted without effort the dark flames dancing in the pitch black air beyond the night.

The sensations kept revealing themselves to her, some solidifying, others dissolving in her dreamscape. Papers, words danced before her, becoming meaningful, changing, transforming into images, understanding. A smile transformed her face, the most terrifying smile she had ever known.

William Synos stepped out of his car late at night after a particularly harrowing workday. He unlocked and opened the door to his house and rushed inside, closing and locking the door behind him, leaving the keys shaking in his hand on the table by the row of clothe hangers. Shaking feet steered him through the hallway and into the living room. He went straight for the rack and the locked upper shelf. He unlocked and opened it, and grabbed the bottle of Scotch there. He found a glass and poured himself a strong drink.

It burned on his tongue and in his throat. He had another sip as he walked to the chair and sat down. The hand holding the glass kept shaking.

He turned his head and looked out of the window, his eyes drawn in the direction of the sound he had heard. It had sounded like branches brushing against the window, but the nearest tree or bush was far away. There was nothing there that could account for the sound. He had another sip, a bigger sip.

The eyes, the dead, dead eyes of a child, a little boy accused him. They burned into him, and he couldn't avoid their stare. It was everywhere, wherever he turned his head. A long row of other eyes joined them, and he gasped in a horror that couldn't be denied.

One head caught fire, burning away all the flesh, until, until only the skull remained. Its eyes stared at him and burned holes in his sore, sore skin.

He looked at the shadows out there, imagining they were moving, closing in on him.

A loud hum reached his ears. He imagined he heard a woman's voice, but couldn't say for certain.

Something hissed at him from the shadows of the room. He jumped in his chair, spilling some of the liquor. This time it definitely sounded like an animal. He stared at the deeper shadows. They were fairly well lit, really. There was nothing there, nothing to see.

He drank about half of what remained in his glass. It burned in his mouth and throat. He started coughing. The stench of his own sweat stayed noticeable, pervasive.

Something made him look out the window again, and there she was, a shadow in the moonlight. He saw her dark, twisted features incredibly clear. The big eyes looked at him. The creature's head was slightly tilted.

– Don't look at me like that! He shouted.

– In what way do you want me to look at you, Billy?

The voice came from his right. He turned in a rush, but there was no one there. He turned back with equal rush. The shadow had vanished.

He jumped on his feet. He spilled his drink.

– You've had bad dreams, haven't you?

He hurried out in the hall, bending down to pick up his shoes. They slipped from his fingers and did a happy dance in the air, before being disposed in the corner. He grabbed the car keys on the table and held on to them for dear life.

The jacket hung on the knack by the door. He reached for it. It… breathed on him. He had no trouble hearing the deep, deep breathing.

– Do you have any idea what I am, Billy? Neither did I. Not until recently. I knew I could draw possible futures, but I didn't know I could turn my creative talent around, that I could actually create the imaginary and impose it on the world.

The jacket grinned at him, a big, big grin with eyes, nose and mouth.

He grabbed the handle and practically tore the door open, practically jumped outside barefoot and without the keys to his door. The fact that it slammed close behind him didn't really register in his feverish mind.

– You're dreaming, Billy, but it isn't really your dream. It is your nightmare, though, one you will never wake up from. Does it help that you know it isn't real, Billy? Does it keep you from sweating an ocean every night and see shadows with sharp, sharp fangs in bright daylight?

He walked with fast, rigid steps to his car, beeping the lock open long before he reached it, the big, strong man tearing the door open so hard that he almost tore it off its hinges.

His hands shook so hard that he couldn't hold on to the keys. They dropped to the floor the moment he sat down. He strived for a long time before he managed to pick them up. His eyes never stopped wavering. His head never stopped turning, attempting to look in all directions simultaneously. He felt like a little kid again, looking under the bed and in the closet before going to bed and falling into a pitiful slumber not granting any rest.

– You were always a bully, Billy, and bullies are always cowards at heart.

He started the car, pushing the gas pedal way too hard. The car slid down the road on spinning tires. He finally gained control just before the first turn and managed to keep the car on the road. The bumper scratched a lamppost and fell off. He drove on, not visibly reacting at all, keeping his eyes forward. He strived to think, to keep his infamous calm, in vain. His mind felt like one, giant pressure cooker.

Sweat kept forming on his forehead, forcing him to constantly dry his brow. Wet palms had trouble holding on to the wheel. He eventually got a sense of direction, and realized that he was on his way to the headquarters and he nodded to himself. That made sense, made a lot of sense.

– BOO!

She shouted straight into his ears.

He lost control of the car. His hands couldn't get a grip on the wheel. The car slid across the street and hit another one parked there. The crash roared in his mind. His head hit the wheel, and he lost consciousness.

The darkness lasted forever in his mind. He could sort of experience it. It replayed itself endlessly in his tortured consciousness.

The headache revealed itself only a few seconds after he reopened his eyes. He sat in the wreck, stuck in the seat folded against the front.

He struggled to get free. He remained stuck. Labored breathing turned even more so. He hammered at the door, the already half broken door. It gave, he knew it did and applied even more force at it.

It fell off. He pushed himself out of the car. The pervasive stench and smoke from the engine made him cough, cough hard. He swayed a bit before he was able to stand somewhat steady. Looking around, he saw that he was familiar with the area. There was a bridge nearby. He practically saw it in his hazy vision.

He rushed forward in a somewhat steady walk. Sweat kept pouring from his brow and into his eyes. The more he dried himself, the more there seemed to be of it. His right sleeve had become soaked, and he switched to the left. He tore the lower part of his shirt from the pants and used it to dry himself thoroughly and methodically.

A chill touched him like a cold, cold hand. He stopped and looked up and there she was, floating, suspended in the air. She looked down on him with those staring eyes of hers, and he couldn't move a finger.

– Tell me about Genesis, Billy!

Her voice sounded so… normal, as if they sat around a table and enjoyed a pleasant conversation.

She lowered herself to the ground, and he realized startled that she was finally here, in her physical form and not the formless, untouchable spirit. He drew his gun from the jacket. She made a small move with her hand. Pain shot through him and the gun fell from his weak grip.

– Rhonda gave me the unedited report. I didn't understand at first that the experiments were conducted on humans and then I didn't understand what type of humans it was talking about.

The visuals of red folders and pink sheets filled his mind.

– It wasn't exactly being kind to people either way. Torture, dissections, the works… and you oversaw all of it. No wonder the report had to be locked away in a vault and not even touch a computer.

He bolted and ran, fleeing the fastest he was able, with hardly any sensible thought raging through his heated, heated mind.

A phone, he needed a phone. He ran, ran hard towards the bridge. An image of a phone stuck at the forefront of his consciousness.

He turned around and cast a panicked glance behind him. She wasn't there. He looked up, to the sides and in front. She wasn't there. He choked in relief, but kept running, hardly able to breathe due to his ongoing panic attack. His feet carried him past the houses and out in the open, towards the bridge not far ahead. The bridge, the bridge, the bridge.

He saw it, a very distinct impression, sensation in his mind, mind, mind. He ran, ran, ran towards the lifeline not far ahead. It seemed to take forever. He turned his head and cast a fearful look behind him, and there she was, walking casually, chasing him, chasing, chasing him forever.

He took the one, final step forward, and stepped at nothing but air. The bridge wasn't there anymore. He stepped off a tall wall towards the river, and it was a far, far, far stretch down.

She watched him fall, watched him hit the concrete far below with a dump sound. The loud wail was cut off abruptly, as if a cord was severed. She stood there for a while, admiring her work.

Now, Lori knew what was real.

Part three: Awareness burning

«Dissolve the modifications of the mind, and an infinite power will be unleashed in you». Patanjali 150 BC.

Chapter Sixteen

Lori heard the music, a prevalent low, intense shaking of the air and the flesh and the vibrating mind. The shadows, transparent and not roamed her vision, her senses. Sometimes they were mere shapes, then faces, with notable features she could almost make out.

They woke up in the morning filled with energy and enthusiasm. Many migrated to the Serpentine in Hyde Park. It had used to be open only in the summer months, but this year there was still summer. Many people joining them there agreed.

The water boiled between the swimmers. They took both long swims and stayed closed to land, staying together, as they usually did wherever they went. Lori felt the bubbles caress her skin and touch her mind, as if each was one, exclusive world. Each bubble wore a face, and a pair of eyes, a nose and lips, and ever-shifting features. Many bubbles became one, but that one was still only one in the multitude surrounding her.

They dried each other with large towels, not in a hurry getting their clothes back on. It felt so good to feel the wind against bare skin. She felt the heat from nearby bodies stronger than from the sun above. People stared, but they ignored that, too. They left at a leisurely pace.

– The birds aren't here today, Lisl noted, – at least not in big numbers.

– I think they might only come when there's anything significant to observe, Lori said, – when a truly significant event is taking place. I know they've been following us around before, without much happening, but that felt more like… a test run.

– That feels like a more than accurate statement, Violet nodded. – It felt like they were doing what we were doing, taking a stroll on a nice day or something.

A nervous laughter greeted her words.

– They're either observers or used as observers by… others or both, Lori said, pondering her own words as she spoke them.

The early swimmers returned home for breakfast. It felt, if possible even better than yesterday and the day before that.

– This feels so… over the top that I'm growing downright anxious, Adriana mused with a fluttering voice.

– I understand what you mean, Arthur nodded. – We're taught that good things don't last, and logic suggests that that's true.

– Cheers! Lisl cried brazenly, raising her glass. – Enjoy, revel in the moment and prepare for the future. We will push on, no matter what's awaiting us.

The future is now!

– HEAR, HEAR, the others choired.

Her bold words did encourage them. Glasses met and parted. Cold and hot food was devoured. The early morning felt like a late night, where shadows and fire and pleasant company grew intimate and hot.

Morning, evening, afternoon, night, it dissolved and mixed, becoming one, prolonged experience.

– I feel like I'm high all the time, Lisl giggled happily, – like we've been elevated to a permanent higher state of consciousness.

– In that case we've elevated ourselves, Cathy stated self-consciously. – It's quite something.

They laughed together, like they usually did. Lori saw remarkably small signs of conflict. Conflict was what they faced from society at large, and they didn't back away from it.

They gathered on a small football stadium in Surrey, in full public view, they and others speaking through speakers to a seething mass of participants.

– We choose confrontation, Lori cried. – We have nothing in common with a society without any kind of respect for life and freedom and dignity. This is not United Kingdom anymore. This is not England. Gathered here are many representatives for the various and varied free and independent states of Avalon. This is not a physical «kingdom», but one of the spirit. They can never remove it with their guns and fists and violence. Our movement seeks to avoid violence, but we also acknowledge that our oppressors might not and probably will not meet us with the same consideration. We will match them fist by fist, but with an open hand as well. We will not be tempted to play their game. We don't acknowledge their laws and authority. Arrest or kill us. It doesn't matter that much. There is very little they can do to us worse than what they've already done, by making us grow up in what is basically a fundamentally unjust society. The revolution will move on. We will ignore them as long as they ignore us or don't become an obvious threat to us or our members. Narrow parameters of behavior dominate today's human society. That is neither desirable nor acceptable. It never was and certainly isn't now, when we're all waking up. The future isn't some obscure, distant day when everything and everyone will achieve true freedom, equality and justice, and live in a sane society. The future is now!

The cheering broke the thin ceiling of air easily, and they could breathe even easier.

– The dance, she cried, – the ancient dance begins.

She stepped down from the low first step and down on the grass. Lisl and the others surrounded her instantly in a pleasant bubble of air and flesh.

They didn't keep people from reaching her and interacting with her, but protected her from the worst effects of it. Flesh and mind brushed her, but didn't impose on her in an unpleasant manner.

They circled her, spoke with her, granting her their devotion and respect, in one circle spreading from that warm and fuzzy inner embrace, to what seemed like an endless inner and outer constantly moving wheel.

They, those bold enough and willing and able to cast their fear aside gave their identities to a scribe writing their names in a large book of shadows. The witch was a male, one dressed in hood and robe, cloaked in shadow. Pleasant shakes rode Lori when she studied him. He was real. A mere glance confirmed that.

– So can I have your name, please?

His voice sounded like he looked, like mist and shadow on a moor or field or dense forest.

– Lori Michaels, I…

– Lori Michaels, she said. – It's my maiden name. My husband and I aren't formally divorced yet. He's being an ass about it, but I will appreciate very much if I can use that from the start. I have my birth certificate, if that helps…

– There's no need for that, he said. – We, all of us choose who we are.

That felt so right. She warmed him with a smile.

– So, what do you call yourself, if I may ask?

– I'm Grant Corvus.

– Corvus is Latin for «crow», Lisl remarked.

– It is? I didn't know that…

A girl, so similar to him in appearance that she had to be closely related sat by his side. She made further notes in her own, smaller notebook.

The event had been filmed, and Lori practically felt how that spread and multiplied as the seconds ticked to minutes and hours and days and weeks.

One blink of an eye, and she had returned to Hyde Park. Women and men danced in the night and in what seemed like a thicker forest with torches in their hands. Fire burned in the mist and the twilight. They had missed fire before, but now it was here, in their very midst, burning the very air between them. The torches paled compared to the dark, dark fire levitating between chanting throats and agile limbs.

Lori knew that now wasn't now, but some future point she couldn't pinpoint. Her eyes reopened and she had returned to the football pitch in Surrey, as she and her companions made their way out on it floating on light feet, with the large crowd turning around its center.

Then, they did revisit Hyde Park. The pitch dissolved and the park appeared. Many other people joined them. The park and even its surrounding areas had become a focal point, drawing people from far and near. Everything and everyone burned with bright daylight. Lori still imagined she gazed at it all cast in Shadow.

The shadow was real, a living, breathing entity that couldn't be denied.

They found themselves at Speaker's Corner. Its attendance had picked up lately, and it was clearly regaining the importance it had once enjoyed.

She noticed it after just a few steps after crossing what seemed to be an invisible line. Everything turned… turned sinister wherever she cast her eyes. Everything and everyone turned gray and… She stumbled and would have fallen if those walking with her on both sides hadn't caught her.

– What is it? Lisl asked anxiously. – Do you need pen and paper?

– Yes, I…

She tried moving her hands into her pockets, but couldn't do it. They just hung there, useless by her side.

The place was crowded. There was no place to sit. She grabbed the pen and paper Lisl handed her. They held the trembling body, as its eyes turned into a vacant stare.

Ravens and crows appeared one by one, ten by ten, flapping hundreds of wings. Lori stared into a million black eyes. People started pointing at them in distress and curiosity.

Lightning struck her. There was no flash, no clouds in the sky. The lightning erupted from her within. The pen and paper slipped out of her hands.

Everything and everyone turned gray and dead, no, not dead, turned lifeless, totally losing whatever life there was. The vision assaulted her in waves, blinking in and out of existence.

A woman stood on the small elevation with the attention of the crowd directed at her.

– Thou shall not suffer a witch to live! She shrieked. – Exodus 22.18 tells it *all!*

Most people were laughing, used to crackpots on this place as they were, but a considerable number of people were cheering, shouting AYE with loud voices, and the mood changed from light to ominous. Many of those present clearly supported the woman and her ramblings.

Lori knew that sightings had picked up lately. People had seen things they couldn't handle, and many, as were often the case allowed fear and hatred to rule them. Lori saw in flashes a public place, pretty much like this one. Night had fallen. Torches burned tall in the crowd's hands. The woman made a noose in her left hand and held a torch in her right.

– The noose or the fire, she hissed. – Tell me, good people and I will do thy will!
– Burn them, the crowd spat as one. – Hang them. KILL THEM ALL!
The woman grinned. She lowered the torch and held up the noose. The cries picked up. She lowered the noose and raised the torch. The cries picked up.
– We will burn half and hang half, she shouted. – We will have our pounds of flesh!
Six sorry creatures swayed on the stage. They were bound and had been severely beaten, and seemed to have suffered prolonged torture.
Lori felt like something tore her apart from the inside, as if she and it were twisted inside out, and it was. A collective gasp rose from the gathering, and they looked around with a stricken expression locked in their features. She realized stunned that everyone saw what she saw, or at least a pale echo of it.
The woman on the elevation burst into flames, but it wasn't flames exactly, but ghostly eruptions from her body centered on her head. Every head Lori saw turned to skulls. There was one big levitating burning skull. It didn't burn exactly. The flames didn't devour it. They just burned, without any visible effect on the skull. She felt its heat. It penetrated her being.
The visions faded, slowly, so slowly. Lori walked to the woman swaying on the Speaker's Corner designated spot, the woman she recognized as one of two in her visions and from her drawings. She levitated slightly, enough to stand face to face, eye to eye with the other.
– It's almost funny, isn't it? She chuckled. – You are what you reviled and spoke against. Your dreams were not nightmares, but visions.
The woman stared at her with insane eyes, through the tons of cold sweat filling and burning her eyes.
Lori lowered herself back to the ground, leaving those who had seen her wondering whether or not they had imagined her ascension. She turned and walked away with her tribe.
Lisl caught up with her, the glow of worship in her eyes stronger than ever.
– You shared your… your visions with us all, friend and foe alike, she said breathless. – That's amazing, just *amazing!*
– Everyone present experienced it, Violet agreed. – They will never be the same again.
The raven revealed itself to Lori in the water mirror reflection, but not in the air above.
She saw in slow, slow flashes the bird's skull revealed.
Its eyes were still there, still staring straight through her.
One minor shift of attention, and she could observe herself through

those eyes. The fear had almost gone away, and the marvel dominated her attention. Looking at herself through a thousand eyes hardly felt disconcerting at all anymore. She looked different at every angle. Every quality of vision brought a different imagery, revealing something not covered by all the other eyes. Ultraviolet, infrared were merely the modest start of it. Her flesh and blood breathed at a faster pace. Excitement made the heart beat faster in her chest and the already boiling blood boil stronger in her veins.

A… bubble seemed to be forming at the top of the rise, an area of brighter air and ground compared to everything around it. She rushed forward and entered the bubble, the brighter sphere. The others looked around with wide eyes.

– It's mine! She stated. – A stray piece of myself.

She recognized it immediately, instantly brought minutes back in time, to the moment she had embraced everyone around her… and released this, a stray given form by her thoughts and will.

– It's like my power, my power's nature keeps changing, she mused. – It isn't necessarily like they're growing, like I'm becoming more powerful… At least that isn't a *given*.

She stopped on the rise. The bubble, the sphere dissolved. Something… it was as if it, whatever it had been… returned to her. She re-experienced the events minutes ago, the sinister vision, the burning skulls. The empty sockets in the skull stared viciously at her.

– The various abilities we exhibit aren't necessarily our true power, she said slowly, – but merely an outer manifestation of something else and deeper.

– Isn't that the same as saying that we are far more powerful than we seem? Violet smirked.

Lori smirked as well, and shook her head in wonder and excitement and a well of other, not so pleasant emotions.

She pondered the issue, running it through her mind, from the first, faint stir of echoes to this moment. It had started, no grown with the first dreams that hadn't been dreams at all. She tried thinking back beyond that night, the days and nights following that one, but she couldn't quite grasp it, grasp her childhood, youth and adolescent memories. It had always been there, she knew that. She just couldn't point at anything solid, until… until her first meeting with Lynn Jenny and Kelly and Julia, and when her children had come of age.

From then it had grown, grown beyond denial or doubt.

– It's stronger when we're together, she mused, – stronger or more easily accessible or both.

Hands touched hands, and they felt it, almost like an electrical charge.

She stood before a mirror. She put one palm on the smooth cold surface. The world turned inside out. It was like she slipped into the mirror, as if she saw it all from the other side. Its world revealed itself to her, in one, prolonged flash lasting forever, until she once again stood before the mirror beholding her shaking form.

In the world of mirrors, she walked down a perfectly ordinary street. Then, in a flash of white and black it stopped being ordinary. As she walked, plants, deep green plants began growing, breaking through the concrete and asphalt until it covered everything on the entire street. It hardly looked like a city at all anymore.

Ten ravens formed a circle around the moon. They squeaked and spoke, and she imagined she almost understood what they were saying.

Shadows cast on a wall had no visible source.

Lisl wet her forehead with a cloth. Lori writhed and moaned on the mat, uncertain of what was real.

– Seers have always experienced their visions in agony and sweat, Lisl said softly. – Swimming through the Dark River is always a trying feat, I would surmise.

Some of the newest arrivals fled from the circle, their fear overwhelming their curiosity and hunger. Lori looked at their backs as they ran, as if she was there and she knew in her heart that they would never return and be doomed to a mediocre and scared existence. Her eyes cleared as she looked up at Lisl. The girl noticed after just a few moments.

– In a primitive tribe, I would have realized my potential in my teens and become the new medicine woman or shaman in training, and been far better suited to deal with… with the power.

– Now, you need to struggle like the rest of us, Lisl said softly.

Lori nodded. She heard voices, light, excited voices from far away. She frowned. A few seconds passed, until she realized the voices were real, that whatever happened, happened right now.

Emily rushed into the room.

– Come and see, both of you, she cried with blushing cheeks. – You must see this!

At that moment, everything came into a terrible focus to Lori.

She entered the other room, where everyone had gathered in front of the small laptop.

– There's an ill wind blowing across this country, this world, Richard Marx said on television.

Lori stared at it, at him, at those standing behind him, utterly fascinated.

She recognized Lynn Jenny. She saw Janice, a young woman she had only drawn before for the first time in real life.

They were at what seemed like a press conference, giving their story to a room filled with journalists and recording crews.

– It's already uploaded to Avalon Rebels, Arthur said. – Some people claim Marx did it himself only minutes after the press-conference.

Avalon Rebels was a rogue media sharing service without censorship, without the limitations of law-abiding services. Governments and corporations had attempted to shut it down from day one. It had only been up for a month, but had already become immensely popular all over the world.

– What you've just seen is actually just the modest start of the presentation of events I will reveal to you today, Richard said. – The five people you see behind me, Trevor Leonard, Janice Steerdink, Eldora Johnson, Justin Masters and Lynn Jennifer Stafford were the one targeted by the paramilitary strike force you've just seen in action. Janice's traveling companion Ruth Aldearsee has vanished. Janice last saw her when she left for the Netherlands some days ago, but she never arrived. Her ticket hasn't been used. And this is merely one case of many I've felt compelled to compile lately, Ladies and Gentlemen. Please observe the screen once more.

He looked slightly different compared to the man Lori remembered, more assertive and aggressive.

Violet looked astonished at the screen, then at Lori and then back at the screen.

The footage shown was very detailed, impossible to misunderstand. A group of uniformed men and woman raided an apartment complex. They were being filmed from across the street, through a camera placed close to street level. A few minutes passed by, before they come back out, clearly empty-handed. Lori recognized startled the uniformed man crossing the street towards the camera. He had been filmed closeup as he bent down and picked it up.

– This man has many names. Mark Johnson, Eric Powers and Laurence Eastborne are just a few I've managed to dig up. He and his accomplishes have quite a long list of «sins» to atone for. You'll find a complete dossier in the provided folders.

– Marc, Lori snarled softly.

The others stared at her.

The broadcast moved from the press conference to a police station, where Richard, accompanied by his entourage of unusually hungry newshounds and freak show and lawyers dropped off the indictment. He held up the papers.

– I charge the government and clandestine parts of the government with harassing and persecuting innocent people. I charge them with domestic terrorism and unlawful secrecy, and murder most foul…

The recording ended. They watched it several times on repeat. Lisl turned to Lori, to Lori standing there frozen.

– What is it? She wondered.

She touched her shoulder. Lori shook and turned her head and looked at her friend with wet, insane eyes. She stood like that for what seemed like an eternity, while everyone else also turned towards her. A million thoughts raced through her head, and she couldn't catch any of them.

– I'm not certain I can put it into words…

– Try! Lisl quietly besieged her.

– What we saw is an important, even crucial event, and as I saw it, it was as if… as if my visions and my present became one and the same.

Repeated chills passed down her spine, spreading to her entire body and self.

– What does it mean? Slater wondered.

– I have no idea!

There was no understanding, no lightning bolt from the sky. She shook her head in frustration.

– It is as if my power to gaze potential futures… has been… nullified. There's not even a sense of it anymore…. as if I've become blind or something.

She rose into the air without effort. The outpouring of energy remained strong and potent, but there were no visions, no itch to draw or anything. She lowered herself back to the ground.

They surrounded her, comforted her in all ways and she felt comforted, felt the smothering, the soft embrace of the tribe.

– Your visions have always seemed to have a life of their own, Lisl, said cautiously, – going all over the scale. It isn't unfeasible that this would be happening at some point.

Another chill trickled down Lori's back, and she wondered if it was instinct or just common human insecurities. Lisl's words echoed in her mind and made her frown.

– You're implying that my visions shut themselves down… deliberately?

– That certainly isn't unfeasible either. Lisl shrugged. – Lately, they've been so powerful that they've literally crippled you, made you unable to act on anything. So, yes, they or rather you, yourself, a part of you, you have no conscious access to, shut them down in order to put a stop to that.

Lori shook her head with a sore smile, acknowledging her sharp intellect, her astute, analytical mind.

Lori's mind kept working, her thoughts kept flowing. That hadn't stopped. The sense of urgency kept haunting her.

– I've drawn a few sketches I didn't understand at the time, she said slowly. – They were all from the upcoming five days and nights of the Samhain festival and showed me alone, without your company on various places. They all make sense, now!

Anxiety graced everyone's faces. Lisl's frown grew deep and sore.

– I must leave for a few days, Lori told them curtly, – leave alone.

That hurt them a little, but they were used to her wiles and let it go.

– Is that wise? Lisl said, clearly fighting to keep her voice even. – Some of us should accompany you.

– I can take care of myself, Lori shrugged, – and I can *cut loose* without worrying about hurting any of you.

They understood what she was saying. A catching formed in her throat.

– Rest assured that I will be back…

An odd smile accompanied her words.

A feather-light invisible hand touched all of those present. She saw them react to it with an excited smile, as she left them, as she practically forgot they were there and after just a few steps found herself on the outside. Just like that and she was gone. It had happened so fast, and was so irreversible. She wore her light jacket and had her shoes on. Everything was set. A tinge of loneliness troubled her a moment or two, but no more than that. She didn't look back.

For the first time in months she was alone, not surrounded by the warm, warm cloud of other people, of her tribe. This was early day. Stores had opened and been open for quite a while. The streets were filled with people wherever she looked. They seemed empty to her, empty shells of nothing.

She stood on the spot where she had drawn herself just outside the Queensway Underground Station. It didn't dawn on her that she had actually stopped there before she had stood still for a few seconds. The newspapers show the same date as in her drawings. She studies herself in the indistinct window mirror image. Her sense of self remains strong. Her lips are drawn into a long, thin smile.

Queensway opened up to her as she walked down the street. It hadn't changed in significant ways since she had first seen it as a teenager. Most Londoners never came here. They left it, in good conscience and spirit to the tourists and to those profiting from them.

Now, though, a strange mood lingered in the air, a residue of a presence

Lori could easily pick up on. Even though she couldn't actually see it because of her current limitations, she imagined she saw Lynn stand surrounded by flames on all four sides. Her memory easily called upon her old vision. The streets she walked through didn't seem unfamiliar at all. She had walked this path a thousand times in a second while writhing and sweating in Lisl's care. She dimly recalled her life of flesh and solid brick before her visions began. The burning images and sensations had threatened to take her over completely, and she didn't want that, and had stopped them cold.

The hospital wasn't that far away. She walked there without exerting herself, recognizing the building she had never seen at a glance. It glowed in her mind, so much more than three dimensions. She walked inside, into the fairly chilled reception hall.

– Hi, she greeted the man behind the desk, giving him a flashing smile, – my name is Lori Michaels. I'm an old friend of Eldora, Eldora Johnson. Is she here today?

He did check, did tap the info on his computer.

– I'm afraid not, he said dryly. – She's on sick leave and hasn't been in since…

– Since the *incident,* Lori completed the sentence for him. – I know. But she isn't at home either, and I wondered if she had returned to work, after all.

– I'm afraid she hasn't, he said and shook his head in what seemed real regret.

His anxiety was visible as well, visible to her, and she knew she wasn't the only one that had come here and inquired about Eldora Johnson lately.

– Thank you very much, anyway, she said, giving him a sweet parting smile.

She left, leaving the building behind before she had reached the exit. The long October morning shadows greeted her outside, for some reason so much more potent now compared to before she had walked inside.

– I know him, Violet said in her head, holding up the drawing of the dead man no longer dead. – I wasn't certain, or didn't want to admit I was, but he's a partner, a junior partner in one of my uncle's firms.

This had been well over a month ago.

Lori returned to Queensway. She walked into Whiteleys, a modern shopping center with a long tradition and presence in the area. She found the exclusive store easily enough.

An employee met her five steps from the entrance, clearly acting fast in order to keep from ruining the store's reputation further by allowing her access.

– Good morning, Lori said good humored, returning to her cultivated language. – I would like to buy an entire new wardrobe, please.

That made the eager beaver pause and consider.

– You're Larry, right? I've heard good things about you.

– You have? He said stunned, unable to quite pull himself together.

– Yes, they say you're quite good at knowing what a woman wants.

He beamed at her. She managed to keep a straight face.

– You do cater to tall and full-formed women, right?

– We do! He coughed.

– Thank God! She exclaimed. – It can be such a bother to find such places in today's world of size zero models.

The contempt in her voice was palatable. He nodded in solemn agreement.

She nodded, too. They were on the same page. That was all that mattered.

He started showing her various clothes and collections. She enjoyed that, briefly imagining she was back to the person she had been so very long ago, before she and the world changed.

The mirror didn't seem quite real to her. She didn't need it either, in order to see herself from the outside.

– I think I'll go for the modern executive look, she informed Larry.

She added two sets of more common clothes as well, just for the heck of it. She paid for it all with her platinum card, the one she had kept all this time.

Wearing new clothes and carrying two bags of new clothes, she left the place, and went to the hairdresser just a few steps away.

– I want you to remake me, she told the woman.

She left herself in her skilled hands. In her mind, she flipped the pages of the book she had made with her drawings, like she had done a thousand times already. Hair fell off her head and hit the floor, making a black, black sea.

The mirror image afterwards brought a soft, pleasant shock. She could hardly recall the features facing her in the mirror. The woman looked so young and vulnerable and certainly not like the shrewd executive she dimly remembered.

She didn't rush it, but made her way at a casual, languishing pace. She walked up the street, to an entrance by the parking garage. Quite a broad staircase led to the next floor. She walked up there and found herself in what had to be one of the best kept secrets when it came to restaurants, a very luxurious and exclusive place where only the wealthy could afford to dine.

A waiter is awaiting her by the entrance.

– Is there anything I can do for you, madam? He says with a pleasant voice, not even hinting at the skepticism she can easily spot in his eyes.

– There is, actually, Lori said equally pleasant, returning to her cultivated language. – You're Grady, right? I'm Lori Russell. I'm here to see Emerson and associates on behalf of Trevor Leonard.

She strived a bit with her dialect again, but managed.

– One moment, madam, Grady said.

She watched patiently and displayed herself in the door as he walked to the four men sitting around the table across the room. Grady finally returned.

– Mr. Emerson and associates are ready to see you, now, Mrs. Russell, he said.

He knew exactly who she was.

She followed him, at a relaxed pace across the room to the special table and the men gathered around it.

Grady stepped aside and she stepped forward, sitting down in the one, available seat.

– Gentlemen, she greeted them frivolously.

They studied her. It didn't faze her.

– You're the prodigy, Knowles said, more than a little condescending. – You've been away for a long time.

– I've been working with a special project, Lori said.

– Is that so? Emerson mused with audible irony in his voice.

Lori didn't say anything.

– You claim to come here with a message from Trevor, but why, if I may ask isn't Trevor coming here in person?

– He has been kind of occupied lately, Lori shrugged.

– So, we've heard…

Lori leaned back in the chair, enjoying the moment.

– You've long since suspected that Trevor has an ace up his sleeve. Well, I'm it!

They exchanged glances, torn between greed and skepticism. She sensed their doubt, their uncertainty.

– What's the message?

Grady arrived with Lori's tea. She grabbed the cup and raised it to her mouth. It was too hot to drink. She put the cup back on the small plate.

– Don't buy Coleman Industries. It's about to take a fall.

– That's it?

– For now…

She grabbed the cup again, and sipped the tea. It was excellent!

The eerie smile lit up her face. Her awareness of it made it even more pronounced. They stared distressed at her.

Grady had rushed to the table almost before she had decided to call for him. She shook her head in amazement.

– I'll have the veal, she said. – Well done, please! And a Guinness.

The meal arrived, after a time she couldn't quite measure or perceive. She fed, well aware of the fact that they saw it like that, no matter how much she used fork and knife, and appeared civilized.

– I'm considering going to the party tonight, she remarked. – You are as well, I presume?

– The p-party, Usher stuttered. – You know about that?

She just looked at him with scorn in her dark eyes.

She dipped her lip into the Guinness froth and drank with vigorous enjoyment. The meal proceeded the same way, alternately with drink and food.

Then, with one blink the world changed. The restaurant looked like it had decayed for years. Broken furniture, holes in walls and ceiling and floor appeared everywhere. People became skeletons clothed in dissolving fabric. With each new blink, it changed further. Two, three blinks down the road the building had become ruins hardly visible anymore in a landscape covered by growth.

– You were far away just now, Yates said, doing his best to entice her with what he perceived as boyish charm, but that to her was just boyish.

– I was dreaming.

– What were you dreaming about?

– Whatever I desire.

The implication of her words and the slutty look she sent him couldn't be misunderstood. He turned red above the collar. Emerson stared at her, clearly displeased with her stealing his thunder, unable to hide it.

– What's your secret?

– What do you mean? She responded with a lazy, relaxed smile.

He was tall, handsome and physically fit, but not attractive in her dark eyes.

– Our paths have crossed several times…

– We've met, you mean? She grinned.

– … and you looked nothing like this. Quite frankly, you don't sound and seem like the same woman.

– I think you're probably right about that, she shrugged. – I have indeed reached quite a few watersheds, lived through several paradigm-shifts lately. It has been most illuminating and rewarding.

She rose.

– Shall we, gentlemen?

Yates rose fast and made a point of taking her arm, of grabbing his prize. She granted him a sweet smile.

They walked out of the restaurant, down the stairs and appeared on the hot and steamy street. The air darkened further around her. She felt it easily, without straining herself, with a casual glance. Her companions were clueless, of course. They studied her, their eyes glued to her breasts and the curve of her hips and radiant face.

She started humming as they walked down the sidewalk. Each step felt like a dance.

– Can you hear the music? She asked them.

They looked nonplussed at her. Of course, they did!

– I'm afraid not, Yates said with regret.

– I can! She grinned brightly. – I hear it all the time!

The big, tall mature woman they occasionally perceived as a young girl and her enthusiasm both interested them and caught their ire. Her smile widened, even as she basically ignored their interest, even as she kept flirting with them.

The music showed her more than, or at least almost as much as her eyes did. There were no more premonitions, or anything even resembling any, but she still felt like she painted her surroundings. The drawing of herself accompanied by the men appeared in her memory just like they passed Bayswater Station, where the drawing had depicted them. The faces, almost all she looked at also looked exactly like they had in her drawing. Only a few didn't.

The discrepancies, though notable didn't seem important. The general, flowing series of images and sensations persisted.

Each time another confirmed itself felt good, felt exhilarating.

The party was held at a modern five stars hotel nearby, at one of its bigger conference halls. She spotted the building from far away. It, like many visuals before it, joined those in her memory, her detailed recall. The insides did as well. The hall in the basement appeared just as dark and dank as she had pictured it in her drawings.

To everyone else it looked bright and stylish, like any official and boring get-together. There were those recognizing her and whispering among themselves.

Her companions noticed the glances as well.

– It's so nice to be remembered, isn't it? She mused. – Months away from the grapevine, but never truly far away.

A waiter offered cocktails on a tray. She grabbed a glass and raised it to her «admirers». A few mirrored her action. She took a sip. It was sickeningly sweet. She turned the glass upside down and its content decorated the floor. Her present companions looked anxiously at her.

– They truly serve all kinds of shit these days, she said aloud.

Her casual pointed stare and wicked grin shook everyone present.

It was as if they could all see her, as if they couldn't avoid looking at her.

Charles Reddham stood right across the room, not exactly staring at her, but certainly sweating, sweating a lot. She imagined he left an entire waterfall on the floor. He left the gathering with fast steps.

The lights blinked slowly, or so they imagined. At least it turned significantly darker in the entire hall. Mr. Reddham walk turned into a rush. He disappeared through the opposite door.

She turned to Yates.

– Let's do the scenic tour. Why don't you introduce me, my dear?

They walked arm in arm with her giving him a smile making him sweaty and uncomfortable. She took a closer look at the gathering. This looked like the typical corporate crowd. She had seen that with one glance, and the impression didn't change with the second, third or tenth.

In spite of that, the familiar feeling of something *other* entered her. She turned her head, turned her head again. She couldn't identify or locate its source.

The backdrop was all there, inside, outside, but the symmetry was all wrong. There was no balance, nothing she could grab and steady her vertigo, her unsteady, shaky legs.

Three young girls, obviously secretaries or something rocked on their chairs, rocked to a melody reaching their ears through the sharing of four ear plugs. A woman in a blue dress had beaten all others to the punch bowl and started drinking. She looked quite a bit out of it, visibly so, as if being unable to lift a heavy load off her mind.

A bit off to the right a Spanish couple seemed immersed in their private conversation. No one present understood shit about what it was about.

Yates led the two of them to a group by the dinner table. Everyone, every single one there focused their attention on her. She recognized them from the relevant drawing. The miserable woman in the blue dress. The three girls dancing to their private tune. The couple prattling on and on in Spanish. They had all been a part of her extensive pre-made pencil art.

Her dark tunnel vision pushed her forward and she looked neither up or down or to the sides. Yates, as if sensing her rock-hard determination glanced uneasily at her. She granted him a disarming smile.

The room appeared empty just then, and with moss and growth on the floor and walls.

She knew how she appeared to them. Her eyes, her deep, deep eyes grew until they filled their vision. A huge, dangerous smile spread on her face.

The smile helped, helped her keep contained the deep dark mood striking her in waves. It had a physical effect, spreading benevolent chemicals in her blood.

She grabbed another glass from a passing tray and emptied it in one go, not really tasting its content.

The ants crawling through her veins, the bad mood she recalled from many late office hours… returned. She calmed herself with an effort and was finally able to stand still, to stop constantly moving her hands.

– Hello, everyone, in case you don't recognize her, this is Lori Russell. You won't believe this, but we met by unforeseen circumstance earlier today.

They greeted her and their greeting was as dry as wood. She returned in kind, not really there anyway.

The two of them joined the table. There was no fixed seating. Everyone sat down wherever they might fancy. She certainly did. A giggle worked itself up her throat.

Most of the seats were eventually filled

Dinner was served, and people began eating. Lori did as well. It hardly mattered that she had just recently eaten. This dish was quite small, not really designed to fill people's stomach, but more like a part of the design than actual food, quite the typical setting at such gatherings.

The Spanish couple kept speaking, kept prattling on endlessly, and she had no idea what they were talking about. Looking at them, listening to their voices, it seemed terribly important.

– So, what have you been doing lately, Lori? The wife of a terribly important man inquired.

Suddenly, all eyes pointed at the unexpected guest.

– I can't say too much, but I certainly remain in charge of the Genesis-project and quite committed to it.

– Is that what it's called? I've heard so much about it, but I've never heard that name. I'm *dying* to hear more.

– That it is, and I can assure you that you will hear more about it.

Lori's grin then didn't exactly make people less uneasy.

She took part in the light conversation without straining herself, without being the slightest distracted from what was churning through her head. She played Yates's companion without batting an eye, even though he did frown occasionally, even though he could never tell why.

The two of them were dancing, moving back and forth on the floor with slow, relaxed movements.

She looked at him with large, lupine eyes.

The language… started making sense to her. Spanish turned out to merely be one more dialect she could easily understand.

– I want to kill them, the woman snarled. – I want to kill them all!

– One more negative thing about capitalism is that it turns everything and everyone into commodities, Lori told Yates. – It's diminishing us, making us less and less and less human.

She emphasized *less* every time, making it more than a spell than a part of a language.

– I want to roast them, the Spanish man spat, – roast them over open fire until they're nothing but blackened remains.

She knew they were still speaking Spanish, since no one else understood anything. That much was clear from the unconcerned expressions of those sitting close to them.

The words and their meaning echoed within her, expanding upon an already expanded mind. She felt it as it happened and didn't have to strain herself in order to make it happen anymore.

The party ended slowly, fizzed out to the nothing it had always been. People began leaving, either alone or in groups or two and two. Lori allowed Yates to drag her off. They met a couple in the hallway. A woman with half of her dress gone released a shriek of laughter. They walked down the hallways to the rooms. Yates pushed Lori at the wall outside his room. She allowed him to do that, to kiss her neck and fondle her all over the body.

She grabbed him, turned them both around and pushed him, pushed his back at the wall. Her deep, huge eyes stared at him. He froze mesmerized. She kissed him on the lips. Her lips burned. She knew he felt that even stronger. He became like putty in her hands.

– We're burning with dark fire, she hissed at him with her deep voice. – That's the only thing that matters!

She kissed him, kissed him again and again and again. He turned hard below. She felt it as she pushed against his groin. An expectant smile darkened her face.

The door opened. They stumbled inside. His hand reached for the light switch. She grabbed his wrist and kept him from switching on the light. The door closed and locked. There were no windows. The room turned dark. Lori heard his breathing, sensed his skin against hers, and right now; that was all that mattered.

She felt him against her fingertips, at the tip of her tongue and tasted his skin and blood as she bit into his shoulder muscle. They stumbled down on the bed. She hit her head on the wall. It didn't matter. Her temporary dizziness didn't matter. Her awareness quickly returned. Her eyes glowed in a dark light. She saw them through his. It was as if she was both of them simultaneously.

Sleep came. She sensed it long before it came, while they were still moving and pushing and touching and breathing in the pleasant, pleasant night. Her eyes saw him, as she moved on him. Open or closed didn't matter. The vast, prolonged dream opened her further. He vanished under her, but she kept moving, up and down, up and down, even as she was falling, even as she was rising, soaked in sweat, as the dark fire warmed her and disintegrated him and she wet his ashes and her head hit the pillow, and she fell asleep there, on the bed.

She woke up startled, like she knew she would. It didn't even take a second for her to get her bearings. She dressed in a daze, in her new, more mundane clothes, leaving behind her executive look, not looking at the still form on the bed, not even once. The different attire, look burned at her from the mirror forming, reforming in the air in front of her. The room faded around her, the stench of smoke filling her nostrils. She walked through the streets. The hotel burned down behind her. The dark fire burned her and strengthened every piece of flesh and bone she possessed.

Chapter Seventeen

She had a large Latte at Roscoe.

The taste and heat of the coffee burned pleasantly on her lips, tongue and in her throat, spreading from her stomach to her entire body and self.

She sat there, studying people outside and inside. A girl in a red skirt crossed the street, seemingly heading for the coffee bar, but turning just before reaching the door. A man carrying an umbrella stopped for a moment outside the window, but kept walking not long afterwards. Another man sat by a table without touching his coffee. The hot drink slowly turned cold. Lori sat there dreaming herself away. When she «woke up» several minutes had passed. The hands at the clock on the wall had moved significantly.

Her stomach growled, making its hunger known. She sat there, inactive for a while longer, before standing up and walking to the cashier.

– I'll have the Greek salad, please.

The vegetarian dish was, as always more than a full meal. She practically devoured it, and slowed down deliberately in order to enjoy it more, to better appreciate the taste and her surroundings between the mouthfuls.

The food still faded from the plate like moisture on a summer morning. She sat there, looking at it for a while, enjoying the sensation of the food being digested in her system. It felt pleasant, even as hunger kept haunting her.

The push started in her arse. She walked to the solid toilet door and pushed the code. The door opened. She walked inside. The door closed behind her. She locked it and walked to the toilet bowl, pulling down her pants and panties and sat down. The shit poured from her arse fast and furious, without much hassle. It felt good emptying herself. Thoughts slipped away as well. She rose and dried herself. The stench filling the small room felt pleasant in her nostrils.

She walked through the space of coffee drinkers. They watched her. At the very least a couple of them did. Their features burned on her retina. She returned to the street outside. The stench of smoke and ashes lingered in the air. The snarl of a smile crossed her face.

The young man standing across the street with the sack on his back stood out to her, like an intense glow in the night. It was bright daylight and it didn't matter.

She crossed the road and stopped in front of him, giving him her best smile. He looked at her with curious and skeptical eyes.

– You have a great butt, she told him.

He turned deep red.

– You're cute, she told him.

The major power of laughter echoed through the air and the ether.

She grabbed his jaw.

– I've seen you around the tower a lot lately. Come and check us out on a deeper level when you're ready.

He looked beyond bewildered at her, unable to take his attention off the mirage in front of him.

– What's the matter with you? She grinned. – Aren't you used to women taking the initiative?

– You're so much more… intense, he marveled.

She grinned wolfishly at him, allowing him to study and appraise her. He finally reached out for her, but by then she had turned and walked away. Her loud chuckle echoed in his warm, warm ears.

He faded behind her, like all the rest. She searched for the nurse, revisiting the hospital, met with nothing but shaking heads and disapproving looks. She walked up and down Queensway again, like she had done so many times in her thoughts and memories, in her nights of future past.

She sensed something on some spots, seeing Lynn burning again, but only as pale remnants, not like anything happening right now, nothing but echoes.

Queensway Tube Station embraced her with its cool shadows. She cast a glance behind her in order to see if anyone was following her, but she saw and sensed no one.

The elevator brought her downwards. She imagined that it fell like a feather, and hit the ground like one as well. It drew to a halt. The doors opened and she stepped outside, into the vast setups of tunnels. A short walk brought her to the waiting area, just before the train stopped. The doors opened and she stepped inside the central line train to White City.

She felt a… pull as she sat down and tensed. A voice spoke in her head, but didn't make sense. She relaxed again and leaned back in the seat.

The hot October days became shadows. Two trains passed each other in the darkness of muted sound and electric sparks. Lori sat in her seat, lost in thought.

The train pulled to the stop, the first stop on Lori's journey.

– This is the Central Line train, a very formal, very businesslike voice sounded through the speakers. – This is Nothing Hill Gate. This train terminates in White City.

Lori imagined she heard several people giggle, giggle very loud. She drummed her fingers on her knee. It sounded like a drum.

She gasped then, without knowing why. It was as if she suddenly could hear someone breathing. She blinked, and she imagined she sat in another coach staring at Lynn and Janice, at them both simultaneously, as they stared at each other through each other's eyes, even as she realized that Lynn wasn't there, but Eldora was.

They were here, on this train. She realized that startled, undeniable.

The two of them spoke to each other, but it seemed faint, distant, as if she couldn't quite catch it in the wind. She sat in a daze, unable to do anything active with her mind or body.

– This is a Central Line train, the voice said through the speakers. – This is Shepherd's Bush. This train is terminated in White City.

Lori suddenly understood what she didn't quite get earlier. Awareness grew to a crescendo in her memory and consciousness. What had been muddled turned to certainty. The train pulled to a halt.

She rose, and left the train in a fairly relaxed pace. The doors closed behind her just as she stepped down on the platform floor. The train started moving again. Lori started running. Janice and Eldora are also running. No one else is.

– She said terminated, Janice cried. – I'm positive!

Lori nodded to herself.

– I can't say I heard that, Eldora mused. – Are you sure?

– I've never been more certain of anything in my entire life.

The young woman's voice brimmed with confidence, with certainty.

They ran upstairs. Lori chased the other two. They ran through the street.

– Taxi! Janice shouted, rushing into the street without looking left or right. – TAXI!

Lori caught a glimpse of them as they jumped into the black cab ahead. She waved down her own car, more than a little brutal. It stopped with screaming tires.

– Follow that cab! She told the driver.

She was evidently very persuasive. He stepped on it.

The sense of urgency prevailed and grew as she sat there, not for a moment removing her eyes and attention from the cab ahead.

The ground shook. She saw it, saw the cars swerve on the suddenly slippery ground. They crashed into each other and lampposts and walls. The explosion reminded her of a sound of thunder. Suddenly, the street was completely blocked with wrecked cars.

Lori saw how Janice opened the door and jumped out, and Eldora following her not far behind. They ran. Lori followed them at a distance. She floated a bit above the ground. No one noticed or even bothered looking at her. All three of them moved into the melee, a world of smoke and screams and haze. Most people ran in the opposite direction. Others just stumbled ahead with empty eyes.

A man approached Janice. He waved his right arm. His left was gone, completely gone. Blood gushed from the stump on his shoulder.

– BOMB! He shouted.

He kept repeating it, until he fell over and fell silent. Janice and Eldora stopped. Lori hovered in the air and studied it all from a distance. They couldn't see her, but she knew that Janice could sense her.

The girl looked around with a pained expression in her eyes, but also with a frown.

There were bodies and parts of bodies everywhere. There was a large hole in the ground not far ahead. Wreckage was unevenly distributed across a vast area.

– The entire station is gone, Eldora cried in distress.

– What's that stench? A man choked.

Janice knew what it was. Lori saw that with one glance.

[It's blood!] Lynn stated.

Lori heard her this time, at least in part. Lynn and Janice had another private conversation of the mind.

[You shouldn't be alarmed by its presence, sister], Lynn stated.

Janice frowned, attempting to focus her thoughts, to form a coherent phrase.

[What?]

[Death, sweet girl. It's always there, with us, one way or another, and will always be.]

Janice blinked and suddenly, for a brief moment Lori could see what she saw, could see Lynn Jenny and the rest outside the old church.

[See? See how it empowers you, opens you up to what lies Beyond? You see, Death is merely a trifle, an obstacle for a witch on her or his quest. Each time we're reborn we grow stronger, more powerful than ever!]

Lori watched Janice, saw how the girl disoriented and dizzy attempted to get her bearings and lost contact with Lynn and her own, deeper self.

The wall to the right crumbled. Janice (and Lori) noticed the long, deep tears and it collapsed before their eyes. The vision lasted two, three seconds, while she blinked again and desperately attempted to clear her eyes, and then the building was back up, a little dusty here and there, a little damaged, but basically whole. It was as if it had never fallen, and it hadn't, except in their vision.

Janice gasped and had trouble breathing. Eldora grabbed her gently and pulled her away, away from Death, from the Wasteland the city streets had become.

Lori allowed herself to fall back on the ground. She pulled back, away from the other two, following the drawings in her memory.

Loud, very loud sirens filled the air, filled Lori's mind. She walked in the opposite direction of the approaching cars, joining the many fleeing from the death and carnage. They were heading east, passing the closed Central Line tube stations back to the central part of the city. All stores closed, as if by quiet agreement, doing so long before the heavy military presence filled the streets.

She walked, walked long distances, like she had done so much the last months. It hardly felt like an effort or even tiring. A man rushed outside and left the trash in the can, and hurried back inside. A man walked fast and furious through the streets, dragging his little daughter with him. The child laughed, laughed loud and carefree… and wicked.

Lori walked on, on light feet. The giggle kept working itself up her throat.

A loud voice on repeat and broadcast through powerful speakers eventually filled the streets, filled her ears wherever she walked.

– AS OF TODAY, AND UNTIL FURTHER NOTICE, THERE'S A CURFEW FROM SIX IN THE EVENING TO SIX IN THE MORNING. PLEASE BE AWARE THAT ANYONE GOING OUTSIDE IN THAT TIME PERIOD WILL BE SHOT WITHOUT FURTHER WARNING BY PATROLLING SOLDIERS OR LAW ENFORCEMENT AGENCIES.

Lori's giggle turned to loud and visceral laughter. People looked at her as if she wasn't right in the head. She laughed even harder.

She heard many foreign tongues. They rushed towards her on a soft wave. She couldn't quite tell what was what, but she knew some of them were there and some of them weren't. It had nothing to do with the actual difference in language.

The giggle persisted. It made her smile, smile, smile…

Six o'clock had passed some time ago. She kept walking deserted streets. She encountered no soldiers or uniformed people of any kind, no public officials what so ever. There were some civilians. They usually crossed a given distance from house to house in a rush, casting anxious glances in all directions.

She heard shots being fired. Her ears caught the occasional loud scream. She moved on.

The detachment kept touching her from time to time. She could not help herself or stop that, not completely and she didn't want to. From time to time… she stopped and turned distant. She heard the sound of heavy boots stamping on the sidewalk nearby. Her pace picked up and she removed herself from the patrol, the women and men with big, ugly guns roaming the streets of London. Clarity brightened her eyes. The detachment didn't return.

A bird passed over her. She didn't spot it until it was close by. It had a huge wingspan. She saw it with utmost clarity. It was an eagle. She looked wide-eyed at it.

She watched it as it flew towards a derelict industrial site ahead, one that already had quite a few trees grown tall in the ruins, penetrating the holes of collapsed roofs. Once again, the chuckle worked itself up her throat. The smile spread on her face.

She sensed them, sensed them while still walking through empty ruins. The wind was blowing. It ripped into her clothing and rustled her hair. One wall had a smooth surface. The reflection of the sunlight on both walls made a circle in something resembling or imitating a mirror. The bright light turned dark, inverted, becoming the spinning dark wheel in her eyes.

They sat on worn benches, around a worn table. Everyone turned their heads and looked up when she stepped across the threshold to the open space.

– I come here as a seeker, she greeted them, – seeking others not fearing the night and the bad women and men with guns invading it.

One man stood up.

– Then you've come to the right place.

He sat back down. She joined him, joined the circle of wanderers in the night.

– Let's light a fire, she suggested.

They looked stunned at her, but she saw that her suggestion sounded very much appealing to them.

She looked around, and they did as well. They noticed, half distant that there was no lack of dry wood around. Everyone, by quiet agreement began gathering it, using it to create a rather large heap. They picked dry, yellow grass and placed it between the dry wood and branches.

A second, almost as tall heap formed close to the first.

The man lit the biggest heap with a lighter from three different sides. It started burning with an even, steady flame. A couple of minutes later that flame had grown to surround the entire heap. It danced in everyone's faces and its shadows darkened the open space and everyone within its brittle walls.

– Can you hear the music, she asked them, – feel the very vibration in the air?

Some of them nodded, some doing so eagerly, others hesitant.

– I'm not certain, the man frowned. – I believe I hear something, but shouldn't it, if it's real remove all doubt from my mind?

Lori nodded. Others nodded as well.

– I *do* hear it, she stated, – hear it almost without pause. I know from experience that it might be difficult to perceive at first, but rest assured that it will assert itself and that certainty will come!

They watched her, studied her, some of them like hawks filled with both wonder and suspicion. She waited, enjoying the heat from the dancing flames, enjoying them as they touched her, as they warmed her bones.

Far sounds echoed in her ears and her mind, in the deepest recesses of her mind, and she sensed her power awaken anew. It had waited patiently for this lone moment.

– So, how did you get here? A woman asked straight out. – How did you find this place? It isn't exactly a well-known route or destination.

– It will be, in time, Lori shrugged. – It will be something akin to a shrine, one that people will seek across vast distances.

– You sound pretty certain of that, as if…

Lori pulled a folded piece of paper from her pocket. She unfolded it and showed them.

Their eyes widened.

It showed this place, but clearly years from now, the ruins even more pronounced, but unmistakably this exact place.

– You will be convinced of my legitimacy soon enough, she stated. – You will doubt for a while, but then you will know beyond any reservation, and in the meantime, you will serve me and our tribe well enough.

– T-this drawing is amazing, a man stuttered.

– Thank you, Dusty, Lori said softly. – What a nice thing to say.

Dustin Cramer's mouth didn't close.

– I know the deepest secrets of you all, the witch, the priestess stated, – and some of them are a doozy, but I won't expose them for all to see and hear. Eventually, we will all know everything about each other, but by then it won't matter. By then we'll be united in an unbreakable fellowship of fate the world has hardly ever seen.

Fear and doubt and anger and everything in-between surged through them, as they sat there, unable to take their eyes off her.

– No, I'm not threatening you. I will never reveal your secrets to anyone, except to those of you harboring those secrets and doubting me. You will! You will do so with joy in your heart.

– If this is an elaborate hoax, you're good, Dusty said. – You're great. But the motive of it eludes me. We aren't wealthy, have no important jobs or anything… A hoax seems like such a colossal waste of time. I wouldn't rule it out, with the world being like it is… but I do doubt it.

– You will laugh a lot every time you recall those cautious words, she teased him, – in the many years to come.

She studied them, each and every one of them in an open and frank manner making both women and men blush, more than imagining that she repeated actions already made.

They began picking from the small heap, using that to sustain the fire. There was still a lot to go around. The fire never shrunk from a given desired level.

It began or proceeded slowly, rising from a single infinite point within. She started *sweating*. Soon, from one moment to the next, every piece of her skin was soaked in sweat. The echo of the lowest sound echoed in her sensitive ears, and she could easily differentiate between each and every one.

They all saw it, how shadow fire began dancing on her skin and that it didn't burn her clothes. Her eyes turned dark, even in the white. They all gasped aloud.

– Good, good, she spoke with her ghostly voice, – I have your complete attention. Is that not true, Leslie Newton?

– Yes, the woman hastily replied. – Goddess, yes!

Unrest shook Lori. Unable to help herself, she refrained from speaking.

– The forces shaking me aren't easily controlled, she explained. – I'll probably never gain complete control of them. Who can control the wind, the lightning burning the very air? We may be able to harness it to a point, but we can never control it. Control is an illusion, and once you've realized that, control is yours to enjoy.

She grinned, the silent snarl exposing her fangs.

The dark creature in their midst leaned back a little and began its tale.

– It's the October full moon and the start of the festival of Samhain, the season of the witch.

She calmed herself with an effort and was finally able to sit still.

– Chills of awareness assault me. I can't help that. My old self will, to a certain degree always remain. That fact will be both good and bad, will both aid me and hold me back, me and all the others destined to shake this world to its foundation.

She reached out, reached out with her shadow fire and touched them, and it felt like nothing to her. They released tiny whimpers. Chills of awareness assaulted them. The silent snarl shook them.

– Now, now, you know a tiny piece, a pale echo of what I feel, know enough to know that the season of the witch will be something special this year and all the years to come.

She showed them, being kind, revealing slowly parts of the bigger world to them. Time trickled like a river on even ground as she filled them with her vision. It wasn't hard, wasn't easy. She just did it without concentrating or focusing in any significant manner. The veil flickered in the quiet wind and a vast space appeared behind it, behind wide open eyelids. A carpet was pulled from its spot on the floor, and an immeasurable depth revealed itself below.

Distant voices, mumbling came closer, turning into music, music ripping into them, filling their minds, leaving no room for anything else.

Doubt faded away. Certainty ascended. They nodded to themselves through the pain and noise rising from the Abyss below, choking in distress.

One voice spoke. They recognized Lori's voice.

– Choose! She stated. – Choose not to choose.

They shook their heads in confusion, unable to take their attention off her.

Blood boiled and hurt in their veins, making them whimper and heave. A giant hand printed with blood had been drawn on the wall.

They believed they opened their eyes again, until it dawned on them that they had been open all the time.

Lori had left. They searched for her, but found her nowhere, seeing her everywhere. Everyone looked bewildered and distraught at each other.

She stood face to face with Dusty. He shook in despair.

– Where were you? We looked everywhere for you.

– I was There all the time, she replied calmly, casually, indifferent. – Why didn't you spot me?

He faded away once again, and she forgot about him, or at least delegated the memory of him to a remote spot in her consciousness.

She walked through a busy street. People crossed her line of vision in a constant flow. It was a familiar, comfortable pattern to her. The sun broke through the clouds. Its bright light didn't blind her. She spotted Lynn Jenny at the gate across the street. Suddenly, the scream penetrating the world and a deep, snarling bass were close. It made her shake in shock.

– On a long, dark road of shifting shadows I hear your steps.

Lynn Jenny said.

She faded away into empty air, and behind her stood revealed only the bare brick wall.

The boy appeared from a mist, or something resembling one. His mouth opened impossibly wide. His face twisted into terrifying features and he screamed, a scream piercing everyone's eardrums, doing so in a wide circle, like violent rings in the water.

Walls and the very air shook, each wave changing the very reality around them all. The scream seemed endless. People screamed, even as Lori was unaffected. Vastly different landscapes and imagery revealed themselves, briefly, before fading. Visuals of realms far from Earthly experience revealed themselves. In one of them she glimpsed or imagined she glimpsed her son.

The scream stopped. The boy's face returned to normal and he collapsed on the spot. He knelt there heaving for breath.

Lori walked to him. He looked up as her shadow fell on his shaking figure.

The boy stared at her.

– I feel light, he gasped, he pondered, – as if I can't touch anything, as if I'm not quite here.

– Your impressions echo mine, she remarked. – Come with me!

He fought himself up on weak legs. She turned and walked away. He followed her, slowly regaining a somewhat steady walk. People stared at them in horror and shock. No one attempted to approach or chase them.

A man carried four garbage disposal bags. He was tall, big and muscular, handling the heavy load easily. Her eyes were drawn to him, as he crossed the street in front of her and her companion. He was wearing a coat, a thick warm coat clearly making him sweat. The content in one of the bags moved. She blinked slowly. The movement repeated itself, confirming it beyond doubt.

Two armed constables appeared from the opposite corner, giving everyone a hard stare.

The big man stumbled and lost his grip on the bags. One of the bags was ripped open. A nude and moaning half unconscious girl was revealed bound and gagged. Most people in the street gasped and pointed accusing fingers at the man. The coppers froze and directed their semiautomatics at him. He snarled and reached inside his coat. They fired at him, even as he attempted flight. He was hit by both salvos and fell to the ground.

Lori and her companion moved on, leaving the ruckus behind. They weren't followed. The two coppers had other things on their mind, as they stood there beaming, congratulating each other with their catch.

The wounded man bled out on the sidewalk. The girl attempted to pull away from him, managing the feat somewhat. The coppers made no move to aid her.

Lori and her companion left the scene. It faded behind them, lingering, not fading completely. Half an hour later, she could still glimpse the fading mirage.

– What did he want with them? The boy wondered, clearly shaken.

– He wanted sex slaves and fresh meat, she shrugged.

It didn't exactly bring him peace.

– What happened to me? What is happening to me?
– You touched the hidden realms and revealed them to everyone close by, she replied. – You awoke to your power and it's a sight to behold. Be proud!
The roar of the truck passing by briefly drowned her voice, but he still heard her, and it made him crash and burn in repeated shakes.
– Your power, your mighty power will continue manifesting and bringing calamity and disarray to the world, and its beyond stunned creatures.
Her quiet, confident statement brought even more anxiety to his already anxious expression.
Time passed slowly. She could practically count every single second and even moment, but it still felt to her like time was racing, ticking away.
Timeless was existence, was reality behind the veil.
She noticed the street, each piece of it, every single brick, photographing it yet again in her mind. Every feature swarmed her consciousness.
They sat in a quiet, dark cafeteria an immeasurable timespan later, devouring giant sandwiches hardly fitting their tiny mouths.
The girl on the floor danced to the beat with misty eyes, so immersed in the music that she hardly noticed anything around her.
Lori noticed her and everyone in the room, even as she focused on the boy.
– I try to make it happen again, he said, clearly frustrated, – but I can't.
– Push, she told him, – push it away from you and it will emerge, never to go away again.
He did, did make the attempt, clearly struggling. One of his hands or at least the air around it started shivering. The tiny blast lit up the entire room. Lori smiled and he returned the smile in a state of mind akin to ecstasy.
The music from the speakers made her drowsy and inattentive. She had trouble dealing with it, grasping her surroundings. The dancers, suddenly more than one, suddenly many didn't look like they were there at all. Eyes stared at her from everywhere. Focusing took an effort. She finally shook herself out of it.
The music… penetrated her. She sat there rocking on the chair.
Her attention was directed at a candle on a neighboring table. Its flame flickered, burning so much faster, shifting in just a few seconds.
The growing flame turned green and darkened the room. The noise, the wretched noise made her ears bleed.
A girl started burning as well, surrounded by that selfsame green, eerie flame. It was obvious that it didn't harm her and that her clothes remained intact. She sat there and listened to the music brought to her through the earplugs, so immersed in it that she hardly noticed anything around her.
The wretched noise turned quiet, and a sense of well-being entered Lori.

– Go to her, she told the boy, – ask her to join us.
He hesitated a bit, just a bit before he rose in a rush and walked to the nearby table. The girl removed her earplugs. Lori didn't hear the words, but she saw the girl crack a smile, and join him as he returned to Lori.
The girl stopped and hesitated a bit, and stopped before Lori. Lori moved her hand, displaying the whirlwind shadow. The boy revealed his hand trick as well. The girl's smile grew to astonishment and excitement. She sat down in a fast and furry movement, anticipation dominating her features.
– You are…
– We are like you! Lori stated. – We're all the same.
– What…
– We're the Earth and sky, day and Night, Lori stated. – We're the new order.
– I can almost understand what that means, the girl frowned.
The waitress put three pints of Guinness on the table. Lori grabbed her glass and raised it. The others did as well. Glasses met and parted. They drank.
– I had a very encouraging conversation with a new fellow warrior today, Lori said. – He sat there rocking in front of the fire. He sounded like he got it, you know, finally got it. He realized how the current human world works, how it no longer should be allowed to work.
She grabbed the girl's hand.
– You know it, now, don't you, know how it tastes?
The girl allowed the dark fluid to linger in her mouth, and she nodded with wide eyes.
– Then you can hear the music.
Lori rose from the brittle chair.
– Phillip and Caitlyn may wait here, wait together. Lori will be back, will return soon.
Lori turned around and walked away in one single fluid movement.
She got hungry again and regretted that she hadn't fed better before leaving the cafeteria.
Feet moved her around, back and forth, circling a wide area, before she found what she was looking for.
She found a garbage can and began searching through it, and hit paydirt quickly. The piece of meat felt so good in her hand. She began devouring it in savage bites.
The low rumble shook her eardrums, her very feet as she moved down a dark street. She felt sleep come, felt how her elevated energy levels depleted her. She was alone, with no one to guard her, and her surroundings suddenly appeared threatening and terrifying, but she couldn't keep her eyes open.

Her eyes and mind sought shelter and found one, a locked door in a rush. She opened the lock. It hardly took a shift of focus at all.

The dusty, abandoned office welcomed her. It changed in her vision, perception to suit her, fitting her perfectly. There was furniture, chairs and tables and couches covered by white sheets. She smiled and placed herself at the center of the open space revealing itself. Her voice, when it made its pitch sounded strong and confident.

– Who will call my name at the gates of death? Who will support me unconditionally?

It pushed easily beyond the room, the brittle walls, to the endless streets and avenues and forests and plains outside.

It was right outside, no farther than the closing and opening of eyes.

The Gypsy, dressed in a very expressive outfit stood in the circle, her body bathing in the silver light of the full moon. She wasn't alone, and beyond the flesh and bone and mind surrounding her, Lori could glimpse the walls and floor of the old church.

– This is the first night, only the first of five, of the many to follow, Gypsy, Lynn Jenny cried within and beyond the ancient walls. – We've all come to this place, searching for something we may never find.

The choir rose and filled the air around her.

– MAY NEVER FIND

The sight and sensations faded away. Only the empty room remained. Lori grabbed a sheet and pulled, uncovering the couch, the inviting couch.

She felt the lethargy come, how her elevated energy levels depleted fast and furious the remains of her strength. She was alone, with no one to guard her, and her surroundings suddenly seemed threatening and terrifying, but she couldn't keep her eyes open. Her body practically fell on the couch. Her head hit the soft fabric and her eyes closed, and she felt sleep come.

Her dreams and visions mixed. She was pulled into it like a leaf in a storm. Confusion mixed with clarity haunted her as faces and sensations chased her relentlessly down the drain of her consciousness.

A woman stood before her and displayed her wicked grin.

– The new world that has always been here is coming.

Lori frowned, recognizing her own face, her devil-may-care grin, but probing deeper, she didn't really recognize this woman.

– Don't be daft, Lori, the Lori in the shimmering mirror, made of air and mist taunted her. – Would you from six months ago have recognized you from tonight?

Lori, the Lori no longer certain she was actually sleeping found herself nodding. It, the statement made sense, no matter its blatant obscurity. The frown didn't go away.

– The Dark River is flooding all fields, flooding and soaking previously dry city streets, making way for the Earth and sky, day and Night, making room for you.

William Synos was running. She was stunned to watch his scared to death visage. She spotted herself in his huge bulging eyes. He hardly seemed like the same man anymore, but like a scared child running from his most terrifying nightmare. She found herself grinning wickedly. They had a conversation, quite the one-sided conversation, where she did almost all the talking, and it was such a pleasure, such a delight to behold.

He fell and hit the concrete far below, just one more spot on her windshield. She shivered and shook and chuckled and cackled, and it was all so very, very funny.

When she woke up the next morning there was hardly any sense of interruption, only of continued, ongoing movement. She walked through the streets again and it felt like her walk had never paused.

The dark men brought the change. She watched it as it unfolded. What for a long time had been hidden and denied rose to the surface. She watched yet again the girl bursting into green flames and she saw the burning man, saw his clothes and surroundings turn to ashes and crumble and fall. The bubbles that for so long had been rising to the distant surface suddenly broke the thin film of water, and the water started boiling, from the bottom to the steamy air, a womb soon to give birth.

Halloween paraphernalia, like skeletons and stuff had become pronounced during the night, but even that seemed like a natural progression from the modest start she had spotted the day before.

Kids seemed bolder, far less intimidated by the adult world than they usually revealed themselves to be. They shouted with loud, daring voices and excessive moves their presence to the surroundings. Others returned the greeting equally undaunted.

– Isn't this early? A man said to his companion. – They don't usually start this early… do they?

Lori smiled to them, grinned to them, and they saw it, experienced it, and their anxiety grew further.

She sat on some sidewalk cafe somewhere and devoured a huge baguette and a huge cup of coffee. The dressing and vegetables and everything melting in her mouth flowed down her throat and into her stomach, where it spread throughout her body, and she felt the spices everywhere. She sat there for a while, enjoying the meal long after it was done, giving her such a great sense of well-being.

People sitting close or passing by revealed themselves to her by a casual glance. They were hardly anything but distractions on the path revealed to her. One brief closing or half closing of the eyes and it once again closed off everything else.

She was walking again, and her time sitting at the sidewalk appeared like just one more blink in eternity.

– Please help me, a man begged and shouted, as he stumbled across the street.

He grabbed some of the people he passed, and some of them might have been willing to help, but he ran on before they got a change to even respond.

– PLEASE, HELP! He shouted in absolute desperation and insanity.

He was gone from her view so fast that Lori didn't feel confident that he was actually real. A drawing, a meaningless drawing had more substance. He had seemed and seemed ethereal to her, like a snapshot of a life.

She walked on, and as she did so she realized slowly that she had become more alert, that the man, the ghost of a man caused that to happen, without her being able to tell why, and she started sweating a bit more. It took a while longer to realize that she had started noticing in more detail the areas she moved through, as if she was… marking them, leaving a trace of herself as she walked. The walls, the brick and mortar changed and so did the flesh close by.

The walk brought her far, farther than she would have dreamed possible only a short while, months ago.

People stared at her as she approached the building. They stared at her with wicked eyes.

She returned to the so called alternative bookstore she had visited like a dabbler ages ago. It did point to itself, exposing itself to her. She stepped inside, a little on edge, without being able to tell why. It was on her path, she knew that. The interior as it currently presented itself looked just as familiar to her as the front of the building.

People glanced at her with curious eyes. She noticed that without straining herself. Something had changed, had changed here as well. She realized that they looked at her with… with respect.

The very nature of the store and its people, both customers and staff had changed. The books offered, the inventory, the very mood of the place had become vastly different compared to the superficial, smooth surface it had once been.

As below, so above, the strange, unknown woman in the air stated. As within, so without.

A woman stepped forward, slightly reluctant, slightly awestruck.

– Greetings, Genesis! Welcome to our humble store.

– Thank you for your kind welcome, Pamela Weller, Lori said. – It's appreciated!

The woman gasped a little, as her name was pulled out of the magician's hat.

Lori kept looking around, committing all of it to memory.

– Is there anything… anything we can do for Genesis?

– Not right now, thank you, Lori replied, more than a little distracted, – she has mostly come here to observe the changes, all the great changes with her own eyes.

She fell easily into the… into the role playing, the role playing becoming real, becoming true.

One ring of a soundless bell and she took in the sight of all the people in the store, the basement, the upper floor, every possible angle and viewpoint, once again doing so with a casual glance.

She probed beneath their surface without trying. They felt the intrusion, and the moment they did so, it grew far more pronounced.

The book placed on the table by the stairs pointed to itself. It was old, decrepit and covered in equally old protective, part transparent paper. Its markings and decorations were beyond elaborate and mysterious. The letters and signs burned in her vision. Its pages were flipping in a sudden burst of wind. Dust rose in the bright air as its movement ended on one particular page.

The stairs went up and down and to the sides in a many-dimensional space Lori had no trouble seeing. The writing on the old, yellowed paper burned itself into her mind.

The moment she closed her eyes, her visions grew in strength and complexity. The letters caught fire.

Whisper these words of malice and spite and dream them true.

They kept repeating themselves in her vision until they turned audible, like curses in the night.

Whisper these words of malice and spite and dream them true.

She returned slowly to the woman and the man standing side by side.

They looked at her with expectation and fear in their wet eyes. She was used to that and found that it sat well with her.

– What does Genesis see? The man wondered.

She pondered his question at some length before replying.

– All… or almost all the old stories, mankind's oldest delightful and frightening legends are true, she said slowly, startled, – or at least have some basis in facts, in real events. Centuries, ages have passed since they were commonplace, and they've mostly been forgotten, but now, as they're resurfacing, they will be forgotten no more.

They and quite a few of the others present understood, clearly or vaguely what she was saying. Yet another brief, casual glance told her that.

– My compliments, Pamela and Hamish, she said, – you've gathered quite a well of fairly advanced arcane knowledge here.

It appeared like he hadn't actually heard her at first. Then he caught himself and finally responded.

– We decided to make that extra effort, he said, – combing off-library sources. There was a surprisingly high number of them. Many libraries have also struggled with public funding lately and wanted to unload what they see as redundant material.

– Your hard work paid off, Lori praised him and he blushed like a young, inexperienced boy.

Several other people joined them, joined in on the event haunting the store. She smiled to them. They returned the smile with adoration and awe in their eyes, in their very being.

She walked among them, was walking among them even after she had left. Their presence lingered at the tip of her awareness, like her pervasive presence kept overwhelming them.

– Chills of awareness are assaulting me. I see the great and horrible events to come.

– The new world is… coming?

– The new world isn't coming, isn't on its way. A new world is right here, in the tunnel and the shadow at its end.

She showed them. It didn't take much effort. They gasped and shook during the vast hurricane, the relentless onslaught.

Some of them followed her. She allowed it. They trailed her, stumbling in her wake.

She heard the screeching of wheels, sensations and screams of pain. She saw smoke rise from a completely different part of the street. The stench of blood and gas reached her from everywhere. She exploded in spontaneous, carefree and wild laughter. It broke and flowed from a place deep within her and spread to her surroundings.

– The moon is shining through the curtain at the wild beast in me, she cried. – The moon is shining and the grass is red, and it's such a delight!

Her companions felt her delight, felt it in their innermost self.

She crossed and crisscrossed her tracks. The ground brightened and darkened like a path before her, by a light, a shadow coming from nowhere, nowhere observable, shifting in an impossible to fathom pattern. She watched her roaming from above. The sounds, sight, taste, scent and sensations invaded her wherever she roamed. She marked her territory with scents more powerful than any chemical.

There was a distinct, qualitative change. She noticed it on a deeper level, beyond the senses at first. One blink and her senses did as well, following the clues of her depths. Streets, people and buildings, everything in her vision burned with clarity.

The light turned red. It practically blinded her. Lori stopped. She frowned. Moments passed until she realized that everyone else kept walking, until it dawned on her that to everyone else the light remained green.

– Stop, she said with a normal voice, until repeating it with a loud shout. – STOP!

All those following her and quite a few others turned and stared at her.

– Get off the road, NOW!

They did, even as there was a loud crack somewhere, and a screech of metal against the ground.

An overturned truck slid down the street, covering the entire road and opposite sidewalk. Many people were hit and were crushed to a pulp.

Screams filled the world (the worlds), fading only slowly. The echo lasted forever.

The truck finally stopped its prolonged flight. The screech came to a startling halt. Silence reigned supreme.

Everyone, absolutely everyone turned to Lori.

– Genesis…

A young male bowed and called her name.

She acknowledged him and the rest with a barely recognizable nod, before turning away and moving on. When she walked down the street and crisscrossed some more in her disparate kingdom, far more followers had joined the long, long trail in her shadow.

They walked on, she relentless, without pause, fatigue or consideration, they stumbling close to exhaustion behind her. All of them glimpsed what she saw some time or another, seeing for a pale moment the world as it truly was, as if was quickly becoming. Parts of reality so far concealed to them revealed themselves, the misty worlds of shadows, the mundane world of brutality and a bias bordering on full-blown hatred for anything different. Everything reached them undiluted, or at least less diluted.

The police assaulted protesters. Bones and skulls broke and voices cracked. The stage seemed completely insane, a vision from the worst kind of hell, distorted beyond belief.

It happened fairly far away from them, but it still touched all of the wanderers, invading them on the most basic level.

– You're not a proper police officer until you're covered by brain mush, she stated.

The sound of breaking bones and skulls and horrible screams echoed in the ether.

The red carpet… the red carpet was soaked in blood.

The mood changed further when they approached another gathering at Nothing Hill Gate.

– Thou shall not suffer a witch to live, a voice hissed just a few steps away.

And then the loud cry sounded through the streets.

– KILL THEM, KILL THEM ALL

They imagined it to be even closer.

– You've joined the witch on her Long Walk, Genesis called. – I salute you! You will be tested far beyond what you believed to be the limits of your endurance.

Fatigue didn't merely touch them. They had become fatigue. The witch moved so fast, with such speed and agility that they needed to run or at least to jog in order to keep up. Some of them fell and didn't get back up, but many held on and stayed on the misty swamp her path had become.

They walked along cars on their way through heavy afternoon traffic, the engines muted in their ears, the stench of exhaust making them gag. Lori hardly felt it, felt any of it.

Today, the endless walk brought Genesis and her companions to another old, derelict and empty building where twilight gathered early. She felt the lethargy come again, the inevitable lethargy she seemed unable to counter.

Birds squeaked. Ravens landed on the roof and entered the building through window frames without glass. The weary but excited human beings gathered in a dusty central hall, where half the roof was gone and the other cast the ground in shadow. Lori sought the shadow, its deepest corners.

A deep yawn worked itself up her throat and was released to the air and reached attentive ears. She sat down on the cold floor, in the dark corner.

Two indistinct shapes knelt by her sides. She noticed, somehow, how they exchanged glances.

– We will aid her, one said, – care for her.

Someone put a bottle to her lips. She drank, sweet lemonade moving down her dry throat. They fed her various foods. She chewed and swallowed whatever was put in her mouth, and felt how it dissolved in her stomach and strengthened her on all levels, even as she fell asleep on the spot. They packed her in blankets and put her on the floor, surrounding her with their own bodies, their heat warming her and soothing her. It felt so good, so incredibly

Chapter Eighteen

She remembered falling asleep. She woke up, without remembering anything in the interim.

The rest, the deep, deep rest had been total. There had been no dreams or visions or anything. She felt alive and ready, as she sat up and fixed her relaxed stare at the two standing in front of her.

– We guarded you, the female said. – We could hardly see you breathe or feel your heartbeat, fearing you were… dead.

– But we knew you weren't, the male said. – We waited for you to wake up.

– Thank you, she said softly. – Thank you for guarding me.

The rest woke up as well, as if their sleep had been keyed to hers. There were lots of yawns and smiles and affectionate touches. She returned them, making a point of hugging everyone present. It took its sweet time, but no one seemed to care. No one was in a hurry anymore. And the scent from the other nude bodies was so pleasant, like a burst of hot desert wind.

Others returned with food, with loads of food and drink.

– We stole it, at a nearby storage, a boy said with excitement and mischief in his eyes, – making sure there would be more than enough for everyone.

They fed, devouring each piece like beasts in the wilderness. All of it was cold and some of it raw, but it didn't really matter. Each piece melted fresh and tasty on their tongue.

She felt the cold floor at her butt. It didn't matter. Her warm, warm body kept burning in the morning chill. It didn't matter. The moisture in the air felt dry as it reached her throat on its way to her lungs and bloodstream. Thoughts kept racing and speeding up, as she kept waking up.

The music rose in her ears and silent ears once again.

She stood up, embracing everyone with one glance.

– You made it, she declared, speaking casually, – made it through the first gate, the initial level. I'll be leaving now, and you will stay here, preparing for what comes next.

The word next echoed through the hall, flesh to flesh.

– You make a stake on this place and fight for it.

– Yes, Genesis, Hamish said, – trust us, we will!

Lori turned and walked away. They faded behind her, like all the rest.

She sat on a bench in a green area somewhere. The sound, the voice reached her ears long before she could hear it. The imagery reached her eyes long before she could see it. The extrasensory sensations flooded her being. It turned dark. She drowned in shadow in the midst of the bright sunlight.

– I see death, Eldora said in the deepest night, – see it a lot…

The shadow crosses her face. Lori didn't merely see it, but experienced it as well.

– And during a night, not that long ago, I saw it closeup. I saw a man white and cold. He was dead beyond recovery. He hadn't been dead a few minutes, but more than an *hour*. People have returned to life after being dead for a few minutes, and after having been found in cold water, but I've never seen anything like this in any official record. He was shot asunder, and bled dry. They were about to put him in the freezer when he twitched, and opened his eyes, and sat up on the stretcher. That man is with us tonight…

Everyone turns towards Trevor, curiosity and awe present in their eyes.

– I dreamt, he, the Dark Man said. – I dreamt of me rising from the grave. I dreamt of a woman in a castle, surrounded by knights. In her right hand she holds a sword, and in her left hand a wand, a wand with a skull on top. I dreamt of buildings crumbling to dust, and the world changing before my eyes.

The darkness faded. The bright daylight reasserted itself.

Her feet touched the pavement. Her hands touched the ether. She felt it at her face, at the edge of her eyes. A van crashed through the window of a store, crushing people inside. The stench of blood ripped into her nostrils. The sound of machinegun fire sounded muted in her ears. Beyond it all she sensed the movement of time. She couldn't catch it, but could touch its firmament, the firmament of forever.

The day passed briefly, unimportant to her.

She slept or believed she slept. The sun set and rose again. The moon kept rising on the sky.

It hovered above Hyde Park, above the city itself, much closer than she had imagined it would be. She imagined she could reach out and touch it. Its dust brushed off her fingertips.

She stood by a window, watching the big, big moon.

Suddenly, she saw herself in the open bedroom window, seeing it from the onlooker's point of view, seeing his thoughts, sensing his emotions. She turned her head slightly, looking directly at him, leaving no doubt whatsoever that she knew he was there. She smiled, a slow deliberate grin, scaring the shit out of him.

– Peek-a-boo, she called. – I can see you.

And he ran, and she was with him for a better part of that panicked run. And…

She felt the Power.

The pale, yellow disk turned bright and distinct and dark in the sky, far brighter than the tiny lamp brightening the day. Its silver light cast shadow everywhere, not just on the tiny spot where she walked and breathed.

She looked from above, at those below, a Shadow far more extensive than the one her flesh and bone body cast on the ground.

– Existence is vast, she told a few people gathered in front of her. – This world is an illusion, not in the sense that it doesn't exist, but in its true significance. It's no more important than countless other worlds and planes of reality out there, in a Universe far vaster than most people can even begin to imagine. Existence is truly endless, infinite, with no beginning and no end and this reality, this entire reality is no more than a philosophical pinprick in that infinity times eternity *squared.*

They faded, not truly disappearing, but delegated to the background of her attention, her ever-expanding vision.

She studied them, and they knew.

– You know! She giggled. – My imposing presence contaminates your perception, and makes you see or at least glimpse reality as it truly is: infinite!

Suddenly she exploded with yet another burst of laughter laughter laughter. She bowed down in a completely uncontrollable outburst, hitting her right thigh with her hand, hardly registering the pain, the sweet pain, watching as waves of mist spread like rings in water.

When she after a while straightened the body, she continued to laugh, loud and bold.

– Do you know, know what it takes of courage to laugh openly, in a public place, unafraid and free?

They looked at her with confusion in their eyes. It wasn't gone, even though there was less of it, that the fact was they had begun to glimpse the bigger truth and they could never more forget.

– I know something about it. I never dared doing it before. Now, I'll never forget and neither will you.

You you you

The word echoed in eternity.

She walked to a woman, stopped before her like a specter, a dancing mist never quite settling.

– You, Oxydan Merryweather will accompany me on the immediate upcoming distance of my long walk. Your old, pallid existence has come to an end. Your life begins now!

She turned and walked away and knew the woman was following, trailing her.

Look at me, she thought.

She knew the woman did.

– It's so funny. I'm walking with my back to you, but I can still see you.

Oxydan's frown grew deep. She couldn't quite liberate herself from her preconception of what the world was, but her eyes were opening, a little bit more for each new second as the moments ticked away.

Time for sleep and dream. The realization came to Lori without resistance. She became increasingly familiar with the process, with the new demands her more powerful mind and flesh placed on her body.

Her yawn echoed in eternity.

– Why is the world filled with stupid love songs? Can you tell me that, Oxydan Merryweather?

The woman looked nonplussed, distressed at her.

– That one is easy. Those in charge want it that way.

The woman looked at her with sudden clarity in her eyes and mind, awareness striking her in soft, soft waves that wasn't Lori's imagination. She was certain of that much.

The longer I reach, the farther I flow from myself, the less certain I become. My reach is powerful, but it isn't infinite, isn't eternal.

Words she spoke to herself raced through her synapses far faster than echoes.

– Guard me while I sleep like the dead!

She crouched on the moist, warm surface she had chosen as her cot. Her eyes closed. They stayed open.

The late October sun rose above the cityscape, the giant tombstones towering above the people walking the emerging streets of fire and shadow. The seat shook beneath her. The train made its way from Waterloo station to Hampton Court.

The fire and the shadow burned her eyes and chilled her bones. Music played somewhere. She heard it as if it was right by her ears, a slow, haunting song. She couldn't help but humming.

She sat alone in the coach. Shadows, dark men filled the space between the spaces. They stared at her with their unfathomable expression. The slow smile broke on her face.

People entered the coach, but they didn't stop, didn't stay. Everyone walked straight through in a fast and anxious pace.

She slept. It was just like before, totally involuntary. She couldn't keep her eyes open. The eyelids fell, feeling heavy like bricks. She didn't fall asleep completely, but experienced the twenty-minute train trip as a kind of waken dream, a daydream cast in darkness. The sun blinded her when she opened her eyes.

The train approached the intimately familiar, the area she had lived for most of her adult life, the place she hardly recognized except as something out of a long removed past life. It faded into her view infinitely slow. The train station at the end of the line was the same, with the same small parking lot and ramshackle building. She left the train, left the station, the stench of the diesel engine not really leaving her nostrils.

The man pushing a baby stroller and the dog by his side walked up and down the street without pause and deviation. He didn't vary his pattern at all, while she watched him, but eventually faded behind her like all the rest.

The ants crawling through her veins, the bad mood she recalled from many late office hours… returned. It felt like an invasion, the most horrible imposition, almost translating into physical pain. She scowled at an old lady she encountered. A dizzy spell almost overwhelmed her. She stumbled and almost fell. The visions began again, violent, repeated attacks on her psyche ripping her apart. The beastly shriek sounded nearby. Mad drumming and music imposed itself on her in violent ways.

She began moving to the beat, synchronizing herself to it, humming its insane melody. It sort-of worked. The dizzy spell persisted, but she gained some modicum of control of it.

The burned-out piece of real estate she remembered was gone. A shiny new house had taken its place. The lawn had once again grown green and healthy, with no trace of the fire visible anywhere. Her vision cleared. Some people saw her and recognized her. They didn't wave or attempt to make contact, but more or less ignored her. The lawnmower didn't move. It stood still by the garage. Its infernal sound no longer filled the entire neighborhood with noise. The dry leaves blew slowly across the lawn.

The vision of the giant, downtrodden airport with its long dusty hallways filled her consciousness in a moment lasting forever. A few bulbs still worked, blinking on and off. A piece of the ceiling fell and hit the floor with silent thunder.

She walked to what had once been the Russell family home. It was clearly deserted, abandoned. She walked to the door and put a hand on the lock. A click and it unlocked. The door slid open. She walked inside.

Impressions of her now quiet, former home hit her softly. Nothing had been changed since she last saw it. Not a single item had been moved that she could see. She walked through the long hallway, into the living room. A glance and she saw the wound in the air, a portal in time and space where her son had vanished, appeared and vanished again. She was still unable to access it, but could now sense it, easily see it for what it was. Her hand reached out and practically touched what to her senses felt like hard air, touched the still sizzling energies. She realized it would always be there, always be accessible to her and others under the right circumstances, by the right set of actions.

A fine layer of something resembling ashes covered her fingertips. It dissolved slowly as she watched.

The parrot, its voice and its cage were gone. Everything here felt empty, abandoned.

Impressions of the past existence imposed themselves on her. In the kitchen, she imagined that she could see a mother and daughter preparing a meal, sharing a quality moment. The catching in the throat came unbidden, quickly fading away.

She walked to the guest bedroom. A very deliberate walk brought her to a drawer in the low sections of the closet. She pulled it out. The confidential part of the Rodham-report, the Genesis project from her former workplace that Rhonda had slipped to her through proxy revealed itself. She picked it up and began flipping the pages. The content didn't seem that important anymore. She knew what it said, what it conveyed to those with the necessary ability to understand.

The entrance door opened. She heard it easily enough. It had been locked. She had locked it. Hands moved by themselves, putting the report back in the drawer, pushing the drawer back in and closing the closet. She left the bedroom and walked into the hallway, almost bumping into her husband.

He looked at her as if he couldn't quite believe his own eyes.

– You smell! He said puzzled.

– I do, don't I? She chuckled.

Her fairly recent upgrade at the beauty parlor long gone, her hair had become greasy, disheveled, suggesting that she had gone far longer than just a few days without cleaning herself. It felt like that.

– I've tried contacting you for *months,* he practically shouted, easily falling back on his old control-freak pattern.

– Likewise, she shrugged. – It doesn't really matter, anyway, anymore.

He caught it, how he didn't matter to her anymore, not even as a source of aggravation and animosity. He crumbled on the spot.

– What happened to you? He whimpered.

– That one is easy to answer. I woke up in a very bad mood one day without knowing why, until the obvious struck me: I can hear the loud scream of pain and suffering filling the world. Thus, I liberated myself, free to roam existence itself.

– You're crazy, he gasped beyond distress.

She stared him down with her insane eyes, and he crumbled before her to nothing, to insignificance.

– I found purpose through my damnation, and joy beyond the darkest fire.

She made her way back to the living room. He followed her like a dog with his tongue hanging out.
– You're nothing, nothing but yet another blood sacrifice.
Reality turned itself inside out the moment she crossed the threshold to the bright room with the portal.
– There you are, a female voice filled with triumph spat.
Toni's twisted features filled Lori vision. They were no longer in the living room or just in the living room, but in Toni's aerie as Lori recognized it from the tower.
– I saw you on TV. I still couldn't get a grip on you, on your location. The people surrounding you created a massive disturbance. To my seeker sense it was as if you didn't exist.
The twisted grin twisted even more.
– But now you're here. Now, I've got you, and I'll never let you escape again.
Lori was frozen in her daughter's merciless grip. She sensed how everything shifted and moved.
– What is this? Tom said stunned. – What…
– Oh, be quiet you simpering idiot!
Toni waved a hand and her father dissolved in flames. His ashes rained down on the non-existing floor between places.
Lori was moved without moving. Resistance was futile.
– «The master made me powerful beyond words».
The spiteful words from long ago repeated themselves in her feverish mind.
She stopped struggling and allowed herself to be pulled away. Two more shapes faded into her consciousness. She recognized Kelly and Julia through a haze of a thousand years.
Lori stopped in front of the trio, the powerful triad combining their powers into an irresistible force.
– There you are, mother. I'm so pleased to see you. I've missed our little talks.
Lori floated in the air, unable to move, hardly able to think. A thought, a desire by the triad, and she floated close to them. Toni stopped her forward momentum with a wave of her hand.
– I can hear the heart hammering in her chest, Julia chuckled wickedly.
– She's so cute, Kelly said.
– She fled in terror from the master like prey from the predator, Toni said, – not knowing that her doom was inevitable.
A hand touched Lori's cheek, but there was no kindness there. A soft touch didn't have to be kind. But on the contrary, be yet another act of malice and

conquest.

– The master will transform you into a fierce and wicked beast, like he did us. You'll want for nothing more!

They grabbed her and pulled her with them, leaving the room. She kept floating, light as a feather. They didn't have to carry her, only pull the feather in whatever direction they desired. Their surroundings changed. Lori got a sense of them. Other females surrounded them, humming like excited peacocks. The luxurious interior imposed itself on her, tempted her, her wiles.

She heard his voice already. Even though his voice came to her from far off, or seemed to, she imagined he already stood right in front of her. She blinked, even though her eyelids didn't move. The humming from what sounded like a thousand throats began. She entered through another door, crossing one more threshold, into what looked like a chapel or a very good imitation of one.

People filed in from all sides, filling the empty benches. Their open mouths added to the choir, the insane choir.

He stood by the altar, surrounded by more concubines, by the singers of the song. Lori's attention was locked on him, eyes, ears, taste and smell, and she couldn't unlock her gaze.

The voices and the buzz faded and the room fell silent. Everyone present had their attention locked on him, unable to avert their blind stare.

– We have another bird with us tonight, he cried, – one that will benefit us all greatly.

Everyone locked their stare on her. She felt x-rayed a thousand times.

Sights of numerous curvy creatures with big bellies cramped her extended vision. It dawned on Lori that the triad was pregnant, that many of the present females were.

He waved a single time, in what seemed like he was waving to her, but was in truth waving to Toni, Julia and Kelly. They brought her to him, brought her before him, like an offering, a tribute. Huge eyes below bushy brows filled her attention, her very consciousness.

She stood frozen before him, her once so elegant hairdo in tatters.

– One falcon flew away, he said. – One falcon returns, like I knew she would.

A cold, hard stare imposed itself on her, doing so from one moment to another, making her shake in her bones.

He began speaking, began doing his thing of compulsion and coercion, the invasion of her mind and being.

She felt what he did. Whatever it was… unlocked her and everything she was flowed to the surface. She still didn't hear all the words, but caught phrases and bits and pieces, and she did understand. The music became her, she became the music, beyond intense and wild. She grew to a giant in her own mind, and she grinned in triumph and expectation.

He frowned. It was all he could do. Suddenly he was the one frozen.

– With one decisive act I destroy myself, liberate myself. I make all words dead and void.

Her words spoken like gibberish, like hexes, derived from a long dead language flowed from her lips.

He gulped. Blood flowed from his mouth. He just fell apart, disintegrating before her eyes. She stopped speaking. He collapsed, crumbling to dust and wet rags, dead long before he hit the floor like decomposed garbage.

The room fell silent, degenerating into total silence.

Lori Michaels turned and faced the gathering, the triad trembling before her.

– She killed the Master, Toni said sullenly and awestruck.

– Yes, Genesis killed the «master», Lori stated calmly, – and he was hardly worth the effort. She killed him as an act of mercy.

The buzz and choir once more filled the room and now it was for her, in her honor.

– On your knees, she bid them, she heard herself say casually.

They obeyed instantly, fearfully, staring blindly at their Goddess, even as they kept humming, kept chanting their song of submission.

– GENESIS, GENESIS, GENESIS!

The puzzle completed itself, still unfinished.

Toni glanced up at her, quickly directing her vision back at the floor, paralyzed, frightened out of her wits when Lori scolded her with both her superior mind and flesh.

– I don't have time for you guys right now. You just stay put. I'll come and fetch you when the time is right.

There was nothing there, nothing left of the people they had been. He had taken it all, and taken it with him to the grave.

She ignored the chill touching her depths and left them there, in the pile of their own ashes.

The wind caught her hair outside. A small tear fell from her left eye, and on a branch sat a raven.

She walked and kept walking through a new land not entirely new, not to her. Ages of memory coursed through her as she crossed its streets and roads. She made it hers, more and more with each new step, every time her feet touched the ground.

The dentist, she sat in his chair, glancing anxiously at his bushy brows. X-rays penetrated her skin and her vast mind, and turned everything inside out. She remembered it vividly. It felt like it had just happened, like it was actually happening right now, and she wasn't completely certain that it didn't.

Everything had become easier. Lifting a rock felt like lifting a feather. Loose items rose into the air all around her. They danced in her honor and sang her praise, as she walked on.

A rock floated into her hand. She grabbed it, studied it and proceeded to crush it to dust in her hand. It took her no effort at all. The powder fell between her fingers to the ground.

She moved within what seemed like a dark cloud. It took only a slight concentration, and she lowered it all to the ground, and she hardly looked any different than all the others walking up and down the street. She enjoyed the warm, warm sunlight on her body.

A dove stopped on the exact spot making the sliding door of an office building open. She stepped inside as the most obvious thing in the world. The male courting her hurried in after her.

– Did you see that? A boy said incredulous to his girlfriend. – It was as if that bird actually knew that its move would make the door open.

– Don't be silly, the girl chided him.

Another unprompted chuckle rose from Lori's throat. They heard her, and exchanging anxious glances, they rushed in the opposite direction from where she was headed.

The pyre, she feels the pyre consuming everything former. She sees it burn in the night on All Soul's Night, senses more than she sees the gathering of shadows.

– The past is prologue, the gypsy brazenly declares.

Lynn Jenny looks at her, at Lori, as she lights the fire.

They drink, drink tea, and Lori does as well. The tiny cup doesn't touch her lips, but its content still flows down her throat. She isn't there. She's There!

– I can feel someone sit by my side, Trevor says.

But there's no one there. Lori looks at him from afar, from closeup.

She sees herself enter the old church, sees herself stand there covered in dust and blood.

– I've walked for days, another Lori says. – I can't remember when I began. During all that time, I saw only the image of this place in my mind, and I sought it with the exemption of everything else.

– This is Lori, Gypsy says to the other four gathered in the old church, – Lori…

– I'm Lori, Lori says to the four she hadn't met before, - Lori Michaels. I'm one of you.

Lori walked in daylight, in firm control of herself and her might. The wilderness across the river, the suddenly so wild river displayed itself to her senses, her vast and acute senses.

The Coleman-building rose slowly from the ground as she walked, as she crossed the small bridge to the outside parking lot. She was calm, a raging sea stirring the sky itself. It rose within her, rose within her yet again. Frustration, the tip of her tongue she still couldn't catch kept riling her.

For some reason, some insane, unfathomable reason she sees Mrs. Rutherford walk her dog. Both Mrs. Rutherford and her dog stare at her with vicious eyes.

The entrance door slid open, parting the moment she crossed the threshold. The raven didn't have to stop in order to make the sliding doors move aside. One, ten, two steps more and she entered the elevator. Its doors closed and it brought her up, up into its master's aerie.

She stepped into the unfamiliar office landscape. Silent drums hammered her. Everyone, even those looking away stared at her. The silent crescendo filled her ears, her very consciousness. She walked the long road to the door at the end of the hallway. Ethereal, bony hands reached for her from both walls.

Lori Michaels stepped into Marco Coleman's office, doing so time and time again until the shifting images and after-images settled into a perceived calm. The shadows on the floor had turned dark and threatening. It didn't move her. She focused on the man sitting behind the desk at the opposite side of the office.

The door closed. It didn't startle her. She just registered it calmly, anxious, like she did everything else. Firm, unshaken feet led her close to the man she had admired with nauseating zeal almost her entire adult existence. She stopped before him, facing him, looking at him with unwavering eyes.

– Hello, Marco, she said casually.

– Hello, Lori, he said in exactly the same pleasant manner, – it's so good to see you again.

– I'll bet!

She said.

They both smiled.

– What do you think of my redecoration? He wondered.

There was no actual physical redecoration. The colors and the carpet and ornaments were exactly the same. Not a thing had been changed or moved.

– I love it!

The shadows, both of this world and others engulfed her. She felt them, their powerful presence, their seething energies. And then there was that something else she both grasped and not. It seethed somewhere below and touched her in both familiar and unfamiliar ways, empowering her further, and she could hardly believe how much.

– Do you feel it? He asked.

He wasn't really asking. She didn't have to reply or voice a reply. The answer was self-evident. She shook in something akin to cramps and feared her menstrual blood would flow.

– What is…

– Why do you ask a question where you know the answer?

She nodded slowly, staring at him with a remote expression in her eyes.

– It's you. You are Genesis, or at least one of its foremost long-term projects. Do you remember the tests you took when you visited us the first time?

She did, and everything, even more of everything suddenly made sense to her.

– I realized early that I needed to be patient. I was even marred with uncertainty for a very long time of trial and error, until confirmation finally hit me between the eyes.

She frowned, a frown cutting deep. It was there, now, right in front of her, one more detail that she hadn't been quite able to grasp.

– You *groomed* me!

He didn't voice a response, she couldn't read his features.

– You were behind the facility in Hackney?

He didn't reply.

– Perhaps you weren't, but you certainly loved the opportunity to study the result. Not that your *observer* fared much better than your colleagues there.

She recalled the observer's final night as a living being with utmost clarity.

– It was at that very moment I knew I had succeeded, he said. – You were ready and you exceeded my wildest expectations. I practically watched how the song, the song of power filled you, and you winked and made both the special and the mundane fall before you like rotten fruit.

She walked around the desk, stepping close to him, to the calm, smiling man sitting relaxed in his chair.

– You goaded me ever longer, until you got me exactly where you wanted me, she said enraged.

– I did, he grinned, – but I didn't truly succeed until you found your true calling, until this very moment.

She tried striking him with her hand, but the moment she did, she felt like she was hit by an invisible force and thrown across the room and pushed at the wall. It did hurt, but she hardly noticed. She snarled at him, a growl shaking air and walls alike.

He chuckled pleased.

– Look at that rage. It will take you far. I sensed your potential the very first time we met. You know what I'm talking about. It's defining you, defining your nature, even more than your power.

She felt it rise within her, but no matter how angry she grew, she couldn't break free from his mental and physical chokehold.

He let go of her, just like that. She dropped to the floor and steadied herself, looking sullenly at him. He rose from his comfortable chair.

– Come with me. I want to show you something.

She was breathing hard. Major parts of her body hurt. She stumbled behind the broad back out of the office and down the long hallway, catching up to the man she had had nosedive admiration for as long as she had known him just as they reached the elevator.

The doors slid open. He stepped inside. She followed him, not taking her eyes off him for an instant.

He wasn't that much taller, but she still felt like he towered above her. He grabbed her, grabbed her hard. She felt it, body and soul. He kissed her on the lips. She was burning, crumbling in his arms, helplessly returning his affection. He let go of her. She gasped and kept gasping, looking at him with shadows dancing in her eyes.

– You had all this power all the time?

– No! He shook his head. – Or I would surely have used it.

He pushed an inconspicuous button on the panel, one of those without a number. She knew with herself that she had noticed it before, but not really paid any attention to it, not on any of her many trips up and down the elevator.

It raced past the floors, not showing any sign of slowing down. She looked at it as it passed the ground floor and continued on its way down, and she recalled her dream.

The retardation began after what felt like forever, but that she realized was hardly more than seconds. The elevator stopped. The doors slid open and revealed the basement of her dream. They stepped outside. A man met them there. She recognized Wilson Florie, a young man she and her former colleagues had deemed to be «on his way up».

– Mr. Coleman and Miss Michaels, he greeted them. – Welcome!

She looked at Marco, not the boy.

– I never saw Tom as a proper mate for you, he shrugged. – His test results were promising as well, though, enough to be deemed your worthy genetic match. It was an unqualified success. Your children are all remarkable.

His words kept hammering her, and she found herself smiling in enthusiastic, growing delight.

– We will have many more children, he stated, – even more remarkable.

Heat and expectation and arousal swept her and gathered between her legs. A silent gasp escaped her open mouth.

They followed Florie down the hallway. The walls, everything here spoke to her. She couldn't keep out the voices, the whispers, the hisses and didn't want to.

It filled her.

Florie opened several locked doors with his security keycard. They flipped open and closed and locked the moment the three of them had walked through. Her hands itched. She scratched them. It did her no good. Marco studied her.

– The walk feels like it lasts forever, she said softly. – Don't worry, I get a lot of that.

The large hall opened up to them. Her eyes burned with the sight of it. A well of unidentifiable emotions rose from her core, her burning core. People strapped to beds filled her vision. They were sedated. Needles stuck in their arms provided drugs to their system. They weren't exactly unconscious. Open eyes stared at the ceiling.

– They're awake, but not aware, he said with pride in his voice, his very being, – the exact state of being of most use to me… to us.

She looked at him, at them, and back at him.

– You can feel it, he stated. – I know you can!

– I can, she said slowly. – It's such a rush!

It flooded her.

When she looked at her hands, she saw the invisible flames without effort.

– I've become skilled in the art of utilizing them, he told her. – I can do so without effort, easy as blinking or twitching a finger.

She felt arousal merely by looking at him.

– Yes, he said excited, – you feel it, feel our attraction.

His eyes burrowed into her. She felt their hooks.

– It does feel right, she admitted, giving him a huge, sensual smile, – so very right.

– And it will feel even more right as our agenda progresses, he beamed. – With our combined power and my *guidance,* we will be unstoppable. We will bring these… batteries with us. They will sustain and empower us wherever we go, aiding us greatly in our…

– … our conquest, she choired with him.

He beamed at her, so very pleased with her, with himself.

She could practically see it, see her drawings making the future. Her eyes moved. She glanced shyly at him, fearing she was practically dissolving in his presence. Cold heat and hot chills surged through her. She certainly would have… if… if… she hadn't polished and kept polishing that hard cold and hot emerald deep within, made it harder than steel.

The smile came easy to her. She posed for him, displaying herself with pride and confidence.

Even though it feels right, it might not be.

She thought.

He took the first step forward, reaching out a hand to her. She stepped forward as well, reaching out to him, signaling her desire to meet him halfway.

Her hand rolled into a fist. Power surged through it. The moment she directed it forward, deadly energy was fired like blades at her opponent, her mortal enemy.

Hard air hit him, cutting into him. He was pushed backwards, even as the charge kept hitting him, even as he deflected most of it. Walls cracked. Blood flowed from his broken skin. He hit the wall hard. There was a loud crack when his shoulder-bone broke.

He landed on his feet, even as her second attack hit him. It bounced off his shield, but not completely. More wounds appeared on his big and heavyset body.

She could see his shield, his defenses. They were telekinetic in nature, like she had surmised and couldn't completely shield him from her far more versatile power. She felt his counterattack. Blood flowed from her nose, from her wrist. More of the walls and ceiling cracked. One burst of power broke through all the way to the outside. Bright daylight flooded the dark bright room. It amazed her, amazed her that she no longer seemed to have limits, even though she knew well that she had.

A strike hurt her. I have no limits, she thought. The limits are only in my mind. She acted on it.

She glimpsed the world outside. The images assaulted her. Buildings far away were shaken, hammered by the power. Distance didn't seem to matter.

His arm broke. Sweat drowned his brow and pain clouded his eyes. There was no speech, no attempt at verbal communication in the infernal noise. Wilson Florie's life was snuffed out. A random flying piece of metal hit his head and crushed his skull. The building shook. Raw amazement touched the combatants' features. She pushed on.

A piece of her ear was ripped off. A tooth was shaken loose. Blood flowed from her arm. A part loosened from the ceiling. It just bounced off the seething energy surrounding her. She screamed in pain. It felt like her hip was ripped out of her body. She fell to the floor with hazy vision.

Rage sustained her. Her power, moving through air and through other worlds and dimensions hit him head on, moving straight through, cutting a path through his very flesh. His scream, the scream itself hurt her. His power was sound, hard sound as well. Amazement kept mixing with fear and desperation and full-blown hatred and contempt at her volcanic forge.

One finger was ripped off her right hand. She screamed in pain and rage, using it, using everything it granted her to renew the onslaught she subjected her enemy to. Pain dissolved in the forge burning at her core. Power reached her undiluted from everyone present, including Marco. The power of everyone present surged into her, into him. The partly sedated people on the tables shook, shook like ragdolls in a storm.

One of them opened his eyes. Clouded eyes turned crystal clear in a moment. He broke the straps binding him without effort. He attacked Marco Coleman viciously, totally beside himself with rage. Marco sent one piece of shrapnel right through his chest, killing him instantly. Pain shot through both the combatants, as his death reverberated through them. Marco was distracted only for a moment. It was long enough. Lori sent a barrage of wreckage and lethal energy at him. One big piece hit him directly in the chest and squashed his ribs. He yelped in pain and horror. Blood flowed from his mouth.

She hit him again. A considerable piece of his head was torn off. An eye jumped from the socket. His breathing turned labored. He fell, collapsed on the ruptured floor. More and more pieces dropped from the ceiling, hitting two more of those trapped in trance. He couldn't move, couldn't act, as the fury approached him, as she floated through the air like a shadow, an angel of vengeance.

His power fizzled and died, fizzled and died, as life faded from the beyond mangled body. He tried moving, tried fighting, in vain.

She stood above him, the very image of cold and hot rage, her lips twisted in disdain.

– They never strike twice.

– Huh?

He looked dazed at her, through the thick film of blood covering his remaining eye.

– In the movies. They immobilize the villain and then flee. Then the villain wakes up and keeps chasing them.

She struck him again, hard, crushing his skull and killing him instantly. Then, pondering it for a moment, she stepped hard on his neck, separating his head from his body.

– If you return from this, I'll kneel before you, she mumbled.

She stepped on other parts of his body, separating each one with a meticulous dedication she didn't really question or ponder.

The pieces erupted in intense flames, burning to ashes in just a few seconds. Marco Coleman was snuffed from this earth. She stepped back.

– Better safe than sorry, she shrugged.

Another loud, louder crack and the building shook even harder. She looked at those on the tables, those still breathing. She turned and walked away, starting on the long climb into the distant daylight. The power kept surging through her, but she needed to be cautious when it came to utilize it. Its use made the unstable building even more unstable. The people on the tables opened eyes already open, opened them one by one. Her power, her godlike power faded slowly but surely, moment by moment.

She landed on the ground outside, crying out in pain as she put weight on her hip and right foot. People fled in panic from the building, the doomed building. She stood there for a moment or ten, breathing hard beyond hard, admiring her great work.

Giant pieces of the once so proud Coleman-building floated and shook in the air, an honor guard paying their respects.

To her!

They descended slowly, only slowly to the ground. A few stayed afloat, not falling at all, as if gravity itself had been suspended in Lori's close proximity.

The building collapsed. Piece by piece fell from high above. More screams filled the air.

Flares in the air opened rifts, offered glimpses into other realities. Unfathomable, frightening and mundane images appeared. People stared as they ran and turned their heads at the beyond frightening sight.

Lori started walking, limping, stumbling across the cracked parking lot, levitating across the worst divides, doing so without trouble, without major effort. Debris covered the ground in a wide circle around the failing building. The first of those who had been trapped below began emerging from the wreckage. She addressed them with a silent greeting, even as she kept stumbling forward on her uneasy path. She blinked with sweaty and bloody eyes.

Ten years ago, this had been practically untouched, pristine land. In two generations, it would be so once more.

She entered an area only resembling a street. Even here, this far from the epicenter of the fight some of the buildings had been reduced to rubble. She froze, even as she kept moving forward, doing so like a force of nature clothed in flesh. Her eyes caught the sight of a dog, a petrified, frozen dog. It stared at her with dead eyes.

One hundred ravens flew slowly across the street.

She and her mirror image became one. It, appearing in mist became flesh. She, coated in flesh became mist.

Sensations kept assaulting her as she moved, sensations of death and life and everything between and beyond, breathing air, soil and water and growing fire everywhere, thinking thoughts new, startling and powerful. She knew what she was.

The image of the tree will be with me forever.

She embraced it, both the physical and the spiritual, metaphorical aspect of it. Many trees surrounded her, but they were all one.

The puzzle made sense to her, now, finally made sense.

She crossed the ridge. Debris and dust and remains drifted in the air around her, as she made her way further into the City, into its heart, its heart of stone.

The Season of the Witch had begun.

Author's word

I woke up one morning in early 2001, and realized that I would soon turn forty. This story began roaming my increasingly active mind not long after that. I decided I wanted to write about people my own age and set out to do so.

More questions quickly presented themselves: what if I had taken a different turn in life and had joined mainstream society in my youth, becoming pretty much like everyone else? Where would that have brought me? Would I have become just like them, or would there still be a spark left… waiting for the right moment to ignite?

The story has taken a very long time to complete. When I wrote first draft of chapter 2 in 2002, Warner Bros Village Cinema was still where Vue Cinemas is now. The fact is that I've only written one chapter on average each year or rather every eleven months. The main reason for that is that I've written several stories about witches, sorcerers, «witchcraft» before and have worked hard to make this one different from those. I always work hard to make my current story different from all the rest, but this time I've worked harder than ever.

There are elements, themes here I haven't touched before or not touched in quite this way. It is its own story, with its own dynamics, and tides and eddies and everything. Lori is really completely different from Afterglow, Lillith and Chloe Webster, for instance.

Another reason is that I have not visited London as often as I used to do in recent years. When I have, I've literally walked in the characters' footsteps and the story has been given a hard push forward. I walked in Hyde Park during a twilight moon and misty summer night. I walked from A to B with them, street by street, corner by corner and dark shadow.

The last few pieces and elements and additions to the story came to me during editing. I've found that that is usually the case. When I look at the whole picture, everything often comes into a razor-sharp focus for me.

I also added to the upcoming Earth and sky, day and Night series of novels and movies as a whole.

BTW, all the names of the restaurants and bars and bookstores and discos are fake. I usually don't advertise for anyone if I can avoid it. The places, however, are real, or they once were.

This is a London story, and the city is just as much a character, a part of the story as all the rest.

Yes, a true new age, part great, part sinister beyond words is coming upon mankind, whether mankind wants to or not.

2001-01-19 - 2017-04-16
Printed version ready 2017-05-30
Final proofreading complete September 20, 2017

Earth and sky, day and Night, second story:

Resurrection dreams

The Season of the Witch is here, an ongoing, lasting fact in human society, an approaching, sinister wave.

The dark men are coming.

Beware of the riders at dawn.

Who and what they are, aren't clear, are a mystery for the ages. They may be two different groups, or be one and the same. People speak about their existence in whispers, in fear and awe and shock and longing. They are coming, may already walk the streets of London. That much is clear. Nothing else is.

Trevor is walking those streets. So are Janice and Ruth, Gypsy and Eldora. Ugly Jenny is shouting her curses and beyond obscure messages at those encountering her, leaving no one or almost no one the wiser.

The dead man died and dreamed his resurrection dreams. They say he was shot, and succumbed to his injuries, but was up and going before his body turned cold. He fell, but is walking still. They all are! What they once believed to be only dreams and nightmares becomes real, a tangible reality they can't escape. The five of them, and many others, are the Earth and sky, day and Night. They glimpse truths never spoken, see things never glimpsed, see existence as the infinite, unending reality it is.

They say that London is filled with living and dead spirits, and that everything is up for grasp. Everything possible and impossible is lurking in the deepest shadow, the brightest day, the misty night of this place of dust and decay.

Yes, a true new age, part great, part sinister beyond words is coming upon mankind, whether mankind wants to or not.

To be published 2019-04-30

EARTH AND SKY, DAY AND NIGHT

Existential horror.
(ten stand-alone, interrelated stories
about the beginning, the returned Power,
at the twilight of the modern world)
(novels, TV, Internet, serializing)

Season of the Witch
Resurrection Dreams
Burning in Gray
A Night in Hyde Park
Dead Woman Walking
The Twilight Storm
The Path of Shadows
The Returned Power
Winds of Change
(blowing wild)
The New Barbarians

Other published and upcoming novels by **Amos Keppler** from **Midnight Fire Media**:

The Janus Clan - (ten chapters about the Wild Man in the modern world, a world balancing on a razor's edge):

The Defenseless
The Slaves
Birds Flying in the Dark
At the End of the Rainbow
Lewis of Modern York
The Werewolf of Locus Bradle
The Valley of Kings
Eye in the Sky
The Iron Cage
Phoenix Green Earth

The Defenseless

The two rivers meet and join in the city of Denver, becoming one...

The two dark brothers, growing up with their sister Linda in a mundane, average suburb, a place well entrenched in modern United States and the world, have since their moment of birth been at odds with the world... and with each other.

Mike and Ted Cousin are not who they are. There is a mystery here, one of birth and upbringing, one of fate. Violence and death, blood and fire follow them all the days of their lives. The fire is resting somewhere inside... waiting for the Spark.

Their parents know something, but are not telling it. The policeman Mark Stewart and their aunt Trudy do, too. Everybody knows something, pieces of the whole, but nobody knows the whole truth, nobody telling it.

The ancient power is returning to the world, a world massively suffering from physical and spiritual poison, on the brink of collapse and a collective tailspin suicide run without its like in human history.

Magick is returning from its long exile. Thus begins the story of the wild beasts rising from their ashes.

The Spark is struck, horrible and terrifying.

First book of ten in the Janus Clan series: Ten stories of the wild man in the modern world, forty years of wandering, before the Phoenix is rising from its ashes.

ISBN 978-82-91693-08-8

Shadow Walk

The world is changing. They know this, in their core of cores, where everything moves and shifts. Night and fire have followed them all the days of their lives.

What they carry inside has always scared them, always intrigued them...

They have always felt different, apart from the crowd. And here, now, they get the confirmation they have always wanted, always yearned for, that they are truly different, a breed apart. The metamorphosis begins. Their minds, their bodies are changing in shocking and unpredictable ways, as what's on the inside is brought to the outside. And as they themselves are changing they are also changing the world.

Danger awaits them, Life awaits them, in the small, backward New England town. Magick and Mystery may be found beneath unturned stones.

People, young and old, are descending on the small, insignificant town of Northfield, New England.

Boys and girls, students at the school of Life, Seekers, yearning for what's different, what's hidden.

They're seeking within and without, high and low.

And here, in this dusty, remote place they're finding it, turning the stone, finding the strength within themselves to be themselves, to break out of confines, to the world beyond. And in time, after the initial, tentative steps, pushing down paths new and undreamed of.

And the present-day order sees them for what they are... Agents of Change, a threat to any establishment, any imposed reality. The heatwave, the worst in living memory, is nothing compared to the boiling within the human heart. The Indian Summer heralds the twilight of mankind.

ISBN 978-82-91693-12-5

Your Own Fate

From The Book of Fate:

In the Book of Fate there is everything. Every incident, all times, everything that has been, that is, that will ever be, everything that might be, everything that could have been.

But who is writing it? Who is penning it? Who is turning page by page, too many to be counted, blowing in the wind? Does it perhaps write itself, with a pen moving across the yellow sheets? Or is it a hand moving the pen, one unseen, one stretching back into the past, back to the time before everything was created, creating itself from nothing?

Timothy Joyce is an enigma, a man without a past, appearing from nowhere, to go on a rampage in an astonished world.

Jeremy Zahn is hunting Timothy Joyce. It seems like he has always been hunting him, from old London, from the island of angels, where it is said they met for the first time, to the city of angels, California, the new world.

Here, on this shaky ground, following confrontations spanning the globe, its time and space the two will fight for the last time.

And the world is watching, its people shivering in their frozen hearts.

ISBN 978-82-91693-05-7

Night on Earth

This is said to be the age of enlightenment and reason...
A culmination of thousands of years' development and illumination.

The hunters are dying off, they say. Their day is done, in favor of the new, enlightened time of neon lights, technology and civilization.

But a hunter is stalking the streets of London. A creature without form, eyes and skin. In a city on the brink of chaos, of social and economic collapse, it is stalking cops, killing them in ever more horrible ways. Sheila Watts is a hunter. She's a cop.

Sheila is lost, losing herself further by the second. She's losing herself, finding herself, as she's closing in on the creature of the night, as it is closing in on her.

Sheila Watts can taste the sweet blood in her mouth...

ISBN 978-82-91693-07-1

Dreams Belong to the Night

New, emerging urban rebel guerilla groups, freedom fighters, called terrorists by enraged authorities are overwhelming Europe.

What is, in truth terrorism? Who does it to whom?
How much can a human being take of bondage, injustice, degradation and destruction of spirit… before being fed up?

Present day society is a wound not closing.
In a modern world society destroying everything making life worth living there are those, who, through coincidence and fate, have decided not to take it anymore.
And as they are making that decision, together and as individuals, they are also starting on a journey, a journey back to humanity's roots.
Judith, Sivert, Kim, Willhelm, Anya and many more.
A handful of people against an entire world.

This is their story…

ISBN 978-82-91693-11-8

Experience the defeat of civilization, of tyranny, of anti-life in:

Thunder Road - Book One: Ice and Fire

Damon Terrill is the Storm Child. He is born into the life hostile civilization's last years, as humanity starts on its return to nature, return to Life.

It started with the need for Freedom, the passion of life, and went from there, in new and unforeseen directions, in one, final attempt to get it right.

– It's the human being's path through life, Anya told them. – What challenges, destroys and strengthens it.

The Thunder Road is making a turn. It always is. Burning Ice, Biting Flame...that is how life began. And that's how it will renew itself. No matter where humans are going. And now the blade is laid bare, ready to be tempered once more. Humanity's idiocy, their hubris has finally and fully been visited upon them. The End Time, the final hour, Ragnarok is here. The sea is rising, winds are increasing in strength. A thoroughly rotten society is collapsing under its own weight.

Humans are natural nomads. Now they become nomads anew, pulled together in small tribes once more, pulled into a fellowship of fate in a final, desperate attempt to survive, to live the life humans are born to live. Finally. Damon, Anya, Andrè, Myriam and many others have started on their way Home.

ISBN 978-82-91693-21-7

Alarums of reality

The end is the beginning. The beginning is the end…

The once so great Caine Manor has become a ruin, one only fit for carrion birds and revenants. No one but daring children and crazed souls dare breach its confines.

The proud and shiny Caine Manor is an outstanding example of renovated architecture at the heart of the city.

Looking at the building, the house, resembling a castle, hidden in a strange, illuminated mist, squinting your eyes, it's often hard to tell what's illusion and what's real. Reality shifts and burns around the Caine Manor, either ruin or proud house, reaching out with strands of night and fire to the surrounding areas and to existence at large. It is the center, or at least one center, in an ever-shifting world.

Is Chloe Webster dead or alive? Is Marion Dexter? Is Marlon Caine? Or David Fallon Somby? Are they perhaps both? Or neither? What is the world? Is it a brick, a hard, impenetrable wall or closer to something akin to mist and shadow? Existence might make sense, to us, to them, but only in glimpses, only in passing, beyond a corner somewhere ahead. They may wonder. They may die clueless. Because they don't know, don't know why terror strikes them and makes their heart beat like a sledgehammer in their chest.

From a place unbound by time and space alarums of reality are reaching out to touch and ultimately engulf them all.

ISBN 978-82-91693-13-2

FALLING

She can not rid herself of it, the sense of falling. It is lurking in her dreams, every time she looks at the world from the edge of her vision. The old, cruel oracle at the fair did not tell her anything she did not know.

Janet of the Blue Flame is born a sorcerer, one with powers of the mind and the body far exceeding those of most others, one in a line reaching far back in antiquity.

In this modern age she, like many others is virtually unaware of the potential resting in the murky parts of her being. She may know, deep down, but she is not aware… not until the day Malone the Sorcerer comes for her.

Malone is dark and powerful. His skills and might are unquestionable. His power speaks to her, to her murky depths, roaring in her consciousness like a storm. Janet is only Sweet Sixteen and is overwhelmed in Malone's presence. When he offers to train her, for her to become his apprentice she consents with an eagerness of a mule chasing the carrot. He is everything she is not, everything she has ever dreamed of being. She leaves her friends and family, leaves behind everything she knows and joins the mighty and enigmatic sorcerer on his quest. His harsh teaching takes her far away, into the nine realms and beyond.

He gives her her devoirs, gives her everything he promised and more, wishing her good luck, leaving her to pick up the pieces of her life.

Janet of the Blue Flame is ready for the world.

ISBN 978-82-91693-19-4

AFTERGLOW DUST

She has died a million times…

Someone is stalking her. She knows this, knows it at the edge of her vision, where nothing really is seen, only dreamed. Her nightmares give her no peace. She turns and looks behind her. There is nothing there her eyes can see. But in the wind, she can hear the wailing cry, the cry of Death. Sniffing that wind, she can smell the blood in her nostrils.

There is truth in flesh, they say… and there is truth in that. But there is also substance in what cannot be seen, cannot be touched. Claws and fangs cut ceaselessly through the night, looking for her. A silent cry is heard in the dark.

Someone… or something is stalking her.

She remembers a kind touch and a slap in the face, and hardly anything else.

Kathryn Caldwell is Afterglow, a woman of undetermined age, a strange creature wandering the dark corners of the world. Something happened to her once, something horrible, something she can never forget or put out of her mind. It is haunting her every second of her dark days, every moment of her pitiful sleep. She has become an empty shell, a pale imitation of the human being she once was. Long ago, as she measures time, she lost everything valuable in a human being, saw it fall through a crack, irreversible, never to be found again.

So she is wandering the darkened streets of the modern world, aimlessly, adrift, hardly ever seen, hardly ever there. People cannot see her, but she is there, present in their daily lives, an open wound that will never close.

No one is safe for Afterglow…

ISBN 978-82-91693-16-3

Black Dragon

One unexplainable, beyond mysterious event changed the world. In one moment, lasting an eternity the Earth and all its creatures was cast in shadow. The sun was blocked out in the sky, and people could only glimpse each other as flickering shapes in a seemingly endless night.

They called it the Great Darkness, and spent years and countless hours attempting to explain it, speculating in vain on its origin.

The results of the event weren't instantaneous, weren't obvious, but in the years to come many people transformed, and gained new and startling abilities, powers of the mind and body never before seen on this Earth.

Lady Grace, Flight Captain, Gimmick, Oracle, The Bowman, Raven Bird and many others rose from the sea of mankind, creatures straight from people's imagination, the fantastic writings of the world, crime fighters, vigilantes and master criminals similar to those previously described only in comic books living the life of their dreams.

The world changed, irrevocably, each new big and small dramatic event removing it further from what it had been, its status quo and social relations altered forever.

Unsettling dreams began haunting them, first at night, in their sleep, and then, slowly, spilling over into their days and waken lives. A creature, a terrifying nightmare rose from the primordial consciousness of them all.

They called it the Black Dragon…

ISBN 978-82-91693-18-7

Secrets

These are descriptions of what cannot be described.

These words within deal with the current world as it is, its prevalent and extensive alienation, inequality and injustice, its ongoing destruction of both spirit and flesh, of everything making life worth living.

But most of all it's about the Night, the great darkness, the dark passions ruling us all, what those in charge more than anything want to take away from us.

Words have power...

Contains 140 poems written from August 2003 to July 2013.

ISBN 978-82-91693-15-6

www.ingramcontent.com/pod-product-compliance
Lightning Source LLC
Chambersburg PA
CBHW060605310726
48982CB00008B/1242/J
9788291693224